The Boulangerie on the Corner

Also by Susan Buchanan

STANDALONES

Sign of the Times

The Dating Game

The Leap Year Proposal

THE CHRISTMAS SPIRIT SERIES

The Christmas Spirit

Return of the Christmas Spirit

A Little Christmas Spirit

A Taste of Christmas Spirit

THE JUST ONE DAY SERIES

Just One Day – Winter

Just One Day – Spring

Just One Day – Summer

Just One Day – Autumn

DREAM DESTINATIONS SERIES

You Can't Hurry Love

The Boulangerie on the Corner

SUSAN BUCHANAN

Copyright

First published in 2026 by Susan Buchanan

Print Edition

A CIP catalogue record of this title is available from the British Library

Paperback – 978-1-915589-06-4

Dedication

For the Molinières family
For taking me into your home, your heart
and for inspiring this story

About the Author

Susan Buchanan lives in Scotland with her husband, their two young children and a crazy Labrador called Benji. She has been reading since the age of four and had to get an adult library card early as she had read the entire children's section by the age of ten. As a freelance book editor, she has books for breakfast, lunch and dinner and in her personal reading always has several books on the go at any one time.

If she's not reading, editing or writing, she's thinking about it. She loves romantic fiction, psychological thrillers, crime fiction and legal thrillers, but her favourite books feature books themselves.

In her past life she worked in International Sales as she speaks five languages. She has travelled to 51 countries and her travel knowledge tends to pop up in her writing. Collecting books on her travels, even in languages she doesn't speak, became a bit of a hobby.

Susan writes contemporary romantic fiction, partly set in Scotland, usually featuring travel, food or Christmas, but always with large dollops of friendship, family and community. When not working, writing or caring for her two delightful cherubs, Susan loves reading (obviously), the theatre, quiz shows and eating out – not necessarily in that order!

You can connect with Susan via her website www.susanbuchananauthor.com or on Facebook www.facebook.com/susancbuchananauthor and on Twitter @susan_buchanan or Instagram authorsusanbuchanan.

Acknowledgements

Huge thanks to

Claire at Jaboof Design Studio for my gorgeous cover – again!

Paul Salvette and his team at BB Ebooks for book formatting www.bbebooksthailand.com

Catherine Ferguson, Katy Ferguson, Heather Harkin, Susan Allan, Wendy Janes and Anne Pack for agreeing to beta read for me.

Mairibeth, Rachel, Sophie, Susan (again!), Mary, Vanessa and Victoria

The Scottish chapter of the Romantic Novelists' Association

The Romantic Novelists' Association – generally!

My ever-expanding Advance Review team and my newsletter subscribers

Rachel's Random Resources for always providing such wonderful blog tours and all the amazing bloggers who take part.

Sue Baker of the Riveting Reads and Vintage Vibes Facebook group for my launch day celebration

Thanks to the following Facebook groups:

Susan Buchanan's Bookworms

Lizzie's Book Group, run by the amazing Lizzie Chantree, for constant support.

The Friendly Book Community

Chick Lit and Prosecco, run by Anita Faulkner

To all of my super-supportive fellow authors who kindly help spread the word – I have your back, and I know you have mine!

Most important of all – the kids. To Antonia for writerly chat and to Luke for distracting me with Yahtzee and Qwirkle when I need time away from my desk.

And last, and by absolutely no means least, my readers. Thank you for your continued interest in my books. It means the world to me, as do your lovely comments. I hope you enjoy the new European Escapes series. If you'd like to connect with me about my books, you can always contact me on susan@susanbuchananauthor.com

Chapter One

'I can't believe it, Jules. Three years together. Three months in this flat together. And now, all the hassle of having to sell it. And I gave up my own flat to move in with him! I loved my old flat. It's so unfair.'

I know I sound like a petulant child, but I can't help it. I did love my old flat, and were it not for Freddy F-word, my ex, I'd still be in it.

Now I have to not only deal with our breakup, but look for somewhere else to live – again. Pack – again. Fork out for solicitors' fees and stamp duty and get another mortgage approved – again. My head is pounding thinking about it.

'I know, Lia, but you're strong. You can deal with it.' Jules rubs my arm in a gesture of solidarity. 'You know what you need?'

I raise my eyebrow at her. 'No. What?'

'A holiday.'

'You've got that right.' I down my espresso in one, now it's cool enough.

Jules taps her finger three times on the café table, a quirk she has when she's in earnest about something. 'No, I'm serious, Lia. You need a break from all this.'

'But I don't have any annual leave booked,' I protest.

'Maybe not, but get in quick before Eric lands anything

else on your plate. Your latest project was completed nearly two weeks ago. Remember how stressed you were going in every day, especially after your breakup?'

Oh, I remember, and how. I had to ignore everyone's nosy, inquiring, well-meaning glances. Although I didn't unburden myself to anyone at work, I couldn't mask the puffy eyes or the general air of sadness enveloping me.

Maybe she has a point. I'll check with work tomorrow.

'I'm sorry I wasn't around when this all kicked off,' Jules says before taking another sip of her coffee.

'Don't be silly, Jules. You were in Minnesota. There wasn't much more you could do, but it did help having you on the other end of the phone.'

She gives a sad smile. 'I suppose. And thanks for organising that plumber for me whilst I was away. How unlucky am I to have burst pipes twice in two years?'

I lean forward. 'Jules, you are always there for me. Sorting out something as basic as a plumber is a lot easier than you sorting out my love life – or lack of one.'

Jules releases a breath. 'I always did say Freddy wasn't good enough for you. Are you sleeping any better yet?'

My mouth downturns and that's enough for Jules, who sighs and says, 'Eating more than a couple of spoonfuls of Cornflakes?'

I wish I hadn't confessed to that now, but when Freddy left, I simply couldn't stomach food; I couldn't get it to go down, and I lost weight I could ill afford to.

I am improving, although my appetite still isn't back to what it was. I keep waking up and turning to talk to Freddy, then remembering we're no longer together and he's no longer there. Every morning it's like a sucker punch to the chest and my heart physically aches. I've taken to running in Kelvingrove Park to clear the cobwebs and prepare myself for the day. I'm sure the pain will pass in time, but for now it's as raw as steak tartare.

I nod to Jules, confirming the appetite is back on track, and I'm about to return to our earlier topic of holidays when Jules' mouth forms an O, and if I could lip-read for sure, I'd guess she'd just muttered 'Oh shit!' under her breath. I turn to see what has caused her reaction and my heart lurches. Not ten yards away, crossing the threshold of Brava, is Freddy. And he's not alone. He's smiling down at a petite brunette, who looks to be about ten years our junior.

Gianni passes the new arrivals, carrying a tray of coffees. His smile falters as he spots Freddy, and confusion crosses Freddy's face as he greets him. Freddy scans the café, his eyes finally meeting mine. I inhale sharply. His face turns the colour of dried cement. Serves him right, because the girl hanging on to him is very familiar with him, her arm draped casually around his waist as she nestles into his shoulder.

Bile rises in my throat and I struggle to swallow. I'd escape to the toilet to hide but I don't trust myself to stand, never mind walk.

Gianni swiftly sizes up the situation, requisite professional that he is, and guides Freddy and his 'friend' to a table on the other side of the café, almost, but not quite, out of view.

'Lia, are you OK?' Jules asks, but her voice sounds very far away. Air whooshes in my ears and I gulp down the bile.

The great thing about having Jules as a best friend is she gets me. She knows me. I don't need to explain anything to her. Without a word, she helps me to stand and guides me by the arm through to the ladies, which thankfully is empty.

As I brace my arms against one of the sinks, tears leak out of my eyes and run down my face, and soon Jules turns me to her and cradles me against her chest, not batting an eyelid at the fact I'm soaking her top.

'Do you think…?'

'Shh,' soothes Jules. She knows what I was going to ask. Is that girl why Freddy left? Was all his, 'It's not you, it's me' as bullshit as it sounded and has he just been the biggest cliché ever?

'I can't go back out there,' I say, panic clawing at my chest.

Jules looks at me, her serious face on. 'Lia Abernethy, we are going to make you presentable again, then we're going to walk out of here, heads held high, pay the bill and go, but only because F-word is here and we won't be able to enjoy ourselves. We'll get a bottle of wine at the shop and go back to yours. OK?'

Numbly, I nod, not trusting myself to speak.

Once I've washed my face, I walk out of the toilets, Jules right behind me … and run straight into Freddy.

There's only a slight intake of breath from him before he says, 'Lia,' then his lips press together in a tight line.

I say nothing, just incline my head.

'Sorry you had to see me with Macey, but it was inevitable, I suppose.' When I remain silent, he elaborates. 'I've rented a flat for a couple of months in White Street, so we may run into each other now and again.'

White Street! Could he have moved any closer to me? What the heck is he playing at?

With great self-possession, I finally manage, 'That's

nice for you. Excuse us.' And just as Jules suggested, with head held high, I walk towards where Gianni is standing at the counter, ready to settle our bill.

As we spill out onto the pavement, I hug Jules then say, 'Let's go back to mine and look at holidays. I really need one now.'

Chapter Two

It's the start of a new week and I hope the beginning of a fresh start for me. Jules came up with the winning idea yesterday of me going to stay at hers in Edinburgh for a week. I can spend some time with her in the evening, and I can float around the capital taking in museums and visiting bookshops. I might even have time for a run up Arthur's Seat.

Hopefully, Eric will sign off my annual leave. I know it's short notice, but as far as I know, no one else in my department is off next week, so I have my fingers, as well as everything else, crossed that he'll say yes.

'Morning!' I greet our receptionist as I swing into the office. She raises a hand in recognition whilst she speaks into her headset, directing calls.

I drop my things at my desk, noting no one else is in yet, and grab a coffee from the jug. Fortunately, our receptionist always has coffee on the go for us. Perhaps it's written into her contract. I sip my coffee and sit down at my desk, feeling energised for the first time in months, and in control for the first time since … well, since Freddy split up with me. I shake my head as if to dislodge his image from it. He's not worthy of my thoughts.

Since I'm super early, I have no qualms about checking

out places of interest to visit in Edinburgh on my PC. I'll bask in the knowledge I'll be putting my out of office message on relatively soon, and browse bookshops and quirky cafés to take in whilst I drink my coffee. Then I'll be in an even better frame of mind for attacking the day with vigour.

As I read, I can't stop the smile from spreading across my face. It's still there when my boss, Eric, comes into the office.

'Morning, Lia. Good weekend?'

Dark circles ring his eyes, as if from lack of sleep. That reminds me of someone else. With a jolt, I hope his wife hasn't left him, but then I remember he has a six-week-old baby.

'Actually, yes.' I smile at him, but don't miss the worry lines on his forehead. 'Do you want some coffee? I'm going to grab another.'

Relief crosses his face, and I wonder what's up with him. You'd think I'd told him he's won the lottery. It's only a cup of coffee. Maybe he didn't have such a good weekend.

'That would be good, Lia. Thanks.'

As I make us both coffee, it hits me this could be a good time to ask for my annual leave, before the day gets underway and my colleagues arrive.

'So, Eric, I was wondering…' I start, as I place the coffee mug on his desk.

His eyes widen as if he's wary of what I'm about to say.

'You know how the Hannigan project is finished, and we have ages before the deadline for Mercury?'

Again, he has that hunted look. I frown, wanting to ask about using up some of my holiday allocation, but curious to know what's up with him. Perhaps it isn't a good time after all. I hesitate, then realise I haven't spoken for a few seconds when he prompts me. 'Yes?'

'Well, I was thinking about taking some time off.'

He visibly deflates, blowing out a breath, then laughs, but it's a humourless sound. 'Time off?' he finally croaks.

'Yes.' I'm feeling uncertain now. Do we have something more pressing coming up I've forgotten about? Wasn't he as happy with my work on Hannigan's as I thought he was? I'm feeling wrong-footed here, but I have to plough on, so I say, 'I have quite a bit of annual leave accrued, and I was hoping to go on holiday, next week, if possible.'

Silence.

I rush on. 'For ten days.' That should give me enough time away from Freddy to have more perspective on things.

His eyes flutter closed for a moment. Surely it's not that big of an ask? I only want what's due to me. I feel a stab of indignation. Please tell me he isn't going to say no.

Eric sighs. 'Lia, sit down.' His face is so absent of colour, he's almost cadaver-like.

'What is it?' Now I'm worried. Is he sick? Has his wife left him, after all?

Eric blows out another breath then says, 'There's no easy way to say this, Lia. I'm putting you on garden leave, effective today.'

'Garden leave?' My brain tries to digest what he's just said. Is this some new company bonding exercise?

He nods gravely. 'I'm sorry. At the meeting in HQ on Friday, I was told I needed to cut our department in half. No one else knows yet. I was going to announce it later today. I've barely slept all weekend.'

'Garden leave,' I say again, seemingly stuck on this phrase. 'As in redundancy, garden leave?' Thoughts of green fingers and mucking around in allotments with my colleagues fly out the window as what Eric is trying to convey to me sinks in.

I've just lost my job.

'Jules, it's me, can you call me back? It's urgent.' I try not to sob.

I told Eric I needed some air, so I'm outside taking in huge gulps of the stuff. He probably didn't realise I meant literally. It's the shock. Here's me asking for holidays, and I get fired. What am I going to do now? I've worked as a graphic designer here for five years. I haven't left and tried to go further up the career ladder as they treat you well and the pay is decent, and I love my job. It has been stressful recently, though, but I'd hoped the increase in workload was only temporary, as it hasn't been quite as much fun working here the past few months. I'm beginning to wonder if that's related to the 'garden leave' Eric has now dumped on me. Was Universal Vision's vision to squeeze every ounce of energy and strength from their employees in the run-up to downsizing the division?

Tears trickle down my cheeks, and as I swipe them away with my freezing cold fingertips, a packet of paper tissues appears in my eyeline. I look up to see Chris, my colleague, gazing down at me in concern.

'Hey, Lia, you OK?'

I nod mutely and fumble with the packet to take a tissue out then wipe my mouth.

Will Chris be losing his job too? Oh God, now I know

something I'm not meant to know about the company, I can barely look Chris in the eye. What a day.

My phone rings. I shoot Chris an apologetic look and say, 'I have to get this. See you in there, and thanks.'

As I answer the phone to Jules, I pray Chris doesn't lose his job. He's too nice a guy.

'Lia! What's so urgent? Ooh, I know, you got the holidays. Excellent, we're going to have so much fun. And I'll see if there's anything good on at the theatre. We could take in a show one night.'

I try to interrupt Jules a couple of times, but she's on a roll, and when she's on a roll, it's best to let her get it out of her system.

When she finally draws breath, I say, 'I think I can come and stay with you.'

'Yay. Wait, but you don't know for sure?'

'Jules.' I sigh heavily. 'I'm on garden leave.' Then I burst into noisy sobs, and this time I'm not even embarrassed by the odd looks passers-by direct at me.

'Garden leave!' Jules says, aghast. 'But … but … but … garden leave! Your company is doing so well. Isn't it?'

Through strangled sobs, I manage, 'I thought so, but this morning, when I went to ask Eric for holidays, it all came out. No one else knows yet. What am I going to do? No job. No boyfriend. Soon to be no flat.' I sob harder now, my reality overwhelming me.

'Right, Lia, listen to me.' Jules adopts her business persona. 'Go see what Eric says are the terms of the garden leave and what else you have to do, and see if he'll let you take some leave straightaway. Come to mine tonight. I'll finish my meetings and be back by lunch. Call me when you're on the train and I'll come meet you.'

'Jules, I can't ask you to do that,' I say.

'You're not asking, I'm offering,' she says firmly. 'You'd do the same for me.'

Grudgingly, I admit she's right.

'Now, I need to go but let me know what Eric says.'

'I will, Jules, and thanks. You're one in a million.' She really is. I'm so glad she has my back, and I'll always have hers.

Chapter Three

I laze in the hot tub with Jules, admiring the backdrop of Edinburgh Castle above us, and reflect on how lucky I am.

It helps me forget, along with the wine, how crappy my life is right now. I've asked the estate agent to do any viewings this week. One less stress, for now, at least.

Jules raises her glass of champagne, and I raise mine in turn, and relax back into the bubbles. This is the life. The knots in my neck have finally unknotted, and the crick in my shoulders has gone. I feel the most carefree I've felt in years. I don't ever want to go home, particularly when I know what awaits me.

'Penny for them.' Jules waves her hand in front of my face to attract my attention.

I blink. 'Just thinking how relaxing it is here, and how much I don't want to go home. Part of me wants to get out of the hot tub and go lie on one of the sofas with a fleecy blanket, and drift off to the glow of the log fire, but I can't will myself to get up.'

'I know the feeling. I don't get the chance to use the hot tub very often, what with me travelling so much. This is so nice. We should do this more often.'

'Hmm,' I say. 'Although I'll need to concentrate on getting another job first, and sort out somewhere to live.'

'Details, details,' says Jules. 'Someone will snap you up in no time. You're too talented.'

Let's hope so. Yes, my team has won quite a few awards for their projects, but despite the sector being far from saturated at the moment, I know of others who've tried to move jobs without success. Plus, the current economic climate doesn't bode well for me gaining a well-paid job I enjoy.

'But seriously, Jules, what am I going to do when I go back?'

Jules tuts. 'You're here to relax, to take your mind off things. Stop fretting. Plenty of time for that later.'

She's not wrong there, I think glumly.

Jules must catch sight of my forlorn look as she says, 'You need some distance from your situation, not to be pulled back into it too soon.' She stares off into the inky blackness.

'Go on then.' I raise an eyebrow at her when she regards me quizzically.

'What?'

'Hit me with it. You had that look in your eye, the one meaning an idea is percolating in that brain of yours.'

Jules grins. 'Ha! There's no hiding anything from you.' She pauses as if debating something with herself. 'OK then, let's play a game.'

I groan. 'Must we? I'm tired.'

'Yes, we must,' she says firmly, warming to her theme and sitting upright in the hot tub. How she dares, I don't know. It's bloody freezing once your shoulders are out of the water.

I burrow deeper into the bubbles as she says, 'Indulge me.'

I huff out a breath, making it patently obvious that's the last thing I want to do, since what I really want is to wave a magic wand and be transported close to the log fire inside and already in my silky PJs, with my hair and body dry.

'Fine,' I say eventually.

'Right, close your eyes.' Jules warms to her theme, all business.

Well, that's easy enough, I'm sleepy as heck as it is.

'Good. Now, imagine a happy place.'

I'm not into this mumbo-jumbo, visualisation or whatever. Or is it manifestation? Suffice to say, I'm far too logical to believe in all that New-Age stuff.

'Lia, happy place.' Her voice holds a warning note.

The annoying thing about your best friend knowing you so well is sometimes it's too well. She knew I was daydreaming. Aargh, I'm doing it again! Happy place, happy place. Hawaii. Maui.

'Remember it has to be your happy place, not somewhere you've never been,' Jules says.

Like I said, bloody annoying that she knows me so well. OK, so I've never been to Hawaii, but it does look pretty idyllic. I don't think a caravan in Portobello is going to have quite the same impact. I know. I'll use here, in Edinburgh.

'And not here. It's too recent.'

'Crikey, are you clairvoyant?' I ask, a note of irritation slipping into my voice.

Jules smirks. 'Well, you know there are rumours my nana was a seer.'

If we were in the living room, I'd throw a cushion at her, but since we're in the hot tub, I have to settle for splashing water at her.

'Hey!' she yelps, laughing. 'Right, focus. I'm serious.'

There's no messing with her once she gets her teeth into something, so I decide to get it over with.

I lie back in the water, allowing the tensions caused by my crappy situation to flow out of me. I'm so tired I could almost fall asleep right here and now.

As the bubbles roil around me, a few images flit through my mind. The Lake District – Lake Windermere and chocolate-box cottages, roaring log fire – I'm seeing a pattern here. I clearly like log fires. But most of the memories there are tied up with Freddy. Damn it!

The vineyard we visited in Chianti comes into view and I can almost taste the fruity red as I recall the amazing food we sampled at the *enoteca* there.

'C'mon, there must be somewhere.' Mild exasperation laces her words.

'Don't rush me.' I don't even open my eyes.

'I'm not. Think of the people you meet, or met, who surround you,' she says softly.

She falls silent – a first – so I take advantage of that fact and allow myself to drift. Although I've met some pretty great people, the ones who mean the most to me are my family and friends, but that's obvious surely.

And then a wave of calm descends over me. The place I've conjured up wasn't calm, far from it, but it was filled with love, laughter, delicious food and joy. That's the only word for it. Pure, unadulterated joy. The *pains aux raisins* in the morning, fresh from the oven; the crunchy baguette that made the most marvellous cracking noise as you tore it in half. If my eyes weren't already closed, I'd need to close them in bliss. I have never tasted bread like it since. The heavenly aroma of the freshly baked *pain de campagne* wafting up towards my attic bedroom at five in the morning. No need for an alarm clock. I'm practically salivating at the thought.

The boulangerie. Toulouse. The Molins family. The Gascon countryside. The terracotta buildings of the pink city.

Fifteen years ago, fresh out of university and before starting at the job I'd been working towards, I decided to pursue my love of languages in a rather novel way. I answered an advert where a family was looking to house students of French, in Toulouse, half board, or self-catering. I foolishly chose self-catering, but the mother took one look at me trying to boil water for pasta one night, with a pre-prepared sauce, and told me to grab a plate from the cupboard and go sit at the table, whilst she took my water off the boil. Thereafter, my love affair with French food and cookery began, although I do recall I wasn't particularly fond of pigeon, or grated horse. I also recall Madame Molins kept that quiet until after I'd eaten it. And I recall how much I freaked out when I realised I'd eaten horse. The memory makes me chuckle.

'You're smiling. I'm taking that as a positive sign.' Jules interrupts my reverie and my eyes fly open.

My smile broadens. 'It is.'

Her eyes widen and she makes a spinning motion with her finger as if to tell me to hurry up.

I decide to put her out of her misery. 'Do you remember when I went to France for three months after uni?'

Her eyebrows knit. 'Yeah. Toulouse, wasn't it?'

'That's the one. And I lived with that family, the

Molins, who virtually adopted me.'

'Yeah, I do, lucky cow. Free food and an annoying wee brother to boot.'

I grin. 'He wasn't that annoying. He was adorable in a play-a-prank-on-the-visitor kind of way.'

'Rather you than me,' Jules says. 'Although the fresh pastries, copious amounts of different freshly baked breads and hot Frenchmen, I could live with.'

I roll my eyes. 'Jules, you're incorrigible.'

'Why, thank you, my dear.' She bats her eyelashes at me.

'It wasn't a compliment,' I say, shaking my head at her.

She winks. 'I know. So, talking about the hot Frenchmen…'

I frown. 'I didn't realise we were.'

'Lia, I'm always talking about the hot Frenchmen.' She waggles her eyebrows at me and I sigh.

'Your happy place is the boulangerie. You should go visit your adoptive French family.'

'I don't know, Jules. It's been fifteen years.'

'Lia, I'm telling you, revisit your past and find your future.'

My smile drops. 'Did you get that from a fortune cookie?'

Jules smirks. 'The fortune cookies never lie.'

Happy her work is done, Jules sinks into the hot-tub bubbles as I ponder what she has said.

Ten minutes or so later, I'm vaguely aware of Jules talking about something.

'You haven't been listening to a word I've said, have you?' she scolds me.

'No, but I have decided something. I'm writing to the

Molins tonight. Where are those postcards you bought today?'

With renewed energy and resolve, I haul myself out of the hot tub and pad through to the living area. Time to pen that postcard.

Chapter Four

Garden leave isn't as much fun as it sounds. And I've not been in the garden as it's the wrong time of year. Why would I be out in my garden, in Scotland, in early March? The temperature has barely risen above freezing in a month. Now I'm back home, and dealing with the drudgery of everyday life post-Edinburgh mini-break is taking its toll, not least because I have no job and the estate agent keeps phoning to arrange viewers.

I can't bring myself to show any more people the flat, no matter that the estate agent says that's their preference, and apparently has a higher success rate, so I skulk in local coffee shops and even at the library in an attempt to avoid bumping into glowing, enthusiastic couples, or worse, newlyweds looking for their first home. I haven't reached that place yet where I can be happy for others finding happiness. I'm too self-centred – sorry, not sorry – at the moment. I hate being like this, but I need something, or someone, to help me out of my funk.

The doorbell rings. Excellent, Jules is here. That'll pull me out of my slump.

But when I open the door, it's my neighbour, Josh.

'Hi, Lia. I've been away and the postman put this through my letterbox by mistake.' He passes me a letter and we chat for a few moments until footsteps on the stairs alert us to Jules' presence.

'Hi, Josh,' Jules says, a faint smile on her lips. She has always had a bit of a thing for my hunky neighbour.

'Hi, Jules.' He smiles back and she almost melts on the floor. I prevent her from making a fool of herself by saying, 'Well, nice to see you and thanks for my letter,' then usher Jules into the flat.

'So–' Jules indicates the letter '–who's that from?'

'Nosy!' I start to open the letter but then notice the '*par avion*' and my heartbeat accelerates. The Molins.

I rip the letter open and find a reply from Madame Molins, then translate for Jules' benefit,

My darling Lia,

How wonderful to hear from you. All is well here. Life has changed a little since we last heard from you. Suzanne and Matthieu are running the boulangerie, whilst Dominique is now constructing houses in New Zealand. Sarah and her husband live with their daughter, Elodie and son, André, in Gascony. Charles, who was only a toddler when you lived here is now at university in Strasbourg.

We would love to see you again. The boulangerie and the apartments haven't changed, so there is plenty of room for you if you come to stay. Everyone is very excited to hear from you. Sarah has said she will try to arrange for her and her family to see you too. Here is our new phone number, and I even have email now. It should be quicker than waiting for the post.

Estelle signs off with big hugs and kisses.

'Are you OK?' Jules asks.

I look up. 'Sorry?'

'You're crying.'

I lift my hand to my face. It's wet, and I can't decide if the tears are of joy or sadness that I lost contact with this wonderful family. But that's what happens – life gets in the way. I'm only glad we're now back in touch.

'Jules, pass me my laptop. I'm going to Toulouse.'

Chapter Five

I'm standing at baggage claim at Toulouse Blagnac airport, waiting for the belt to come around again. Please God, let the airline not have lost my luggage. Then I see it. It's hard not to. After years of struggling to spot my black mid-size suitcase with its array of stickers of places it had travelled to, on baggage carousels, I finally treated myself and bought a purple case with white polka dots. How's that for standing out? As it sails towards me, the tension in my shoulders eases.

Ever since I booked the flight, to whoops and hollers from Jules, I've been afraid something would scupper my plans. Part of me knows I should simply embrace the fact my trip hasn't been blighted by catastrophe, but the reticent part of me is always expecting my bad luck to rear its head again, hence the panic over my luggage arriving.

Case in hand, I stride towards Arrivals. I can't believe I'm actually here. I'm doing this, and I'm so excited, if a little nervous, about seeing the family who took me in fifteen years ago, and treated me like their own.

Since I decided to take a taxi to save lugging my suitcase on the tram or bus, my first stop will be the taxi stand. However, I'm no sooner through the Arrivals gate than Suzanne and Estelle descend upon me, babbling away in French at high speed, hugging me as if they haven't seen me in, well, fifteen years. When we finally break apart and I draw breath, I beam at them. Their eyes fill with tears, of happiness, I hope. I hold their hands and the three of us look at each other.

Oh my goodness. I can't believe how right this feels. I try out my halting French – I've been practising feverishly for the past six days but still, I have a long way to go before I'm proficient.

'You look amazing,' I say to them both. Suzanne has hardly changed.

'I love your hair,' Suzanne says, pointing to the long pink streak running through my rather boring brown hair – kind people call it chestnut. On a whim, I had a section dyed pink to pep it up some.

We hug again and it feels like the reunion it is, but more than that, like an understanding between souls. It's almost impossible to describe. I have a home, well, I had a home, but being among these people feels like coming home. It's like only a few weeks have passed since I last saw them, instead of fifteen years. Suzanne is still as lean as ever. If possible, she looks even more cool than she did as a teenager. How unfair is that? Her unruly auburn curls spill over her shoulders as she chatters away animatedly in that typically French way. No nonsense. No lack of confidence. Happy in her own skin. Estelle, well, Estelle is the quintessential French mum. She has dressed up a little more than I recall. Perhaps because she's away from the boulangerie, but she's wearing black boots with a heel, black jeans and a three-quarter-length Herringbone coat. She's even wearing sunglasses, although they're on her head. It is only March.

I'd never really considered Estelle to be particularly chic in the past, certainly not when compared with Parisian women, but she could give them a run for their money today. She looks incredible for sixty. If anything she looks better than she did when I lived with them. Her skin is flawless. What's her secret? I need to know.

As we drive to their home, which is attached to the boulangerie, we cram in as much information as we can about the past fifteen years. We did keep in touch, initially weekly by phone, for the first few months, then the calls became less frequent, then they petered out eventually too, not because we had no desire to keep in touch, but simply because life became too busy.

Estelle tells me about the new additions to the family, and how Sarah lives further away now, and how Dominique now lives in Rotorua. It sounds like it's not only my life that became too busy to maintain the contact there once was. It's a pity I won't get to see my 'annoying wee brother' all grown up, but what a life he must be leading in New Zealand.

There's a crunching of brakes – Estelle's driving has always been harrowing to experience – and Suzanne shoots me an apologetic look, but my attention is captured by the wonderful sight of La Boulangerie au Coin de la Rue. It's almost exactly as I remember. The purple and lilac striped awning of the boulangerie extends round the corner to the entrance to the house, which is on the other side, through a black wrought-iron gate leading to the courtyard garden, and beyond to the kitchen door. I almost want to clap my hands together in glee at how familiar it is. Memories stream in from every side, jostling for room in my head. Matthieu arriving in the kitchen, dusting his hands of flour on a towel before washing them and sitting down at the table to eat lunch with us all; how we'd all eat lunch together, whenever possible; the joshing that went on between me and Dominique in particular, the heavy sarcasm Suzanne applied to her mum, but in a good-natured, albeit teenage, way; how eating at the table, sharing the stories of the day, was the cornerstone of their lives, my life, too, when I lived there. It all comes flooding back and tears prick my eyes as the emotion threatens to overwhelm me.

Suddenly, a shadow looms over me. Matthieu. '*Salut,* Lia.' His gruff voice startles me at first, but then, as his face broadens into a wide smile, I collect myself, greet him and give him two kisses, one on each cheek. He fires off a torrent of French at me, and I panic slightly. His accent has always been harder for me to understand than that of Suzanne and Estelle, perhaps because I spent so much more time with them, and I struggle to keep up with what he's saying.

Suzanne rolls her eyes at her dad. '*Papa*, not so fast.'

Matthieu throws me an apologetic look and his pace alters, so I'm soon able to follow what he's saying. I work out he's happy I'm here and he doesn't think I've changed at all. Yeah, I wish. Just the presence of a few wrinkles. The kilos I'd gained in the past fifteen years, I've lost in the past few weeks after my split from Freddy.

Matthieu ushers us to the table and he and Estelle, once she has divested herself of her coat and washed her hands, prepare us an impromptu snack of *pain de campagne* with fresh tomato salad, whilst Suzanne opens a bottle of red wine. Négrette. Back when I lived here, I wasn't a connoisseur of wine, not that I particularly consider myself one now, but I do now know more than wine is just red, white or rosé. I note the wine is local, and it warms my heart to remember how for the Molins, sourcing everything locally and supporting their community, even within the city, their small area of Chalets, is all-important. Usually, it's produce from a friend's farm, or a cousin's apiary, or a neighbour's orchard. The cheeses the Molins used to put on our lunch and dinner table were incredible. I salivate at the thought and then, as if conjured up by my desire for them, Estelle brings over a platter of cheese.

And just like before, Estelle is centre stage, doing what she does best. She really is my second mum. Whilst Suzanne speaks English, neither of her parents do, so they assume, as they rightfully should, that I'll understand their French.

Estelle begins. 'This cheese is from the *fromagerie* next door. You remember?'

I nod. How could I forget?

'It is a creamy Roquefort with an intense flavour, kind of like burnt caramel. The second one is Ossau-Iraty – from the French Basque Country. Sheep's milk. And the third one is Rocamadour, which is sweet and tastes of hazelnuts.'

I'm suddenly starving. Suzanne and I wash our hands companionably, as we used to do when called to table, and Matthieu passes me the bread. Gratefully, I tear off a piece, cut myself some Roquefort, haphazardly slather some on the *pain de campagne* and then bite into it. Oh my God, it tastes like – actually, I can't describe it. Nothing would do it justice. How can I have been eating the pretender from the deli near my flat and enjoying it? That shows how poor the other offerings have been in the UK. I moan with pleasure then catch myself, embarrassed, but it's clearly the right reaction to have had, as all three are staring at me, smiles on their faces.

Estelle winks at Matthieu, who grins, then Suzanne joins in and says, 'Welcome back.'

An hour later, replete and not a little inebriated – that Négrette is more potent than I'd anticipated – I finally move from the table when the house phone rings and Estelle goes to answer it.

'It's Sarah. She says she's coming over on Monday. She can't wait any longer to see you.'

My heart melts. Sarah was always the responsible one, such a sweet nature. The eldest. She and Suzanne used to help Matthieu clean out the bakery after he'd finished 'creating' for the day, ready for the next day's work. It's all coming back to me how gruelling it must be for them. As a young tourist, all I focused on was eating the spoils. I make a pact with myself to help out more, and with that in mind, I rise to clear the table. But Estelle admonishes me with a wag of her finger. 'No, you are a guest.'

Some things never change.

'Why don't you go unpack instead? I've given you the same room,' Estelle says with a smile.

I give in. She's very convincing. I squeeze her hand lightly as I pass her and then climb the three sets of stairs to my attic room. Given I'm out of puff by the time I reach the top, I'm delighted Matthieu has carried my suitcase up for me. I am so out of shape.

My room is exactly as I remember. A cluster of French novels – both classics and popular romance novels – adorns the white bookcase, pretty yellow and white gingham curtains flutter in the breeze from the open Velux window, and a pristine old-fashioned white eiderdown covers the bed. Rich ruby-red satin cushions and a matching bed runner complete the look. I sit on the bed and drink it all in, then I take a few snaps as my heart soars and I text Jules.

I'm here. I can't believe it. They're as wonderful as ever, my room looks the same and the food is amazing. Thanks so much for making me do this. Love you, L x

When I return to the living room, we settle down and continue catching up, the room quickly filling with animated chatter and laughter.

The doorbell rings and Matthieu frowns, raising his chin in a question to his wife. Estelle shrugs and looks at Suzanne, whose mouth downturns in an 'I have no clue' expression.

Matthieu hauls himself out of his chair and goes to open the door. Soon there is the sound of laughter and friendly banter, and I'm curious as to who is disturbing them so late on a Saturday night, particularly when usually they'd be in Gascony. I'm guessing it's not someone hoping for a late-night pastry.

Another memory – in southwest France, the *pains au chocolat* aren't always called *pains au chocolat*, but *chocolatines*, or *chocos*. They taste so much better than the poor substitutes we get back home. I'm hoping we'll be having some tomorrow, even if the boulangerie is closed. I'm guessing Matthieu keeps some for Sunday breakfast.

Matthieu returns to the room, and Estelle is about to ask him who was at the door, but the question has barely begun to form before a tall, slim guy with brown spiky hair, and the most gorgeous smile, causing laughter lines to crease at his eyes, follows Matthieu into the room.

Estelle rises from the sofa. 'Jean-Luc. How are you?' She embraces him then kisses him on both cheeks. 'What brings you here tonight?'

'I had to return to the *fromagerie*. I'd forgotten some cheese I was supposed to take to a friend in the Lot tomorrow.'

'Ah,' Estelle says as if that explains everything.

That's when Jean-Luc's gaze meets mine. 'Oh, I'm sorry, you have guests. I don't want to intrude.'

'Not at all,' says Suzanne. 'Come, sit with us. We never get the chance as we're always at *Mémé* and *Papi*'s at the weekend.'

Jean-Luc nods. 'Thank you.' He takes the red wine Estelle places in front of him. 'I saw the lights on and was surprised. I wanted to make sure nothing was wrong, but I see everything is just fine.' His eyes twinkle, and is it my imagination or was he looking at me as he said that?

'Sorry, Lia, how rude of me. Of course, you have not met Jean-Luc. Jean-Luc, this is our good friend, Lia, all the way from Scotland. She is here for a couple of weeks. She came to live with us fifteen years ago for three months, to learn about France and the French. A gap year, or in your case, Lia–' she turns to me '–a gap three months.'

I smile and although I'm pretending it's at Estelle's comment, it's because Jean-Luc's presence is making me feel things I haven't felt in a long time. A really long time. Fleetingly, I realise just how over my relationship with Freddy was long before he broke up with me. I don't remember the last time he made me feel like this, if ever.

'Hi,' I venture shyly in French. I can manage that. I'm

too tongue-tied for much else right now.

Estelle turns to me. 'Jean-Luc's family has had the cheese shop next door for three generations.'

'Your cheeses are incredible,' I say.

'Thank you. Perhaps sometime I can give you a tour of where we make them. Show you the real France.'

I manage to croak out, 'That would be lovely, if you have time.'

'Oh, I'll make time,' says Jean-Luc.

I flush to the tips of my toes. I can't make eye contact as I know my neck is bright red and my face will follow suit. I only hope I can pass it off as the effect of the Négrette.

Jean-Luc is good company and he regales us all with tales of disasters in the cheesemaking process, a new member of staff, and the time a cheese rolled away at the market when a mastiff careened into his stall and sent everything flying.

Talk soon turns to Saint-Sauvy in Gascony, where Estelle's parents' home is, and where the Molins usually retreat to at the weekend, and where it transpires we'll be going first thing tomorrow morning to check on the grandparents. With my arrival today, they've rescheduled, and I feel bad for upsetting their downtime and family routine.

Suzanne scoffs, 'Don't be silly, our grandparents will be having a great time, playing cards with friends, gossiping and drinking wine. They're probably relieved we're not there to keep them in check.'

Everyone laughs and when I sense Jean-Luc's eyes on me, a warm glow suffuses my face. This trip is already turning out to be more interesting than I'd first anticipated.

Chapter Six

The toll of the church bells wakes me. Immediately, I realise it's Sunday, as when I lived here, on every other day, it was the aroma of baking bread or freshly prepared *chocolatines* that roused me from my slumber, not the bells.

Sleepily, I try to return to my dream, since I'm pretty sure the guy in it was Jean-Luc. A bit early for him to be strolling through my dreams, but as dreams go, I'll take it. Damned bells. Maybe something would have happened if they hadn't woken me. I know it was only a dream, but I can imagine, right? I count the number of times the bells peal out. Eight. Hmm, time for a little more shuteye or should I make an effort and get up?

Eventually, I decide to get up, although the sky is only beginning to lighten. I'd forgotten sunrise is a good half-hour later than in Glasgow, and the lack of light confuses me for a second.

It takes me all of two minutes to throw on some clothes, splash some water on my face and trot downstairs, past everyone else's bedrooms, to the bakery floor, and then on into the family kitchen, where Estelle is already preparing breakfast.

'Good morning, *ma fille*, how did you sleep?'

It warms my heart that she calls me 'ma fille' – my

daughter. When I lived here, I always felt just like one of her children. She and Matthieu couldn't have made me any more welcome.

'Really well. I was a bit worried for a second as the mattress is a lot firmer than the one I have at home, but I fell asleep almost straightaway.' I falter over the word for 'firm', but I think she gets my meaning.

'Good. Omelette?' She indicates the frying pan where she is adding peppers and tomatoes to her eggy mix.

'Hmm, yes, please.' The heavenly smell is already assailing my senses and I breathe it in. I hadn't realised I was so hungry.

'Where is everyone?' I ask, assuming they aren't in bed as no one in this family ever had a lie-in the whole time I lived here. There was always too much to do.

Estelle stirs the omelette. 'Suzanne is still asleep. We were doing the accounts late last night, and as we're not in Saint-Sauvy this morning, she's taking the opportunity to catch up on her sleep. She doesn't usually stay overnight since she lives with Patrick, her fiancé, but as we're all going to visit my parents later, she decided to sleep in her room.'

'I haven't heard much about Patrick. What's he like?'

'He's from Mauritius originally, forty-two and an architect. They met when they were both on holiday in Italy, but they were with their partners at the time.'

'That must have been interesting.' I laugh.

'Yes, there were some tense moments, but fortunately, it has all worked out.'

'*Salut, les filles.*' Matthieu comes into the kitchen, hair still wet from the shower.

'Morning.' I smile as Matthieu kisses the top of Estelle's head and then grabs her hand and tries to dance around the kitchen with her.

'Get off!' She swats him away good-naturedly and his shoulders heave with laughter. 'I've omelettes to prepare.'

'My favourite.' He raises his chin in his signature Gallic way.

'Lia, coffee?' Estelle asks.

I stand up from the table. 'Yes, but I'll get it.'

'No, you are a guest, Lia,' Estelle says, same as last night.

'Yes, but I want to do my bit.' I can be just as stubborn as her. 'And anyway, I'm sure Matthieu has other things to do.'

Matthieu sits down at the table. 'Like eating omelette.'

Estelle flicks a tea towel at him and we all laugh. I love their camaraderie. Growing up, I didn't experience this, at least not beyond the age of eight, when Dad died. Sometimes I find it hard to recall his features, never mind any heartwarming family tableaux.

'Everything all right, Lia?' Estelle's concerned gaze is focused on me.

I blink and a lump forms in my throat. This is obviously why it was so easy to slip into family life here with the Molins. Although Mum and I are close, I definitely felt that gaping hole from having no father figure. Mum did her best, but there was only one of her, plus there were two of us, me and my sister, Samantha, who was only two when Dad died. It was a lot for Mum to deal with on her own.

Estelle and Matthieu know my dad died when I was young, but I didn't dwell on it with them when I was here last time, and I don't intend to now.

'Yes, just reminiscing.' I smile. 'That omelette smells

incredible, Estelle,' I say, changing the subject.

As with anything related to her cooking, Estelle beams. 'You can give me your mark out of ten once you've tried it.'

She splits it in two and gives half to me and half to Matthieu.

I frown. 'Aren't you having any?'

'Oh yes, I'm going to make another couple.'

I dig in, and remember not to groan. It's very difficult not to have food orgasms when living with the Molins, as everything tastes amazing. Although they run a boulangerie, both Estelle and Matthieu are also excellent cooks. The omelette's incredible and I enjoy every morsel.

'Lia, we're going to head to Saint-Sauvy in an hour. Is that enough time for you?'

I nod, unable to speak due to the quantity of omelette in my mouth.

'Sarah usually goes to her grandparents' at the weekend too, but Elodie had a football tournament so that's why she's coming here tomorrow instead.'

I can't wait to see Sarah. Last night, Estelle showed me some pictures of her and her beautiful family. Her face shone with pride as she spoke of them.

My phone buzzes with a message. Jules. Who else? Mum is away on a cruise with a friend, so she's unlikely to be texting me. When she found out Freddy and I had split up, she was all for cancelling the cruise, but I wouldn't let her, and although Samantha and I are close, I haven't told her yet that I've come to France. She helped me enough just by keeping in touch by text after I split with Freddy. I don't want to be a burden to her, or Mum. They have their own lives to lead and life is busy. Well, mine was. Now, not so much, what with the garden leave. I smile at the thought of what that garden leave has led to. Every cloud definitely does have a silver lining.

Samantha's halfway through a Masters in Creative Writing at the University of Bath, so she has her own stresses.

How was your first night? Did you wake to the smell of baking bread? Was it heaven? x

I obviously didn't tell Jules there's no baking on a Sunday. Sleeping in my old bed, as I've come to think of it, was heaven though – despite the firmness of the mattress – right down to the rain pitter-pattering off the Velux window in the middle of the night. I drifted back to sleep each time, barely aware I'd awoken.

Hey Jules, how you? Fabulous to be back. They haven't changed a bit. Neither has my old room. Yes, it was wonderful, although no fresh bread. And I met a gorgeous man. He's a cheesemonger. It's Sunday and the boulangerie is closed. Off to the country in an hour. Will send pics xx

Immediately, Jules pings back a reply. *A cheesemonger, get in! Give me the rundown.*

I chuckle at her quest for details and type back, *Later,* knowing the one-word answer will frustrate the hell out of her.

When I've finished my omelette and eaten part of the second one, plus polished off two large cups of coffee, served in blue and white ceramic mugs, I offer to help Estelle, and she directs me to loading up the car with what we need for the grandparents.

They probably won't remember me. Estelle's mum and dad must be in their late eighties, early nineties now. I should probably ask. If I recall correctly, her dad was René and her mum Alexine. I wonder how they're doing. All I remember, apart from a treasured photo taken of all the women on the last Saturday I spent here fifteen years ago, was that I really struggled to understand them. Because of where they live, and given their age, they speak patois, or more correctly Gascon dialect, not French. I did manage to glean a few bits and pieces, but only because I speak Spanish too, and the dialect in Gascony is like a mix of French and Spanish. I suppose that was inevitable with its proximity to Spain. Plus, I was genuinely interested in the variety of dialects. I have such respect for the lengths people in these communities go to in order to keep a language alive.

Suzanne bops downstairs, looking like a teenager with her youthful demeanour and slim build, effortlessly chic, in only a pair of jeans and a plain white tee. I so wish I could pull that off. Perhaps it's years of having to wear suits for meetings, but I simply can't get away with that. I've opted for straight-legged denims, a cashmere jumper and a scarf jauntily knotted around my neck, so it looks like I know what I'm doing. I probably look like a total idiot.

'Ready?' Suzanne asks as she grabs an apple from the fruit bowl and takes a bite.

She sees me looking at her and pauses mid-bite. 'What?'

When I say nothing, she points to the fruit bowl. 'Take one if you want.'

I shake my head. She doesn't realise I was just thinking how much like an advert for good living she is. Maybe I can strive towards that, too, now I'm here in France, eating the Mediterranean diet, for the most part. Not sure the croissants and *chocolatines* count as Mediterranean though, or a good diet.

We all pile into Matthieu's Renault estate. Estelle, as usual, is chattering away as if her words will be rationed soon. I half-listen as I roll down the window and take in the sights, sounds and smells as we begin the hour-long journey to Estelle's parents' house in Saint-Sauvy.

Soon we leave the city behind and pass field after field of reddish brown or bare soil. Suzanne tells me if we were a few months later, they'd be filled with poppies and sunflowers, but it's still too early, although we do spot some snowdrops. The earlier rain has given way to glorious sunshine and I know there's no place I'd rather be. The only thing, or rather person, I wish I had with me is Jules. She'd love this, but this trip to France is one I have to make alone. This is my metaphorical as well as physical journey. I'm hoping it will be cathartic and I'll be able to offload some of the recent negativity that has plagued me. I'm still waiting to hear what will happen definitively with my garden leave, and until I know the outcome, I'm a little in limbo, and it's not a situation I enjoy being in.

The fields give way to vineyards, the vines held up and strengthened by plastic ties, and I can't help but wonder how much each field is worth.

Suzanne notes me looking and says, 'These are the Cabernet Franc grapes. They are the most exclusive. St Émilion, the most expensive wine in France, contains at least thirty per cent Cabernet Franc.'

'Oh?' I say. I know nothing about grape varieties apart from those of the wines I like to drink. And the only percentage I know about when it comes to wine is the alcohol percentage.

Suzanne nods. 'Yes, the majority is Merlot, about sixty per cent, with around thirty per cent Cabernet Franc and ten per cent Cabernet Sauvignon.'

'I didn't know that. I'm a bit clueless when it comes to wine,' I confess.

Suzanne laughs. 'Don't worry. Hazard of being from this area. We know a lot about wine, cheese, foie gras and, in our case, baking.'

'You sure do,' I agree. 'And although you can keep your foie gras, I'm happy to sample as many of the other three as possible.'

'There's a lot of money to be made in foie gras.' Suzanne grins. 'But where there is money to be made, there are always crooks. So I'm glad it's not something we're involved in.'

I couldn't agree with her more. Yuck. Foie gras. The very thought makes my stomach heave.

As we drive, Suzanne fills me in on the other crops Gascony is famous for. Some of them are plain to see as the golden brown of the wheatfields and the pale green of the cornfields stretch for miles ahead of us, the new stalks of corn barely beginning to push through. I'm also keen to try the locally grown fruit after what she's told me.

'We also grow walnuts and have a lot of chestnut trees. There is nothing better in winter, or in autumn even–' she corrects herself '–than roast chestnuts.'

I'm almost salivating at the thought. The morning's drizzle isn't such a distant memory that I can't imagine how comforting those would be when it's cold and bleak.

As we enter the town of Mauvezin, I feel as if I've had a lesson from a great teacher en route. The more I discover about the area, the people, the more I want to learn. It's considerably different coming back here at thirty-six than being here at twenty-one, I'm discovering. Twenty-one-year-old me clearly missed so much, and I have this urge to make up for it. I want to understand everything. The need to know more is almost like a drug coursing through my system. Fortunately, I have Suzanne on tap for that, and she appears ready to play her role as guide.

Suzanne points out the château of Mauvezin and gives me a potted history, as I try, and largely fail, to recognise landmarks other than the castle. However, the more she explains to me, the more fascinated I become, particularly with the history, and already I'm wishing my trip to France was longer than two weeks.

Chapter Seven

We draw up outside a smallholding. I only have the one memory of it – that photograph, taken fifteen years ago, of all the women standing outside.

I take the opportunity to feast on the view when we get out of the car: the gently undulating hills of Saint-Sauvy and its environs, with the yellow flowers of the rapeseed fields, pockets of woodland and forest and a church spire or two from the neighbouring villages. It's so peaceful here. No wonder the Molins come to visit their parents and grandparents each week.

Matthieu unloads the car as Estelle and Suzanne go indoors to greet Estelle's parents. I follow a few paces behind.

Alexine, whom I recognise, but who has notably aged, pushes past Suzanne to reach me. 'Lia, it is good to see you,' she says. I just about make that out. It may take me a while to acclimatise to the dialect again.

'And you,' I say as she embraces me. She is so small against me. She can't even be five foot. Even though it's not particularly cold, she's wearing several layers. She feels much more insubstantial than last time I saw her, although then she would only have been early to mid-seventies. Her hair, however, is immaculate, but free of product, if I'm not mistaken. In the countryside, the focus on style is replaced by practicality and comfort, but that doesn't mean she doesn't look neat. She's rake thin, but there's a kindness as well as an intelligence in her eyes that shows you should never underestimate her. I imagine she was a formidable woman when she was younger. In fact, she may well still be.

Her welcome warms my soul and the fact she remembers me after all these years melts my heart. I try my best French on her, hoping she'll understand, even if she responds in dialect. She pats my arm and her face creases into a wide smile, revealing perfect tiny teeth. Her movements are unsteady and as she moves away from me, back towards the house, I reach out an arm behind her, ready to catch her if she stumbles.

'Come,' says Alexine. 'René is waiting to see you again.'

Privately, I wonder why he didn't come out with her to greet me. However, no sooner am I indoors than I see why. He waves at me from his bed in the living room. If I thought Alexine had changed, René is a shock. My memory serves up a robust, confident but quiet man of the land – his family business agriculture, rather than the boulangerie – but René is a shadow of his former self. He seems shrunken, significantly so. It's clear he is very ill, but I don't want to ask and can only hope Suzanne or Estelle will enlighten me later.

My train of thought is broken by Suzanne throwing her arms around her grandfather. '*Papi*, how are you? Do you need some help?'

René shakes his head and Estelle chooses that moment to say, '*Maman*, come help me prepare lunch. Matthieu has brought some special things today. Your favourites.'

Where the sparkle had disappeared from Alexine's eyes only a moment before on seeing her husband's discomfort, and possibly pain, now her eyes shine, and I think what a wonderful daughter Estelle is. In fact, she's generally awesome: great mum, great daughter, great friend, great 'adoptive' mother in my case, and I wonder when she gets any time off.

What a shame. They work so hard, and then even at the weekends they have to look after their families. First it was their children and now the parents and in-laws.

I sit with Suzanne and René as Matthieu tends to some plumbing task René has told him needs doing. The banter between grandfather and granddaughter flows easily, and it's lovely to see their rapport, although I can't help but feel wistful I've never had that. My grandparents lived too far away for me ever to have that relationship. I only saw them fleetingly at Christmas and perhaps once during the summer holidays.

'Everyone, to the table. We will eat outside,' Estelle says when she returns. She moves to the veranda as Matthieu passes her with a wheelchair, which he directs towards René's bed. As I pass over the threshold, I risk a glance back and see Matthieu transferring his father-in-law to the chair with such care and tenderness, it makes me want to weep. Again, I wonder what illness he has to render him so incapacitated, but I'm sure I'll find out in good time.

I take a seat at the black oval wrought-iron eight-seater table and over a lunch of salad, with mountains of creamy Roquefort, tomatoes on the vine and baguette, as well as paté and houmous, we chat animatedly about Scotland – Alexine has always wanted to go but never been – and I try to learn more snippets of dialect. With Matthieu as designated driver, Suzanne, Estelle, Alexine and I have a couple of glasses of wine from the Gaillac region. It's like stardust. And this is their lunch wine. God only knows what they drink when they go out for a meal then.

We're rounding off our meal with a digestif, and René is flagging, his eyes heavy with tiredness, when the roar of a car's exhaust breaks the relative silence. A Porsche, not sure which model, pulls in next to us. My heartbeat picks up when the new arrival steps out of the car. He is bloody gorgeous and a dart of longing shoots through me. Close-cropped brown hair, with precision-groomed facial hair and the most piercing emerald-green eyes. He can't be far off six feet tall, too – another thing I like. Taller than me, but not too much taller. And he's very tanned; in fact, he's so tanned he may actually have some Middle Eastern heritage in him.

What is wrong with me? I've only just split up with Freddy. The last thing I need is to embroil myself in some scenario with some random French bloke. Two random French blokes, my memory tells me, as I recall the night before with Jean-Luc. Maybe I'm on heat, or going through early menopause. That's meant to make you super horny, right? Whatever the reason, I can't help the feeling this guy has created in me.

'Madame Bouchard, *bonjour*,' he calls.

Oh crap, and a super sexy voice to boot.

'Théo, what a surprise.' She beckons him over with a finger and he strides towards her, throwing a glance in my direction as he passes. My breath catches and I lower my eyes, fearing I may blush.

He bends to kiss her on both cheeks, as I take in his long, muscular legs encased in designer jeans, the immaculate crisp white shirt and the navy cashmere sweater he has artfully draped around his shoulders, almost in the Italian way. He then greets René – formally, again, I note.

'*Papa* sent me with some Armagnac for you. It's the new vintage.'

Alexine bestows a fond smile upon him. 'Your father is so kind, Théo. Tell him thank you very much. Wait and I will get something for you to take back to him.'

I studiously ignore Théo. I'm not meaning to be rude; it's simply that I don't want to embarrass myself further by flushing pillar-box red.

Alexine returns shortly afterwards with a bottle of white, with a handwritten label, and some homemade bread, which she hands to Théo. 'Why don't you put that in the car and then join us?'

I glance up at that moment, not sure whether what I feel is hope or despair. All I know is my heart is racing. Théo hesitates then Alexine says, 'Oh, and we have a visitor, Lia. She's staying with Estelle and Matthieu for two weeks.'

Théo turns to me and his lips edge up at the corners. '*Enchanté*, Lia.' He then spouts a torrent of rapid French that I don't follow. My panic at not having understood pretty much anything must become apparent as Alexine intervenes.

'Lia is from Scotland. She speaks French, but I think perhaps you are going too fast for her.'

'In that case, Lia, may I offer my apologies?' Théo says in English with barely a trace of a French accent.

I smile and shake my head. 'No need to apologise. Nice to meet you.'

'No, the pleasure is all mine.' His eyes rest on me for a

millisecond longer than would be usual for an introduction and that feeling of lust strikes me again. I almost want a fan. Thank God I didn't meet him on a summer's day or I'd have combusted.

Matthieu rises. 'What would you like to drink, Théo? I'm guessing no wine for you since you're driving.'

'No. Perhaps some orange juice.'

'Coming right up.' Matthieu turns back. 'Would you like something to eat?'

'No, I'm good, thank you.'

As René and Alexine talk with Théo, I notice Suzanne is very quiet. I wonder how old Théo is, but I don't imagine there can be so much of an age difference between them, and it makes me question why Théo didn't greet Suzanne or she him. I'm probably just being silly. It's the analytical part of my brain. I'd have been a great detective story writer, I'm sure, as I'm always analysing everything, often seeing patterns or clues that aren't actually there.

'Isn't that right, Lia?' Alexine says.

'Sorry? I was miles away,' I say, guiltily. I don't want them to think their conversation isn't interesting enough for me to join in; I simply have a habit of daydreaming, especially when in the presence of a hot-looking man. And if there's one thing Théo is, it's hot. Wait until I tell Jules. She'll never believe me. Not one but two hot men in two days. She'll be on the next flight. I try to stem a grin but it slips out.

Théo raises an eyebrow, clearly wondering what has caused me to smile.

'I was telling Théo you stayed with Estelle and Matthieu fifteen years ago for three months and now you're back for a trip down memory lane.'

'That's right. I loved it here, the boulangerie, the countryside here in Gascony–' I spread my hands expansively to encompass my surroundings '–the language, the people, the way of life.'

Théo's eyes meet mine. 'So, you're interested in French culture, cuisine, history, too?'

I nod. 'Of course. I'm hoping for full immersion in all things French the next couple of weeks.'

He inclines his head and looks thoughtful.

Suzanne clears her throat. 'Top-up, Lia?'

I glance down and see my glass is empty. 'Sure, thank you.' I hold out my glass and she refills it.

'Théo?' she asks as if saying his name causes her physical pain and I wonder at the atmosphere between them, although, the frostiness seems to be one-way, coming from Suzanne, which is odd as she's usually so laid-back.

'I'll get myself some more orange juice from the fridge.'

As Théo goes indoors to refill his drink, I study Suzanne. She's scowling so hard she may turn him to stone if she continues. No love lost there then.

When Théo returns, he smiles warmly at me as he strolls back to the table, and shyly, I smile back. As Jules would say, he's all man. Testosterone fuelled. Not my usual type, I must admit, but he has a certain *je ne sais quoi*, and I'm not only saying that because I'm in France. He has a sophisticated air. I realise I don't know what he does for a living, and as if he has read my mind, Théo starts discussing wine with René, whose body may be enfeebled, but whose mind certainly isn't.

I don't catch everything they say, but I glean enough to know Théo is a vintner in the family business. He does look the type to be swanning around a vineyard, checking the temperature of his grapes as he escorts enthused tourists around, or maybe he's the one who cuts multi-million-euro business deals for the family brandy. Whatever the case, he exudes a certain something that reels you in, and he seems a natural extrovert, fitting in with the Bouchards and Molins with ease, Suzanne excepted. One day I'll ask her what her gripe is with him, but I don't want anything to spoil today.

The sun is shining. We're replete with delicious food and I lean back in my chair, close my eyes and raise my face to the sky, eager to feel the sun's warmth as I listen to everyone's chatter around me.

My phone beeps and my idyllic moment is shattered. Freddy.

For God's sake, will he get out of my life already?

Hi, Lia, the estate agent phoned. Someone is coming tomorrow to view the flat. Can you bake some bread or something? Let's hope for a quick sale, yeah?

Is he for real? I hadn't bothered to tell Freddy I was coming to France, as it was none of his bloody business. I'd told the estate agent I was still contactable, although I'd be out of the country, so they knew the score, but since they were doing all the viewings, I didn't think it was a big deal.

And bake bread. Do I look like I'm Freddy's bloody servant? Plus, what gives him the right to think he can breezily ask me to bake bread to have a welcoming aroma greet the viewers? We no longer live together. We are no longer a couple. He is banging someone else and probably was for part of the time he was with me. Red mist descends and I have to put my phone back in my bag before I send Freddy a string of expletives. Ignoring him is more powerful, but it doesn't stop my heart rate picking up in anger.

Suzanne gives me a knowing look, her eyebrows scrunched. 'Everything OK?'

'Yeah,' I mutter unconvincingly.

I sense Théo's eyes on me as Estelle talks to him about a wine delivery for a friend's birthday.

'Oh, I didn't realise the time,' Théo says, jumping to his feet. 'Apologies, everyone, but I need to be at my brother's for dinner soon.'

As we all say goodbye, Théo stops by my chair. 'Lia, could you help me with something from my car, please?'

Taken aback, I almost say, 'Me?' but stop myself in time. 'Sure.'

I follow him to the boot of his car, which he opens then rummages around in. 'For you, to take back to Scotland.' He hands me a bottle of Armagnac.

'Oh, I couldn't possibly. But thank you.' I make to hand it back to him, but he says, 'Please. I will be offended if you don't accept. It's a gift.'

His gaze is so earnest I relent and thank him.

'Could you take this bottle for Estelle as well, please?'

'Sure.' I hold out my hand.

'One last thing.' He moves closer to me, and lowers his face as if to whisper something to me. It's surprisingly erotic, and I catch the scent of his aftershave. Woodsy.

I wait, almost holding my breath, which I fear will whoosh out of me any second.

'Will you have dinner with me?' His voice is soft and sexy and every wild ounce of me wants to say yes, despite the unexpected invitation, but my analytical brain makes me say, 'But I hardly know you. I just met you half an hour ago.'

His emerald eyes sparkle as he says, 'Ah, but strangers

are simply friends waiting to be made, isn't that how the saying goes?' His hand touches my shoulder in a gesture of camaraderie, at least I think that's what it is, but the jolt that shoots through me must be visible.

'Apologies, I have overstepped myself.'

I give my head a slight shake. 'No, it's OK. I simply wasn't expecting...' I don't want him to know I wasn't expecting to feel that sensation when he touched me, so I let my thought hang unfinished. That way he can wonder if I meant, expecting him to touch me.

He quirks an eyebrow. 'So, dinner? Friday? Five o'clock? I'll pick you up from the Molins'.'

I dither for a second, then he gives me such a disarming smile, I cave. 'Dinner,' I say, then I walk slowly back towards the family, almost swinging my arms holding the two bottles of wine.

Looks like I've got myself a date. Wait until I tell Jules.

Chapter Eight

I call Jules first thing before she starts work. When she's in the country, Monday is always her busiest day, with lots of meetings. She's a total powerhouse, but then she didn't get to be running her own successful PR firm and have legions of people below her to do her bidding without making lots of sacrifices. I'm sure she sleeps less than five hours a night.

'You've what?' cries Jules.

I smile at her indignant expression, grateful for video calling. This is priceless.

'I've got a date, on Friday, with a handsome Frenchman called Théo.'

'Christ, I thought I worked fast, girl, but this is fast work indeed. Well done. And he's a cheesemonger, fabulous. Bring loads back with you when you come home.'

I accept Jules' praise then correct her. 'Actually, he's not a cheesemonger, he's a vintner.'

'How did you mix that up?'

'Hmm, funny story, but I didn't mix it up. It's two different guys.'

'Lia Abernethy, you total tart.' I note a hint of respect in Jules' words. 'How can you have gone to France and in two days met not one but two hot men? Let me check flights.'

I listen as she fires a torrent of questions at me.

'Well, I met Théo in Saint-Sauvy, in Gascony, when I went to Suzanne's grandparents' country home.'

'Right, and how did you get from meeting him to him wanting to get into your knickers?'

'He does not want to get into my knickers,' I scoff, secretly hoping there may be the future possibility of him wanting to get into my knickers, the very thought of which makes me go warm in places I'd rather not discuss with Jules. I'm also wondering if I have any appropriate knickers with me on this trip, or if I may need to visit a lingerie shop.

'Yeah, right. He so wants into your knickers. Tell me all the details.'

'I don't really know anything except he's picking me up from the Molins' at five on Friday, and taking me for dinner.'

'Five? Isn't that a bit early for the French?' Jules asks.

'That's what I thought, but what do I know? Things may have changed since last time I was here.' Plenty has already. I think back to René.

'Did you take anything suitable to France with you to wear?' Jules presses.

Honestly, not that I'm aware of. The last thing on my mind when I came here was going on a date. I've only just got shot of Freddy.

'Not really. Maybe I can pick something up.'

'Good plan. And how are things with the family?' Jules asks.

'Great. As if I've never been away.' Happiness floods my system as I realise the truth of this. I love this family as if they were my own and it doesn't feel as if fifteen years have passed since I last saw them. Instead, I feel as if I've been on a gap year and have just returned home.

'Aw, that's good. Which one is Suzanne again? The younger one?'

'Yeah, she still works in the boulangerie.'

'And what does she think about your date with the fabulous Théo?' Jules grins as she says 'fabulous'.

'I haven't told her yet.' I realise this only now, but am questioning whether subconsciously I held the info back because of her attitude towards Théo, or if I was too caught up in the moment and forgot.

'Why not? Get on it as you'll need her advice, not only with fashion tips, but for how French guys behave on dates and what they expect, and what you should expect.'

Jules has raised a valid point. The rules of dating may be worlds apart from what I've become accustomed to in the UK, not that I have much of a handle on it there, what with being in a relationship with Freddy F-word for the past three years.

'And whilst we're on the subject of hot French men, what about the other one? The cheesemonger?'

'He was only being friendly when he was at the Molins' on Saturday night. He offered me a tour of the cheese process.'

'I'll bet he did.' She gives a saucy wink.

'Enough, you,' I say. 'He's lovely and sweet and he works next door, so it'll be nice to have a friend close by.'

'Wouldn't mind a friend like that myself.' Jules grins.

'Anyway, Julia–' I use her given name to pretend I'm annoyed with her '–can't stay chatting to you. Much to do, hot men to meet.'

'Talking about men, and not hot ones, have you heard

from F-word?'

'Yes,' I say, my voice rising in pitch. 'Do you know what he bloody well did?'

I relay the details of Freddy's text and Jules is rightly as outraged as me. 'Want me to go round and spill a drink over him in Brava if he dares show his face again?'

'No, but thanks. I've ignored him.'

'Well done. Tough, I know, but necessary. Right, let me know how the viewing goes. The sooner you get shot of any link to that idiot, the better.'

'Don't hold back, Jules, now, will you?'

She tilts her head to one side. 'I only speak the truth.'

'Right, I really am going now. I want to have a walk down by the river and explore a little before Sarah arrives this afternoon.'

'Fine, text me later.'

'Yes, Mum.' I salute her.

'Love you.'

'And you. Don't do anything I wouldn't do,' I say.

'That's not exactly leaving much, is it?'

'Ha bloody ha, now beat it.'

'Going.' She blows me a kiss and I reciprocate.

'Suzanne, you busy?' I ask as I pad into the living room. She's sitting with a stack of receipts in front of her.

'Afraid so. I have to finish this and then I'm off to the supplier to pick up some flour.'

'No worries. I'm going for a walk down by the river and to see the market in full swing again.'

She smiles. 'Place du Capitole has changed a lot in the last fifteen years. The market is still there, but it's a lot more professional now, with vans and fixed stands, rather than the wooden tables and canopies that could be dismantled each day.'

'Progress, eh?' I say.

'Yeah, not always a good thing. But maybe we could do something together another time. I have a few things I'd like to show you.'

'That would be wonderful, thank you.' I lean down and hug her then pop my head into the boulangerie through the beaded curtain after checking for the sound of customers and hearing none.

'Estelle, I'm going into town. Do you need me to pick anything up?'

'No, no, thank you.' She then comes forward to kiss me on both cheeks. 'Have a good time.'

'I will, thanks.' As I turn to go, Estelle says, 'Actually, could you get some garlic, some spring onions and perhaps some tomatoes, from the market?'

'Of course.'

She rummages in her bag for her purse, but I lay my hand on her arm. 'Let me.' She goes to protest, but I insist. 'It's the least I can do. Really.'

I hug her and head out through the front door of the boulangerie, but not before I study the array of goods lined up beneath the glass countertops and inhale the amazing aroma.

I meander along the network of little streets, going from memory, occasionally taking a wrong turn, but revelling in the luxury of not having to be anywhere by a certain time. I'm still early enough to make the market in plenty of time. I drink in the smells, the sounds, including the occasional frantic horn. Stereotypes are stereotypes for a reason and the French's impatience in traffic is legendary. I love absorbing the spoken French as I amble along the streets, unhurriedly. This is the life. I pass a playground where young mums are pushing their children on swings, chatting with friends, whilst others walk around the park with their dogs or with babies and toddlers in pushchairs.

The sun rises high in the sky and beats down on me. It's warmer than I'd expected and I wish I'd worn a T-shirt as was my original plan. A school looms ahead of me, where outside in the playground some children are playing with skipping ropes whilst another group is chasing one other. I smile at the obvious fun they're having.

Finally, I arrive at Place du Capitole. It's even more magnificent than I remember, and it seems fitting that as I reach the main square, church bells toll the hour. It's almost like a declaration or a celebration of my return to this place which I loved so much. Suzanne is right though; it has changed. My gaze sweeps across the square, from the market, which is still going, but doesn't seem to be quite in full swing, to the perfectly positioned permanent stalls. Elderly men and women mix with young mothers buying the freshest vegetables of the day. I try out my best French on the bemused stallholder at the vegetable stall as I struggle to recall the French for spring onions. She gleans from my description what I want and produces them from the other side of her stall. I pay and thank her, putting them in the basket I brought with me, along with the garlic and tomatoes.

I stroll round the square, taking in the majestic building of the town hall. A wedding is taking place, and I admire the bride's dress and how handsome the groom and groomsmen are.

I stop at each stall then buy some Toulouse sausage from the *charcuterie* to take back as a contribution for the Molins. I skirt a few stalls that have suddenly become busy, but as I pass the final one, a flicker of recognition ignites and I spot Jean-Luc serving a customer. His eyes meet mine and his lips curve into a smile. He bids the customer good day and I wander over to him.

'Fancy meeting you here,' I say, hoping that didn't sound too flirtatious. I do, after all, have a date with Théo on Friday.

He grins and says, 'I'm filling in for my colleague. He usually mans the stall but has a doctor's appointment so I'm the emergency cover.'

'I see. Well, I'm having a little trip down memory lane. The square has changed a lot since I was last here.'

He sticks out his bottom lip. 'It has indeed. We've only had this type of stall for about five years. I think I prefer the old way, more traditional, but this is what people want, and it can be moved easily, from place to place.'

I see the rationale behind his response.

'Anyway, I won't keep you. I'm going for a walk along the river, down to Pont Neuf whilst the weather's fine.'

'Good plan. I wish I could go with you, but...' He shrugs and holds up his hands, indicating the stall and Place du Capitole.

'No problem. I know you have work to do. See you soon?'

He nods, his smile broadening, showing those perfect white teeth, although now I look more closely I see one of the bottom ones has a tiny chip out of it.

I wave goodbye and set off to explore, my thoughts full not only of my late morning adventure, but of Jean-Luc's smile and his kind eyes. God, I'm making him sound like a Labrador. It's hard to explain, but I feel as if he and I would get on well as friends. I suppose it's good I've friend-zoned him as I have a date with Théo on Friday, not that it has to go anywhere. An impulsive decision to have dinner with an unknown man in a new country doesn't need to lead anywhere, although a naughty little voice tells me*, a snog might be quite nice.* I snort. A snog. What am I? Fourteen?

No, I'm putting down my overexuberance with the opposite sex – first Jean-Luc then Théo – to the fact that Freddy F-word has completely knocked my confidence, and seeing him with Macey was a double whammy.

Time to eliminate Freddy McKenzie from my life, once and for all.

Chapter Nine

'Sarah!' I drop the bag of vegetables onto the kitchen table and rush forward to greet her.

'Oh, Lia, it is so good to see you,' she says, hugging me to her.

I hold her away from me to study her properly. 'You look amazing. How can you look this amazing when you have not one but three children?'

She laughs. 'Practice. No, I'm kidding. It's running around after this lot,' she says as her youngest child, André, hares into the kitchen. Estelle had shown me who everyone was in the family photos. When I was here, Sarah only had Charles. Then she had Elodie a few years after I left, so she must be around eleven or twelve, and then André not so long ago, so I think he might be around five or six. It's hard to keep up.

It also makes me realise I haven't asked Suzanne about kids, but since she's divorced and now with Patrick, plus no one has mentioned kids, I'm guessing not.

Estelle wanders in from the living room with a long-limbed, lithe girl. Elodie. She is stunning, with her mum's eyes and her father's colouring, a golden hue matching that of demerara sugar.

I'm never sure how to be around teens or pre-teens.

Don't they start acting like teenagers earlier these days? I don't want to condescend to her, so I say simply, 'I'm guessing you're Elodie.'

She nods mutely and puts an arm around Sarah, as if for moral support. Her shyness is endearing and I warm to her instantly. She has definitely inherited her mother's nature.

Sarah bids me sit down then makes coffee for the adults and pours some orange juice for Elodie and milk for André, who is still haring around, chasing a remote control car, which bumps into every possible wall and door.

'André, sweetheart, come up to the table, please,' Sarah says, and it warms my heart how easily she switches from friend to mum. I remember her doing a similar thing with Charles.

As we sip our drinks, Sarah fills me in on the last fifteen years. The information whooshes out of her at an incredible speed, which amuses me as she was always so quiet; Suzanne was by far the chattier one. How this woman has grown, certainly in confidence. Being a mother to three children must do that to you, I suppose, and distractedly I wonder if motherhood will ever be a chapter in my own life.

'So, what have you been doing since you arrived?' Sarah asks.

'Well, I was down by the river there. I walked along to Pont Neuf, and before that I was at the market in Place du Capitole. Oh–' I turn to Estelle '–I saw Jean-Luc at his stall.'

'Ah, yes, the boy who usually runs the stall for him was at the doctor's.'

'Yes, Jean-Luc told me.' I turn back to Sarah. 'And of

course yesterday we went to see your grandparents in Saint-Sauvy.'

'How is *Papi*?'

Estelle's mouth downturns. 'As well as can be expected. Dad helped him outside for lunch.'

Sarah nods knowingly and sighs. Then turning to me, she says, 'You'll have noticed *Papi* isn't in very good health.'

'I did, actually. Such a shame. They're lucky you are all able to go and help out each weekend. It must be tough on Alexine too.'

Estelle blows out a breath. 'Yes, my mother is strong, but she's not getting any younger, and she's stubborn about giving up the pocket of vines they have. Of course, she has someone else manage the manual labour for her, but she's too old to be running a business and trying to look after someone as unwell as my father.'

'I can imagine it's hard trying to tell her she's getting too old for it, though.'

'Ha! I wouldn't dare, and I consider myself a strong woman,' says Estelle, 'but my mother has that inner strength that women from Gascony have. An indomitable spirit too.'

Sarah nods in agreement as the children sit at the table quietly and sip their drinks.

'Did you go to *Papi*'s yesterday?' Sarah asks Suzanne as she walks into the kitchen and plonks herself down.

'Of course I did.' Suzanne seems a little defensive, as if questioning why she wouldn't have visited.

'Sorry again I couldn't be there, but I'll definitely be there this weekend, if you and Patrick want to do something together. You could take a day off.'

'Ha!' Suzanne mirrors her mother's earlier comment, and it strikes me again how alike they are.

'What's wrong?' asks Sarah, placing her arm on her sister's.

'Nothing, but maybe I will take next weekend off. At least that way I won't bump into anyone I don't want to.'

'Oh?' says Sarah.

Suzanne lets out a sigh. 'Théo was there.'

There's a moment's pause before Sarah crosses the room to put her arms around her sister. 'Don't let Théo Martin get to you. He's not worth it.'

Suzanne nods silently, and a mixture of unease and curiosity courses through me. What's the history between those two, and have I just made a huge mistake by accepting to go on a date with him?

Sarah turns to me. 'Do you want to help me prepare lunch, Lia? Suzanne has to clean down the bakery ready for tomorrow.'

'I'd love that, thanks,' I say with a broad smile. Privately, I'm hoping the cuisine has moved on from pigeon and grated horse.

As I bustle round the kitchen, directed by Sarah, I enjoy the camaraderie between us. Coq au vin is on the menu today. Estelle is still out front in the boulangerie and I hear her chatting with customers, the singsong lilt of her voice carrying through the beaded curtain to the kitchen. I feel so at home here, almost as much as I did in my own home, growing up, I realise.

Mum wasn't very adventurous in the kitchen, always cooking the same relatively plain food – she isn't any better now – and I didn't learn my love of food and cooking until I came to France the first time, and where better to learn to cook? I decide I'll make a concerted effort these two weeks I'm here to learn as many recipes as I can, and put them into practice when I return home.

'Elodie, why don't you get some art materials from the drawer in the bureau, and you and André can draw whilst we make lunch?' Sarah suggests.

Elodie's lips curve into a smile, and she unleashes a torrent of French to André, who beams at her and takes her hand as they walk into the living room together. They're good kids.

I fetch the seasoning for Sarah, and she goes through the various stages of preparing the coq au vin, as I'm sure she has done a hundred times before. As I help her, it occurs to me that everyone has their role. Matthieu is napping, I know, having baked from 2 a.m.; Suzanne is handling accounts and keeping the bakery clean as well as fetching items from the cold store for her mother as she needs them, plus she has already been to the supplier. Sarah, although she has her own life, her own family and her own job, and no longer works or lives in Toulouse, quickly resumes a role she held in this house as a young woman. It's heartwarming to see how everyone in the family pulls together to keep the wheels of the business turning.

The children sit and draw at the table as we cook. Finally, Estelle closes up shop at two and then Matthieu joins us and we sit down to eat.

The coq au vin is delicious, served with Parmentier potatoes and asparagus.

'So, Lia, what's next on your list of things to do in Toulouse?' Estelle asks, amid the chatter going on around us as we all tuck in to our coq au vin.

At the back of my mind is my date on Friday with Théo, but given I know something's going on with Suzanne, I'm certainly not bringing that up. Perhaps I'll try to speak to Sarah on her own before she leaves today to get to the bottom of that story, so I can decide what to do. Should I cancel the date? He seemed really nice, if a bit forward, and quite frankly, he was as hot as a habanero chilli pepper.

'Lia?' Estelle asks, an eyebrow raising in question, and I realise I've gone off into a daydream.

'Sorry, I was miles away. Well, I was hoping I could help out in the boulangerie.'

Estelle's eyes go wide in surprise, and I hurry on. 'I know my French isn't very good, but I was hoping if I listened to you speaking and I understood the terms used, then perhaps I could pack the pastries and bread, or something, maybe at your busy times. Take the pressure off you a bit.'

Estelle purses her lips. 'If you're sure you're happy to spend part of your holiday working, that would be much appreciated. I never turn down offers of help. Do I, girls?'

In unison Suzanne and Sarah say, '*Non*, *Maman*.'

'That's settled then. When would you like to start?' Estelle asks.

'Since you get busy in the afternoon, how about today?' I suggest.

Estelle throws her hand out in a gesture of acceptance. 'Looks like I have a new staff member. Now, eat up and then, Sarah, you can help Suzanne clear whilst I show Lia the ropes.'

'*Bonjour*, Madame Leclerc,' says Estelle when an elderly lady in a dog-tooth three-quarter-length coat enters, a wicker basket slung casually over one arm.

'*Bonjour*, Madame Molins. I'd like a *pain de campagne*, two baguettes and two *pains aux raisin*.'

As I reach for the large round sourdough closest to me, she suddenly seems to notice me. I'm not sure her expression is approving.

'No, not that one. The one behind it,' she says in rapid French. 'I like it better.'

I replace the one I'm currently holding in the tongs and pick up the one she has indicated. She appears satisfied with this one as she inclines her head, so I put it in a paper bag. I then say, 'Are these two *pains aux raisins* OK for you, Madame?' I gesture to the two I think look best, and when she nods, I do the same for the baguettes, and almost grudgingly, she replies, 'They will do.'

Praise indeed. Not.

'You have a new staff member?' she asks Estelle, almost incredulously.

'Yes, this is Lia, all the way from Scotland.'

Instantly, her demeanour changes, as if a switch has been flipped. 'Ah, Scotland, how I have wanted to visit it again.' She leans forward and her voice drops almost to a whisper. 'Many years ago, I had a dalliance with a Scotsman. I was–' she stops to think '–twenty-four, I think. Yes, I have very fond memories of Scotland.'

Clearly. Naughty minx.

Estelle and I exchange a bewildered look over her shoulder as she rummages in her bag for her purse.

When we've said goodbye to Madame Leclerc and waved her off, Estelle and I turn to each other and burst out laughing.

'Twenty-two years she has been a customer here, and never has she shared anything so personal. You must be a witch, Lia, making people part with their deepest, darkest secrets.'

I take a bow. 'Guilty as charged. A fully-paid-up member of the coven.'

Estelle and I work companionably side by side for the next couple of hours when I'm required. When I'm not needed, I sit in the living room, reading a French romance novel, or talking to Suzanne.

I'm thoroughly enjoying myself, refilling the window displays with the various items of *viennoiserie*, although I do manage to sneak a *pain aux raisins* for myself. I'm sure Estelle won't mind. It's so good. I also have my eye on a delicious-looking apple pastry, but that'll keep until later. I'll need to watch I don't eat all the profits, or ask Estelle to install an honesty box for me. No wonder the place is always so busy – I wouldn't be able to resist if I were passing by on my way to or from work. And I remember from the past how even as you enter the boulangerie, the wonderful aroma of freshly baked bread and *viennoisserie* reaches you.

Their hours are staggered. Matthieu obviously puts in the super-early shift; Suzanne from 5 a.m. and Estelle from just after breakfast at 6.30 a.m. so that the boulangerie is ready for the day ahead. It all seems to run like clockwork, with each focused on their task, whilst facilitating the others to do theirs.

We've had a run of customers, then suddenly all falls quiet.

'Excuse me a moment whilst I go to the bathroom,'

says Estelle. 'If anyone comes and you're not confident enough to chat with them, call me and stall them.'

'I will.'

No sooner has she left than the bell over the door jangles and I look up to see Jean-Luc standing before me.

His face splits into a smile. 'This is a surprise.'

'A nice one, I hope.' I can't help flirting a little.

'Oh, definitely a nice one.' His smile broadens and the hairs on my arms stand on end.

Whoa! Is it hot in here all of a sudden?

'How was the market?' I say, trying to deflect the sexual tension.

'Good, thanks. I like doing the market stall occasionally, plus I love being out in the fresh air.'

Another tick. Outdoorsy type. 'Even when it's raining?'

He laughs. 'No, I'm not that virtuous. I hate it when it's raining, but at least we have a canopy. And I hate it when it's cold, too, at the market. I like to be cosy.'

'I'm not a fan of the cold either,' I confess, although privately I wouldn't mind the cold if it meant Jean-Luc could heat me up. I cough. Get a grip, Lia.

'So, how have you ended up working in the boulangerie?'

I flash him a smile. 'Simple. I asked.'

Jean-Luc's eyes crinkle as he opens his mouth to say something, but then stops.

I scrunch up my eyes, and my actions mirror his. 'What?'

He pauses then says, 'Nothing.'

'No, go on,' I say. I'm not letting him get away with that. Something's on the tip of his tongue and I want to hear it.

'OK. Well, I was thinking, I liked your forthrightness and I get the impression you're confident in asking for what you want.'

If only he knew. God, I know what I want right now, and I most definitely can't ask for that. I settle for, 'Hmm, sometimes.' And, in for a penny, in for a pound, I check out my flirtometer again, 'And what about you, do you always get what you want?'

His lips curl up at the edges. 'I like to at least go after what I want.'

My God, if ever there was a conversation more loaded with double meanings, double entendres and subtext, I've yet to be party to it.

I flush to the roots of my hair, which I artfully rearrange to hide my discomfort as Estelle bustles back into the boulangerie. 'Jean-Luc, *ça va*?'

Whilst Jean-Luc chats with Estelle, I take a moment to compose myself and calm my racing heart. Who knew life in France could get so complicated so quickly?

The doorbell peals again and another couple of customers come in. Estelle greets them and I check to see if she needs me to pack anything yet, but she's busy chatting with them about their uncle who has moved to the Basque Country.

Jean-Luc turns back to me and asks for a baguette and a *pastis Gascon*.

I glance around, trying to work out which one that is, but luckily, Jean-Luc comes to my aid.

'It's that one. Apple pie with a hint of Armagnac. Delicious,' he says. 'And my favourite.'

'That's so funny. I was considering having one of those.'

'Really?' he says, and when I nod, he continues. 'You've got good taste.'

Don't I know it. Down, girl.

'Actually, I came to see you.' His eyes hold mine for a second too long and I almost stop breathing as I wait to hear what he has to say.

'Me?' I lick my lips involuntarily. Christ, he'll think I want to eat him alive. Oh, God, thoughts, please don't go there. Too late.

'Yes, the tour of my production facility in Gascony. Do you remember?' He rakes his hand through his hair, looking uncertain now. My heart skips at how charming and endearing the gesture is.

'Of course I remember. When were you thinking?'

He holds his hands out to the sides and shrugs. 'Is now a good time?'

Estelle's bat ears kick in. 'Jean-Luc, are you taking Lia to Gimont? Wonderful idea. Lia, you've been so helpful today, go and enjoy yourself, and we'll see you later.'

That's me told.

I gulp. 'Let me get my things.'

The sexy half-smile he gives me makes my insides turn upside down as I head to my room to grab my cardigan and bag.

With a jaunty, '*A bientôt*, Estelle,' I follow Jean-Luc out of the boulangerie, my stomach jangling with anticipation and more than a little lust.

Chapter Ten

'So, where exactly is your *fromagerie*?' I ask as we leave the boulangerie.

'It's just outside Gimont.'

I don't know where that is. 'How far away is that?'

'Forty minutes.' He stops beside a moped. 'Here, put this on.' He hands me a helmet.

Oh my God, oh my God, oh my God. We're travelling forty minutes on a moped. I'll have to hold on to him tight, is my first thought; my second is that I want to hold on to him tight, and that makes me exhale more loudly than I'd expected.

'Everything OK?' He peers into my face, which I'm sure must be as white as the Cliffs of Dover by now.

I nod silently and repeatedly as Jean-Luc studies me, a look of concern on his face. 'You have ridden on a moped before, haven't you?'

'Eh, no.'

'Really? You're a moped virgin?' he says, his eyes brimming with amusement.

I don't think I can cope with any more double entendres. My insides are fizzing as it is.

I clear my throat, unable to speak, and nod again.

He chuckles. 'I'm glad I'm your first.'

I flush lobster-red, and even the tips of my ears feel warm.

'Lia, I'm teasing. So, are you getting on?'

I can't say no now, can I? From somewhere deep down inside, I find my nerve, put on the helmet and slide on to the moped.

Jean-Luc gets on the front. 'Hold on tight. This goes much faster than you'd expect.'

I grip on to his leather jacket as I half tuck my cardigan into my trousers so it doesn't flap too much in the wind. However, as the moped speeds away along the street, I realise that's not going to be enough and I slip my arms around his waist and hang on for dear life.

His rib cage heaves as he laughs. 'I'll go easy on you, but it's good to see I don't need to tell you twice to hang on.'

Eventually, I relax into him, even loosening my grip so I'm not pinching his skin, as I'm sure I must have been earlier. I thought mopeds were sedate numbers. He's right; this one is speedy, and he navigates with ease the network of streets until we reach the main road out of the city towards Gimont.

As I lean into him, I breathe in his aftershave, citrus – lemon with a hint of honey? Whatever it is, it's delicious. Who needs an aphrodisiac?

Plane trees whizz past then fields and fields and yet more fields. Looks like we're going to the countryside.

The wind picks up as the sun goes down and I bury my face into the back of Jean-Luc's jacket, inhaling deeply as I do so. He smells divine and a heady sensation comes over me. I'm going to have to rein myself in or I'll be jumping the poor boy. My arms, however, fit perfectly around his waist, my hands resting on his stomach, very much at home there. His leather jacket isn't zipped up and I can feel his abdominals through his T-shirt. I need a cold shower.

At one point his stomach tenses and I wonder if this moped ride is having anything like the effect on him that it's having on me.

My legs are right behind his and the heat from them radiates into mine, which is just as well as the biting wind is beginning to make other parts of me bloody cold indeed.

He partly turns around and shouts something to me, but his words are lost on the wind and I shake my head and manage a tiny shrug. For a moment, his face is so close he could inch forward and kiss me, but he turns back to keep his eye on the road.

Eventually, he draws to a stop outside a cream building, which in swirly writing reads Fromagerie Rochefort, then dismounts and offers me his hand to climb off.

'Thanks,' I say as I take off the helmet and shake out my hair, letting it tumble over my shoulders again.

His eyes never leave mine and he coughs before saying, 'Here we are.'

I wonder what he was thinking, but we've been down that route before and perhaps I'm better not knowing.

Jean-Luc takes me through the *fromagerie* room by room. As we walk, I realise I could listen to him talk all day, whether he's talking about cheese or about sandpaper. His accent is really hitting the spot.

'Thanks for the tour,' I say as we prepare to head back to Toulouse. It's starting to get dark now, and I'm apprehensive about travelling by moped. As if sensing my unease, Jean-Luc says, 'Don't worry, you're with me. I'll keep you safe. Like I said before, hang on tight.'

'OK.' I climb on behind him again, hyper-aware of how close our bodies are. It's startlingly erotic. I honestly don't think if we were naked, I could be any more turned on.

As I alternately hug his waist and chest, I realise how much I like him. He's so easy-going, so decent, not to mention sexy as hell.

Jules is either going to give me an almighty telling-off, or be my biggest cheerleader in advocating I go for it. Well, it's not as if I have anything else to do with my time. Here, in France, I'm at my leisure, and I can do what I like. Although, a little voice reminds me, *you're only here for two weeks. Don't be a tart.* Who said anything about sleeping with him? A snogathon might be nice, though, and maybe a bit more, if those abdominals I felt earlier are anything to go by, plus he wears clothes as effortlessly as a fashion model, but without the pout and attitude, or the hefty price tag.

My hands rest easily on his waistband, but I can't help but wonder what would happen if I slid my hand inside his T-shirt, either up or down an inch. Oh my God, I have got it bad.

We stop outside the boulangerie and Jean-Luc parks up, then takes my helmet from me.

'Thanks, that was so interesting. I had a really good time.'

'Me too.' He pauses and I stop, just as I was about to make a bid for freedom. I'm not sure I trust myself around him.

He looks at me in that unnerving way he did earlier, as

if he's about to say something. I'm on the verge of asking him, 'What?' when he says, 'Do you fancy a drink?'

I must look puzzled, or as if I'm about to say no, as he continues, 'Just one. In Place du Capitole.'

I hesitate, but only for a second, before I say, 'Why not?'

We start walking and I shiver at the cold. My thin cardigan gives me little protection against the wind.

'Here.' Jean-Luc takes off his leather jacket, his white T-shirt riding up as he does so. 'I don't feel the cold.' He drapes his jacket over my shoulders despite my protestations. It's as if it was made for me, and there's something ultra sexy about wearing a man's leather jacket, and at him offering it to you. Chivalry isn't dead, after all. I'm all for feminism, believe me, but I also like to be warm. Something tells me if I'd gone inside to retrieve my jacket from the Molins', I'd have found an excuse not to go back out, and I think Jean-Luc had some intuition around that too.

Whatever sorcery was at play, here we are, walking towards Place du Capitole, me wearing his leather jacket, him lying about not feeling the cold. Didn't he tell me earlier today he liked to be cosy? And I wonder if he too recalls his passing comment.

It's not long before we reach Place du Capitole. Jean-Luc seems to know half the people there as they greet him, some eyeing me curiously. He introduces me to his friends and explains I'm staying with the Molins.

Interestingly, we don't stay with his friends, and once he's chatted a few minutes with each of them, he finds us a table and asks me what I'd like to drink.

'Wine?' I say.

'What kind?' he asks.

'Can you recommend something?'

Give me two minutes.' He flashes me a smile, and as he walks away, I think how I could lose myself in those dimples.

Chapter Eleven

Jean-Luc returns a few minutes later with two glasses of red.

'This is a Saint-Sardos. Hope you like it,' he says. '*Santé!*'

'*Slainté!*' I say.

He eyes me quizzically and I laugh. 'It's Scottish for cheers.'

'Ah. I like it. *Slainté*.' He rolls the word around on his tongue. '*Sláinte*.'

His attempt to pronounce Scottish Gaelic makes me smile, but fair play to him for trying.

I take a sip of the wine, which is divine – there's no other word for it. Fruity and floral, and something else.

Being like velvet, it slips down all too easily, and soon I'm asking Jean-Luc if he wants to stay for another glass.

'Sure.' He moves to get up, but I rest a hand on his arm. 'My turn,' I say. 'Same again?'

He nods and I head to the bar, trying to once again calm my beating heart.

When I return with the drinks, Jean-Luc is on his phone. He hangs up and says, 'Estelle, wondering where you are.'

'Oh God, I forgot to tell her I might not be back in time for dinner.'

'It's fine. I told her you're still with me and I'll bring you home safely.'

I don't doubt it for a second.

'But I also told her we might order some food here, if that's OK with you, since they've already eaten.'

When I don't immediately reply, mainly because I can't force the words out of my mouth, Jean-Luc rushes on, 'Or we can go back after this one, and you can grab some leftovers. I'm sure it'll be delicious. It's *canard à la cuisse*. Cooked duck.'

'Do they serve food here then?'

'Yes, and one of my friends is the chef. It's nothing elaborate, but it's tasty. You like omelette?'

I nod, unable to speak as my eyes rest on his tanned, toned arms and the way his T-shirt stretches across his abdominals as he bends down to pick up the menu he inadvertently knocked off the table with his elbow. Gulp, gulp and gulp again.

When he straightens up, he asks if I'm allergic to anything, or if there's anything I don't like. Since I like pretty much everything, he orders us a cheese, tomato and peppers omelette. My stomach rumbles. I know it's not so long since I had cheese at the *fromagerie* facility, but I'm starving nonetheless.

Whilst Jean-Luc is at the bar, Jules messages me. *What are you up to? You've gone quiet on me. How are the men in your life? I need details!! Life is lonely here without you. I need some good gossip to keep me going x*

I chuckle. Jules is a riot. She'll be out for dinner with friends most nights I'm away. Although I'm her bestie, I'm not deluded enough to think she's pining for me. I do, however, know she definitely wants details. I'll drip-feed them to her.

I'm kinda busy right now x

Busy? What kind of busy? Man busy? Am I interrupting something? Oo-er? Have you rumpled any sheets yet? x

I'm not sure what kind of trollop Jules thinks I am, but I've only been here a few days. I'm not that fast a worker. OK, I am currently out with a gorgeous man, having a drink and some food, and almost had an orgasm on the back of his moped, but she doesn't need to know that. Those are exactly the kind of details she wants, but I can't tell her that. Not yet anyway.

Laters xxx I type as Jean-Luc returns.

My phone beeps as I sit down and I just manage to see Jules' *???!!!* before I turn my attention back to Jean-Luc.

'So, Estelle tells me you studied in the States. Whereabouts?'

'Atlanta. I went to university there, did a course in liberal arts before I realised I really did want to be a *fromager*. But I got the education I wanted, improved my English, had a lot of fun, then came back and did my *fromager* training here, which largely meant travelling around France learning about cheese.'

'That sounds incredible. I'd love to do that. Eating cheese all day, for work.' He laughs then I say, 'I've never been to America, although I'd love to go. Did you go to any of the other states?'

Jean-Luc nods. 'I travelled a lot by car there. It was easy enough for me as they drive on the same side of the road, and they have such huge highways compared with here.'

I smile. 'Yeah, I've never been good at driving abroad. It freaks me out too much, what with having to drive on the opposite side. Fortunately, my best friend, Jules, takes it in her stride, so she's our designated driver. Where did you go?'

Jean-Luc pauses for a second, as if gathering his thoughts, then says, 'Well, we toured South Carolina, North Carolina, Florida and I went to New York once, which was fun, but I far preferred the Deep South.'

'We?'

'Yes, I had an American girlfriend for a while. We met in the university cafeteria. Cherry.'

I chuckle. 'That's—'

He cuts me off. 'Very American, isn't it? Makes her sound like a brand of soft drink. I used to call her Cherry Coke, and it drove her crazy.'

'You're so mean.' I glare at him and give a mock eye-roll. 'And where did you like best?'

He muses this over for a minute or so. 'Honestly, I liked being in the Carolinas – Asheville, the Blue Ridge Mountains. I do like the great outdoors, so it was so awe-inspiring. Sure, we have the Pyrenees here, but it was different, an untamed wildness.'

I nod. 'I can imagine. I've been to the Alps, but the mountains of Scotland are beautiful, too, though they're very different: the landscape, the smells, the sounds even.' I sigh. 'I love travelling.'

Jean-Luc gives a wistful smile. 'Me too, although I don't get to do enough of it now as I have work commitments.'

'Responsibility is a bitch,' I say. 'Does that translate?'

He laughs. 'Yes, in fact it does. And anyway, sometimes when you say things in French, I understand what you mean because I know the English you're translating from.'

Instantly, I switch to English. 'Ah, you're taking advantage.' Momentarily, I think he can take advantage as much as he likes. I blink to clear that vision from my head and continue. 'Seems unfair we're always speaking French when you could easily be practising your English. You know, since you lived in America and all.' I lend an American drawl to that last part.

He grins and takes up the challenge. 'OK, you're on. So, apart from helping Estelle in the boulangerie, what plans do you have during your time here in Toulouse?'

Guilt sweeps over me as my imminent date with Théo pops into my head. For a millisecond I consider cancelling, then I shoo the idea away, as, apart from not knowing how to contact him, it would be rude, and it is only dinner. I'm not planning a night of mad, passionate sex with him or anything. Although the more time I spend with Jean-Luc, the more the idea appeals of engaging in those activities with him; pity then that I'm going out on a date with another man.

'Well,' I stall, 'I'd like to see a little more of the surrounding countryside as well as visit some of my old haunts from when I lived here. But time passes quickly, so I may not manage to see as much as I'd like.'

Jean-Luc looks pensive for a moment. 'Hmm, shame you can't extend your stay.'

Was that a suggestion? An invitation? A declaration of interest?

'Yeah … shame,' I say vaguely.

Jean-Luc eyes me curiously. 'I mean, I suppose you need to go back to work at some point.'

When I remain quiet, he says, 'Don't you?'

Rather than answer his question, I respond with one of my own. 'Do you know what garden leave is?'

Confused, he shakes his head.

'It's when your company pays you to stay home from

work during your notice period.'

His eyes go wide. 'So you've lost your job?'

I purse my lips. 'More or less. I had a few weeks' holiday still to take, so that's what I'm doing now, but I'm supposed to return to work, even though I won't physically be at work, but I think I'm meant to be on hand if they want to talk to me. Honestly, I don't know. I need to talk to my solicitor about it. It's all a bit of a nightmare.'

Jean-Luc's lips downturn. 'I'm sorry to hear that. That does sound tough. And there's no possibility you could stay on in France, since you don't *need* to be at work per se?'

I definitely detect hope in his voice this time.

'That would be lovely.' I look him right in the eye. 'Do you know what? Maybe that's what I need. Perhaps I could book into a *pension* for a few weeks. Maybe Jules could come out with me, if she can take any time off.'

Jean-Luc's smile broadens. 'Now, that would be wonderful. I mean, I really want to meet Jules now too. She sounds incredible.'

'Oh, she is, and she'd love to hear you say that. Perhaps you can tell her in person one day.'

He chuckles. 'I look forward to it.'

The frisson between us is so tangible I feel as if we would give each other an electric shock if we touched right now.

'Jean-Luc, how are you?' A man in chef's whites stops by our table, holding two heavenly-smelling omelettes, which he places in front of us, before Jean-Luc stands and they embrace each other.

'Good. You?'

The chef rolls his eyes. 'Busy. You know how it is.'

'I do.' Jean-Luc turns to me. 'David, this is Lia. She's

visiting from Scotland.'

'Ah, Scotland, Lia, nice to meet you. I hope to go to Edinburgh one day. The castle looks incredible.'

'Nice to meet you too. Your food smells amazing. And yes, Edinburgh Castle is incredible. So atmospheric.'

His smile reaches all the way to his sunken-in eyes. I'm guessing it has been a long shift. 'Thank you, Lia.'

He turns to Jean-Luc. 'I like castles. I've visited forty-seven so far, but mainly here in France.' He speaks animatedly to Jean-Luc for a few minutes in rapid French. I understand very little of the conversation and realise I have a long way to go before I'm fluent. I make out 'think', 'glory' and 'good luck'.

David then seems to recall the passage of time, turns back to me and points to the food. 'Excuse me, once I start talking, I cannot seem to stop. Enjoy your omelettes.'

Once we've said goodbye to David, we dig in to the food and it is every bit as flavoursome as its aroma suggested.

A couple of glasses of wine follow the food and finally we decide, reluctantly on both sides it seems, that we should make tracks, and Jean-Luc signals for the bill, which he promptly pays.

I realise how cold it has become as we leave and my conscience doesn't let me keep Jean-Luc's jacket.

'No, Lia, I insist. You have goose pimples.'

I look down to where my cardigan has ridden up my arms and I do indeed have goose pimples.

'All the more reason for you to wear it, or you'll be an icicle.'

He grins. 'It's not so far. C'mon. Tell you what, I'll wear my jacket, on one condition.'

I quirk an eyebrow. 'Oh?'

'You give me your arm as we walk so you can get some of my body heat.'

Oh, help. What an offer. I'm sure I visibly gulp. My throat goes dry and I don't trust myself not to squeak instead of speak, so I simply smile and nod.

I take off his jacket and he slips it on as I say, 'I want to pay half of the meal.'

'No need. Uh-uh, don't insist. When in France…' He lets that hang in the air and I wonder what it means.

Finally he says, 'And if you really feel you want to go fifty-fifty, maybe we can go for omelette another night, or we could eat something else, doesn't have to be omelette.' He's babbling now, and I'm pleased to note I'm not the only one who gets tongue-tied.

I shiver and his arm instantly goes around my shoulders as we walk companionably and slowly back to the boulangerie. I'd like to say the heat from his body is warming me up, but it isn't, I'm bloody freezing, so I think warm thoughts instead. In fact, some of my thoughts are very hot indeed and have bog all to do with the outside temperature.

He adjusts the position of his arm so it's slung around my back and waist, hugging me closer to him. I nestle against him and we fit so well together.

I almost want our steps to slow further, as I don't know what to do when we get back to the boulangerie. Every fibre of me, every molecule, wants Jean-Luc to kiss me. Do I need to wait for an invitation? Am I brave enough to initiate things? If I've misread his intentions, I could make a huge fool of myself, which could make things rather awkward, what with his *fromagerie* being next door to the boulangerie. But, on the positive side, I'm leaving France in less than ten days, unless I extend my stay, and I wouldn't have to see him ever again if I didn't want to. God, I'm overthinking this. Just let it play out, Lia. Dampen down your inner analyst. It has killed most of your relationships so far.

We reach the boulangerie, and neither of us seems to want to break apart. Finally, I say, 'Thanks, Jean-Luc. I had a really good time.'

He gives an oh-so-sexy, lazy smile and his eyes don't leave mine. He's going to kiss me. I know he is, and I bite my lip and wet my lips slightly with my tongue. Anticipation has never felt so good.

A piercing voice rents the air. 'Jean-Luc, there you are. I need a lift home.'

I peer in the darkness to where the voice is coming from, then I see a woman, possibly a little younger than me, with a caramel Afro blowout and the most piercing green eyes, which look as if they could skewer me right now, as she approaches us. She's heavily made up, wearing designer clothes, if I'm not mistaken, teetering on the most ridiculous high-heeled shoes, which aren't needed anyway as she's almost the height of a giraffe. She must be just shy of six feet, without the heels.

'Gloire!' Jean-Luc's voice has a sharp, almost resigned edge to it. 'What are you doing here, and at this time of night?'

'I was in the neighbourhood,' she says breezily.

Personally, I'm wondering when this area became the red-light district, but I say nothing.

As she reaches us, she scowls. 'Who's this?'

Jean-Luc sighs. 'This is Lia. She's staying with Estelle

for a few weeks.'

She glares daggers at me then at Jean-Luc.

I'm not sure what I've done to attract her enmity, but if looks could kill…

'Lia, this is Gloire.' He hesitates as if he was about to say more.

'Yes, Lia, I am Gloire, Jean-Luc's girlfriend.'

Nausea rises from my stomach. He doesn't deny it; he just looks wretched.

'Gloire… Lia…' Jean-Luc looks between us.

My phone rings. Saved by the bell.

I take out my phone. Freddy. I glance at Jean-Luc and Gloire. 'So sorry, I've got to take this. It's my boyfriend, Freddy.'

And without a backward glance, I let myself into the boulangerie and close the door.

Chapter Twelve

In the end, I didn't answer Freddy's call as a maelstrom of emotions was coursing through me. Jean-Luc has a girlfriend. He was about to kiss me. I know it. I still feel quite sad at the thought that I believed I'd made a good friend, but yet again I've been a gullible idiot. I really liked him too, but I've made sure to avoid him the past few days.

Jules is gutted for me. She thought I'd found a hunky Frenchman to take my mind off Freddy F-word. I joke with her that I still have an option in Théo, although somehow I'm not as excited about my upcoming date with him as I should be.

At least something good has happened this week. Freddy was calling to tell me a viewer wanted to make an offer on the flat, so fingers crossed, soon Freddy and I can definitively go our separate ways. I can't believe I was taken in so readily again, after Freddy. God, I must be desperate for affection and love.

Despite not wanting to, when I've been in the boulangerie during the day helping Estelle, I've thought of Jean-Luc often, of the lovely evening we spent together, our almost kiss, and of how his body felt against mine on our moped ride. And it hurts. It hurts that the rapport I thought was developing with Jean-Luc was all in my head.

It hurts that once again I let my heart rule my head, and I berate myself for allowing myself to feel this strongly about someone so quickly. Plus, it proves you can never really know a person. And I've known Jean-Luc all of two minutes.

Jules is much more philosophical than me. She's a great believer in what's for us in life won't go by us.

And I kicked myself the day after my non-date with Jean-Luc, when I realised David, his chef friend, had been talking about Gloire, his girlfriend, when we were at the restaurant. I thought it was something to do with glory, but 'gloire' means 'glory'. What an idiot I am. David must have been wondering what Gloire would think of Jean-Luc having dinner with me. I bet they had a right old laugh about him cheating on Gloire, although if I'm honest, Jean-Luc didn't strike me as that kind of guy. My head hurts. I'm fed up analysing this over and over. Men. They're not worth it. And that makes this evening's date with Théo that little bit more difficult to stomach. I also realise I have no idea where we're going, so I have no idea how to dress.

With the events of Monday and being busy in the boulangerie, I haven't even contemplated shopping for clothes. He'll have to take me as I am. I'm feeling quite bolshie at the minute, so if he doesn't like it, he can lump it. My heart's not in it. If I'm honest, my heart feels broken. There, I've said it. I thought I had a connection with Jean-Luc, but I was taken in by his boy-next-door persona. I won't make that mistake again.

I'm in the boulangerie listening to Madame Leclerc chat with Estelle and trying to work out what she needs, when the landline rings. Estelle asks me if I can answer it, so I do.

It's Sarah.

'Hi, Sarah, how is everything?'

'Good, thanks. I wanted to invite you over at some point before you go back to Scotland.'

'I'd really like that. And it would be nice to see Florian again.'

'Yes, he's looking forward to catching up. Unfortunately, Charles is at university and won't be back until after you go back to Scotland. He's quite different now to when you last saw him.'

'I bet!'

'So, what have you been up to?' she asks. 'I didn't get to say goodbye the other day. Mum said you'd gone to Jean-Luc's *fromagerie* near Gimont.'

'Yes, it was so interesting.' Clearly, I don't tell her about the awkwardness that ensued afterwards, with the arrival of Gloire. To change the subject from Jean-Luc, I say, 'And I've been continuing to work in the boulangerie, which has been so much fun.'

'Ooh, don't let *Maman* keep you inside the whole time. You're only here for two weeks.'

'I know, don't worry. I've ventured outdoors a few times too. In fact, I'm going out tonight.'

'Oh really? Where are you off to?'

Inwardly, I smack my head off a wall. I didn't want to broadcast my date with Théo, given Suzanne and he don't seem to see eye to eye, and I haven't found a way to bring it up with her. Nor did I manage to speak to Sarah about it before. Now, I've kind of shot myself in the foot as there's no real way, apart from lying, of evading this question.

'I'm going out for dinner.'

'Is Suzanne taking you to the Mongolian place I recommended?'

Awkward. 'I can't say she's mentioned that.'

'Oh, so where is she taking you then?'

Oh crap. 'Actually, I'm not going with Suzanne. She's doing something with Patrick tonight.'

There's a pause as I imagine the cogs in Sarah's brain whirling. 'So, are you and Jean-Luc going out again? People will be talking.' She laughs.

Hardly.

'No, I'm not going out with Jean-Luc. I don't think Gloire would be very happy about that.' I decide I can't put this off any longer, and since I'm not doing anything wrong, I spit it out. 'I'm going out with Théo.'

Silence. Then Sarah says, 'Théo Martin?'

'Yes, I met him at your grandparents' at the weekend. He asked me out to dinner, and I figured why not?'

More silence. It's really quite unnerving. 'Is something wrong, Sarah?'

She exhales loudly. 'Not wrong exactly, but Théo and Suzanne have history.'

My suspicions have been confirmed, but Suzanne is with Patrick now. So what's the problem? I say nothing, hoping Sarah will enlighten me.

She exhales loudly. 'He didn't treat her very well.'

Crap. That's not what I needed to hear. 'I'm so sorry,' I say. 'Oh, Sarah, I don't know what to do. He's due any minute, and I have no way of contacting him to cancel and no time to let Suzanne know he asked me out. I've had a few things on my mind this week, and it didn't even occur to me to discuss my date with you guys.' I feel a bit guilty for fudging the truth, but sometimes needs must.

'Look, it was a long time ago. For all I know, Théo has changed. Just, let me talk to Suzanne about it. I know how to handle her. Go, enjoy your date, make up your own mind.'

'Are you sure?' Because I'm not now.

'Yes, positive. One thing, though, why would Gloire be upset at you going out with Jean-Luc?'

My mouth downturns even though I know she can't see it on the phone. 'Perhaps because she's his girlfriend.'

'Gloire isn't Jean-Luc's girlfriend. Not any longer,' says Sarah.

'She isn't?' I say, confused.

'No, she's his ex-girlfriend. They broke up three months ago after she slept with some footballer. She keeps trying to get back with him, though, but he, understandably, isn't entertaining the idea. He was always too good for her anyway.'

Gloire isn't Jean-Luc's girlfriend. Jean-Luc is single. Fuuuuck!

Oh God, my head is throbbing. I'm about to go out with Théo when I fancy the pants off Jean-Luc and it seemed like he rather liked me, but now I've misread the situation because of his crazy ex-girlfriend. What a mess.

'OK, thanks, Sarah. You've certainly given me lots to think about.' I'll say.

I hang up and stare at the phone for a long moment. What am I going to do now? I shake my head as if doing so will provide some inspiration – or knock some sense into me – then slap my forehead. Shit! I told Jean-Luc my boyfriend Freddy was calling. What the hell will he think of me? I was practically eyeing him up for my supper the other night, and then I made out I had a boyfriend. Crikey, exes have a lot to answer for.

The doorbell tinkles in the boulangerie.

'Théo! How are you?' Estelle asks.

Oh no. He's early. Fifteen minutes early. I don't even have time to compose my thoughts properly now.

'I'm good, thanks, Madame Molins. You?'

They chat for a few minutes, then Estelle asks what she can get him.

I hear him say, 'Actually, I'm not here to buy anything. I've come to take Lia out for dinner.' That's when I remember I haven't told Estelle either. Oh my God, I'm useless.

'Lia?' I hear the puzzlement in Estelle's voice.

'Yes, didn't she tell you?' He sounds unsure now.

'Of course,' Estelle fibs. God, what a tangled web I've woven. 'Let me go get her.'

I pad to the kitchen so it's not obvious I overheard.

'Lia, are you there?' she calls from the living room.

I pop my head round the living room door. 'Hi, Estelle. Everything OK?'

'Théo's here for you.'

'Ah, that's right. We're going out for dinner. Oh my goodness, Estelle, I'm so sorry, I forgot to tell you. I don't mean to make a habit of this,' I say, thinking back to Monday evening with Jean-Luc.

She dismisses my concern with a wave of her hand. 'Have fun.'

'I will.' I won't. I kiss her on both cheeks and walk through to the boulangerie, where Théo smiles when I enter.

'Hi. Ready to go?'

'Sure. I hope I'm suitably dressed. I'm not sure where

we're going.'

'You look stunning,' he says. Flatterer. I look passable at best.

I skip out of the door after Théo, willing myself to enjoy tonight. Théo turns back to me and I smile at him, just as I hear a door opening. I swing back, expecting Estelle to be behind me, but it's Jean-Luc, his face frozen in horror. A horror which must match mine. I try to speak but no words come out. How to explain, apologise? How to convey what I feel, what I thought happened the other night, why I've been avoiding him, and why I'm now leaving the boulangerie with another man.

'Théo,' Jean-Luc says curtly.

'Jean-Luc.' Théo's acknowledgement is equally brief.

Jean-Luc regards me coolly. 'Lia.'

'Have a nice evening, Jean-Luc.' Théo's tone is saccharine sweet. 'Shall we, Lia?' He hooks his arm in mine and almost pulls me away. I can only glance behind me helplessly at Jean-Luc's forlorn yet angry expression as Théo and I walk towards his car. What a bloody mess I've got myself into.

I'm quiet in the car, my head spinning with so many different thoughts, as well as questions. Jean-Luc and Théo know each other then? But Théo lives in Gascony, doesn't he? They didn't exactly welcome each other warmly. What's all that about?

I half-listen to Théo as he tells me where we're going. A restaurant in the mountains. His friend owns it. As we twist and turn on the hairpin bends, my stomach lurches and I find myself longing for the moped ride with Jean-Luc.

Many women may prefer a Porsche, but I'm not one of them. I'm not impressed by labels and brands, not even high-end sports cars. What's more important to me is keeping the contents of my stomach where they belong.

I sneak a peek at him as we drive. He oozes sexuality, raw masculinity encased in designer clothing, and would get any woman's pulse racing. He's wearing black jeans, which look brand new, and a pristine baby blue shirt, which sets off his colouring. He looks good, but he knows it. Ah, I'm being uncharitable. I just wish I didn't feel so conflicted.

After an eternity, the car screeches to a halt and I gaze up at the restaurant, which sits beside a lake, overlooking the mountains. The Pyrenees? It's awe-inspiring and I don't know what to say – which doesn't happen often. My jaw drops as I gaze at the panorama before me. Although it's already dark, the beam from the Porsche's headlights illuminates the view. The mountain is reflected in the aquamarine lake – a perfect mirror image. Théo couldn't have chosen a more romantic location for a date, and I resolve to be kind and engaged, irrespective of my feelings for Jean-Luc. Jean-Luc isn't here, Théo is, and if the way Jean-Luc looked at me earlier is indicative of his feelings for me, romance, if it ever was on his mind, is off the menu.

Théo opens my door and I climb out. I feel underdressed, but there's little I can do about it now. I stand and stare at the lake for a moment. I hear the cascading waterfall as it tumbles down into the lake, before I see it. Théo comes to stand beside me. We remain like that, not touching, simply admiring the spectacular view before he breaks the silence. 'Every time I come here, it takes my breath away.'

I can completely understand that.

'Shall we?' Théo puts his hand in the small of my back and guides me gently towards the restaurant.

Chapter Thirteen

I'm more than a tad nervous as I follow Théo into the restaurant. It's not huge, perhaps about forty covers, but the décor is so authentically mountain lodge, and I love it.

The maître d' leads us to our table, which overlooks the mountain and the fabulous reflection in the lake. It seems almost fitting for a proposal not a first date.

'I usually opt for their speciality of the week,' Théo confides, once we're seated. 'It's always delicious.'

If the aromas I can detect are anything to go by, he isn't wrong. I glance towards the table next to us and realise I'd happily eat any of the dishes, as they look and smell incredible.

The waiter brings a menu and Théo explains the items I don't recognise, since there is no English version of the menu, something I always prefer as it generally means the restaurant isn't a tourist trap. That said, we're so far off the beaten track here, it would be hard for there to be much passing trade.

In the end, we both settle for the specialty of the week which is *agneau de Pauillac*.

'The lamb is from Pauillac, which is very close to here,' Théo explains. 'It's superb, I promise.'

The conversation flows surprisingly easily. Théo is fun,

flirty and fascinating. He tells me tales of his youth, asks me about my life in Scotland, regales me with the history of wine, but also checks I'm not bored by his droning on – his words – and the evening passes rather more quickly than I'd expected.

'So, you grew up, splitting your time between Toulouse and Saint-Sauvy then, like the Molins?' I ask.

'That's right. We all used to hang out together when we were younger.' He's smiling but I notice a tightness around his eyes.

I'm dying to ask him about Suzanne, but I don't.

'I guess that's how you first met Jean-Luc too.'

A shadow flits across his face and then it's gone. 'That's right. Would you like some dessert?' He picks up the menu.

If that wasn't a dramatic change of subject, I don't what is.

When the meal is over, we walk out into the night and I assume we'll head straight for the car. Instead, Théo offers me his hand, which I take, and we stroll down towards the lake, which is even more sensational now the moonlight is dancing upon it.

'Are you honestly only here for one more week?' he asks.

I nod. 'Unfortunately, yes.' I avoid his gaze and stare out at the lake and the imposing mountain above.

I startle as he circles my palm with his thumb. It's unbelievably sexy. I clear my throat, which is suddenly dry.

Théo angles me towards him, then raises his hand to my hair and takes the pink streak between his finger and thumb. 'I like this.'

'Thanks. One aims to please.' I'm not sure if my humour translates. Unlike Jean-Luc, as far as I know, Théo hasn't lived abroad, although he does speak English pretty well.

He is so close to me now I can barely breathe, and I realise I do want him to kiss me. All doubts from earlier in the evening have vanished, and in this one moment, I want nothing more than Théo to take me in his arms and kiss me.

He nudges my forehead gently with his, then looks into my eyes and smiles. Our lips are less than an inch apart. Then slowly we meet in the middle and our lips touch. Zing. He kisses me ever so gently, then I respond, leaning into the kiss, wanting more. He kisses me more deeply and I groan, and I feel the corners of his lips curve up against mine. Then he kisses my neck and I know I'm lost. This man knows how to kiss. I'm in trouble – again.

It's long past midnight when Théo and I arrive back at the boulangerie. He doesn't immediately say goodnight or get out of the car when we stop, and I feel awkward for a moment. We enjoyed some rather passionate kisses in the mountains, but the further and further we got from that spectacular vista, the more it held a dreamlike quality. I almost wondered if it had happened at all as we resumed our small talk on the way back to Toulouse.

I've never liked first dates; I've always felt too nervous to enjoy them properly, but I actually did enjoy tonight, even if we had a bit of a wobbly start, with my head not being in it, nor my heart. But now I've resorted to type and I'm feeling antsy and the urge to babble to hide my discomfort is strong.

Théo fortunately steps in and saves the day. 'Lia, I like

you.'

Well, that was direct. No messing about with our Théo here.

'Er, I like you, too.' I wouldn't have kissed him if I didn't.

He smiles and his perfect white teeth almost glow in the dark. 'I'd like to see you again, but I don't want to put pressure on you, so here's my number.' He writes it down on a piece of paper and hands it to me. 'This way, you have my number, and you can use it if you want to.'

Wow, that's so considerate, and the kind of thing I'd expect of Jean-Luc.

Jean-Luc. God, I can't get him out of my head.

In a moment of impulsivity, I take out my phone and tap in Théo's number then send him a text saying *Bon nuit!*

When his phone beeps, he smiles.

'Thanks, Théo.' I wait for him to kiss me but he doesn't; instead he hops out of his side of the car and comes round to open my door for me. Then once I'm on the pavement he gives me a chaste kiss on the lips and says, 'See you soon, Lia.'

As he gets back in his car, I notice a light on next door, in the *fromagerie*. And I'm not sure if it's a trick of the light, but I'd swear the curtain moved. No matter. I shake my head and put my key in the boulangerie door.

I've closed the door and am about to walk across the boulangerie to the living room when I hear a tap at the door. Immediately, my hand flies to my side. No, I've not forgotten my bag. I wonder what Théo wants. A tiny prickle of irritation goes through me. Sighing, I open the door.

'Jean-Luc!' I take an involuntary step backwards.

'Lia, can I come in? I have some news.'

My first thought is what news can he have that can't wait until morning? Did he see me with Théo? No, that wouldn't be enough reason for him to knock on the door so late at night, would it? Plus, I'm not even sure he cares.

I take one look at the distress etched into his face and my heart plummets. 'What's wrong?' Nausea rises in my throat.

'It's René.'

Chapter Fourteen

Jean-Luc follows me inside then exhales heavily and sits down. His eyes search mine. 'René has been taken to hospital. His kidneys have failed.'

'Oh my God!' My eyes well with unshed tears. 'Poor René, poor Estelle and Matthieu.'

Jean-Luc shakes his head. 'I know he hasn't been well, but I didn't realise this was a possibility.'

'Are Estelle and Matthieu at the hospital?' I ask.

Jean-Luc nods. 'Yes. Alexine phoned them after she called the ambulance. I think Sarah managed to get there first, though. She helped her grandmother until the paramedics arrived, although I'm not sure how much they were able to do. I wouldn't know what to do in that situation, would you?'

I shake my head. 'No, I wouldn't have a clue.'

'I hope you don't mind, but I told Estelle that you and I will somehow, between us, manage the boulangerie tomorrow. Suzanne is still coming over as she has to make the *chocolatines* instead of her father, and she'll bake the bread and everything else, but then she'll be exhausted, so I said since you've been working in the shop already, you could probably hold the fort, and I'd be next door for help if you needed it.' He peers into my face anxiously. 'Was that OK? I didn't speak out of turn?'

'No, no, that's absolutely fine.' I'm terrified at the thought of being left in the shop on my own with my patchy French, but I'll muddle through somehow. There's always Google Translate, and like Jean-Luc said, he's only next door. Plus, on a positive note, I do like a challenge, and I have been enjoying working in the boulangerie. It's simply a case of donning my big-girl pants.

'Poor Suzanne. It'll be the last thing she feels like doing.'

Jean-Luc dips his head. 'Quite. Anyway, I should let you get some sleep. Will you be OK here on your own?'

I hesitate. I don't want him to leave, not only because I don't want to be alone in a strange house, but because I'm unsettled by the news he has given me, and because I fear I may burst into tears at any moment.

What I'd really like is a hug, but I don't feel I can ask for one, particularly since I've just come back from a date with another man.

I bite back a sob. Jean-Luc instantly comes towards me. 'Hey, hey, come here.' He envelops me in his embrace and I lean into him, relishing the heat from his body as a torrent of sobs bursts forth from me. And I'm not only crying for René, I'm crying for the mess I've made of my friendship with Jean-Luc, the chaos I've left back home in Scotland with the death of my relationship with Freddy – having to sell the flat, and also discovering his new girlfriend in our favourite coffee shop with him. Losing my job was simply the icing on the cake.

'Sorry.' I sniff as I pull back from him. He doesn't let go of me, though, and his eyes are so intense, questioning, that for a moment I think he's going to kiss me. Then he seems to collect himself and says, 'René will be OK, I'm sure of it. He's in the right place.'

Numbly, I nod as my eyes roam the living room, taking in the happy family photographs, where René features in so many of them.

'I'll stay,' Jean-Luc says, 'if you want me to. I can sleep on the couch.'

'Really? Are you sure you don't mind?' I look at the couch, trying to assess its suitability as a bed as opposed to somewhere to snuggle into whilst watching TV.

If it were my house, I'd have said he could sleep in one of the other bedrooms, but it seems too intimate, too personal, and I don't feel I can take that liberty.

'Good, it's decided. I'll text Suzanne so she knows I'm here when she comes over and doesn't get a shock when she hears a man snoring in the living room.'

I manage a small smile at Jean-Luc finding some levity in this difficult situation.

'Would you like a nightcap before you go to bed? You've had a bit of a shock.'

I hesitate. Spending more time with Jean-Luc right now perhaps isn't the best idea, especially when I'm already emotional, but it's only a drink and he is doing me a huge favour by staying overnight. 'Sure.' I pause then say, 'Thank you, Jean-Luc, for everything.'

He gives a little smile, but it seems sad almost, and I wonder what he's thinking.

As we sip our cognac, we run through what I need to know for the next day. Jean-Luc tries to keep things simple. Suzanne will fill me in on most things before she leaves to go home to bed, apparently, but she won't be with me in the boulangerie itself.

'So, I'll gauge how busy it is in the *fromagerie*, and if it's quiet, I'll come in and help if you need me, but in any case, if you get stuck, you can either text me or come in. Here, let me give you my number.'

I glance up and my eyes meet mine. 'Your number?'

'Yes, in case of emergency.'

I find I rather like the idea of having Jean-Luc's number and also the idea of being able to call on him in case of emergency, but I'm not only thinking of in relation to the boulangerie.

As we drink our cognac, Jean-Luc asks me how I'm enjoying my time in France. He avoids asking me about Théo, or what I was doing tonight, and I'm grateful for that, as I honestly don't know what's going on. Maybe life in Scotland wasn't so tough.

I try to keep the topic neutral and focus on the time I've spent in the boulangerie, helping Estelle. I regale him with funny stories of the clients, and sometimes I try to get him to guess who I'm talking about by describing them, their words, their clothes, their attitude, when really what I want to do is tell him how much I enjoyed spending Monday with him and how gutted I've felt since the misunderstanding about Gloire. I realise he still thinks I have a boyfriend, and in an attempt to clarify things between us, as he'll probably think I'm cheating on my boyfriend as well as going out with Théo – what a bloody mess – I tell him I wish I could stay in France longer and not only to avoid having to return to the mess of my life in Scotland.

Jean-Luc listens as I tell him some, but not all, of the details. I'd like to keep some of my street cred intact, and would prefer not to come off as a total loser. I tell him that in addition to having lost my job, I split up with my boyfriend three weeks ago and we're now having to sell the flat we only bought three months ago, and how being in France is a lovely escape from it all.

I see the cogs in Jean-Luc's mind whirring into action. I'm not cheating on my boyfriend. He's my ex-boyfriend. The same as Gloire is his ex-girlfriend. For a second, a light appears in his eyes and then the shutters come down. He's thinking about tonight and Théo. I'll cross that bridge when I come to it, but at least for tonight he knows I'm not some unfaithful witch, and that's enough for me.

It matters to me what this man thinks of me, because I like him. A lot. And I think he may like me. But then there's the difficulty of us living in two different countries, and the fact I've just been on a date with Théo, someone he clearly doesn't rate. I want to get to the bottom of that story. No, I need to get to the bottom of that story. Why does everyone dislike Théo so much?

'Exes are the pits.' Jean-Luc toys with his tumbler, swishing the amber liquid back and forth. 'For the record, Gloire isn't my girlfriend. She hasn't been for a while.' He sighs. 'She's also very high maintenance and has misplaced hopes of us getting back together. It's not going to happen. She did something unforgiveable.' He doesn't know Sarah filled me in, but I act sympathetic without probing.

He sighs again. 'People change. Gloire used to be a sweet girl, but then she started hanging with a pretentious crowd, and, well, she changed. She got a modelling contract and, well, let's just say, she wasn't short of interest from other men.'

I rest my hand on his forearm in a sign of solidarity, then say, 'Yep, exes are definitely the worst.'

As we drain our drinks, I don't want our conversation to end, but I know we must get some rest, plus Suzanne will be here in a couple of hours to start baking the bread and making the *chocolatines* and other pastries, and since I need to get up and prepare the boulangerie for business, I'll probably need to get up relatively early. And my still being up means Jean-Luc can't go to sleep on the couch either.

With great reluctance, I say, 'I think we should go to bed. I mean, we both need to go to sleep. I mean, you here and me upstairs.' I'm blushing furiously. I can feel it.

Jean-Luc's lips twitch and I know he's laughing inside, and now it's my turn to create the levity, and I'm glad I've done so. René is important to Jean-Luc too, and he'll be concerned not only for René, but for the entire Molins family. They're so close, almost like family, especially working next door to each other.

'I know what you meant,' Jean-Luc says, his lips curving upwards.

As I stand to leave, he does too. He kisses me on both cheeks and wraps his arms around me and we remain entwined for what feels like several minutes but is probably only ten or twenty seconds. I wish we never had to move apart, and I get the impression he feels the same way.

When we do finally draw apart, I say, 'Jean-Luc, can I talk to you about the other night?'

He sighs then says, 'Lia, I don't think tonight is the right time. And I don't know about you, but I'm pretty tired. Can it wait?'

'Of course.' I can't help feeling a little deflated at how readily he shuts me down, but I do my best not to let it show. I need to put this right, but Jean-Luc's right, first, we need to know René is going to be OK.

I head to bed, my hand raising to touch where Jean-Luc kissed my cheek. Somehow I feel sleep won't come easy tonight.

Chapter Fifteen

The tantalising aroma of freshly baked bread assails my nostrils in an all too familiar tableau. Yet as I rouse myself, the memory of last night's events kicks in and I recall it's not Matthieu who will be baking the bread, but Suzanne, taking her father's place as he keeps a vigil at his father-in-law's bedside in hospital.

My eyes feel glued shut and I give a huge yawn. I'm still exhausted and wryly reflect that if I'm exhausted, how must the others be feeling. I fumble for my mobile phone to check the time. My alarm hasn't gone off yet, so that's something. I don't need to worry about opening up the boulangerie late, although I dare say neither Suzanne nor Jean-Luc would let me sleep so late I didn't open up on time.

After throwing on some clothes and dragging a brush through my hair, I tentatively head downstairs, holding on more tightly than usual to the wooden handrail on the steep steps down from my attic bedroom. The smell of the *chocolatines* is even more heavenly than before, and my mouth waters. But first I need to freshen up.

I splash cold water on my face, several times, before it has any impact, then brush my teeth until they gleam. Murmured voices come from the main part of the house.

Since I didn't see Suzanne in the bakery area, I can only imagine it's her and Jean-Luc talking.

Once I'm semi-presentable, I slink into the kitchen, where Jean-Luc is seated, his clothes rumpled from sleeping on the sofa, the lines under his eyes indicative of how few hours rest he managed. Suzanne can barely keep her eyes open and covers her mouth with a hand as she yawns. Not even the ultra-strong coffee she has brewed – the aroma alone is enough to keep me awake, hopefully – is working for her.

'Morning.' I place my hands on Suzanne's shoulders in a gesture of support and kiss her lightly on the cheek. 'How is your *papi*?'

She turns to me slightly and her tired eyes meet mine. 'He's stable at the minute, thank God. *Papa* is still with him, and *Maman* is with *Mémé*.'

I exhale heavily. 'That's good about René. How is Alexine doing?'

She shakes her head wearily. 'Not great. Despite always seeming so strong, and being strong for *Papi*, *Mémé* has been having problems with her heart the past few years.' Tears fill her eyes and she quickly wipes them with the edge of her sleeve. 'I'm scared we'll lose them both.'

Jean-Luc, whom I haven't made eye contact with until now, covers Suzanne's hand with his own, whilst I wrap my arms around her trembling body.

'Shh, you can't think like that. René is where he needs to be, with specialists who do this every day. And your mum will take care of *Mémé*. She won't let anything happen to her.'

Suzanne sniffs then nods in agreement. Jean-Luc hands her a paper tissue and she blows her nose noisily then excuses herself to go to the bathroom, leaving Jean-Luc and me alone.

I sigh and sit down at the head of the kitchen table, between their seats. Jean-Luc absentmindedly strokes my hand in a gesture of solidarity. We're all caught up in our thoughts about the elder Molins. I risk a smile, which may have manifested as more of a grimace. Jean-Luc looks at me wordlessly, his eyes searching mine, then as if corralling his energy from somewhere, he says, 'Coffee?'

I nod gratefully. It's not the tiredness that is weighing me down but the fate of this family whom I adore so much. If all I can do to help this situation is keep their boulangerie open for them, then I'll do it to the best of my abilities, even if I am nervous as hell about being left in the shop alone, with my pitiful French and my lack of know-how.

'What time is Suzanne heading off?' I ask as Jean-Luc pours me coffee, and I add sugar. I need the injection of it and the caffeine to get me through the day.

'Soon. She has been up for more than twenty-four hours already.'

'Why doesn't she sleep here? She still has a room here and she sleeps here sometimes anyway,' I suggest.

'I don't know. Maybe she wanted to be home so she could be with Patrick.' He lowers his voice. 'Particularly in case there's any bad news.'

My eyes widen and Jean-Luc rushes on. 'Not that there will be. René's relatively stable now, I believe, but perhaps that was her line of thinking last night. Or maybe she wants to pick up some fresh clothes.'

I nod. 'Did you sleep OK?'

'It took a while for me to fall asleep, but I think the cognac helped in the end. Once I was asleep, I didn't even wake when Suzanne came in. I was out cold.'

'He was,' Suzanne says, re-entering the room. 'And what a pity I couldn't even appreciate a half-naked man in my parents' living room. Those days are gone.'

I give a faint smile at her attempt at levity, whilst I wonder which part was the naked part and why.

'I was boiling and I couldn't find the thermostat to turn the heating down. It feels like the Tropics in here. Eventually, I had to take my T-shirt off as I was sweating like a pig. How attractive.'

'Don't worry, I'm used to rooms smelling of sweaty men. First, I had to grow up with Dad and Dominique, and now Patrick.'

He doesn't smell too bad from here, despite him still wearing last night's clothes. I can't help wondering what he'd look like without his shirt on, though.

'How are you going to work in the *fromagerie* today if you don't have any clean clothes?' I ask.

'Oh, I always keep a clean set at work. For cheese-related disasters, you understand.'

He manages to make me smile, and I'm grateful for it.

'Suzanne, you must be shattered. We were thinking, why don't you sleep here? You're probably safer too, rather than driving when you're this tired.'

She lets out another huge yawn, unable to cover her mouth in time. 'Sorry, yes, I am. I have no idea why I didn't think of that before. And fortunately, I, too, have clean clothes here. I'll text Patrick and tell him I'm crashing here today and I'll be back tonight.'

I'm much happier with this plan.

'And you can always come and get me if there's any problems in the boulangerie,' she says.

'Not a chance,' I say as Jean-Luc shakes his head vigorously. 'You need to rest. Jean-Luc and I have it under control.'

Suzanne glances at him and he gives her a double thumbs-up. I think she's so tired, she has completely forgotten what was arranged for today. She definitely needs to sleep, so I shoo her off to bed and she goes without much resistance.

'Right, what time is it?' I ask.

'Quarter past six,' replies Jean-Luc. 'Time for one more cup of coffee and some of those delicious *chocos* Suzanne has made, then we need to get ready for work, and I need to change.'

'Sounds like a plan. Thank you, Jean-Luc.'

'No need to thank me, Lia.' He stands and busies himself pouring us more coffee whilst I fetch the *chocolatines* from the bread bin where I know Estelle usually stashes the selection reserved for the family. Out of force of habit, Suzanne has done the same.

We chat whilst we eat breakfast, and it seems like the most natural thing in the world for me to be eating breakfast with this man, and I know it's an image that will fill my dreams for days to come, despite the initial reason he's there.

Two hours. I glance at the boulangerie clock again. I haven't stopped for two hours. I dab my forehead with my sleeve. I'm sweating. Who knew serving in a shop by myself could be such hard work?

Don't get me wrong, I'm loving it, not even the embarrassment of my not yet fluent French is holding me back, but I'm exhausted. All I hear is the ping, ping, ping of the bell over the door as yet another customer comes in. There have been queues, for goodness' sake. I chuckle to myself. I didn't remember Saturday at the boulangerie is by far the busiest day, but then perhaps it makes sense as it shuts at one, only re-opening at six thirty on Monday morning. I'm actually feeling quite proud of myself that I've handled the masses all on my own. Plus, every time I package up one of the various artisan breads and pastries, it makes me want to create them myself. I'll need to ask Suzanne and Matthieu for lessons.

It started off sedately enough this morning, with the first trickle of customers a little before seven, and I was feeling quite smug, thinking I could handle it all and I'd probably spend most of my time reading a novel next door in the sitting room, waiting for the ping of the doorbell, but come half past seven, it was as if someone had deposited a coachload of tourists outside the boulangerie's door. The bell must have dinged every thirty seconds, and the leisurely '*Bonjour*' and two-minute chat I was having with each customer descended into a foot-tapping, huffing, exhaling loudly queue of impatience.

I've already had to text Jean-Luc twice as I've been unable to leave the shop to fill up the bread and pastries from the stock-room. He has been wonderful, popping a back-in-five-minutes sign on the door of the *fromagerie* and stepping into the breach to help me.

How Suzanne has slept through all this, I don't know. She must have ear plugs in, as even exhausted, I couldn't sleep through the sound of that bell constantly going off.

Jean-Luc has also worked alongside me, babbling away in dialect to some of the older customers, who don't originally hail from Toulouse by the sounds of it, and chatting away amiably to others in French I can just about understand, despite the speed.

From what I can gather, him helping out in the boulangerie has them tickled pink, but once they understand why he's helping, their whole demeanour changes, and they fall into one of two camps: those who're genuinely concerned for René's wellbeing and that of Estelle and the family, and those who are adding another snippet of gossip to their repertoire. Generally, the latter are few and far between, as the Molins are clearly much-loved in this neighbourhood.

By the end of the morning, we've pretty much sold out of most items, and when the clock strikes one, I turn the Open sign to Closed and lean back against the door with a sigh of relief. A tap at the door has me spinning around, thinking it's yet another customer I have to tell we have nothing left, but no, it's Jean-Luc. His grin is wide and I think I'm falling for him a little bit more.

When I open the door, he says, 'I brought lunch.' He holds up some cheese and a bag of tomatoes. 'I didn't know if Estelle had any, so I added these.'

I take them from him. 'Thanks.'

'Do you think I should wake Suzanne?' I ask, listening to see if I can hear her padding about upstairs, but there's no creak on the floorboards.

Jean-Luc shakes his head. 'Let her sleep. They may be visiting round the clock. It depends how severe René is.' As he speaks, he takes plates out of the cupboard, with a familiarity which makes me smile. He's obviously at home here, and well-thought-of by the family, if he knows where everything is and he can come and go as he pleases.

We sit down to an impromptu lunch as Jean-Luc tells me of the antics in the *fromagerie* this morning. Apparently, everyone was abuzz with the news of a new girl working in the boulangerie, and the fact she wasn't even French. I smile, hoping it's not too big a negative. The last thing I want is for clients to leave the boulangerie as they can't make out what I'm saying. When I voice my concerns to Jean-Luc, he laughs and says those who were talking about me were either charmed by me, interested in my being Scottish, or correcting my pronunciation of certain words.

'I hope you stood up for me to that last group,' I say, mock indignantly.

'But of course. I simply asked them how good their English was, and if they'd be able to step in and help out in a friend's shop in England, or Scotland, if there was an emergency. That soon shut them up.'

We giggle like two schoolchildren at his audacity, and a warm glow floods my system. I feel as if I've been back in Toulouse months, not a week.

The tomatoes marry perfectly with the crumbly cheeses Jean-Luc has brought, and we wash lunch down with a glass of Fronton, which induces a memory of picnicking near the country house in Saint-Sauvy with Suzanne and Sarah, all those years ago. We take our time and when we've finished, I'm almost ready for a nap, something Jean-Luc picks up on.

'Right, let's get this lot washed up, then we're going for a walk. Sitting around waiting for news won't help us.'

I frown at him. 'But don't you have somewhere you need to be? No plans this afternoon?'

He shakes his head. 'Nope. I was going to have a lazy afternoon, for once, but I think what's called for today is some exercise.'

I have worrying visions of him taking me to the gym, or on a hike.

'Have you ever been to the Japanese garden here?'

I purse my lips. 'I don't think so.'

'Excellent. It's beautiful, and so relaxing. Right, grab a jacket and once I've washed these dishes, let's go.'

I don't usually go for the bossy type, but there's something attractive about him taking control of our afternoon, in such a natural way, as if we've been dating for years, instead of not at all.

'Let me just scribble a note to Suzanne.' I scrawl: 'Gone to Japanese garden. Hope you had a good sleep. Some lunch in the fridge for you. No news yet. Please ring me when you hear anything. Lia x.'

I weight the note down with a mug then follow Jean-Luc through the boulangerie to see what delights await us at the Japanese garden.

Chapter Sixteen

'How did I not know this was here? It's gorgeous.' I squint at Jean-Luc in the sunshine, shading my eyes with my hand.

'Didn't I tell you it was worth seeing?' Jean-Luc beams at me.

'You know how lucky we are to be visiting it today, don't you?' I say, to which he nods. 'It has rained four out of the seven days since I arrived.'

We amble along at a snail's pace almost, taking in the beauty of everything around us. I must have been super self-absorbed to miss this place completely when I lived here, or perhaps student me wasn't interested in the swaying blossom trees and their delicate pink petals. It's true we don't take time to admire the beauty of nature all around us, usually. But today is different, and today I am drinking it all in.

'I'd have shown you the garden when you lived here, if I hadn't been studying in the States at the time,' Jean-Luc says. 'It's one of my favourite places in the city.'

'No wonder. And I can't believe it's so close to the boulangerie.'

He laughs. 'Sometimes we miss what's right in front of our noses.' The way he says it is so earnest, it makes me wonder if he's saying one thing, but inferring something else – something between us perhaps.

Oh God, why do we women always do this to ourselves? We read too much into things. I know I do, for sure. I tell myself I'm overthinking things and settle in to our walk again.

As we wend our way through the garden, I sight a red bridge in the distance. It's suspended over a lake and to the left of it, the branches of a cherry tree, heavy with blossom, droop forward, almost touching the water. It would make a fantastic photograph.

A young couple are taking a selfie, all smiles, and I can't help but think that it's the perfect romantic backdrop.

'Oh, wow, look at the little bridge.' I turn to Jean-Luc and plead with my eyes for us to see it close up. He takes the hint and we meander along the tree-lined pathways until we reach the centre of the bridge, passing the couple, who have now finished their photo shoot.

I look down into the water, where water lilies bob on the surface. All that's missing is for a hardy frog to come along and perch on one, or are all my imaginings conjured up from Disney movies? It's hard to tell. *Your prince is already here*, my inner voice says, but I quickly quiet it.

Jean-Luc leans over the wooden rail of the bridge, gazing into the water, copying my stance. 'I like to come here to think. This place calms me.'

I turn my head to look at him and am struck by how right it feels being with him, right at this moment, in this beautiful place. Finally realising I'm staring, and haven't acknowledged what he said, I inhale deeply and say, 'I can see why.'

We stay like that, leaning on the bridge, watching the

turtles swim past, then we turn towards each other, as if each deciding at the same time we should move on, and trying to figure out in which direction we should go next, when two women stop next to us.

'Would you like us to take your picture?'

'Er—' I hate having my photo taken.

'That would be perfect, thanks.' Jean-Luc hands her his phone and shows her how to take a photo with it before putting his arm around me and posing for the camera.

Thanks, Jean-Luc, but soon I'm so entranced by the feel of his arm around my shoulders that I couldn't protest even if I wanted to.

One of the women snaps a few shots then hands Jean-Luc's phone back to him, as her friend says, 'What a beautiful photo. You're such a lovely couple.'

'We're not…' I start, just as Jean-Luc bestows a dazzling smile on me. I can't complete the sentence. Plus, I like the idea of leaving that thought hanging in the ether. What is it they say? Fake it till you make it? Maybe I can pretend Jean-Luc and I are more than we are, until perhaps one day we will be.

Jean-Luc shows me the photos. They do look good. I'm actually happy with a photo of me, for a change.

'Can you forward that to me, please?' I ask.

'Sure.' He sends it straight over and then says, 'Ready to see the temple?'

'Absolutely. Lead the way.'

Jean-Luc hooks his arm through mine. 'Let's go.'

We wander off the other side of the bridge to the temple. The last people are just vacating it, so we have the whole place to ourselves. We sit down side by side, embracing the tranquillity. I'm wholly relaxing into the zen moment, enjoying just being, when my phone rings. René, is my first thought as I grab my phone. But it's not news of René – it's Théo, so I don't answer.

Jean-Luc raises an eyebrow. 'Do you need to get that?'

I shrug. 'Unknown number. I'm enjoying living in the moment. We're slave enough to our devices.'

His lazy smile sends bolts of lust sparking through me. I feel as if flames must be shooting out of me, I'm so hot.

'True. Today should be about relaxing. There'll be time enough to get caught up in the fray soon enough.'

I sigh as my thoughts return to René. I hope no news is good news. Jean-Luc catches my eye. 'Ah-ah-ah! No moping. Right, we need a drink.'

'We do?'

He nods. 'Most definitely. Up to you, can be a coffee or alcohol, but I need to keep an eye on you and ensure you relax.'

I like the sound of that, so I take the hand he offers me and let him pull me up. As I jerk to upright, I stumble and throw out my arm to steady myself, but Jean-Luc catches me as I fall against him, and my breath hitches as we remain like that for a second too long, before we break apart.

I cover my discomfort in the usual way. 'Sorry, I'm so clumsy.' Then I readjust my hair over my face so he can't see me flush the colour of vine-ripened tomatoes.

'*Allons-y.*' He takes my hand and it seems so natural for me to slip mine into his and leave it there. It's warm, strong and masculine. Not too large, not slender, just right. God, I feel like I'm comparing him to bowls of porridge in *Goldilocks and the Three Bears*.

Jean-Luc steers us down a couple of side streets I don't

recall coming across before, until from the hubbub I'm certain we must be close to Place du Capitole, then he stops in front of a gorgeous little café, Café Joli, and I can't help but think it definitely lives up to its name as it's so pretty. Flowers in assorted colours spill out of ceramic pots of various sizes placed symmetrically around the outside. Patio heaters tower overhead, but don't detract from the frontage whose windows display signs advising patrons they offer crêpes and galettes.

Soft classical music emanates from within, and it's soothing; I can't quite place the composer, but I recognise the piece. Yes, I could definitely while away some time here with Jean-Luc. It has to be far preferable than fretting back at the boulangerie over the situation with René. I'd prefer to be in company, and Jean-Luc is easy company to be in. He's so chilled. With all the uncertainty in my life at the moment, I could be doing with taking lessons from him on how to achieve this. He could be the perfect antidote to my screwed-up life, but then I chide myself. He's a person, not a cure.

'What do you fancy?' Jean-Luc asks once he nabs us a table inside. We've decided it's still too chilly for us to sit outside.

Undecided, and unwilling to tell him exactly what I fancy right now … I say, 'What are you having?'

He towers over me, dimples forming in either cheek. 'Well, I know we just had lunch, but the crêpes here are the best in Toulouse.'

'In the whole of Toulouse?'

He inclines his head and puts his hand on his chest, where I imagine his heart to be. 'Would I lie to you?'

Honestly, I don't think he would. Ever. Jean-Luc is one

of those ultra-dependable types, but hot with it. Crikey. Could I just stop thinking for one minute about what his smile and the expression in his eyes do to my insides?

'So, you're having the crêpes?' I check.

He dips his head. 'I am.'

'OK, make that two.'

Jean-Luc half-turns to indicate the board. 'What filling?'

It's a little far away but I manage to read the choices: butter with sugar; lemon and sugar; Nutella; salted butter caramel. Mmm. The last one hits the spot.

'Salted caramel for me, please.'

He turns one of his sexy smiles on me again. 'Good choice. I'm having the Nutella.'

'Good choice,' I parrot back to him as he pivots and goes to place our order.

Whilst he's gone, I check my messages. Jules, Freddy, the estate agent.

Jules first. *How was your date? Did you get it on? Details!!*

I smirk. That girl is unbelievable. Was it really only last night I went on my date with Théo? It seems such a long time ago. So much has happened since then, and how I feel has dramatically changed. Deciding not to reply for now, I skip to the photo Jean-Luc sent me of us in the Japanese garden earlier. It's such a great photo. I don't often post on social media, but this photo makes me want to. I hesitate then decide if Jean-Luc's OK with appearing on my feed, I'll post it, since I look as relaxed and happy as I remember ever seeing me in a photo. It's a totally natural shot.

Jean-Luc reappears, interrupting my thoughts, his long legs sliding beneath the table and nudging against mine as he adjusts his chair.

'Sorry! Anyway, order placed and should be here shortly.'

'Don't worry about it. Listen,' I say, turning my phone around, 'would you be OK if I posted this on my social media?'

His cheeks pinken and I rush on. 'It's just it's a good photo, and I love the backdrop of the bridge and the blossom, plus I hate getting my photo taken and I quite like this one.'

He shrugs. 'Sure.'

'Thanks.' I tap a few keys and turn the phone back towards him. The post reads *A relaxing walk in the beautiful Jardin des Plantes in Toulouse. How cute is this bridge?*

Jean-Luc's lips – which are very full, I now realise – curve into a smile. 'Looks good.'

'Almost as good as these crêpes,' I say as the waitress brings them to the table. My stomach rumbles and heat creeps up my neck.

Jean-Luc laughs. 'Clearly, it was a good call to have crêpes now. I obviously didn't feed us enough at lunch.'

I hit send on the photo, pick up my cutlery, ready to dive in, then say, 'But it was so good. It must be all the hard work that's making us so hungry.'

Jean-Luc eyes me thoughtfully. 'Must be.' After a moment's pause, he says, 'Do you want to go half and half, or are you one of those people who never shares food?'

Sharing food has always felt intimate to me, but Jean-Luc and I have already shared a few intimate moments, and they've felt entirely natural, so I don't hold back. 'I can share.'

He cuts his crêpe in half, then gestures for me to bring my plate closer. When I do, he slides half of his onto my plate, and then glances up at me, seeking permission to cut mine in half and claim his portion. I nod and he slices it in half then drags it onto his plate.

I take a bite, of mine first. It is sublime.

'This is *so* good.' I half-cover my mouth so he doesn't get a glimpse of me chomping down on my crêpe.

His eyes twinkle. 'I don't like to say I told you so, but…'

'Yes, best to finish there.'

We eat in companionable silence for a few moments and my thoughts are torn between how things are going with René at the hospital and what's going on with the gorgeous man in front of me. Single. Not in a relationship with Gloire. Lovely, both in nature and to look at. Where's the catch, and why hasn't someone decent and normal – not Gloire – snapped him up already? It's like having a really good-looking best friend, but one I'm insanely attracted to. To be fair, I'd need to be a nun not to be attracted to him. He looks good, he smells divine, his touch sends shock waves through me, his voice I could listen to forever, and … I bet he tastes good too. Gulp.

He places his knife and fork on the table. 'That was even better than I remember.'

I'm still chewing so simply nod.

'I lost you for a moment there. What are you thinking about?'

Well, there's no way I can divulge that, is there? I flush at the prospect. 'Wondering how René is getting on, how things are going at the hospital.'

Jean-Luc's expression turns solemn and the sparkle goes out of his eyes. 'Yes, we should probably call Suzanne to see if there has been any news.'

I finish my crêpe as Jean-Luc throws a few notes on the table and signals to the waiter, who comes over. Whilst they chat, I pick up my phone and note the barrage of notifications on my post. I'm obviously not the only person who appreciates beautiful gardens in France.

I open the notifications.

Wow – gorgeous. Love the blossom. And the guy isn't half bad either.

Who is he?

You look amazing, and your partner is rather tasty too.

New love interest?

Way to make Freddy jealous! You look incredible.

Who is the hot guy with you?

Glad to see you're living your best life.

Fabulous photo of you both. Haven't seen you look so happy for ages x That one's Jules.

What happens in France stays in France. It's followed by a winking emoji.

Is he a model?

With dismay, I note very few of the other comments even mention the bridge, the garden or France itself; they're mainly focused on Jean-Luc. Maybe I should take the post down.

I'm suddenly aware Jean-Luc's hovering at my shoulder – he must have finished his discussion with the waiter whilst I was scrolling through the comments – and frantically, I shove my phone in my jacket pocket. I most definitely don't want him to see those comments. But as we head back towards Chalets and the boulangerie, I can't help wondering why it's such a big deal to me, and why I don't just put myself out there – with Jean-Luc. We're both single, albeit we each have baggage, although mine is considerably heavier than his, and now I've thrown Théo into the mix. My head's beginning to hurt. Or is it simply because I like Jean-Luc, a lot, and don't want to lose him as a friend?

My phone beeps, reminding me we were going to call Suzanne for news. But it's Théo again, and this time, there's a message.

Heard about René. Absolutely awful. I'll swing by around seven and take you for dinner. I know you won't want to be in their way at a time like this, and it'll do you good to be occupied. Théo x

What? No, that's not what I need right now. I bristle at Théo's insinuation I'm a burden on the Molins.

Furiously, I type back, *Thanks, but I have plans.*

'Are you OK?' Jean-Luc asks, the gentle pressure of his hand on my arm startling me out of my thoughts.

'Ye-e-s. I-I just … got a message from my estate agent,' I fib.

Jean-Luc arches an eyebrow. 'Good news?'

I give a slow shake of my head. 'Nothing definitive. Just an update on a viewer.'

'Oh. You looked confused, that's all.'

Inwardly, I take a deep breath, then push on, lie after lie. 'They wanted to thrash out some more details, but I thought we'd been pretty specific already.' I mentally kick myself for my usage of 'we'. The last thing I want is Jean-Luc recalling I'm only just out of a relationship.

I hate lying to him, but I don't want to spoil the day, and I'm certainly not mentioning Théo.

Chapter Seventeen

The mood is somewhat more sombre than before as we walk back towards Chalets. Something has shifted between us, and I can't help feeling it's all Théo's fault – well, not all his fault, I have a certain amount of blame to hold on to as well, but if he hadn't been presumptuous about coming and taking me for dinner, and why, I wouldn't be feeling like this right now. Instead, I'd be continuing to enjoy a wonderful afternoon with Jean-Luc.

Jean-Luc's smile has dimmed considerably and he walks along beside me, in silence, lost in his own thoughts.

Why do I feel so guilty though? I like Jean-Luc, he seems to like me, and I didn't like how Théo's text made me feel, despite having enjoyed his company the other night. There's no mistaking he's charming, but there was no way I was letting another man dictate to me what happens, not after Freddy and his behaviour. I think again of my beautiful southside flat – I really need to get over that, but it's hard. One of the reasons I'm so unsettled is because I don't have anywhere concrete to go back to, once I return to Scotland. Why am I agonising over this anyway? I'll be gone in a week. I almost draw to a standstill. Do I need to return to Scotland so soon? Could I be of some use here? I'm loving being here, despite the many complications in my love life. Could I help the Molins in some way?

Or is Théo right and I'm 'in the way'? The very thought makes bile rise in my stomach. I risk a glance at Jean-Luc. His brooding gaze ahead isn't lost on me. He hasn't spoken a word since we left Café Joli. It's as if he knows intuitively something is up. Yet he's too much of a gentleman to ask. He'll have worked out if I wanted to tell him, I'd have done so already.

Now I just feel awkward, and it's all my own fault. I should have realised agreeing to go on a date with Théo was a rebound response to having met Freddy with his new girlfriend, who's ten years younger than me, so anyone showing me a bit of attention was a welcome boost.

'I wonder if Suzanne is awake,' Jean-Luc says, breaking into my thoughts.

'Yeah, she must be exhausted.'

He stops on the pavement and looks directly at me. 'Will you be spending the evening with Suzanne, or…?'

He leaves the end of his question unasked. What to do? Was he about to ask me to spend the evening with him? There's nothing I'd like more. The short time I've spent with Jean-Luc has been wonderful – fun, pleasant, natural, easy.

I'm aware he's studying me, waiting for me to fill in the blanks. I fumble for the right response then settle on, 'I don't know. It all depends I suppose on what the update is on René.'

Jean-Luc nods slowly. 'Of course.'

'But if I'm in the way, or they have other plans, then perhaps I'm better out of the house – unless they really want me there,' I blurt out. Screw Théo. It just hit me that

I can't have him turning up with Suzanne there, not after what Sarah said. And that's the perfect excuse, or reason, to assuage my conscience. I mentally give myself a shake. Not that I should need a reason. If he hadn't been so presumptuous, I wouldn't be in this quandary.

'Well, you can let me know then. You have my number.'

I do, and my mind flits back to the photo, and comments, on Instagram for a second.

We saunter back to the boulangerie. It strikes me that I don't know where Jean-Luc lives, only where his production facility and *fromagerie* shop are. So I ask.

'Oh, I live in Jolimont.'

'It's lovely there. I had a friend when I stayed here who lived in a beautiful house there.'

'Yes, it's a nice area. I'm very lucky.' He is; it's one of the most sought-after areas in Toulouse.

I raise an eyebrow. 'Your parents' house?'

'It was, but they left it to me when Dad retired.'

I whistle. 'Wow, that *is* lucky.'

He grins. 'I think so.'

Finally, we arrive back at the boulangerie. Is it my imagination or was that the slowest walk in history? I had the feeling neither of us wanted it to end. Already our meander through the Japanese garden seems so long ago. I don't know what to say next, but as I'm about to say something, Jean-Luc leans forward and kisses me on both cheeks.

'Maybe I'll see you later?' The inflection in his voice shows he hopes that will be the case.

I smile again. 'I'll let you know. Are you heading home now?'

He shakes his head. 'No, I have some accounting to do.' He pulls a face and closes his eyes momentarily. I laugh, but my breath catches – he has the longest eyelashes. Criminal really.

'Rock n roll Saturday for you,' I say.

Now it's his turn to laugh and the creases at the corner of his eyes liquefy my insides.

'Anyway, I'd best go see if there's any news on René.'

'Yes, please let me know how he is.' He raises a hand in goodbye and disappears into the *fromagerie*.

I open the door to the boulangerie and immediately the sounds of voices greet my ears. Well, more than Suzanne is here at least. When I pass through the curtain from the boulangerie into the living room, Sarah and Estelle are huddled on the sofa, Suzanne on one of the armchairs. Their subdued expressions lift slightly as they spot me, and my heart both sinks and soars. I hope they're not trying to put on a brave face for me, their visitor. My thoughts fly again to Théo's words about me being in the way and I scowl inwardly.

'How is he?' I ask without preamble.

Estelle sighs. 'Not good. He'll be in hospital a while, then we'll need to look at long-term care, from what the doctors tell us.'

I frown. 'What does that involve exactly?'

Estelle sighs again. 'That's what we're trying to work out. It's too soon to say for sure, but it does look like it will mean a great deal of upheaval and change.'

I take in the tension around her eyes and how she is hunched over. I also note the worried glances both Sarah and Suzanne are throwing her way. This isn't good.

'Is there anything I can do to help?'

Estelle shakes her head. 'No, it's fine. We'll cope.' The unspoken 'as we've always done' hangs in the air.

Suzanne slaps her hands on her thighs. 'Tea anyone?'

Estelle gives a silent nod. Sarah dips her head then moves in closer to her mother, wrapping an arm around her. Estelle seems lesser somehow, diminished. I feel awful. I shouldn't be here intruding on this family at this time. But what to do? Part of me thinks I should change my flight, but then I'd feel as if I were only staying when the going was good, and I'd feel bad for abandoning them in their hour of need, if that's not too dramatic. The other part of me feels, particularly now since Théo has raised it, that I'm in the way. They don't need to be distracted taking care of a visitor, not right now.

'I'll give you a hand, Suzanne.' As I walk to the kitchen, I bash out a message to Théo. *Can't tonight. But thanks.*

'Herbal or English tea?' Suzanne asks.

I look up to see her holding two boxes of teabags towards me.

'English, thanks.'

I take some cups out of a cupboard as Suzanne flips biscuits onto a plate.

'How are you holding up?' I ask.

She shakes her head. 'I don't know, really. There's just so much to think about. Already our time is stretched because of *Mamie* and *Papi*, you know?'

I do. Sarah tends to visit her grandparents in the east more as they are also elderly and not particularly mobile and she lives closer to their home in Verfeil, but each of the Molins in turn also visits regularly, as the only other support Matthieu's parents have is from neighbours and friends, and they're either all elderly too, or they have families to look after as well. If only they lived nearer. If only Alexine and René lived closer too. The Molins are literally playing piggy-in-the-middle.

Suzanne looks so wretched, I hug her to me. As I wrap my arms around her, some of the tension leaves her body and her shoulders relax.

I pull back after a few seconds and say, 'Anything I can do, please, just let me know. I mean it, Suzanne. Anything.'

She nods slowly as if she has really considered what I've said. She turns away, but not before I see her brush her fingertips across her eyes. Suzanne is tough, just like Estelle, but the strain is getting to her. I know she'll be worried not only for René and Alexine but for her parents too.

We finish making the tea in relative silence then I say, 'Who's with Alexine?'

'She's with a neighbour for now. *Maman* has come here to fetch some clean clothes, then she's going to stay with *Mémé*, at least for tonight.' Her voice cracks when she mentions her grandmother.

I want to know how Alexine is, too, but I sense Suzanne needs a break from the subject.

'C'mon, let's take this tea through.' I usher her forward to the living room, conscious of the sombre atmosphere there.

As I sit down, I wonder where Matthieu is and ask.

'He has gone to his parents',' Estelle says. 'He wanted to tell them in person about René. They don't hear so well on the phone and he didn't want to have to explain the news via a friend.'

I nod. Makes sense. But I know it's quite some trek from Saint-Sauvy to Verfeil.

All my problems, with Freddy and the flat, losing my

job, and the pitiful state of my life generally pale into insignificance when I tot up everything this family is going through. They are under so much pressure, and spinning so many plates, it's dizzying.

'Estelle, Suzanne tells me you're going back to be with your mum tonight.'

Estelle raises her tired eyes to me, and I wonder how much she has slept. 'That's right. We'll need to take it one day at a time.'

Sarah adds, 'We're going to have a family meeting tomorrow night to figure out a rota for hospital visiting and running the boulangerie.'

'And looking after Alexine, and the childcare and *Papi* and *Mamie* Molins,' says Suzanne.

'That too,' Sarah agrees with a sigh. 'I'm sorry that things have become so problematic during your visit, Lia.'

'Oh, please don't apologise. I'm just worried for René, and well … all of you.'

As one, all three glances land on me.

'Us?' says Sarah.

'Yes, you're all trying to juggle so much. Let me help.'

When they don't initially answer, my insecurity kicks in and I say, 'Or would it be easier for you if I wasn't here? I can check into a hotel or guest house. It's no problem.'

'No, no, no,' Estelle reassures me. 'You are fine here. We may not be around as much, but you are always welcome here.'

'Estelle, thank you. But if I stay, I must also help. So when you draw up the rota tomorrow, please include me for anything I can help with, whether it's making dinner, going to the cash and carry, or helping in the boulangerie.'

Estelle's eyes mist over and she grasps my lower arm.

'Thank you, Lia.'

'You're welcome. Now, is there anything I can do tonight?'

Estelle shakes her head. 'No, I'm going to *Mamie*'s and Suzanne is going to the hospital then home to Patrick. Isn't that right, Suzanne?' She looks to her younger daughter for confirmation, and Suzanne nods. 'And Sarah is heading home to the children. I think we have the rota sorted for tomorrow. Sunday is simpler as the boulangerie is closed and we're usually in Saint-Sauvy, anyway.' She pauses as if it has cost her mentally and physically to iterate all of this, then she says, 'But if you could be around on Monday at some point to help with the boulangerie, that would be much appreciated. I can't think further ahead than that at the moment.'

'No problem. I'll be here.' I pat her hand.

'Thank you, Lia.' The missing sparkle from her eyes brings a lump to my throat. Estelle, always so full of life and bonhomie, diminished by the problems besetting her family. When there's only so much of you to go around, how do you decide what to do? And she never was a great one for delegating. Typical matriarch, she likes to oversee things herself. However, she has taught her children well.

'Now, girls, I'm going to shower, then head over to *Mémé*'s. Lia, I'm sorry we won't be around tonight, but there is plenty of food in the fridge.'

'Don't worry about me. In any case, Jean-Luc said he'd keep me company if no one was around, but I can take care of myself.'

Estelle nods. 'As you wish. Say hi to him for us.'

'I will. Actually, he wanted me to update him on René, so I'll go tell him in a minute.'

As Estelle heads off, I sit a few moments with Suzanne and Sarah, who are both trying to work out as best they can how they see this rota working, and the potential clashes of timings within it, in advance of the family meeting tomorrow night.

'I'm worried about *Maman*,' says Sarah.

'Me too.' Suzanne stands and begins to pace. 'Even with us all chipping in, this isn't going to be easy, particularly long term.'

'We've got to try to be positive. I know it's hard, but together we can all make it work. Please, let me help too.'

Suzanne gives me a weak smile as Sarah nods at me.

'Good, now do you mind if I nip next door for a few minutes to speak to Jean-Luc? I won't be long.'

'No problem,' says Sarah.

Suzanne is staring into space, lost in thought.

When I knock on the door of the *fromagerie*, there's no answer and for a moment, I wonder if Jean-Luc has gone out or headed home, but as I'm turning to leave, he walks through from the back and his smile lights up his whole face. Warmth suffuses my cheeks at being the cause of it.

'Hey, Lia, come in.' He holds the door open and as I enter, the citrusy aftershave he wears hits me like a drug. Jean-Luc is watching me as I pause in the *fromagerie* and look around, drinking in his space.

'It's a little underwhelming at the weekend. Everything's in the fridge now. You should come back when my wares are on display.'

I follow him through to the back, which is a much bigger space than I had anticipated, and although the square footage must be the same as that of the Molins, the layout is completely different. For one, Jean-Luc's is totally open plan. Where the Molins' space is like a rabbit warren of rooms and staircases, Jean-Luc's is spacious, yet homely and comfortable. It's also bright and airy as a result.

'This is lovely,' I say. 'Is this the same size as next door?'

'Yes, at least the downstairs. I don't own the upstairs. It was designed so the upstairs had a separate door to the flat above.'

That makes sense. I had wondered what he'd do with quite so much space.

'Please, have a seat,' he says, gesturing to the sofa. I do, and when he sits on the cuddle chair opposite me, I feel a pang that he hasn't sat beside me, whilst also appreciating him not crowding me.

'I'm not staying long. For now,' I clarify. 'I just came to let you know how things are with René and to say I'm free later, if you want to … do something together.'

I flush when I realise how that could be misconstrued. 'Watch TV, have dinner, go for a walk, I mean.'

He smiles. 'I'd like that. All of it.' His smile drops. 'But what of René?'

I sigh and tell him the latest update.

He nods gravely when I finish. 'They haven't had the easiest time of it.'

'No,' I agree, 'and unfortunately it looks like that's set to continue.'

Jean-Luc's mouth downturns, and it reminds me of exactly how close he is to the family. Then he seems to decide not to dwell on things, saying, 'So, about tonight, how about coming to mine?'

I'm not sure if something in my expression shows my alarm, or apprehension, but he says, 'No strings. But I do like to cook.'

No strings. Just as well he misinterpreted my expression then, although I can't help feeling wistful at barriers being laid down quite so emphatically. I like him, and I'd like him to like me, as more than a friend. I know my life is way too complicated right now, but sometimes you've just got to say yes to things, and sometimes you've got to grab opportunities that fall into your lap. How could I say no to Jean-Luc? And I don't want to.

'That would be lovely, thanks. Mode of transport?'

He chuckles. 'You weren't so taken with the moped, am I right?'

I laugh and say, 'How did you guess?'

He looks skywards for a second then brings his eyes back to mine. 'I think they call the vibe you were giving off "abject terror".'

I lean forward and bat him playfully on the arm. 'Oi! I thought I hid my terror admirably.' No, I didn't, but I did rather enjoy clinging on to him tightly.

'At least you won't be on the moped for long this time. My house is only ten minutes away.'

For a second, my stomach plummets at the thought I won't have an excuse to be pressed up against him for long. And we're just friends, right? *Despite you wanting more*, that inner voice tells me.

'Is there anything you don't eat?' Jean-Luc asks me.

'No, I'm actually pretty easy to please.' I feel myself redden at the unintentional double entendre.

He smiles and suddenly I'm looking forward to this evening a whole lot more.

'Anyway, I'd best get going,' I say, standing. 'I want to spend some time with the Molins, see how I can help before they all head out this evening.'

'Sure. I'll knock on the door around seven. That gives me time to pick up a few things and finish off here.'

'Great. I'll see you later.'

As he shows me out, there's a definite spring in my step at the thought of the evening to come.

Chapter Eighteen

'You will let me know how things are with René, won't you?' I say to Suzanne, the last of the Molins to leave.

'Absolutely. Now, go, enjoy your dinner with Jean-Luc. He's a nice guy.' She has a twinkle in her eye, and I suppress a smirk. I don't know if she's just enjoying what's potentially going on in my life right now with Jean-Luc as a distraction from all the unpalatable stuff in her own, or if she's matchmaking of sorts, but if it helps take her thoughts away from the situation with René, even for a moment, I'm happy to help.

After being caught out and being frozen to the bone last time I was on Jean-Luc's moped, I've made a point of wearing skinny jeans and a rose-coloured top with a tan leather jacket I've borrowed from Suzanne and my own tan Chelsea boots. I'm opting for comfort over glamour, and let's face it, with Jean-Luc having an ex like Gloire, who could have featured in *Vogue*, it's best I don't try.

I've spritzed myself with the sweet floral and patchouli perfume Suzanne loaned me too, and ready for the evening, I'm just applying a slick of neutral lip gloss when the doorbell chimes.

'I'll get it,' calls Suzanne, who's just about to leave.

Right on time. I almost dance my way to the door, I'm

so keen to get the evening started. I hear murmured voices, then a raised one. Suzanne's. What on earth?

I walk into the living room, through the beaded curtain and into the boulangerie and stop dead. Théo's standing in the doorway talking to Suzanne, and Suzanne's body is radiating tension from every pore. Her face is almost puce. She glances at me and her expression contains a mixture of confusion, pain and something I can't quite put my finger on.

'Lia, Théo is here to take you to dinner,' she says, her voice flat. 'I need to go. Can you lock up?'

I'm so gobsmacked by so many things unfolding all at once, I don't even have time to set the record straight before she's gone, leaving Théo, standing on the threshold, in her wake, my reply superfluous. What must she be thinking? I told her I was having dinner with Jean-Luc. And not only that, Théo of all people, who she has a huge beef with, is here to take me to dinner.

'You look *different*.' Théo comes forward and kisses me on the cheek. I stand and stare at him, dazed and confused. 'And you smell divine.'

'Th-thanks,' I say, still unable to articulate much, my mind racing as I dread to think what went through Suzanne's mind when Théo told her he had come to collect me.

'Shall we go?' he says, attempting to usher me out of the boulangerie.

'Go? Go where?'

He laughs. A strange almost hysterical sound. 'For dinner, Lia, like we arranged.'

Oh no. This is bad. He can't be here. I'm about to have dinner with Jean-Luc. I told Théo I wasn't available tonight.

'Théo, I can't come for dinner. I…' He has just seen Suzanne leave. I settle for, 'I messaged you.'

His forehead creases and a slight tick plays at the edge of his mouth. 'You did?' He checks his phone. 'I don't see any message. What did your message say?'

I did message him, I know I did. I sent it as I went to make tea with Suzanne. This can't be happening. I scrabble in my bag for my phone, open up the messaging app and … see the message definitely sent. Oh my God! What am I going to do?

'Théo, I'm sorry, but I did send you a message–' I show him my phone '–as you can see. I've–' again I scrabble around for what to say '–told the Molins I'll be here for them this evening, and I don't want to let them down.'

He frowns again. 'But Suzanne just left.' He pauses, watching me the whole time. 'And are Sarah and Estelle here?'

Belatedly, I realise he hasn't even asked how René is.

I'm so much out of my depth, I don't even know how to answer him, nor am I even aware I haven't until he says, 'Lia, are the Molins at home right now?'

It's not in my nature to outright lie; the occasional white one, yes, when needed, but I feel as if I'm being interviewed by the secret police, so I do what I would if I were in that scenario: I cave.

'Not at the moment, but they'll be back later.'

He smiles. 'Well, then, that gives us plenty of time to have dinner. And you're in luck. I've booked us into one of the best gastronomic experiences, here in Toulouse, so we can be back in ten minutes, if needed.'

Unable to think of any more excuses, and becoming redder by the minute, and even more panicked at the idea of Jean-Luc arriving and finding Théo here, I say, 'But I'm not dressed for a posh restaurant,' clinging to the hope my attire will be the dealbreaker, and my evening will continue as originally planned. But Théo isn't to be thwarted.

'Don't worry,' he reassures me. 'I know the maître d'. Now let's go. I don't know about you, but I'm starving.'

I barely have time to register what he says before I have to mask my expression to conceal my dismay. Standing ten feet behind Théo, outside of the boulangerie, is Jean-Luc, talking to Suzanne. And he heard every word.

Jean-Luc pats Suzanne on the arm as she speaks to him. I'm not sure what she says, but I do catch one word – Théo. Then whilst Théo fiddles with his jacket, I try to beseech Jean-Luc with my eyes, but he shoots me a look of such disappointment I want to cry, then he turns and heads back to the *fromagerie* as Suzanne strides towards her car. Feeling sick to the pit of my stomach, and with a reluctance I've never felt before going on a 'date', I follow Théo to his car.

As he drives, Théo prattles on about which celebrities have been at this restaurant and how many great reviews it has had, but as I half-listen to him, half zone him out, all I can think is, how the hell am I going to explain this to Jean-Luc?

I have no appetite now. Théo is interesting and pays me attention and he's generous, but I'm not sure he particularly listens to what I want, generally. He recommends what to order for starters and mains, and I go along with his choices – I'll barely taste them, or touch them, anyway, the way I'm feeling. I hope I can at least force something down and that the price tag isn't too hefty. I'm sure in other circumstances I'd love this place, albeit it's a little fancy, but these aren't the right set of circumstances.

I can't help thinking of Jean-Luc, all geared up for us to spend a leisurely evening together, him planning to cook whatever surprise he had decided upon, then us watching TV or chatting, like an old married couple, or good friends, and maybe something more. I guess I'll never know now, as he looked so desolate, so resigned as he walked away from the boulangerie, it made my heart squeeze in agony, especially since I was the cause.

At the first possibility to escape without appearing impolite, I make my excuses and head for the ladies. There, I pull out my phone and text Jean-Luc. *I'm so sorry. I can explain everything. I can't apologise enough. Can I meet you tomorrow?*

I wait for a few minutes but there's no answer. Of course, he may not be near his phone or he may be riding his moped, or he may be choosing not to reply. With no other option, I put my phone in my bag and slink back to the table, where Théo is looking at his watch.

'More wine?' he says, spotting me.

'Yes, please.' Maybe wine will make this whole nightmare situation magically better. I sigh inwardly. I'm not being fair to Théo. He's kind, attentive and interested, and has taken me out to dinner, but my heart's not in it. Not even the beautiful terrace where our table is positioned, or the view from it, or the frankly exquisite food can numb the emptiness I feel at having let Jean-Luc down. But it's my fault – all my fault. I could have been firmer with Théo; I could stop being a screw-up. No wonder Freddy left me for someone a decade younger. What a cliché I've become. I grit my teeth. Now, enough of the pity party. I got myself into this mess and now I have to get myself back out of it. But I'll try to fix that with Jean-Luc tomorrow. Tonight, I need to appreciate the fact Théo wanted to take me out, and play the part of the interested date, even if it means acting, and even if I feel hollow to my core.

I tune in to what Théo is saying. Part of me wonders if he's really very insecure. I mean, he's hot as hell, flashes the cash – not that that has ever mattered to me – and has charm by the truckload, but his constant need to namedrop or talk of how many stars the restaurants that he has visited have, or which restaurants throughout France his family's Armagnac is stocked in is a tad wearing. Why does he feel he has to try to impress so much?

I do my best to engage, when I haven't the slightest clue what he's talking about as he bangs on about the column stills used in the production process, rather than the pot stills used in 'brandy'. I always thought Armagnac was a type of brandy, but to hear Théo talk, I've been sacrilegious to think so.

Not even the second-to-none view of the Garonne river or the sublime gastronomic menu can take this non-date from catastrophe to success. I shouldn't be here, and all I can think of is how I've let Jean-Luc down and what he must be thinking of me. Or maybe I'm not important enough for him to think about. I'm itching to check my phone again to see if he has replied.

Instead, I put some effort into enjoying the amazing food. Asparagus velouté with minted greens – both melt in the mouth and the flavours marry so well.

When I take my first bite of the grilled hake with slow-roasted fennel and orange sauce, I actually moan as it is so good. And I smile a genuine smile at Théo, whose face lights up on seeing, and hearing, my reaction. Despite his flaws, he does genuinely want to please, and the fact I'm enjoying the food clearly makes him happy.

The food also gives us something else to talk about, which is a godsend. In the past hour, I've learned more about Armagnac than someone doing a thesis on it.

The wine pairings are also on point. Well, I guess they should be, given the pedigree of this place, but it's true that the right wine enhances the flavour of the food. As the Iberian pork pluma with fig jam and spicy juice arrives, I'm already filling up. I'd worried I wouldn't be able to eat a bite, such was my guilt over Jean-Luc, but the food is so incredible it would be an actual sin not to eat it and do my best to savour it. Plus, since I'll insist on going Dutch, I don't want to squander money, especially when I have no job to go back to. Momentarily, my thoughts flit to home: Jules, my lack of a job, the flat sale. I seem to have swapped those problems for another set, and I've only been here just over a week. That was clever of me.

By the time the desserts arrive, I've had considerably more wine than I'd intended and I even manage to nibble at the sweet cake with peanut ice cream, which was surprisingly delicious, despite me not being a peanut fan.

I am, however, totally stuffed. If I eat another bite I will combust. I have no idea where Théo puts it all. I mean, I know the portions are small, as it's a tasting menu, but seriously. I've seen more fat on an Olympic middle-distance runner. I drag my mind away from Théo's physique when he interrupts my thoughts.

'Do you want to get out of here?'

I raise my eyes to his. I don't know how to tell him, "Yes, I do, but could you get a wheelbarrow to roll me out in as I can't move", so I plump for, 'Sure.'

He signals to the waiter for the bill and as I bend down

to take my purse out to pay my share, I sneak a look at my phone, ostensibly to check the time, but also in the hope of having received a message from Jean-Luc. One new message. My heart soars. Jean-Luc's replied. I open up my messages, but it's Suzanne. *No change. He'll be in for a few more days at least.*

I sigh. Poor Suzanne. Poor René. Hopefully, being in hospital will do him good and when he returns home, he'll be in much better shape, but the lack of any real news is a worry. I slide my phone back into my bag and take out my purse. When I sit upright, however, and ask Théo to see the bill, he waves a finger at me. 'No. I've taken care of it.'

'But, Théo, no. I want to pay half. It's very expensive here.'

He smiles. 'You're my guest.' He pauses then says, 'I tell you what, why don't we go for a walk along the river, burn off the calories we've just eaten, and if you like, we can perhaps stop in at a bar and you can buy me a drink. How does that sound?'

I glance at Théo's body for a second. He doesn't need to work off any calories. I must ask him how he keeps so trim, and then follow his example. His suggestion will prolong the evening even further, but I'm tipsy by now and he has been very generous with both his time and his money since I've been in France, and it would be churlish not to agree, so I say, 'It sounds like the least I could do. Thank you for dinner.'

'My pleasure,' he says as the waiter brings our jackets and hands them to Théo, who thanks him then holds mine out to me for me to shrug on.

As we walk out of Au Pois Gourmand, I make a mental note to come back in daylight, so I can properly appreciate the building's architecture. All I can see at the moment is that it's colonial style.

'They have three different restaurants here,' he tells me as he follows me to the door.

'Oh, I hadn't realised. Do they all have a view of the river?'

'Yes, but the best view of the Garonne is from the terrace we were on.'

I don't doubt it, but I'd still like to see it in daytime. I wonder if pleasure boats glide by during the day carrying holidaymakers from one part of France to another. My geography is woefully inadequate. I have no idea which rivers join up with others, but surely it must be possible.

We saunter down onto the pathway. A couple of people are also walking along the riverbank but then they branch off at another section – a house? Maybe they live there. If so, how lucky. The houses are gorgeous here along the river, what little I can see of them in the moonlight and the dim light from the streetlamps.

Théo walks beside me, companionably, no pressure, for which I'm grateful. He doesn't take my hand, doesn't put his arm around me, and if I wasn't so mixed up over the whole Jean-Luc thing, and if Freddy's infidelity hadn't screwed me up so much, perhaps I'd be put out at the fact he doesn't, but right now, I'm appreciative. I can just be, and it is a beautiful walk along the river. There's something special about doing this walk at night when hardly anyone is around. All your senses go on high alert – smells and sounds have a way of heightening when you can't see as well as you can during the day. A bat flies low over us and I shriek and cover my head with my hands, my heart pounding. Just as I was enjoying a moment, nature's menace has to frighten me half to death.

Théo, who steadied me as I shrieked and jumped, turns me towards him. 'Careful. We don't want you falling in the river.'

'No,' I say as he takes my left hand, caressing my fingers. God, it feels so good. How can someone caressing your hand feel so erotic? *Because you lived and put up with Freddy F-word for such a long time*, a little voice says.

When I glance up, he's staring down at me, a smile playing on his lips. 'Oh, Lia, if you only knew how much I want to kiss you – again.'

My heart thuds in my chest, my body betraying me. He's bloody gorgeous. It's not my fault. Théo must take my hesitation as consent as he leans down and presses his lips gently on mine, and before I know it, my body is responding and I'm kissing him back. It feels so good, and I moan, a slight catch in my breath, and I feel him groan and grow.

'Come back to mine,' he breathes into my hair when we pull apart. 'Nobody will miss you at the Molins'.'

As if I'm being physically jerked out of the scene by the arm, I pull back. Once again, he has made me feel inferior, obsolete. Whether he meant to or not isn't important, but that's how I feel.

'I'd love to,' I lie, 'but I promised them I'd be back to help, and I have some things to sort out.' Why am I justifying myself to him?

A flicker of irritation flits across his face, but then it's gone. 'Let me drive you home.'

Later, as we say our goodbyes outside the boulangerie and his car zooms away, all I can focus on is the tiny light still on in the *fromagerie* and my heart aches a little.

Chapter Nineteen

I wake late and struggle to get out of bed. I think I'm a little overwrought from the events of last night. At least the boulangerie is closed today.

I sigh and check my phone again. Still no response from Jean-Luc. What did I expect? What must he have thought when I left with Théo? I cringe at the thought. I'm not proud of myself, and I pray I can make things right with him, although I don't know how. I was in a very difficult position. *Oh, Lia, stop justifying it.* The sad thing is, I honestly would have preferred to spend the evening with Jean-Luc. Despite everything, including the ultra-fancy restaurant. Maybe I should take an assertiveness course. It's hard not to be angry with myself. I've let a man manipulate me – again. First, Freddy, when he chose where in Glasgow we should live – the west end, over my lovely flat in the southside. Now, I've let Théo come between me and Jean-Luc. Well, I only have myself to blame, although that doesn't make me feel any better right now.

Anyway, first things first, I need to find out what's happening with René. When I reach the kitchen, it's empty, which is unusual. It's normally a hive of activity. I fish out some croissants and *chocolatines* and make some coffee then sit down to work out what I'm going to do today, particularly with regards to putting things right with Jean-Luc. It's Sunday, so he's unlikely to be at the *fromagerie*.

I have a couple of texts from Suzanne and Estelle, giving me updates, and telling me Matthieu decided to stay at his parents' last night as his mum wasn't doing too well, so I am, in fact, all alone.

I take another sip of my coffee. I may go back to the Japanese garden later. I really enjoyed it there. Particularly my moment with Jean-Luc, when the woman who took our photo thought we were together.

By the time I sort myself out, it's ten thirty. I'd forgotten how quiet European cities, even the big ones, can be on a Sunday morning. As I meander through Chalets, it's almost deserted, the only sound the ringing of the church bells. I decide to grab a coffee first and amazingly find somewhere open, although I appear to be the first customer. The owner gives me a wide smile, takes my order, then I settle down with my thoughts as I await my *café au lait*.

Is it too early to call Jean-Luc? Just as I'm pondering this, I receive a text, which I pounce on, hoping it's either Jules or an update on René. I don't even dare hope it's Jean-Luc. That ship has sailed. But it's Freddy. What does he want?

Couple coming for a second viewing later. Will let you know how it goes. F.

No kiss, I note. It's incredible how you can love someone enough to move in with them, yet only a few weeks later you can't bring yourself to add an x at the end of a text message.

That said, given our last meeting, I wouldn't want it. Jerk. Jules had that right. I don't reply. What would be the point? If there's news, hopefully he'll let me know. It hits me with a sudden clarity that I need to decide, and soon, whether to stay or go, and if I'm staying, I need to rearrange my flight. I'll see what the lay of the land is like back at the Molins. Despite the drama in my life – is there ever a time when there isn't any drama? – my gut tells me to stay in France. Apart from Jules, what is there to go back to? And she'd definitely be up for visiting.

My coffee arrives, and as I sip it, I look out over the little square, watching as the exceedingly well dressed families walk past, clearly having been to church. Their clothes scream Sunday best. A young boy fidgets with his jacket, looking about as comfortable as I was in my skirt and flouncy top back when I was a kid. I hated going to church then, but now I like seeing the inside of them, although that's more for the architecture. They are kind of soothing too, though. I laugh inwardly. Maybe I should go now. Would God have a solution to all the issues I have? Then I berate myself. If I'm going to church, even if just for a few moments, it should be to pray for René.

Decided, I drain my coffee, signal the waiter and pay then head for Notre-Dame du Taur. I remember visiting it once, with the Molins, on the single occasion we didn't go to Saint-Sauvy at the weekend. I wonder if it has changed much.

As I arrive, it's clear this was where the families had been streaming from, as although there is no service in progress, there are signs one has recently taken place – prayer books and hymnals stacked haphazardly by the exit and strewn untidily on pews, and a few stragglers speak in hushed voices in the vestibule.

It's so long since I've been in a church, but today something has drawn me here. I look to see if there is the possibility to light a candle for René – old habits die hard. There is, and I do. I'm not sure whether I believe or not, but sometimes, I find it's a comfort just being in a church. It's like balm to the soul. After I light the candle, I sit for a few minutes in one of the pews, garnering a few odd looks from the remaining parishioners. It's not much of a tourist trap, and it's early, so I probably stand out, but I don't care. I'm here to pray for René. I just hope I can remember the words.

As I bless myself, my phone beeps. Damn it, I forgot to turn it off. I fumble in my jacket, trying to pull it out and switch it off, double quick, casting an apologetic glance to the elderly ladies nearby who are throwing me disapproving looks. I can just imagine they're thinking *disrespectful foreigner.*

I'm about to turn the phone off, when I see it's a message from Jean-Luc. *No problem.*

It takes me a while to remember if I asked him a question. What does the *no problem* refer to exactly? No matter, I need to get out of here. I need to call Jean-Luc and see if we can meet today so I can explain.

As I make my way out of the church, it occurs to me I have no idea how I'm going to do that. I stand outside the church, admiring the decorative arch entranceway and call Jean-Luc. It rings nine times then goes to voicemail.

Deflated, I decide to head to the Japanese garden to cheer myself up, but I've only been walking a few minutes when I hear a raised voice behind me, 'You, Scottish.'

Since I don't know many people in Toulouse, to say I'm surprised would be an understatement. I whirl around to find myself face to face with Gloire and another woman, who is equally as tall as her, both around five feet eleven, but whereas Gloire has a mass of caramel Afro curls, her friend has black close-cropped hair next to her porcelain white skin. They both look as if they'd be at home gliding down the catwalk at Paris Fashion Week.

'Ah. Gloire?'

She juts out her chin, aggressively. 'Yes, I am Gloire, Jean-Luc's girlfriend.'

My brows furrow. 'But I thought you two had split up?'

Her jaw tightens. 'We are giving each other some space. We have not split up. So you … can … keep … your … hands … to … yourself. Understood?'

She punctuates each word with a finger pointed at my chest, her face contorting grotesquely.

'Gloire, Jean-Luc and I are only friends.'

'*Non*, *non*, you are not friends. You will not be friends,' she seethes right up close to me. With her henchwoman in tow, she couldn't be more threatening. I get the message loud and clear.

'Gloire, I am living with the Molins. Jean-Luc's *fromagerie* is next door. We are neighbours.'

'Well, I had better not see you out socially with my boyfriend. People talk. Toulouse may be a city, but Chalets is a village. Don't overstay your welcome.'

With a glare that would freeze Death Valley, she stalks away, her friend mirroring her expression then following in her wake.

I stand for a second, trying to control my breathing.

Did she just threaten me? It certainly seemed like it. I'm not a confrontational person, but part of me wants to run after her, grab her by her frizzy caramel hair and ask her who the hell she thinks she is.

Instead, I gather my wits and walk slowly back to the boulangerie, my plans to return to the Japanese garden forgotten.

When I return, Matthieu is sitting at the kitchen table, a stack of paperwork in front of him.

'Hello, Lia,' he says. 'I'm having a glass of wine, if you'd like one.'

I try to hide my concern at this big bear of a man imbibing at this time of day. Things must be bad.

'Sure.'

When he makes to rise, I wag a finger at him. 'No. I'll get it, thanks. How are your parents?'

He visibly slumps in the chair, his five o'clock shadow notable despite it being nowhere near five o'clock. He's dishevelled and worn-out-looking as if he last had a decent sleep a week ago. Maybe he did. Even prior to René going into hospital, the worries they had with his own parents, and them not being exactly handy to visit daily, must have taken its toll on him, on the whole family, in fact.

'*Maman*'s not as agile as she was and *Papa*'s breathing isn't great. I stayed overnight to keep an eye on them, and because I had to make a note of everything that needs doing. There are so many repairs to make.'

'You all have a lot going on right now.'

He smiles, sadly. 'We do, but we'll survive. We always do.'

They do, but I can't help but worry how they can keep going like this. They are pulled in so many different directions, including geographically. They have to look after their own health too.

'Have you eaten?' I ask.

He shakes his head, so I say, 'Scrambled eggs OK? I know it's not French, but it's what I fancy, and I don't want to embarrass myself by making food you're used to.'

He laughs and I set about preparing us some lunch.

As we eat the scrambled eggs – an odd combination with red wine, I've discovered – Matthieu fills me in on the state of play both with his own parents and René and Alexine. It seems things are more precarious than I thought. From all the stress of constantly running around after their respective parents, and managing the business, Estelle has become an insomniac, and it's starting to tell on her health, and now with René's condition worsening and him requiring long-term care and supervision once he gets out of hospital, the situation will only become more difficult. How much more can this family take?

Chapter Twenty

Next morning, I open the sliding door to the living room and three pairs of eyes gaze back at me. Estelle, Matthieu and Suzanne. Estelle, who would normally rise from where she's sitting to kiss me on both cheeks and wish me good morning, is grey, her face drawn, and she looks as if she has aged thirty years overnight.

'Morning!' I try for breezy and hope it doesn't come across as false or disrespectful. Again I'm struck with whether I should be here or not.

Estelle mumbles something incoherent, Suzanne stifles a yawn and Matthieu gives me his usual gruff '*Bonjour*.'

Usually, I'd ask if they slept well, but looking at them that question has already been answered. Instead I say, 'Coffee?'

I'm greeted by three nods, and as I put the water on to boil, Suzanne sidles up beside me.

'Sorry we aren't more "welcoming" at the moment.'

Privately, I wonder why she isn't having a go at me about Théo, but I'm relieved too. I wave away her apology. 'Suzanne, don't be silly. You've nothing to apologise for. You all have a lot on your mind.'

Distractedly, I think how my problems are so trivial compared with their issues.

'How are René and Alexine?' I ask.

Suzanne closes her eyes momentarily then shakes her head. 'Honestly, I don't know what we're going to do. *Mémé* is starting to show signs of strain, and that's whilst *Papi* is still in hospital. I have no idea how she'll cope once he's home again.'

As I stir the coffee in the cafetière, I say, 'Couldn't they get some help?' I wonder what the carer network is like here, although my gut tells me in mainland Europe, generally it's the families who look after their elderly parents, not carers.

Suzanne shakes her head again. 'They can't afford it. I mean, the ideal would be to have a full-time nurse, but *Papi* wouldn't welcome the intrusion into their daily lives. He'd see it as some sort of failure, but they simply don't have that sort of money anyway, even if he would allow it.'

'Hmm, that is a problem. What do your parents think?'

She gives a humourless laugh. 'They wish they could physically pull *Mémé* and *Papi*'s house to the next street to this one so they could keep a closer eye on everyone.'

'Yes, a genie in a bottle would be handy right about now.'

Suzanne smiles sadly. 'If you find one, let me know.'

'Suzanne, how can I help? Practically. I mean, obviously I can work in the boulangerie, but is there anything else I can do?'

She looks at me for a long moment as if debating something with herself. 'If you're happy to stay, as and when we need something doing, I promise I'll tell you. Believe me, I'm not about to turn down offers of help.'

'Thanks. You and your family have done so much for me, and'—I stop before I say I feel part of the family—'I really am here for you. I know things are tough and about to become even more so, so please, make use of me.'

Suzanne leans in. 'You'll wish you'd never said that,' she says, finally cracking a smile.

We take the coffees through to the others and set to making a plan for the day. I have a renewed sense of purpose. This family means the world to me, and I will do whatever I can to help them.

I've been in the boulangerie for two hours alone, with Suzanne away to the cash and carry again and Matthieu sleeping; Estelle also has gone to grab a few hours' kip at my insistence. Although business was brisk earlier on, and then steady, it has settled to a trickle, and I'm enjoying people-watching. A woman wearing an elegant cream cardigan with only one button done up and a pastel floral scarf around her neck wanders past, a wicker basket slung casually over her arm, pushing a buggy where a toddler is drinking from a sippy cup. A cyclist floats past dressed as if he's going on the Tour de France, all Lycra-clad and tinted sunglasses. He looks rather incongruous here on this sleepy street. A guy in his late teens or early twenties walks past, earphones in, a backpack fit to burst slung over one shoulder, three books cradled under one arm. Guess he's a student then.

Next up, a man around my age, maybe a few years older, with tousled light brown hair, walking a bichon frisé wearing a pink jacket with the name Coco stitched in white. As I'm surreptitiously observing the man – who has the thickest, most luxurious hair I've ever seen not on a woman – a van pulls up next door.

Curious, I watch as the deliveryman goes inside, then realising I've lost sight of bichon frisé man and there's no one else currently to people-watch, I turn my attention back towards the *fromagerie*. I feel a thump in my chest as Jean-Luc comes out, the deliveryman shows him something inside the van, then Jean-Luc takes some paperwork and signs it; all the while, I've been focusing on the thick stubble gracing his jaw, the slight dimples as he laughs at something the deliveryman says, and the golden tan on his bare forearms.

Regret surges up unexpectedly and once again I wonder how I'm going to fix things with him. He hasn't replied to my messages and he hasn't made any attempt to come to the shop today, albeit he also is working. As I'm ruminating over this, he glances up and his jaw tightens, or did I imagine that? He gives me a slight smile of acknowledgement, but it isn't exactly what I'd call friendly, and turns back to the deliveryman. His brush-off hits me like a sucker punch and I'm grateful when Madame Leclerc appears just then. At least with a customer present I can't wallow in self-pity.

'Good morning, Lia. No Estelle today? And how is René?'

'Morning, Madame Leclerc.' I wonder how much to divulge. Finally, I settle on, 'Everyone is a bit unsettled. René is still in hospital and Estelle is having a lie-down. It has been a very busy few days for them all.'

'Poor thing,' she says. 'Please give Estelle my regards and tell her to pass them on to Alexine and René too. Alexine and I have been friends a long time. It is terrible when your husband is so ill. And if I know Alexine, she won't be looking after herself properly.'

On that, I know she's right.

'I will. The usual?'

'No. Today I have a visitor.' Madame Leclerc purses her lips, casts her eyes over our selection of breads and pastries then selects a *chausson aux pommes*, a small baguette and, after debating a few moments, a raspberry tart. I package them separately for her and then bid her good day. As she leaves, I see Jean-Luc cross the road then walk down the other side of the pavement. Did he do all that so as not to walk past the boulangerie? Surely not. I'd just been trying to work up the courage to go talk to him since things are quiet. Well, that's that idea dead in the water.

Deflated, I take one of the *chausson aux pommes* and bite into it, the sweetness of the apple giving me the sugar hit I need right now.

My phone pings. It hurts how much I want it to be Jean-Luc, but once again, I know it won't be. I take it out of my overall pocket. Freddy. What does he want now?

We have progress. The couple who came this morning have already given a verbal offer subject to survey. He quotes their price – it's more than we'd asked for, but not quite the twenty per cent above that most properties in the west end of Glasgow command nowadays, but who cares? It draws a line under us and we can move on. More importantly, I can have my share of the money and buy myself somewhere else to live, get another mortgage. A horrible thought hits me. Will I get another mortgage if I've lost my job? Will having a decent amount of capital behind me be enough? I'll get another job, won't I? I still haven't decided how much longer I'm going to stay in France. *However long the Molins need you.*

I'm busy ruminating over all this when the door pings,

and I look up into those gorgeous brown eyes I've come to know so well, but today the shine is missing from them.

'Hi, Lia,' Jean-Luc says. He's holding a blue and white striped bag from the butcher on the other side of the street. So he wasn't trying to avoid me by passing on the other side of the road. I wish my brain would stop overthinking things.

'Jean-Luc,' I manage, even though I've been holding my breath since he came in, and now it's actually painful.

'I came to see how René is and to ask if there's anything I can do to help.'

I nod. I'm not the best person to answer how he can help and everyone else is either asleep or out.

'He hasn't been great, and Alexine is struggling. She hasn't been doing too well health-wise either.'

His mouth downturns and he shakes his head. 'It's so awful. I hope René improves soon, and Alexine. Please tell Estelle to pass them my regards.' He points a finger in the direction of the *fromagerie*. 'Anyway, I'd best get back.'

I can't let him go like this. This is my one chance to explain. As he turns for the door, I call, 'Jean-Luc!'

He pivots, surprise registering on his face.

I come round the counter towards him. 'I wanted to apologise for the other night.'

He studies me for a millisecond too long for his nonchalant response to ring true. 'Don't worry, Lia. You can date whoever you like.' But his eyes tell a different story. Contempt? Anger? Bitterness? Not expressions or emotional responses I'd witnessed in Jean-Luc until now. No, something else is at play here, and I'd be willing to bet it's not just to do with me, but the dynamic between him and Théo that I noted before.

'But I'm not dating Théo.'

Jean-Luc's eyes display his disbelief.

I rush on, 'I'm so sorry to have let you down, and I really wanted to have dinner with you on Saturday night, but Théo had messaged me to say he'd pick me up, and I'd replied saying I wasn't available, but he didn't get the message—'

'*Salut!*'

I didn't even hear the ping of the doorbell, I was so intent in explaining myself to Jean-Luc.

Suzanne puts down the boxes she is carrying and leans against the counter. 'Jean-Luc, how are you?'

He smiles, this time a genuine smile, the one I thought was reserved for me, but which I now realise is how he greets those he is close to. For a moment, I envy the easy camaraderie between the two.

I watch as Jean-Luc asks after Suzanne's grandparents and she tells him the latest. Her eyes show a hint of tears threatening and Jean-Luc pats her shoulder, then, when her voice breaks, he takes her by both shoulders, looks into her eyes and tells her it's all going to be OK, and she sniffs then nods. She believes him. She trusts him. It's clear they've been friends a long time. It's almost like time is suspended. If it were possible, I'd want to remove myself from the scene as I almost feel like a voyeur, witnessing this emotional moment between them. I can tell they haven't been romantically involved with each other before, they're too comfortable together for that, but their friendship hits me in the chest. I'm so happy for Suzanne that she has Jean-Luc as a friend, and so gutted I've screwed up the chance of having that, or more, with him, because I capitulated to Théo. Well, the next time I see Théo, if I do,

I'll be taking a stand.

'Do you want a hand with these boxes?' Jean-Luc asks Suzanne.

It's like I'm not even there.

'No, it's OK. Lia and I will manage, but thanks,' Suzanne says.

'Remember, anything I can do to help, just let me know.'

'Thanks, Jean-Luc. I appreciate it. We all do.' Suzanne shoots him a grateful look then bends down to pick up a box.

'In that case, I'll see you later.' He heads for the door, his eyes still on Suzanne. Why do I feel he's deliberately not looking at me?

No! I didn't get to finish my explanation.

He turns to me. 'Lia.'

And then he's gone. And once again, I've missed the opportunity. I want to hit my head so hard off the wall, but instead I pick up a box and follow Suzanne through to the living room and then into the storeroom.

Chapter Twenty-one

'Oof!' Suzanne places the box she's carrying on a shelf in the storeroom, before taking mine from me. Then she turns back to me and says, 'Right, do you want to tell me what the hell is going on with you and Jean-Luc?' Her eyes flash, but I detect a glimmer of amusement too. She clearly thinks it's something that can be fixed, or perhaps she doesn't realise how serious it is.

My heart sinks through the floor. How can I explain without going into the whole Théo aspect of it? Ever since Sarah told me about Suzanne's history with Théo and then I witnessed for myself the other night her vitriolic reaction to him, I've been dreading having to come clean about our dates. At least things haven't progressed beyond a few heated kisses. But he is rather magnetic, although I can't exactly tell her that. I'm guessing that's how she got in deep with him in the first place.

Eventually, when Suzanne looks at me pointedly and raises an eyebrow, I have no choice. So I blurt out, 'I was meant to have dinner with him on Saturday night, and I was so looking forward to it, and then Théo arrived to pick me up for dinner and wouldn't take no for an answer.'

Suzanne's posture stiffens. 'Théo insisted?'

I nod miserably and fiddle with the edges of my overall.

'But why was Théo coming to take you to dinner?' Her brow furrows and she absentmindedly rubs at a stubborn piece of dried-in flour on the shelf.

My brow furrows. Didn't Sarah say she was going to talk to Suzanne about this after our first date? I decide against mentioning that though, as the last thing I want is to drop Sarah in it. She has probably been too busy with her own family life and everything extra that has landed on them with René being ill.

I hesitate then say, 'He'd texted me to say I'd be in the way with everything that was going on with your family, and offered to take me for dinner so I could be out of your hair. I'd replied saying I had plans, and thought that was the end of it. But apparently he didn't get the message, and the first I knew of that was when I was about to go meet Jean-Luc and you told me Théo was here for me. After that, you left and I tried to make excuses to Théo, but then I looked up and Jean-Luc was outside talking to you, and saw us together, although Théo didn't see him as he had his back to him, and...' I finally draw breath. I'm aware I was babbling, but once I started I couldn't stop.

Suzanne's face falls. 'So, let me get this straight. Théo told you you'd be in the way here and that he'd take you out?'

I nod. 'He was very persuasive. I kept trying to say no, but he wasn't listening.'

Suzanne makes a sound halfway between a laugh and a shriek. 'Yeah, he's good at not listening and just taking what he wants. I bet he did receive that text, but decided to come anyway. Théo always gets what he wants.'

I straighten a little. 'You think he lied about not receiving my text?'

She studies me for a moment then says, 'Théo's a master at manipulation, so yes, anything's possible. Poor Jean-Luc. And I'm so sorry, Lia, but I obviously played a part in this, as I was so hurt and confused on seeing Théo here, and the fact you were going out with him, that when I was talking to Jean-Luc, I mentioned Théo was there to take you to dinner. I thought for some reason you'd lied, although I couldn't think why you would.'

I nod again. 'I feel terrible. I texted Jean-Luc from the restaurant, trying to explain, but he didn't reply until the next day, and now I've blown it. I really like him. Yes, I might like it to be something more, but I definitely like him as a friend, and I'm so afraid I've lost him.'

I'm on the verge of tears and it hits me just how strong my feelings are for Jean-Luc. I know he'd be a good friend to me – always. Except perhaps if I stamped all over his feelings.

'Jean-Luc will come round, as a friend, but yes, you may well have blown it in the other department,' Suzanne says, then sighs.

'And I'm so sorry to even mention this, when everything else is going on,' I say.

'Don't worry, your drama has distracted me for a second. We all need that right now.' Suzanne sighs again. 'C'mon, let's get some lunch.'

I follow Suzanne into the boulangerie, turn the sign to *Fermé* and lock the door.

As we eat a lunch of cured ham, salad and baguette, Suzanne quizzes me on the whole Théo debacle, and I can tell it has struck a nerve.

Finally, I say, 'Listen, Suzanne, I'm so sorry. I didn't realise you and Théo had history when I first went out with him.'

Her head shoots up. 'First went out with him? How many times have you been out together?'

'Sorry, I thought you knew. Twice.' I run a hand through my hair, playing with the pink stripe, unable to believe I'm having this conversation and potentially causing Suzanne more pain.

'That day at your grandparents'.' I pause then steel myself when I see Suzanne's furrowed brow. 'He asked me out when I helped him get the Armagnac out of the boot of his car.'

Suzanne rubs two fingers up and down the centre of her forehead as if trying to massage away a headache. 'Slick. He really does never miss an opportunity.'

'I'm so sorry. I hadn't long split up with Freddy and him asking me out was so unexpected, I didn't know what to say, and then he told me he'd pick me up here, and by the time I'd processed what was happening, he'd gone.'

'Yes, he's good at that. Going. Total shit,' Suzanne says bitterly. It's so unlike her to be vitriolic, it takes me aback.

'Suzanne, you don't need to tell me, but can I ask what happened between you and Théo?'

She looks at me for a long moment then her gaze drops to the table. 'We've known each other all our lives. He, Jean-Luc, Sarah and I used to hang out, play together as kids up at our houses in the country. Our grandparents all lived in the same tiny village.' She looks up. 'Where *Mémé* and *Papi* live now, in fact.

'Théo and I began seeing each other, then when I was twenty-two, I had to spend more time here studying for my *boulanger* exams and less time in Gascony. He cheated on me not only with my best friend from kindergarten, but also with my second best friend. He was seeing all three of us at the same time.' She juts out her chin. 'That's the kind of guy we're dealing with.'

'Oh, Suzanne, that's awful. How did you find out?'

'Ha! We were supposed to be going on holiday together, on safari. We'd talked about moving in together. Then the night before we were due to go, I arrived at his apartment an hour earlier than planned as Sarah said she'd finish up at the boulangerie so I could start my holiday early.'

Tears brim in her eyes and I swallow the lump in my throat. Poor Suzanne.

'And when I got there, I must have been in denial as Amelie's car was outside, and I wondered if she was looking for me. Given the position I found them in, she definitely wasn't looking for me.'

Tears roll in fat drops down her face, plopping onto her T-shirt. She swipes them away angrily and composes herself as best she can.

'After that, Jean-Luc was the one who looked after me, looked out for me, made me come out of my room, spent the summer with me.' She gives a bitter laugh. 'Well, we consoled each other really.'

'Oh? Why did Jean-Luc need consoling?' But as soon as the words are out of my mouth, I know, and I blurt out before Suzanne can tell me, 'Amelie was Jean-Luc's girlfriend.'

Suzanne nods. 'Yep. We were all friends, but Théo has always been so competitive, always wanted to win at everything. At first, I admired that in him, but he could be cruel with it. As I saw all too clearly in the end.'

I don't know what to say. Théo cheated on Suzanne and Jean-Luc. They were friends, had grown up together. Who does that?

'But why?' I frown. I don't get it.

Suzanne shakes her head. 'Théo wants to have everything, and he hated when Jean-Luc was "winning", to his mind. So, he took Amelie, and ruined everything.' She pauses then says, 'Sorry if that sounds melodramatic, but it really did feel like the end of the world at the time.'

'I bet. What a prick!'

Suzanne laughs. 'Yes, he was that. He is that. I've never seen Jean-Luc so angry and it's the only time I've ever seen him in a fight. Gave Théo a black eye, although Théo did give him that chip on his front tooth.'

So that's how it happened.

'I'm so sorry, Suzanne. That's despicable.'

'Yes, it wasn't the finest moment in my life, but at least I got one of my best friends from it.'

Just as I'm wondering if she and Jean-Luc were ever an item, she says, 'There was never anything romantic between us, but he has always been there for me, before and since.'

I nod, hoping it's not too late for me to repair things with him. Then I lay my hand on Suzanne's. 'Sorry this has upset you so much, but thanks for telling me. And for what it's worth, I agree – Jean-Luc is definitely one of the good guys. I'm disappointed – in fact that doesn't go far enough, but right now I can't think of the word – in Théo, and I knew he was a little narcissistic—'

'Ha! A little? He carries a mirror, for God's sake!' Through her watery eyes, she manages a slight smile.

'OK, a lot narcissistic…'

Suzanne dips her head, as if mollified.

'But I didn't have him down as that. He has rolled out the red-carpet treatment for me—'

Suzanne takes a swig of her juice, gesticulating towards me with her glass. 'He does that.'

'But, Suzanne, why does your family tolerate him after what he did to you?'

She shrugs. 'We have to muddle along. We're neighbours, at least in Saint-Sauvy, and his father's lovely.'

There's a pause between us before Suzanne says, 'Anyway, enough about me. If you don't mind me asking, are you going to see Théo again? And what are we going to do about you and Jean-Luc?'

I shake my head. 'Jean-Luc, I have no idea. Earlier, I was trying to explain what happened the other night…'

'Oh!' Suzanne face-palms. 'I interrupted, right?'

I give a sad smile and tilt my head.

'Timing never was my strong point,' she muses. 'Well, never mind, helping you sort things with Jean-Luc is not only a priority, as he's one of my favourite people, but it gives me a project to focus on. That way I'm not only concentrating on all the negative stuff going on right now.'

I dip my head in acknowledgement. 'Feel free to use me as a guinea pig.'

Suzanne laughs then turns a little more sombre. 'And Théo?'

I sigh and gnaw at a raggedy nail. 'It's time I extricated myself from Théo. But he doesn't make it easy.'

She leans over and puts an arm around my shoulder. 'No, he doesn't, but don't worry. We'll sort it. All of it.'

I hope she's right, because despite everything, I want to

stay in France, and I don't think it's simply to avoid going home to Scotland any more.

In the afternoon, the boulangerie busies up again, with a steady flow of traffic streaming through until at least seven.

I've held the fort whilst Suzanne has fielded calls asking for the latest updates. Sarah will visit her grandfather this evening with Alexine.

I haven't seen Jean-Luc again, although I've received three texts from Théo, which I've studiously ignored. It occurs to me that with Jean-Luc's arrival this morning, I'd forgotten to text Freddy back about the offer on the flat. I glance at the door and see no one is in the immediate vicinity so I tap out a text to Freddy. *That's great. Can you let me know when you have the official offer in writing? Or should I ask the solicitor?*

Suzanne returns for our final hour in the boulangerie.

'I forgot to tell you. We have a verbal offer on our flat.'

Her mouth drops open. 'That's wonderful. You must be relieved.'

'You have no idea.'

She pauses then says, 'Have you thought any more about what you're going to do once you return to Scotland?'

I don't admit that when I'd talked to Jean-Luc, prior to my huge Théo-shaped faux pas, he had voiced the idea of me perhaps not returning to Scotland.

'Not really. I'm going to take some time before I jump into the next big venture, though.' I try not to laugh inwardly at the fact that if Jean-Luc were here and if this had been a few days ago, he might have been laughing –

moving to France is a pretty big venture, but now, talking to Suzanne, I mean taking on another high-profile, demanding job. For what? To return to my little one- or two-bedroomed flat exhausted every evening, possibly resorting to hooking up with guys on Tinder – yeah, who am I kidding? I could never bring myself to do that. I either meet someone the old-fashioned way, by meeting them face to face, in a pub, at a course, or through friends, or even work, but not through an app. I'm happy for those who find someone this way, I'm not judging anyone, but it's not for me.

She nods knowingly. 'Very wise. It's all too easy to make rash decisions when we've had a bad experience.'

I don't quite catch her expression, as she turns when the landline rings in the living room, but I can't help wondering if she's referring to the decisions I've made since I got here. She wouldn't be far wrong if she is.

'*Mais non!*' Suzanne cries.

I rush into the living room. 'Suzanne! What is it?'

Tears roll down Suzanne's face. 'It's *Mamie* Molins. *Papi* Molins thinks she's had a stroke!'

Chapter Twenty-two

I can't believe it. How can one family have so much go wrong all at the same time?

As I cradle Suzanne to me, rubbing her back as she sobs, I'm aware we still have to tell Matthieu his mum has had a stroke. He only just returned from his parents' and was due to go back again tomorrow.

I'm about to wake him, when he appears, tucking his T-shirt into his jeans. He takes one look at Suzanne and from the blood draining from his face, I guess he's assuming the worst about René.

'Suzanne?' A man of few words, Matthieu doesn't do small talk.

'*Papa*, it's *Mamie*. She's been taken to hospital.'

Matthieu's face is ashen. He clasps his hand over his mouth, almost as if he can stem the emotion by doing so.

As Suzanne fills her father in, the big, lumbering man visibly shrinks into himself. He flops onto the arm of the couch as Suzanne tells him what she knows so far. My heart twists for them both as she gives him some of the more distressing details – how his mother was found and when, how long they think she had been there.

'I need to go,' Matthieu says, pulling on his boots.

'Suzanne, why don't you go too?' I suggest. 'We're

almost finished here, and this is more important. I can take care of things tomorrow too.'

'*Papa?*' she asks. 'What should we do?'

I know she's thinking ahead to the morning and how there won't be any *chocolatines* or baguettes except what's left from today, and I also know they'll hate the idea of having to close, but needs must.

Matthieu sends me a grateful look. 'I made some fresh batches earlier this afternoon, but there won't be enough for all of tomorrow. Sell what you can, and thank you, Lia. I'm so glad you're here.' He pats my shoulder then enfolds me in a hug. I know right now that's what he needs so I let him hug me then I hug him back. When we draw apart, Suzanne is standing, waif-like, looking totally lost. No wonder. Her world – her family's world – has been torn apart – again. I wrap her in my embrace then she and Matthieu spring into action and grab bags, jackets, wallets and head off to *Hôpital* Rangueil here in Toulouse.

It has been a hell of a day, and when forty-five minutes later, I shut up shop and flop down on the sofa with a glass of wine, all I want to do is crawl into bed. I don't even know whether I should call Estelle or Sarah. Will Suzanne and Matthieu have done that en route? Estelle is due back tomorrow at some point, depending on what the news is with René.

I pour myself a second glass of wine, text Sarah and Suzanne for updates, then video call Jules.

'To what do I owe this pleasure?' she answers, face side-on to the camera, pretending she is in a huff with me.

'Sorry, Jules. There has been a lot going on.'

She turns to face me. 'Oh? Pray tell. What's the scoop with the hot Frenchman, or should I say Frenchmen?'

I groan and say, 'Don't ask. That's secondary at the minute.' I then tell her about Suzanne's grandmother's suspected stroke and about how things are with Alexine and René and how strung out everyone is.

'God almighty, that's grim. How's the family coping?'

'Not great. I honestly don't think they know if they're coming or going. And now they're so stretched, there's no one here to make the bread or pastries for tomorrow's customers. Matthieu made a few batches earlier this afternoon, but that's all we have.'

'I don't imagine having to close their boulangerie for the day will sit well with them from what you've told me about their work ethic,' she says as she distractedly twirls a lock of curly blonde hair around her finger.

'Quite, but it's not closed for the whole day. I'm filling in.'

'You?' Jules splutters. 'On your own?'

'Gee ta, Jules. Thanks for the vote of confidence.'

'Sorry, sorry. I just hadn't realised your French was back up to that standard where you could happily converse with actual French people all day long in a proper business.'

'It's better than it was and desperate times require desperate measures,' I say.

'Ooh, I see you're on the vino. How is *le vin rouge*?' Jules raises her own glass in a toast.

'*Santé!*' I raise my glass to meet hers.

She frowns. 'Does that mean "cheers"?'

'Indeed it does.'

'Ah. As you know, *vin rouge* is the sum total of my French. Well, that and *bonjour* and *merci*.'

I take a sip of my wine. Phoning Jules was the tonic I needed. She always knows how to lift my spirits.

'Anyway, what *is* the score with you and the Frenchmen?'

I huff out a breath then say, 'You don't want to know. I've screwed up – again.'

'In that case, Lia Abernethy, I definitely want to know. Spill.'

So, I do. I tell her about all the chaos which has surrounded me in the past not quite two weeks. She listens patiently, then says, 'Grovelling usually works. Stroke his ego a little. Jean-Luc will come round.'

I wince as I rest my wine glass back on the table. 'Jules, I honestly don't know if it will. I mean, he's lovely, as a person, as well as to look at, and he's not pretentious or I suppose swayed by material things. He's'—I struggle for the right word—'real.'

She bites her lip. 'Well, we can't have you hankering after a *real* man.' She can't help it; she always jokes, even when serious.

'Jules.' I give her a warning glare.

'OK, OK, he does sound lovely. I'd suggest trying to apologise again, and leave it at that. You'll be coming home in a few days anyway, so unless you're planning to conduct a long-distance relationship with him…'

Wow, has it really been that long since I spoke to Jules that she doesn't know my innermost thoughts about staying a bit longer … or a lot longer?

'About that, Jules.' I pause for a second. 'I'm changing my ticket so I can help the family.'

'That's an excellent idea. Nothing much to rush back here for at the minute.'

I quirk an eyebrow at her and she rushes on, 'Apart from me, of course, and naturally things will be looking up on the job front once you come back and apply for some jobs…' She frowns. 'Lia, what's going on?'

'Nothing,' I say, unconvincingly.

'Lia Abernethy, I've known you since nursery. What aren't you telling me?'

I hesitate a fraction of a second too long before she pounces, saying, 'You *are* hiding something! Right, spit it out, right now.'

Thinking how best to phrase this, I eventually say, 'Would it be so bad if I didn't come back straightaway? Maybe waited a few months before coming back?'

'Months?' Jules' face is a picture. She clearly wasn't expecting me to say that. 'Wow, you have got it bad.'

I give her what I hope is a disparaging look and say, 'No, I haven't.' At her disbelieving look I rush on. 'I just think I could benefit from remaining in France for a while, initially to help the Molins, but then, well, we'll see.'

She pours herself another glass of wine. 'OK. What are you going to do in France?' Then before I can answer, she says, 'And when can I come visit?'

I grin. This is more the chat we need to be having. 'I don't know. It's too New Age to say, "I want to find myself", but I want to have a long think about what to do next before coming back to the UK and getting on the hamster wheel again, if at all. I mean, why am I on the hamster wheel? Is that the only indicator of success?'

Jules shakes her head vehemently.

'And for what? I'm thirty-six, partnerless, jobless, soon to be homeless. Maybe I don't want to be tied down with another mortgage, more costs. Maybe I just want to live a little, and … well, *be*.'

'Lia Abernethy, welcome to the dark side, where we're

all about hedonism and enjoying life. Cheers!'

I'm not sure I'd term what I'm looking for as hedonism, but I'll certainly embrace a life which doesn't feel as if it's all planned out for me, which allows me to be spontaneous and make decisions just because, ones that affect the here and now, and that don't necessarily have to fit into a five- or ten-year plan.

I raise my glass to Jules and we chat until I have to call it a night. Phoning Jules was the right thing to do. She has buoyed me up, as she always does. I know what I want to do, and who I want to be surrounded by: the Molins.

Later, as I pull the bedspread over me and snuggle down, my thoughts are filled with a longer stay in France, how exactly I can help the Molins, and setting things back on an even keel with Jean-Luc. It's only as I drift off that I realise I haven't thought of Théo once.

Next morning, I'm in the boulangerie long before it opens, putting everything in its place, just so, except I keep back two baguettes, a *pain de campagne* and two *pains aux raisins* for Madame Leclerc. She's in every day, and I now know her routine like clockwork. For some reason, she has become my favourite customer, even though she was disagreeable when I was first in the boulangerie. She has softened, and her stories keep me enthralled. I'd hate for her to miss out as she sometimes doesn't come in until later, long after the commuter crowd has been in, buying breakfast or ingredients for their lunch on the way to work.

By late morning, I'm almost out of everything and realise there's no way I'll be able to open up in the afternoon. I'm just writing a sign to read *boulangerie closed this afternoon* when a truck pulls up outside. Another delivery for Jean-Luc, I imagine.

Not wishing to be caught watching like last time, I pass through the beaded curtain to the living room to keep out of sight. But as I'm wondering whether to do some housework this afternoon, or put on a load of laundry to help out, the bell over the boulangerie goes. A customer.

However, when I return to the boulangerie, a smile on my face as I greet the customer, I discover it's the deliveryman from the truck. Maybe he wants a pastry.

'Morning. Delivery for Molins,' he says. At least, I think that's what he says. His accent is so thick and he mumbles. He can't be from this area and it doesn't even sound like the Gascon dialect Alexine and René use. When a stream of words that I don't understand comes out of his mouth and he points to the paperwork then the truck, I realise I haven't understood any of it, so I ask if I can see the invoice.

I read it, but it doesn't make a great deal of sense, and it looks like a very expensive item, over five thousand euros. I can't even work out what it is, never mind sign for it. I don't feel qualified. What if Matthieu doesn't want it? What if it's a mistake? No one mentioned a delivery today, although they may have forgotten with everything that's going on, but still, I can't sign for it.

When I tell the man this, his pleasant demeanour changes, and he marches out of the boulangerie and prepares to unload whatever he's here to deliver.

I rush out after him. 'No. Can you wait, please? I need to call to check.'

He rat-a-tats words that I don't follow and continues pulling the item towards the front of the truck as if to offload it, then he readies a trolley.

'Can you wait, please?' I ask.

He shakes his head and taps his watch.

I try to call Suzanne, but there's no answer. I don't even have an update on Matthieu's mother yet. That doesn't bode well and I hate to disturb them when they're possibly at the hospital or exhausted, but I don't feel I should sign for this, particularly when the man is being so unreasonable.

As he tries to unload, I shout, 'No!' then realise a few people walking past on the street are staring.

I can feel a blush creeping up my neck and when a voice says, 'Is everything OK?' it doubles in intensity and my heart races.

When I turn, Jean-Luc is standing hands in pockets in the chef's jacket he wears when in the *fromagerie*, a frown creasing his face, but with the hint of a bemused smile on his lips.

'Jean-Luc, thank God.' Trying not to talk too fast – something I know I'm prone to do when I'm upset or stressed – I explain the Molins aren't here and I can't contact anyone and the driver is refusing not to offload the gargantuan kitchen item I don't want to sign for without authorisation. I also tell him, in an aside, I'm having difficulty following the driver's accent.

Jean-Luc pats me on the arm. 'Do you mind if I speak to him?'

'God, no. Please do!'

I stand to the side as Jean-Luc engages amiably with the driver, and soon they are laughing and joking and the driver is pushing the item back into the truck. He brings down the sliding door, locking it, then still talking to Jean-

Luc, he heads for the *fromagerie.*

Jean-Luc points to himself then the *fromagerie* as he follows the driver. Did Jean-Luc just manage to stop that driver being a difficult git by offering him some cheese? Surely not.

I return to the boulangerie, affix my sign to the door and lock up, glad to have some alone time to get over the stress of the driver's unwillingness to back down. I'm just glad he did for Jean-Luc. Who says misogyny and chauvinism are dead?

I'll thank Jean-Luc when I next see him. My phone pings. Suzanne. Finally.

Mamie *has indeed had a stroke. She's going to be here a while. I'm staying here for now to look after my grandfather.* Papa *will be home later today – he's going to meet* Maman *there so they can discuss what we do this week about the boulangerie. I'll let you know their ETAs when I can.*

My heart sinks. How on earth are they going to cope with this now?

Chapter Twenty-three

I've done some housework, feeling at least I can be useful in that respect, even if I can't bake pastries or bread. Everything is gleaming and I can see my reflection in the glass of the oven door. Right, it's about time I tried to do something else productive whilst I wait for news, or for Estelle and Matthieu to return. In fact, maybe I could make them dinner.

This time I opt for borrowing Suzanne's bike. I'm sure she won't mind; she never did in the past. I have a notion for cycling along the Canal du Midi. I wobble a little to begin with, but once I make a few rotations, I get the hang of it again. What is it they say? – you never forget how to ride a bike? Well, I haven't forgotten, but I'm definitely rusty. However, as I glide down the streets leading to the canal, I can't help but appreciate the wind in my hair. I do, however, wish I'd ditched the hoodie I'm wearing, as I'm absolutely boiling. Plus, I never suited hoodies, but needs must. I didn't want to freeze to death like I initially did on the back of Jean-Luc's moped.

Thinking of that journey makes me smile and feel a little warmer all at once. I sail past all the traffic and onto the path leading to the canal, which is busy with both narrowboats and barges. I remember Suzanne and I joking when I lived here about how one day we'd cycle to Carcassonne. We were only slightly put off by the fact it took twenty-four hours. Lack of time meant we never got around to it. Now, with the saddle already digging into me, I realise I'll probably never be fit enough to do it, but it doesn't stop me from smiling at cyclists coming towards me and wondering if they have come from Carcassonne or one of the other cities or towns along the route. Medieval towns have always fascinated me, and who knows, perhaps if I stay longer, I can go a bit further afield and explore the *bastides* in Gascony and Languedoc.

Ha! I'm getting carried away, but with the gentle sun on my face and the smell of spring flowers in the air, it's hard not to enthuse about the area and wish I could do this more often. It's certainly taking me away from my current troubles.

Soon fields of huge pink blooms, whose name I don't know, greet me as I cycle past, for now without a care in the world.

I stop to take a sip of water. I think I'm hoping for some divine intervention to help me understand how I can help the Molins. I don't even know Matthieu's parents or I'd offer to help there. I could go to look after Alexine, but I'm sure she wants Estelle with her. If only I could bake, but it's a very tightly regulated profession in France. They have to sit exams and everything to be allowed to do anything beyond simply selling the pastries and bread. Even if they could show me what to do, I wouldn't be allowed to make the products without extensive, and expensive, training. So that puts the kibosh on that.

I cycle along, avoiding some passers-by pushing an off-road stroller housing the cutest baby girl with bright red chubby cheeks. Drool rolls down her chin. She must be teething. A pang goes through me like a blade slicing into my heart. I can't say I'd never thought of having kids with Freddy, but since women are having babies later and later these days, I hadn't felt the rush to get pregnant, figuring I had plenty of time. Now, with our split, and me being alone with my thoughts, and sighting the baby, it brings home to me that the possibility of me having children is drifting further away.

My phone pings as I cycle. I slow then flip my phone out of my pocket. Théo. I don't even open the text. He can wait; I only checked my phone in case it was one of the Molins. I need some space to clear my head and figure out what I want – and where I want to live.

As I cycle, the tension eases in my shoulders, despite the workout. The throb I'd felt begin at my temples during the situation with the delivery guy has gone, and I'm simply enjoying the clean, fresh French countryside air. Well, city, but it's beside a canal, so it feels like countryside.

Thoughts tumble around in my head like in a lottery machine draw: Jean-Luc, René, Alexine, Estelle, Matthieu, Théo, the flat, Freddy, my job, my livelihood, Suzanne, my life, France, Scotland, my family, Jules. Damn, the throb's starting up again. However, I'm enjoying the slight burn in my calves as I cycle. Exercise hasn't been top of my priority list for the past few years, unfortunately, until my recent runs in the park post-breakup. There's always been some other project needing finished, or a few extra hours to put in for some unscheduled piece of work. Much as I'm a grafter and a perfectionist, it is nice, despite everything else going on, to be able to get out in the fresh air and cycle. Back home, I'd have been glued to my desk, or with a client. I certainly wouldn't have been taking a cycle along the Forth and Clyde Canal.

Am I just in love with the idea of living in France or could I do this long term? Could I do it if Jean-Luc and I couldn't at least be good friends? Is this the sort of decision I should be making when I've only been here such a short time and when so many dramatic, and traumatic, events are happening to those closest to me and in my own life? Should I take stock first before making any major decisions? *That's what you're trying to do*, my inner voice tells me.

But why not? Why couldn't I live in France? I could research apartments here. There must be somewhere not too far away from the Molins that would be within my budget. I could enrol in a course to improve my French so I could freelance. I can do my job pretty much anywhere. Why not in France? No actual reason. I've lived here before, and even though I was much younger and much has changed, the essence of the place is the same. The pace of life and the people are almost the same. The lifestyle too.

Do I want to go back to my old career, and if not, what could I do?

I glance at my watch. Wow! I'm impressed. I've been cycling for an hour and a half. That's a lot of thinking. I frown when I realise I haven't spotted any cafés or eateries along the route, not even a kiosk. I curse myself for not bringing anything with me to drink except water. Maybe I should head back. I'd like to freshen up before Estelle and Matthieu return. I'll check how they are and they can update me, but then I think I should leave them alone so they can talk – they haven't seen much of each other for a few days, and the situation with their parents must be so distressing for them both.

As I stop abruptly and turn my bike one-eighty, my phone rings. God, it's going to be Théo, isn't it? He's nothing if not insistent, but although he's extremely easy on the eye and very charming, and a great kisser, he's not the one for me. He cares too much about appearances, who he's seen with and where; although how I fit into that I'm not sure, since I'm hardly a catwalk model.

But when I ease the phone out of my pocket, I see it's Jean-Luc. If I'd answered any quicker, it would have been me calling him.

'Jean-Luc. Hi.'

'Lia, is everything OK? Are you OK?'

I scrunch my forehead then say, 'Yes, I'm fine. Why?' Inside, I'm fist-pumping the fact he cares.

'The boulangerie is closed. It's never closed in the afternoon during the week.'

I sigh. 'Yes, I'm fine, but Matthieu's mother isn't.'

'Matthieu?'

I can just imagine him raking his hand through his hair at the news.

'Yes, his mum had a stroke last night. Suzanne and Matthieu went straight to the hospital, so obviously there was no time to prepare any bread or pastries. Today I sold what Matthieu baked yesterday afternoon before we got the news.'

'Oh no, that's awful. Poor Matthieu.'

'Yeah.' I don't know what else to say, so I say nothing.

'Where are you?' Jean-Luc asks.

I cast my glance around, taking in the narrowboat gliding alongside me, with a family having lunch on the deck. 'I'm not sure exactly.'

'You're not sure?' Amusement laces Jean-Luc's tone.

'No. I borrowed Suzanne's bike and went for a cycle along the Canal du Midi. I've been cycling about an hour and a half, but I'm just about to head back. I thought there'd be cafés or somewhere I could get a drink and sit and watch the world go by for a bit, but there doesn't seem to be much here.'

'Not on that particular section, no,' says Jean-Luc. 'Do you fancy some company later?'

A smile creeps across my face. He's extending an olive branch, and I intend to grasp it with both hands.

'Well, Estelle and Matthieu are both due back later. I was planning on making myself scarce once they've given me any news. Give them some time alone.'

'Sounds reasonable. How about you come to mine or I could meet you in Place du Capitole?'

I'd far rather see his place, so I say, 'If you send me your address, I'll text you when I'm leaving. What time do you want me?'

'About seven thirty. It's not too far. See you later.'

'Bye.' I ring off, wondering what just happened. Has he forgiven me? Have we drawn a line under things? I don't know, but one thing I do know is, I have a second chance, and this time I'm not going to screw it up.

I arrive back at the boulangerie sometime later, having taken a little longer than I'd expected. I wasn't able to cycle back as quickly, despite the incentive. Clearly, I'm out of condition. Fortunately, I make it back just before a heavy downpour; I'd only had some drizzle to contend with en route.

Once I've stowed the bike, I open the door from the courtyard into the kitchen and immediately hear voices. Estelle and Matthieu must be back. But no, wait, that's not Matthieu's voice, although it is Estelle's. It's Théo. White-hot fury courses through me. He has to stop turning up like this. There couldn't be a worse possible time. Matthieu and Estelle need time to themselves. If this is to do with me, and I strongly suspect it is, I won't be happy.

I really want to nip upstairs, have a shower and change, and once more I curse Théo for landing himself on me when I didn't expect it.

'Oh, that'll be Matthieu,' says Estelle as I enter the living room.

'Hi, Estelle,' I say from the doorway. I glance towards Théo and give him a slight nod before moving forward to embrace Estelle. Am I imagining it or did she hold me just a little bit tighter than usual? She has had so much to deal with, so much thrown at her, she mustn't know which way is up.

As I step back from Estelle, I say, 'Théo.'

'Lia, I was just passing and thought I'd come see how René is, but Estelle tells me Matthieu's mother isn't well.'

'No, she isn't. The family have a lot on their plate right now,' I say pointedly.

'Quite.' He turns to Estelle. 'Estelle, please pass on my regards to Matthieu, René and Alexine, and to Suzanne'—I try not to laugh at that—'and Sarah, and Matthieu's parents.'

Estelle is a better person than I am. She pats Théo's hand fondly. 'Thanks for stopping by, Théo. Say hi to your father.'

'Lia, will you walk me out? I think Estelle should rest,'

Théo says.

White-hot fury rises inside me again. He's manipulating me – again. It reminds me of Freddy, which makes my heart rate increase again, and not in a good way.

'Sure.' I follow him out to the boulangerie where he stops. 'So, what's going on?'

I raise my head and jut out my chin. 'What do you mean?'

'Well, you're not returning my texts.'

I try to work out how to couch this in terms he won't take too badly, but already I know his ego won't take it well. Théo is as hot as a piping batch of hot cross buns straight out of the oven, and I don't think he's used to being rejected.

'Théo, I have a lot going on right now.' I point back towards the Molins' living quarters. 'And so do they. I don't really have time for a "friendship" right now.' I lay extra stress on the word so it's clear I mean romantic, without me having to be explicit.

He nods. 'I see. And this wouldn't have anything to do with Jean-Luc?'

I straighten up to my full height. Not that it's any of his business. 'Jean-Luc?'

'Yes, Jean-Luc.' His demeanour has changed notably and there's an undercurrent in his tone I don't like. If I didn't know already, it would have been as plain as a packet of Walkers ready salted that there's major animosity between these two.

'Jean-Luc and I are'—I stop myself before I say 'friends', and instead plump for '—neighbours.'

He raises an eyebrow, scepticism written all over his face. Nope. Didn't think he'd fall for that, but that's what he's getting.

'Théo, I've enjoyed our time together, and I'm sure if I stick around, I'll see you via the Molins, but I need to concentrate on a few other areas of my life right now. I'm sure you understand.' I walk towards the door and opening it, I say, 'Now, I need to get back to Estelle. Have a nice night.'

The incredulity on his face suddenly shutters over, and as if adopting a well-worn mask, Théo says, 'Of course. See you around.'

As I close the door, I can't help noticing he glances in the direction of the *fromagerie*. Well, he won't find Jean-Luc there, as he will have left for the day.

When he has gone, I stand in the boulangerie, hands braced against the counter and take in a deep breath. Finally, I've cut Théo off. His presumption was getting out of hand. He may be exceedingly good-looking, but apart from his charm, the chat was pretty shallow. No, long term, I need someone like Jean-Luc. Not Jean-Luc, per se, but someone like him. Who knows if I'll remain in France? I thought I'd have decided by the end of my cycle journey, but with Jean-Luc's untimely, yet welcome, interruption, it kind of knocked me for six and my brain postponed any long-term decision-making. What I do know is I want someone without drama, with whom things are easy. Don't get me wrong, I don't want the human equivalent of a Labrador, but I do want an easier life than I had with Freddy, and to a certain extent the past week or so with Théo. I could do without the angst.

As I walk back into the living area to Estelle, I'm reminded of the proverb 'from mighty oaks, little acorns do grow'. Hopefully, over time the seeds of my and Jean-Luc's friendship will grow into something more, and I can't wait until tonight to see if he shows any sign that may be possible.

Chapter Twenty-four

Estelle and I chatted and I made her some pasta with peppers and pesto. Her bemused expression as I set the dish in front of her was enough to tell me it's not a common dish in France.

I can't let Jean-Luc down this time, and I'm getting increasingly anxious, as I don't want to leave Estelle on her own, but Matthieu hasn't returned yet.

'Don't worry about me, Lia. Matthieu will be here. He must have hit traffic.'

Matthieu hasn't called, but then he is a stickler for the rules and safety and there's no way he'd answer the phone, or make a call, even on hands-free whilst driving.

I'm about to call Jean-Luc to tell him I need to postpone and why, when Matthieu walks into the living room, through the beaded curtain, unveiled like some noughties game-show contestant.

'Lia.' He nods and smiles, as if trying to act normal, but the dark circles ringing his eyes tell a different story: one of a man who has too many stresses simultaneously, and who is worried sick for both sides of his family.

He reaches for Estelle and they hug. I stay whilst he fills us in on his mum's situation – too soon to tell; he'll need to return in the morning. At his words, I see Estelle crumple, although I know she's trying to be strong. This is an intimate and emotional moment for them. I tell them I'm going to see Jean-Luc and I'll be back later, then I head off. I walk, using the GPS on my phone, to the address Jean-Luc gave me. It's about twenty minutes.

Fortunately, the afternoon's rain has faded to nothing, and as I pass through the centre, the pavement cafés are abuzz with twenty-somethings meeting friends; children and parents eating dinner; and a group of female tourists, I'm guessing Nordic, given the blue eyes, blonde hair and Amazonian stature – they make me look small – laughing and having a good time.

It's definitely not a bad place to live. Much as I love Glasgow, particularly the west end and the southside, the weather is generally atrocious. How much better it would be to live here, at least for the summer, and be able to enjoy all these perks.

When I reach the address Jean-Luc has given me, I stop and stare. In front of me is the most gorgeous townhouse. Jean-Luc lives here? On his own? I gulp and tentatively ring the doorbell, my mind whirring. Excessive wealth makes me uncomfortable; coming from a working-class family it gives me an inferiority complex. I know it shouldn't matter, but it's how I feel.

Jean-Luc opens the door in a pair of soft faded mid-blue jeans and a mint green shirt, with the top two buttons unbuttoned, which gives me the tiniest glimpse of his chest hair. My heart does a little flip and my eyes flick back to his face, which is split by a beaming smile, showing those beautiful white teeth, tiny chip and all.

'Lia.' He bends down and kisses me on both cheeks, then ushers me inside. 'Come in.'

I walk inside, marvelling at how the old is teamed with the new; a walnut table, possibly antique, sits in the twenty-foot hallway, next to a coat stand, where I leave my jacket. I can't help noticing the umbrellas with carved wooden or brass handles. I stifle a smile as I try to imagine Jean-Luc using one of those. He'd look as if he'd stepped back a century, or two.

'This way.'

Jean-Luc's voice penetrates my thoughts, dragging me back from the nineteenth century to the present. An iPod sits in a docking station on a shelf and discreet speakers blend at intervals into the background. Clearly, Jean-Luc likes to listen to his music wherever he is.

The hallway opens into an enormous lounge, with huge windows overlooking a small interior courtyard on one side and a little park on the other. Rigid floral fabric sofas cluster around an enormous marble coffee table strewn with cookbooks and newspapers. It looks lived-in, cosy.

'Come. The kitchen's this way. What would you like to drink?'

I shrug and say, 'White wine, or red, depending on what we're eating.'

'White will do nicely. We're having *poulet à la Toulousaine*.'

'I don't think I ever had it when I lived here,' I say, frowning as I try to recall. Then again, when I was in my early twenties, food was fuel, not something to be savoured. And if the Molins didn't make it for me, I certainly hadn't. 'What's in it?'

Jean-Luc glances back at me as he takes a bottle of

white from the enormous American-style fridge.

'Well, chicken, obviously.' He sets the bottle on the countertop then removes two crystal glasses from a leaded-glass cabinet, opens the wine and pours it as he continues. '*Jambon de Paris* ham, a piece of Toulouse sausage, clove of garlic, some aromatic herbs, salt and pepper. Nothing difficult.' He grins. 'But I hope you'll agree, oh so tasty.'

I'm trying not to salivate, so say, 'I'm sure I will.' My stomach rumbles and I blush as Jean-Luc says, 'I'd better feed you soon.' He peers at the oven. 'Fifteen more minutes. Shall we?' He indicates the sofas and I gladly flop down on one. It has been quite a day, and although I'm delighted to be here and with a bit of luck about to get things back on track with Jean-Luc and clear up any previous misunderstandings, my limbs are all too aware they've been put through their paces more than usual today. My calves are protesting and even my shoulders feel tense from hunching over on the cycle ride.

He sits down on one of the chairs opposite. I like that he hasn't automatically assumed anything and I don't need to feel uncomfortable by him being almost on top of me – now, there's an image I'll struggle to get out of my head – as we sit together.

'So, how are things? Did you see Estelle and Matthieu?'

I fill him in on the latest and explain I'm worried about them, all of them.

He nods gravely then sighs. 'It's a terrible situation for them to be in. How do you provide support to your family and keep your business running smoothly when you're dragged from one side of the region, or out of the region, in such a way?'

'Exactly,' I say. 'I wish I could do more.' I shake my

head in frustration and Jean-Luc leans forward and covers one of my hands with his.

'Lia, they will be so grateful for your support and the fact you're here. If you hadn't been, they'd either have had to close the boulangerie today or Suzanne would have had to stay behind. You gave her the chance to be with her father at this difficult time. Think about that.'

He's right and it goes some way to making me feel better.

'So, have you thought any more about extending your visit?'

Dare I hope he's asking because he wants me to? 'Yes, I'll stay a while longer, at least whilst the Molins need me.'

'You're a good friend, Lia.'

I raise an eyebrow. This is possibly the perfect opportunity to address the faux pas with Théo. 'I don't know about that. I haven't been a very good friend to *you* lately.'

He gives a wry smile and I go on. 'Jean-Luc, I hope to draw a line under this, so it's important to me that you know I really did want to spend that evening with you, but I felt trapped – Théo can be very persuasive. No, not persuasive, insistent. I felt I had no choice, but I realised afterwards I did have a choice, and I chose not to cause a scene. And I'm sorry, because your friendship means a great deal to me.'

Jean-Luc's eyes rest on me as he takes a sip of his wine. He nods almost imperceptibly. 'Lia, I like you. A lot. As a friend, but also, hopefully as something more. I don't often do relationships and I just felt–' he casts around before plumping for '–we clicked.'

'We did,' I interrupt.

'But I need to know there's only me in the equation,' he says, his eyes earnest now. 'No Théo, no Freddy, no third party skulking in the wings. I don't want to be second best or play second fiddle. When I'm in a relationship, I am fully committed to the person, and frankly, I'd want the same from them.' I go to speak, but he holds up a finger to stop me. 'Sorry, let me just say one more thing. I know it's early to talk of a relationship, but when I feel like this about someone, I go all in, and I don't want anyone else. I felt a spark between us the first time I saw you, when I walked into the Molins' living room.'

I did, too, but I've already interrupted him once, so I'm not going to tell him that right now. Let's just pray I have my chance soon.

'I've already had my heart stamped on before, and I think you have too.' He pauses and I give him the slightest of nods in confirmation as I wonder who stamped on his heart. Gloire? It seems unlikely. For a millisecond, I recall Gloire's threats to me. As if she gets to tell me who I can and can't be friends – or more – with. What are we? Twelve?

Then my attention returns to Jean-Luc's heartfelt explanation, and I realise he has finally paused.

'Jean-Luc. I-I-I—' I flounder. 'I completely agree. I like you, in that way.' His lips lift a smidgeon. Was that a smile? 'And just so we're clear, I told Théo today, in no uncertain terms, when I returned from my cycle ride to find him in Estelle's living room, that we can't see each other any more.'

Jean-Luc's eyebrows raise. 'Oh? How did he take that?'

I blow out a breath and say, 'Not particularly well. I don't think he's used to rejection.'

Jean-Luc gives a dry laugh. 'You can say that again.'

'So,' I try, 'do you think we could make a fresh start?'

Jean-Luc's beautiful lips curve into a smile which reaches all the way to his mesmerising mocha eyes, then he says, 'Oh, I think so.' Then he leans over and brushes his lips ever so gently against mine. I'm just about to wind my arms around his neck and pull him towards me when he jumps up. '*Merde. Le poulet!*'

Thankfully, the chicken is fine and our evening is more than fine. After dinner, we sit on the sofa and talk, and talk, and hold hands and kiss, laughing and joking, and every one of those delicious kisses sends tingles all the way through my body until all I want to do is drag him to bed. After all, I'm thirty-six, and I know what I want.

The rattle of shutters being pulled down nearby jolts me sometime later and I glance at my watch. It's past midnight. How is that even possible? Both Jean-Luc and I have to start work early tomorrow. But I sense that like me, he hasn't wanted the evening to end, although I'd be lying if I said I'd noticed how many hours had passed. He's such easy company to be in. Spending time with him is effortless. I don't feel as if I have to make a concerted attempt to measure up, be good enough. I can just be.

Jean-Luc breaks into my thoughts. 'Why don't I walk you back?'

'Oh no, don't be silly. I can walk back myself, or get a taxi.'

'I insist. Toulouse may be largely safe, but it's too dark for you to walk back alone.'

'Who will walk you back then?' I quip.

'Don't worry. Thoughts of you will keep me company,' he says as he passes me my jacket. His comment makes my heart sing. Why didn't I meet this wonderful man when I first came to Toulouse all those years ago? How different life could have looked, and we could both have been spared a considerable amount of heartbreak.

We saunter along the lanes to Chalets, arms linked, bodies close together, almost whispering, as once we pass through the central square of Place du Capitole, there isn't a single person around. It feels like I'm in *The Night Before Christmas* story, and we're being careful not to wake anyone.

When we reach the boulangerie, Jean-Luc turns to face me. I look up at him, at his eyes sparkling with fun and mischief. He's sexy as hell, and I'm not sure he even knows it. Definite boy-next-door material, but with a spicy edge. My heart is pounding in my ears. I've had a lovely evening and I don't want it to end, but it must.

Jean-Luc's lips tick up at the edges before he lowers his head towards mine and I bring my lips to his as we meet, then we're kissing again, but this time after a moment it becomes more urgent, tongues gently probing, then teeth clashing, which makes us giggle. The whole experience is doing unmentionable things to my insides, which are on fire. I want this man and now, but that's simply not possible. How I wish we'd taken matters further earlier in the evening. Now it will have to wait, at least until the next available opportunity. I wonder if I have time for a cold shower before I go to bed, or would that wake everyone?

We pull apart, each staring hungrily into the other's eyes. He feels it, same as I do. It's magnetic, irresistible, and oh so hot. Boy next door just morphed into hot stuff central. Our lower bodies are still melded together, so I can feel how turned on he is. Glad it's not just me. Reluctantly, I drag myself away from him; otherwise I'd have to ask him if he had the keys to the *fromagerie* with him. Actually, that could work. But no, when we have sex for the first time – and I do mean when, not if – it can't be on a cheese counter.

We stare into each other's eyes for a moment, then Jean-Luc's crinkle at the edges and he tugs me towards him again by the lapels of my jacket and rests his forehead against mine. 'What's the saying? The best things come to those who wait?'

'Hmm,' I say contentedly, breathing in his aftershave again.

He pulls back, then as I look up at him, his lips nudge up into a smile and he bends down to kiss me on the nose. 'See you tomorrow?'

My heart soars and I say, 'Looking forward to it.'

As he walks away, I remain at the rear entrance to the boulangerie for a few moments, watching him, then smile as he turns and gives me a wave.

I inch the door closed and almost tiptoe into the kitchen, eager not to wake Estelle and Matthieu, but their voices ring out from the living room as I pass through the kitchen. They're still up? They must be exhausted. I thought they'd have been asleep hours ago. I wonder if there has been more news and that's why they're still awake. I'm about to go and ask when Matthieu sighs and says, 'It's no use. No matter how many times I go over the accounts, I can't find any extra. We're not going to be able to survive dropping our hours to look after our parents and keep the boulangerie going. There's simply no money to hire anyone else. Estelle'—his voice cracks—'we're going to have to sell the boulangerie.'

'No, Matthieu, no.' Then I hear Estelle sobbing, quietly at first then more loudly; her heart is breaking and tears slide down my cheeks. Desperate not to intrude on this intimate moment, I tiptoe up the stairs to my bedroom, where I lie awake for a very long time.

Chapter Twenty-five

The next morning it's a real struggle to get out of bed, despite waking to the aroma of freshly baked bread wafting up from the bakery below. I've slept little and I'm as refreshed as if I've been clubbing all night and then gone on to an after-party. I tossed and turned for I don't know how long, but I only managed stolen snatches of sleep. It would appear Matthieu has had even less rest, if that delicious smell is anything to go by. He must be running on empty.

As I dress, I wonder how to approach Estelle and Matthieu over last night's news. Do I pretend I don't know? I didn't mean to overhear them, and I couldn't have avoided it, but I feel terrible for having witnessed such a raw moment between them, and now I'm in possession of information I shouldn't have. I wish I could talk to someone about it, but that would feel like a betrayal. Even talking to Jules or Jean-Luc is off limits. I'm not sure what to do, but what I do know is I have a commitment to the Molins to open up their boulangerie, for as long as they need me to, whilst they navigate the minefield that is caring for two sets of sick elderly parents who live in different regions.

When I reach the kitchen, Estelle is seated at the table. Her face is drawn and a hopeless air hangs over her. She doesn't even note my arrival, she's so lost in her thoughts. My heart aches for her, for all of them. I'm guessing she hasn't had a chance to tell the rest of the family yet, if she and Matthieu only reached the decision last night. Again, I feel awful for being privy to this knowledge before Suzanne and Sarah.

As breezily as I can muster, I say, 'Morning, Estelle. Would you like some coffee?'

Her eyes raise to meet mine and a smile crosses her lips. 'Lia. Sorry. I was in a little world of my own.'

'No problem. Have you eaten?'

She shakes her head. 'No, I don't seem to have much appetite at the moment.'

I place my hand gently on her arm. 'Estelle, you have to eat. Even if it's something small. You can't afford to fall ill too from not looking after yourself.'

She nods wordlessly. This woman took care of me whilst I lived here, and she has always been the matriarch, the lynchpin, of this family. Now it's her turn to need nurturing. I'm surprised she can think clearly with everything that is being thrown at them – and all at the same time too.

'Suzanne is coming later. Matthieu has been baking since around two, so there will be plenty of stock for the boulangerie today.'

'He must be exhausted. He can't have had…' I stop myself just in time. I don't want to reveal I know they were still up when I went to bed. I heard them finally come to bed about half an hour after I did. They were clearly too distracted to hear me come in, so perhaps I can get away with making out I was at Jean-Luc's even later than I was.

'Neither of us is sleeping particularly well at the

moment,' Estelle says dully.

'Has there been any more news?' I ask as I place on the table a few of the pastries I'd kept back yesterday before the boulangerie sold out, for this very eventuality.

'Matthieu's mum is stable but not particularly responsive at the moment. Sarah went to the hospital last night and stayed with her grandfather. A neighbour looked in on Matthieu's father during the day for us, whilst we try to work out how to manage this new schedule between us all.' Tears spring to her eyes and I reach forward and clasp one of her hands in mine.

'Estelle, whatever I can do to help, please, tell me, and let me. I know how overstretched you all are at the moment.'

Her eyes lock with mine. 'Thank you, Lia.' She leans forward and hugs me and her slight body trembles against mine as she finally lets the tears fall.

Our roles reversed for once, I rub her back until she calms and composes herself.

'I'm sorry. I don't know what came over me,' Estelle says.

'Estelle, you don't need to be strong all the time. You have to let it out sometimes, otherwise your own health will suffer.'

She nods as if digesting what I've said. 'Thanks, Lia. And for listening.' She pats my arm. 'I'm so glad you're here, although I'm sorry you're embroiled in this mess.'

'Don't be silly. And I meant what I said, whatever I can do, tell me. I'm more than happy to take some of the load off you all.'

Estelle's lip quivers and for a moment I think she's about to burst into tears again, but she straightens her spine, gulps and says, 'You have no idea how much that means to me.'

I smile at her. 'Right, I'll make coffee whilst you tuck into those pastries. I'll make some for Matthieu too.'

'Deal. And I know what you can do to help.'

'Oh?' I turn back from the cupboard, two mugs in my hand.

'You can tell me how things went with Jean-Luc last night.'

I can't help the broad smile that breaks across my face, both at her interest and at thoughts of Jean-Luc.

'OK, but what's discussed Chez Molins, stays Chez Molins,' I say.

Estelle seems visibly cheered by the fact there is news to tell, and I grin as I bring over the coffees and set them down.

'You'll have to wait a bit longer,' I tell her. 'I need to let Matthieu know his is ready.'

Estelle rolls her eyes. 'Tell him to come in five minutes. I want time to hear this first.' She props a cushion behind her back as if she's settling in for kids' story time at the library, then takes a bite of a *chocolatine*. Happy that she is eating something, I head off to see Matthieu.

'Matthieu!' I knock on the bakery door and mime drinking coffee. He gives me the thumbs-up and I hold my hand up, splaying my fingers, in the international symbol for five minutes.

He nods and gestures to what he's doing, giving me the impression he has to finish off whatever he's working on first.

As I'm returning to the kitchen, my phone beeps in my pocket. Freddy.

The buyers have put in an offer. I breathe a sigh of relief. Finally, I'll be free of Freddy. Despite everything going on here in France, it still feels like a set of heavy barbells has been lifted off my chest. I still have the uncertainty of what I'm going to do with my future, work-wise – and no news from Universal Vision yet – but at least I'll be free of Freddy and can look into buying my own place again.

When I enter the kitchen, Estelle is wiping crumbs of flaky pastry from the corners of her mouth with a napkin.

'So. You and Jean-Luc,' she says.

I smile inwardly, delighted to see a glimmer of the old Estelle, the dog with a bone Estelle. Her children used to call her the Rottweiler when I lived here, as she was so persistent. She's definitely the glue holding this family together; she always has been.

Deciding to indulge her, I provide a watered-down version of last night's events.

Her eyes widen and she claps her hands together. '*Oh là là!* This is wonderful news, Lia. I love Jean-Luc like a son.' Then she frowns. 'But didn't you have something going with Théo?'

I sigh and begin to tell her the ins and outs of things with Théo as she listens avidly until the sound of Matthieu's footsteps stops me from providing any more details. But Estelle doesn't hold back from telling Matthieu one key point.

'Hey, Matthieu,' she says as she pulls out a chair for him. 'Lia and Jean-Luc kissed.'

The big bear of a man studies me, his eyes twinkling. 'Really?'

A blush spreads across my face as I reply, '*Oui*.'

He nods. '*Bon*. He's a good guy. One of the best.' Then

he shoots me a smile, sits down and begins drinking his coffee. Subject closed. Approval given. How different we women are from men.

Soon we're caught up in discussing their plans for the day: they're heading to the separate hospitals and parents' houses to relieve Sarah and Suzanne. Suzanne's coming back here to help me, but if I can keep things running until this evening, Estelle tells me that would be helpful. They're meeting Suzanne and Sarah midway so they can all have a family meeting. Two guesses what that's about.

'I'll be back tonight, though,' says Estelle, 'but Matthieu will be going to stay with his father.'

I nod, doing my best not to display any sign I know more is going on underneath the surface.

Once we've had our mini-debrief, I help Matthieu carry through all the tantalising-smelling pastries from the preparation area to the boulangerie and display them to full advantage. Matthieu grabs his keys, kisses Estelle, raises a hand to me in goodbye and is out the door less than five minutes later, in an attempt to miss the traffic.

Estelle tells me she has some calls to make and laundry to catch up on, so I tidy up the breakfast things and finish preparing to open up the boulangerie.

As I change the sign on the door from closed to open, the *fromagerie* door opens on my left and Jean-Luc appears. My heart tugs a little as I take in how handsome he is and my eyes widen. He's now completely clean-shaven, and I touch my jaw, recalling where his stubble grazed me last night. I'm not sure if I prefer him with or without the stubble, although I note I can see his dimple better without it.

The sunlight falls on his face as he turns fully towards

me and it's like I've been struck by Cupid's arrow. I'd be going too far to say he looks like an angel, and his behaviour certainly wasn't that of one last night, but he looks pretty damned good.

'Morning!' he calls as he saunters towards me.

A joyful smile splits my face. 'Morning. Sleep well?'

He nods. 'Amazingly.'

I raise an eyebrow. 'That good, huh?'

'Sign of a clear conscience.' His eyes glint with amusement in the sunlight.

'Is that right?' I say.

'That's what I hear. And you? Did you sleep well?'

For a millisecond, I don't answer, recalling the news I learned before I went to bed, then I mask my feelings and aim for bright and breezy. 'Like a baby.'

His smile widens. 'Babies are often up throughout the night. Bawling.'

'True, but I did actually sleep well. I'd had such a relaxed evening, you see.'

'Oh, did you do something nice?'

I think I like this flirting. 'I did lots of nice things last night.'

'That's good. I hope you got everything you wanted,' he deadpans, eyeballing me.

I squeeze my legs together almost imperceptibly and say, 'Not quite everything, but almost.'

His lips twitch as if he's trying to stop himself from laughing. 'So there's room for improvement.'

'Oh yes, practice makes perfect,' I say, wondering how I'm going to stand behind a counter in a boulangerie now, when all my hormones are roaring at me to leap Jean-Luc's bones here and now. But I don't think that's what the regulars expect when they come to pick up their daily croissant, so I may have to resist a little longer.

As if he senses my predicament, Jean-Luc says, 'I need to get back and open up. I can see Monsieur Aubert coming. He'll be coming in for his daily cheese fix. I'm surprised he doesn't have shares in the company.'

I laugh and say, 'See you later,' as Estelle walks into the boulangerie from the living area.

'Hello, Jean-Luc, how are you?' she says.

'Good, thanks, Estelle. How is René?'

'Improving, but slowly. Thanks for asking.'

'I was sorry to hear about Matthieu's mother. Is she all right?'

'Too soon to say. He has just left to go to the hospital. I'll let you know once we know anything more. Or perhaps Lia can keep you updated.' She shoots me a furtive little smile.

'Sure,' I say.

'I believe you had quite the successful dinner last night,' Estelle says to Jean-Luc, and my heartbeat accelerates. *Estelle, shut up! Please don't share what I told you this morning.*

Jean-Luc glances at me before replying, 'I think so. And, Estelle, please remember, if I can help in any way, do let me know.'

Estelle pats his arm. 'Thank you, Jean-Luc. Well, you know, you could keep an eye on Lia for me, help her with the boulangerie if she needs it.'

I don't miss the glimmer of mischief in her eyes as she says this.

'Of course.' Jean-Luc nods gravely, as if it's the most serious matter he has ever had to consider. He turns to encompass me in a goodbye hug and then heads back to the *fromagerie.*

'You're in safe hands there, Lia,' says Estelle.

Don't I know it. My thoughts return to Jean-Luc's hands and mouth and what he was doing with them last night. *Oh là là,* as Estelle would say!

Once Estelle has gone, and Jean-Luc is next door again, a constant influx of customers keeps me occupied, as they drop in for their usual sustenance and supplies. In between the busy spells, my thoughts return to the Molins' dilemma and what I overheard last night. As I'm pondering this, my mobile pings. Freddy.

The potential buyers want to come and have another look at the flat.

Hastily, I type back, *Good, let them.*

I refill the pastry racks from those stacked in the storeroom. Matthieu must be exhausted. He made hundreds and in such a short amount of time. As I place the final tray on the shelf beneath the glass counter, I remember I still haven't changed my flight. A thought occurs to me, then the ideas tumble out one after the other. What if I didn't go home? What if I stayed long term? What if I used the money I'll get from the sale of the flat to invest in the boulangerie? True, I have no idea how much I'd need, but I have quite a bit of capital in the flat, plus I have some savings, and I'm bound to get redundancy, despite the fact Universal Vision has been unerringly quiet on that front so far. Distractedly, I remind myself I need to chase them up.

I'm so deep in thought, I don't even notice Jean-Luc

entering the boulangerie or the overhead doorbell jangling.

'Hello? Is anyone there?' Jean-Luc says, waving a hand in front of my face.

I jerk backwards, startled, and almost fall through the beaded curtain into the Molins' living room.

'Hey! You OK?' Jean-Luc asks, his brows knitting in the middle. I must look a comical sight, almost on my backside half in, half out of the beaded curtain, which I'm clutching part of in my right hand.

He comes round counter-side and frowns. 'Is everything all right?'

'Yes,' I say, shaking my head. 'I was just thinking about something and got a fright when you spoke.'

He smiles. 'Not the reaction I was going for.'

I return his smile. 'What can I do for you? Baguette? *Chocolatine? Pain aux raisins?*'

'Actually, it's what I can do for you.'

I raise an eyebrow and he laughs. 'Not like that – yet.'

When I pout he laughs again. 'I made us some lunch, and since I know you close for lunch at two, I thought we could snag a baguette and eat together.'

'Good plan. Thank you. Are we eating here or at the *fromagerie*?'

His lips quirk upwards. 'Oh, I think we can manage at the *fromagerie* this time. Remember, I do have a room in back.'

My eyebrows raise again and my heartbeat speeds up, as well as the receptors in my nether regions lighting up like a Christmas tree.

'Get your mind out of the gutter,' Jean-Luc says. 'The kitchen.'

I snort then reply, 'Give me five minutes.'

When Jean-Luc smirks, I say, 'Now whose turn is it to get their mind out of the gutter? Now, scram!'

His laugh continues all the way back to the *fromagerie* as I try to marshal my thoughts and return to the subject of the boulangerie and my soon-to-be-enhanced bank balance.

What if I can save the boulangerie for the Molins?

Chapter Twenty-six

'This is quite the picnic,' I say, taking in the array of dishes Jean-Luc has set out for us.

'Just a few things I threw together. Is that for me?' He points to the baguette I'm holding.

'Sorry, yes.' I hand it to him and our fingertips brush, sending a tiny shock through my system. I jump back as though burned. It wouldn't do to get overly amorous during lunch – we have our respective businesses to get back to. I roll this idea around in my head again – our businesses. Could the germ of an idea which has taken root in my mind in the past fifteen minutes really work?

With my garden leave, my despair at the thought of joining the job market back home right now and the lure of France, Toulouse and the Molins pulling me, together with the idea of making a change work-wise, could I take a chance and invest in the boulangerie?

My thoughts have been a jumble ever since Freddy's text sent them into freefall. There has been so much going on, I haven't had much time to muse over the ramifications of the flat selling and what I could do with the money when I get it. It gives me a financial freedom I haven't had … well, since I joined forces with Freddy.

All my life I've been led to believe that doing well in

exams, getting a good job, moving up the career ladder and buying a flat, house, mansion, is the best way to go, but is it? Is it really?

Could success actually look like owning a boulangerie in a sleepy part of Toulouse, France? Could I be happy learning to do this for a living?

'Red wine or white?' asks Jean-Luc, the amusement in his eyes making me wonder if he has been talking to me and I haven't noticed. I'm so consumed by this realisation of the possibility of not only moving to France, but helping save the Molins' business and actively taking a more formal role in the boulangerie, that he could probably have stripped naked and I wouldn't have noticed. OK, I may have taken that too far, but, suffice to say, my brain is filled with the all-encompassing prospect of living here and how I could make that a viable reality long term.

'Red, please.'

I try to compose myself and act natural whilst my mind does its best to process all of the new ideas flitting through it at breakneck speed.

When Jean-Luc places my wine in front of me, I sit opposite him at the bistro set in his bijou kitchen behind the main area of the *fromagerie*.

'Help yourself.' He passes me a plate, which I accept gratefully and begin piling with slices of the mouthwatering cheeses he has put within arm's reach. When I've chosen two or three, I add crackers – of three different types, naturally – and then turn to the salad.

'It's a vegetarian niçoise,' Jean-Luc tells me, then counts off on his fingers. 'Eggs, white beans, olives, mixed greens, tomatoes, cucumber and–' he pauses as if trying to recall another ingredient '–green beans. I like it, because it's very colourful and bursting with flavour.'

'It certainly looks it.' I serve myself a generous helping and add it to the bowl beside my place setting.

Once we both have food on our plates, it's a full three minutes before either of us speaks. That shows how starving we both were. Being a shopkeeper is hungry work. Back home in Scotland, I'd grab a pre-prepared sandwich and eat it at my desk whilst I continued working through a project – it's a gift to be able to stop and savour food rather than only looking at it as a source of fuel.

We sit companionably, enjoying the food – which is delicious – and Jean-Luc talks me through the cheeses he has chosen for lunch. I love cheese and I'm having difficulty not moaning with pleasure as I taste some of these, but I'm concerned it may unleash other sensations in one or both of us, and this isn't the time. We have to go back to work, and I have to sort my head out.

Finally, Jean-Luc says, 'What's bothering you?'

I look into his earnest brown eyes and frown. 'Nothing.'

He sits back then rests one elbow on the table, his index finger tapping his lip, his thumb under his chin as he studies me. 'I don't believe you.'

'Excuse me?' I say, taken aback and more than a tad defensive.

'Sorry to be so forthright, but although I don't know you very well yet'—I like his usage of *yet*—'I can tell something is up. So, do you want to talk about it?'

My gaze locks with his. I'm so torn. On the one hand, I could really use someone else's advice on this, but on the other hand, I'm not sure Suzanne and Sarah even know yet that their parents have no choice but to sell the boulangerie.

Finally, I say, 'Can you keep a secret?'

After I've told Jean-Luc everything, he sits back and blows out a breath. 'That is a lot to take in. Poor Estelle, and poor Matthieu. I knew something had to give soon, what with them having to run around so much, but I never dreamt for a second it would mean selling the boulangerie. They've been here for … well, forever.'

'I know.' I haven't told Jean-Luc yet about my great idea, but I need him to absorb the news first, before I can get his take on my proposal. I also need to sit down and do the maths, and speak to Matthieu to see how much the boulangerie would cost. I know I could contribute, or partner with them, but I'm not sure if I'll have enough to buy the business outright. Plus, it depends how time-critical the sale is for them. It could still take two to three months for the money to arrive. Can they hang on until then?

He watches me carefully. 'Go on.'

'Sorry?'

'There's more, isn't there?' When I say nothing, he continues. 'What else is on your mind? I can almost see you sitting on your hands in an effort not to blurt it out, so c'mon, out with it.'

I smile at his astute observation as well as his turn of phrase then sigh and say, 'My ex texted me to say we have an offer for our flat. I'd already been thinking of staying in France a little longer, at the moment mainly to help the Molins, but if I'm a hundred per cent honest with myself, also to see if I could imagine myself living here long term.'

Jean-Luc's eyes widen and the tiny dimple appears in his cheek. 'Really?'

I grin at the hopeful note in his voice. 'Yes, really.'

Before we can get caught up in the ramifications of that, I move on. 'So, I was thinking perhaps I could buy, or buy into, the boulangerie.'

Jean-Luc's mouth falls open and my eyes crinkle as I try to hide a smile. He looks so adorable, although he'd probably be indignant at me finding him adorable, preferring to be considered sexy.

Once I've dropped the bombshell upon him, Jean-Luc becomes animated and fires questions at me: would I study to become a *boulanger*, where would I live, what solicitors would I need – French or Scottish or both? This is good and exactly the sort of help I need. If the Molins do indeed have to sell, then maybe if it's to me, it won't be such a blow, or maybe with my capital, they'll be able to stay on as co-owners. One thing's for sure, I couldn't be a *boulanger* without the training. Suzanne had already told me in the past of the *boulanger* qualification needed before being able to prepare food in a boulangerie. So even if I do buy the boulangerie, a trained *boulanger* would have to work with me until I've taken and passed the diploma. Something else I'll need to look into.

Determined to have as many of my ducks in a row as possible, I pull out my phone and for the rest of our lunchtime together, we check out the requirements to become a *boulanger* and look into how to overcome as many of the obstacles as we can so that I'm as primed and prepped as possible before I have the discussion with Estelle and Matthieu.

I'm so glad I decided to confide in Jean-Luc. He loves the Molins and will do everything to help me keep the boulangerie in their hands – or at a push, in mine.

Once I'm back in the boulangerie, the rest of the afternoon passes in a blur, with a steady stream of patrons and as many thoughts flitting through my head. Every spare moment I have is taken up with me wondering if what I'm hoping can happen is indeed possible, or too far-fetched.

I'm glad I spoke to Jean-Luc about it, as he was able to tell me about some of the French business regulations, which both gave me food for thought and further inspired me to go down this route. If I do get the go-ahead, I'm not fooling myself this will be an easy task, but I do think it's doable.

It's an hour to closing time when Suzanne stomps in, her face blotchy as if she has been crying. I don't need a crystal ball to know what that's all about.

'Hey, are you OK? How's your grandmother?'

She shakes her head, her unruly auburn curls flying around her, and starts to tremble, and for a moment I wonder if something worse than possibly losing the boulangerie has occurred. But next minute, she says, 'Mum and Dad are selling the boulangerie. It's simply not feasible for them to keep it open whilst having long-term caring commitments to both sets of grandparents.' She pauses, her chest heaving, 'And there will be a considerable amount of caring for both *Papi* and *Mamie*, from what we've managed to glean so far.'

'Oh, Suzanne, I'm so sorry.' I hold out my arms and she steps into my embrace and I hug her quivering body to me.

For the rest of the time the boulangerie is open, I sit in the living room with Suzanne as she pours out her heart to me – about how this is the only home she has ever known, how she doesn't know what she'll do for a job now, wondering how her parents will cope with the loss of their sense of self; her woes are endless, and I'm not surprised. I know what it's like to have the rug pulled out from under you, what with losing my job and my relationship in the space of two weeks, and, well, now my home – although that may turn out to be a blessing in disguise.

I can't yet tell Suzanne my big idea as I haven't fully formulated it yet and there are a lot of gaps in my knowledge. I don't know the best way to tell her and I can't quite decide whether I should wait until her parents are back or not, so I decide the best thing to do is sleep on it. With any luck, I'll have a light-bulb moment by morning.

Chapter Twenty-seven

I've barely slept all night. When Suzanne went into the bakery to start making the bread, instead of Matthieu, at two thirty, I was already wide awake, and the incredible aroma of baking bread rising to my attic bedroom meant there wasn't a chance in hell of me getting to sleep again. I left it a couple of hours to let ideas continue to percolate, but at four thirty, I swing myself out of bed and soon I'm dressed and down in the bakery to see Suzanne. I can't wait any longer. I think I'll explode if I don't tell her. I want to give her some hope. She may not know how much money is involved, or if my offer will be enough, but I want her positive – no, *need* her positive – and firing on all cylinders, if we are to keep the boulangerie.

'Morning!' I call at the door.

Suzanne gives me a wave, dusts her hands on her apron then washes her hands at the stainless-steel sink before coming towards me.

'Did you sleep well?' she asks, the irony of her question not lost on me, given that the dark circles ringing her eyes show she hasn't, and possibly hasn't slept at all. But for now the show must go on, so here she is, prepping the *chocolatines* and baguettes, the *pains aux raisins* and *pains de campagne*.

'Not much, if I'm honest.' I eye her carefully then say, 'Suzanne, can you take a break and I'll make us some coffee?' When she glances back at her ovens and her waiting ingredients, I say, 'I know you have loads to do. I promise it won't take long, but I have something important I want to discuss with you.'

Her eyebrows scrunch up and her head tilts to one side. 'OK. But in fifteen minutes, I need to be back here, or you will run out of stock by lunchtime.'

'Deal. I'll sort the coffee,' I say as I turn and head towards the kitchen.

'I'll bring the pastries,' Suzanne calls from behind me.

A few minutes later, we are both seated at the kitchen table, munching on warm country bread slathered in homemade strawberry jam from Alexine's plants in their garden in Saint-Sauvy.

'So, tell me,' Suzanne says in the style of a busy woman who has another several hundred pastries and loaves of bread to make this morning. I realise I don't even know if she's going to the hospital today, nor which one, or if she's heading home to see Patrick for a bit. But for now, those questions will have to wait; it's time to bite the bullet.

'Suzanne, my ex told me we have a firm written offer for the flat.'

'Lia, that's great news. Congrats.' She leans forward and gives me a quick hug, but as she sits back, her brow furrows. 'That's not all, is it?'

I shake my head. 'No. Suzanne, I want to stay in France. I've been thinking about it for about a week or so.' Her amused expression makes me laugh. 'Yes, I know it might not seem a long time, but I've barely thought of anything else for a week.'

'This wouldn't have anything to do with Jean-Luc, would it?' she says with a sly smile. '*Maman* told me you two kissed.'

I grin. 'Well, it's a nice bonus, but of course I'm not going to make such a life-changing decision based on a man, and particularly one I've just met.' I pause then say, 'But I have been thinking of changing career, what with losing my job, despite having put in a ridiculous amount of my energy into the company and working my butt off. Problem was, I didn't know what I wanted until now.'

Suzanne doesn't interrupt, not even when I pause again. She just continues to take occasional bites of her bread. I can't say I blame her; it's blooming delicious. Another perk I'd enjoy if I moved here.

'I knew I wanted to make a change, but I was stumped as to what. Until yesterday'—I almost said "when Freddy told me about the offer on the flat", but then I remember at that point I wasn't meant to know Estelle and Matthieu intended to sell—'when you told me about your parents having to sell, and as I lay in bed last night, it struck me that with the sale of my flat, I'll have the capital to put towards a new home … or enterprise.'

I pause, this time to allow the words to sink in.

Suzanne's eyes widen. 'Lia, you can't mean what I think you mean.'

I smile and say, 'That very much depends on what you think I mean.'

Her brow creases. 'The boulangerie? You want to buy the boulangerie? You'd really do that? Are you sure? I have no idea how much it costs, how much *Maman* and *Papa* would be looking for it, but I do know there was a boulangerie near *Mémé* that went for around fifty thousand euros.'

That's doable. More than doable. The capital from the flat sale, plus what I have in the bank, and my potential redundancy package would cover that and leave me some wiggle room. I can't help the excitement that surges through me, and I try to tamp it down as I know I need to have a clear and rational chat with Matthieu and Estelle when they return later today.

But then I remember the *Boulangerie Au Coin de la Rue* comes with accommodation, quite extensive accommodation and my heart sinks.

'What's wrong?' Suzanne asks.

'I think it will be much more expensive than that because of the house – it will come as a package. I can't see how legally they can be separated.'

Suzanne's face falls, but about ten seconds later, her lips curve into a smile and she says, 'What if we – me and you – could run it and our family and you could co-own it?'

Well, that thought had crossed my mind, but I have no idea how to split ownership of a property, particularly when it's part business and part residential. I guess that's for the solicitors to sort out, but Suzanne is on the right track, and I love the fact she's so upbeat about it all. We need to find a way, and things certainly appear more hopeful than they did yesterday. So, no, I haven't spoken to her parents yet, who, when it comes down to it, are the owners, but surely the fact Suzanne is on board is a major plus.

'I'd love that,' I say, reaching out to pat her arm. 'I don't know yet how to make it happen, or if your parents will go for it, but I want to put it on the table. It has to be better than losing the boulangerie.'

Suzanne nods vigorously. 'I couldn't agree more. Right, Lia, thanks, and you've given me a lot to think about, but right now, I have to get back to baking, or we'll have lots of disappointed customers this morning.' She stands and takes one final slurp of her coffee before rinsing her mug and setting it on the draining board. Then she comes towards me and hugs me. 'And Lia, thank you, seriously, from the bottom of my heart. You're an inspiration.'

I feel myself colour and I make some dismissive comment then tidy up and go prepare the boulangerie for opening up. Afterwards, I quickly text Jean-Luc to tell him Suzanne is on board and I'll let him know as soon as I've spoken to Estelle and Matthieu. As I open up the boulangerie, I can't help thinking things are finally looking up.

The boulangerie is so busy and in the few breaks I have from the torrent of customers, I talk to Suzanne, who is very animated about the whole prospect and struggling not to call her parents to tell them. This means I don't have time to nip in to see Jean-Luc. I text him to say hopefully I'll be able to see him tomorrow morning before the boulangerie opens but right now, Suzanne is here and I can't get away. He has been sending words of encouragement throughout the day, along with the occasional snippet of information that may help me work out how to make this happen, including information of a *boulanger* course, where I'd have to spend a couple of years learning the craft before I myself would be allowed to create products that could be sold in the boulangerie. And now the seed has been sown, I really want that. I love cooking. I love baking. Why not do it for a living? In France? In the Molins' boulangerie?

After we close up the boulangerie, Suzanne takes a phone call then tells me her parents are on their way back. Nerves jangle in my stomach. Why am I feeling so uptight? Hopefully, I'm helping the situation here. That being the case, I should feel confident, like I do at work – well, like I did feel at work until I was put on garden leave.

'Lia, don't worry, this may be the best news they've had all month, perhaps even all year.'

Her attempt at reassurance is welcome, but somehow it doesn't stop that jangling; in fact, a full orchestra has taken up residence in my insides.

I decide to make myself scarce so Suzanne can pave the way for my suggestion. She can then call me once they've had time to discuss things, and I've also advised her to give them a bit of a breather when they get back and not to just dive in, as they must be exhausted, and their heads whirling, as well as their minds being elsewhere.

Forty-five minutes after the Molins arrive home, Suzanne comes up to my room, where I've been lying on the bed, trying to read a romance novel and not getting past the first page. My mind is too full of broken bottles as my mum would say.

'I think you'd better come down.'

I almost physically gulp at her tone. Shit. I didn't think it was that bad an idea. Are they going to turf me out? Maybe they think I'm here to take over. Maybe I've insulted them. Feeling sick to my stomach, I plod downstairs, my tread heavy, almost like I'm being led to the gallows. Suzanne's expression was so grave, and all the mumbled, hushed snippets of conversation I'd managed to hear were too vague to give me any idea of what the Molins are thinking. Have I done the wrong thing here?

Committed the ultimate faux pas? Snubbed my hosts? I hope not. I adore them and would be devastated if I'd hurt their feelings. My stomach decides right at that moment to rumble and I almost glare at the traitor. I've no time to eat now. I just hope it doesn't do that during this potentially life-changing conversation.

When we reach the living room, Estelle and Matthieu both turn towards me, their faces not as joyful as I'd hoped they'd be at the prospect of me saving them from losing the boulangerie.

'Sit down, Lia,' says Matthieu. Now I know it's serious; it's always Estelle who leads conversations in this family.

'Suzanne has told us about the very generous suggestion you've made about investing in the boulangerie.'

'That's right,' I say tentatively, still not sure how to read the room.

'Lia, I don't want to tell you how to live your life, but this is a big undertaking, and I'm not sure you realise what's involved,' he goes on.

He's right, although I have a bit more of an idea than he probably imagines, since Jean-Luc has been helping me with research and given me lots of pointers already.

'I understand, Matthieu, and you're right to be cautious. However, I've been thinking of staying in France, at least for a longer period, if I'm honest, since a few days after I returned. I'm unhappy with my career at the moment, and I'm looking for a change of direction. Why not the boulangerie?'

I see him try not to roll his eyes and I do my best to tamp down my frustration. 'Matthieu, please don't misunderstand me. I know I can't possibly replace what you do and with no knowledge. This is a long-term plan for me. Eventually, I'd hope to study to become a *boulanger*, but I know that takes years. Quite simply, I want to help you, Estelle and Suzanne. I have the capital from my flat sale coming soon. If I can help and you're not against the idea – and providing the money is enough to allow you to do what you need to do – then, please, at least consider it.'

He taps his fingers against his knee as he thinks. 'But you don't actually have access to the money yet?'

I shake my head, a little deflated. 'No, so it really comes down to how long your cash flow will stay healthy.'

Matthieu then turns to Estelle, who shrugs and smiles before saying, 'We have nothing to lose. Why don't we discuss the financial side of things with Lia? We're not too proud to do that, are we? Her offer comes from a place of love, for us, and for France.'

Matthieu looks at Estelle for a long moment, then at Suzanne, who nods. He sighs. 'OK. Let's have a look at these figures, but, Lia, there is one thing I must tell you. I already spoke to Bernard, my solicitor, today, to see if he could come up with any suggestions of who may be interested in the boulangerie as a going concern. It's only fair to advise you of that.'

I can't admit that I'm a bit crushed by that, but the important thing is to move things along and see if my plan is viable, so I thank Matthieu and grasp Estelle's hand in thanks.

As Matthieu fetches his accounts, I cross my fingers that my plan comes to fruition and that I haven't got everyone's hopes up for nothing.

Chapter Twenty-eight

It's not even eight o'clock in the morning, French time, before I call Jules.

'You've done what?' Her eyes bug out on the screen.

'I've offered to buy into the boulangerie with the proceeds of the sale of the flat.'

Jules' mouth drops open. 'And you're telling me this only now? Wow, that cute cheesemonger really has got you wrapped around his little finger.'

I can't help the stab of irritation that needles me as Jules says this, even though I know she doesn't mean anything bad by it.

'I know. I know. I should have told you, but things have been so crazy, and once Freddy sent me the message saying the viewers had put in a firm offer, everything clicked in my head.'

'But what about the legalities? And what do you know about running a boulangerie, Lia? I'm sorry, I don't mean to put a dampener on things, but it's a lot of money, and I want to make sure you're thinking straight.'

'Thanks, and you're right, it is a lot of money, but I've never felt surer about anything in my life. I think Universal Vision putting me on garden leave was a sign. Now I can only hope the Molins go for it, although after our conversation last night and studying the accounts, it does look possible. Just. I've already rescheduled my flight.'

'Do you want me to come over?' Jules' face is so earnest, I break out in a smile.

'No, it's fine, but can I please rely on you to be on the other end of a phone, as I'll probably want your reassurance now and then – like now – that I haven't lost my mind completely.'

She grins. 'Not any more than usual, you mean.'

'Ha, bloody, ha. Right, I'm going. I have, as you can imagine, a ridiculous amount to do, and still have the boulangerie to open up. Matthieu is dropping in to discuss things with his solicitor this morning, and Estelle is off to the hospital to visit René, then on to see Alexine. I think she may stay over. Honestly, we need an app to keep track of everyone's movements.'

'And what's the deal with the dashing Jean-Luc?'

I can't prevent the smile that spreads across my face.

'Lia Abernethy, you have not, have you?'

'No, Jules, not that, but we have had more than a few moments, and a bit of a heart to heart.'

'Hmph. I prefer when there's less talking, more action.'

'Ha! I know you do, but I'm not you, nor am I brimming with self-confidence. But Jean-Luc is so easy to be with and he has also been helping me with the boulangerie legalities.' I lower my voice when I say this last part, as I don't want the Molins to know I've discussed it with Jean-Luc. I'm sure they wouldn't mind, but I did talk to him about it before I put it to them. However, I genuinely feel if I hadn't, then I might not have had the guts to suggest it to them. At least this way I had the chance to talk through the pros and cons with someone who has some knowledge of running a successful business in France and the issues I might come up against.

'OK, you've convinced me. But get it on with this guy, and soon! He has his own house, right?'

I realise I must have omitted to mention that I'd had dinner there, and how opulent the townhouse was. 'Yes. He lives alone.'

'Perfect. Once you've sorted all this business stuff, get him alone, and…'

'Jules, you don't need to draw me a picture, I get it.'

'Well, you're not getting it yet, though, are you?'

'Fnar! So not funny, Jules.'

'On the contrary, I think you'll find I'm hilarious. Anyway, didn't you have to be somewhere?'

'Crap, yes, I do,' I say. 'Love you and thanks.'

'You too, and thanks for the six thirty wake-up call.'

I grimace. 'Sorry. I forgot about the time difference in all my excitement.'

'Only kidding. Keep me updated.'

'I will.' Just as I'm about to hang up, a flash of what I think is male fills the screen. No, it can't be. 'Jules! Is that … Josh?'

The male dives out of shot before Jules clears her throat and readjusts the duvet saying, 'Actually, Lia, yes. Josh, come say hi to Lia.'

A sheepish-looking Josh pulls back the duvet, his eyes sparkling, bed hair in evidence. 'Hi, Lia.'

I raise an eyebrow and say, 'Hi, Josh. I'd ask how you are, but I see you're just fine.'

Josh grins. 'Jules has been looking after me.'

'I'll bet,' I say as Jules pans the camera back to herself and makes a can-you-believe-it face.

'We'll talk later, Jules.' Now it's my turn to get all the details. I can't believe she has been holding out on me. She may treat them mean and keep them keen, but she has fancied Josh for ages. Interesting.

I hang up and head for the boulangerie to open up, realising I haven't had a chance to meet with Jean-Luc yet. For now, it'll have to be a quick text.

At least Suzanne is here to keep me company once she has finished creating enough pastries to sink a small ship. Stress obviously makes her more productive than her already usually efficient self. She's about to crawl into bed for a couple of hours' sleep when Jean-Luc pops his head round the door of the boulangerie.

'Hi, Jean-Luc. *Ca va?*'

'I'm good, thanks. How are you doing?' he asks Suzanne.

She huffs out a breath. 'Right now, shattered, so, no offence, but I'll leave you in Lia's capable hands. I'm off for a nap.' As she turns back towards me, she winks and I suppress a smile.

'Sleep well!' Jean-Luc calls before shooting me a grin. Once she's out of earshot, he says, 'So?'

I part the beaded curtain to check Suzanne really has gone to bed and isn't still in the living room or kitchen. I don't want her overhearing that Jean-Luc is au courant of the situation.

'Well, I had a good long chat with Estelle and Matthieu, and Suzanne last night, and although they have to speak to the bank to see what's what and how much capital they need to release, potentially we could go into business together. I've told them the sum I'm able to invest, and they were pleasantly surprised.'

He puts his arms around me. 'That's wonderful news, Lia.' I sense he wants to say something more, but at that moment Madame Leclerc enters.

'*Bonjour!* Jean-Luc, do you still work next door?' she asks.

'But of course, Madame Leclerc. How are you today?'

'I'd be better if I could buy some cheese to go with the bread I'm about to buy from Lia, but sadly there's no one at the *fromagerie* next door,' she says pointedly.

'I was … discussing something with Lia.'

'So I see. Are you finished now?'

'Yes, yes.' He shoots me a look and I press my lips together, trying not to snort with laughter. He's like a schoolboy being reprimanded by his teacher for not doing his homework. I forget that Jean-Luc has grown up with all these people around him. My regulars … listen to me – my regulars. I haven't even bought into the boulangerie yet. But, my regulars have been coming to this boulangerie and Jean-Luc's *fromagerie* since he was a child.

'Good. Then I'll see you there in a few minutes. Let me get my order from Lia first.'

Madame Leclerc turns to me, Jean-Luc clearly dismissed. He raises his eyebrows at me and then grins. 'See you later. Lia.'

I smile goodbye to him and turn to Madame Leclerc. 'Good morning, Madame. And how can I help this morning? The usual?'

'Yes, and also, I wonder if you could help me.' She eyes me, then purses her lips. 'I can trust you to be discreet, *n'est-ce pas*?' Her shrewd glance takes me in to the extent I feel a tiny bit uncomfortable.

Despite being a tad unnerved and wondering how I can help her with anything that requires discretion – exactly how secretive must one be when it comes to matters of croissants and baguettes, after all? – I reply, 'Of course.'

She sets her handbag – Prada, I now note – down on the countertop and says, 'I believe the boulangerie may be going up for sale.'

I'm so startled she knows this that I can't help gaping at her. I'm about to ask her how she knows, but she waves her hand dismissively at me, as if anticipating my question. 'Lia, I have lived here a long time, and I listen.'

I nod and wait to see why she is asking. Surely it has to be more than the fact she has concerns over buying her pastries elsewhere.

'Can you please remind Matthieu that not all offers are good offers?'

For a moment I think she's referring to me, and I frown, which elicits a raised eyebrow from Madame Leclerc and a 'Did you hear what I said?' Then I realise she couldn't possibly know about my potential involvement unless Matthieu, Estelle or Suzanne have told her, and I know that isn't the case, so what is she referring to?

'Yes, I'll tell him,' I say, confused and wondering what to make of her interest as I pack her usual into paper bags for her.

A few hours later, I'm serving a young mother, Elise, who comes in most days with her two beautiful yet rascally children, who are around four and six, when to my surprise, Matthieu comes in through the main boulangerie door.

Usually, when he returns, he goes straight through the courtyard and into the house.

'Matthieu, hi. How are things?' I ask after I've taken Elise's money and bid them goodbye, Matthieu holding the door for them and asking Elise how her mother is. It warms my heart how much of a sense of community exists between all the customers here, and I hope I can be a part of continuing that trend.

He nods, his open, expressive face displaying so many emotions at once. Instantly, I sense the news hasn't all been good and my heart plummets to the floor.

'We'll talk properly later, but I saw my solicitor first thing and so far, the feelers he put out haven't drawn anyone's interest.'

My heart both sinks for the Molins and soars for me. 'It's early days, though, Matthieu. But did you manage to make an appointment with the bank to see if what we discussed could work?'

He nods again. 'Better than that. I managed to have a meeting with the manager, as a client had cancelled and so he had a free spot.'

I can't help smiling. 'Excellent.' Nerves set in as I ask, 'So what did he say?'

He hems and haws then says, 'Essentially, from what you're able to invest and what we could leave in as sleeping partners, and to help Suzanne, it's doable. I'll have to speak to Bernard again, now I've met with the bank. Obviously, we need to go over conditions and we have a lot to iron out between us, but it's possible this is the solution we're all looking for.'

'Oh, Matthieu! Thank you, thank you!' I'm so delighted, I come round the counter and hug him. I'll finally get to realise a dream I didn't even know I had until recently.

'We'll get some champagne to celebrate once Bernard confirms it for me,' Matthieu says with a smile.

'I'm so excited. Thank you for not dismissing my idea out of hand.' Then a thought strikes me. I'll need to find somewhere to live, but for now, I don't care about that. I'm hoping the Molins will let me stay for a few weeks more whilst I sort things out, but right this second, all I want to do is tell Jean-Luc, and Jules, in that order.

'No, thank *you*, Lia. Without your proposal, we'd be in danger of losing the boulangerie entirely. This way at least Suzanne still has a job, we still have a home and we still retain some say in the business.'

I nod. 'We both benefit. Matthieu, thanks for trusting me with your business.'

He smiles again. 'I think it's about us trusting each other, but even though you've only come back into all of our lives recently, we've known each other a long time, and the very fact you want to invest in our business, that you've been around to support our family during this very difficult time, speaks volumes.'

'Thank you.' I grin. 'Let's hope we're drinking that champagne soon then.'

'Indeed. Right, I'm going to freshen up and then head off to my parents'. I'll see you tomorrow and I'll let you know when I get a call back from Bernard.'

'Oh, I almost forgot. Madame Leclerc was in earlier and said to tell you to remember that not all offers are good offers.'

Matthieu screws up his face. 'Madame Leclerc? How did…?'

I shake my head. 'That's what I thought. Anyway, I'm only passing on the message.'

'Thanks.'

When Matthieu slips through the beaded curtain to the living room, I almost want to jump up and down with glee or do a happy dance. I'm ninety per cent of the way there, ninety per cent of the way to making my 'dream' of living in France long term a reality. I quickly text Jean-Luc and then Jules. Within less than a minute, Jean-Luc throws the boulangerie door open and scoops me up, swinging me around. My feet aren't actually touching the ground, both physically and metaphorically.

'You did it!' he says, his smile so wide it reaches all the way to the depths of his chocolate brown eyes, which I now notice seem to have flecks of amber through them. A trick of the light?

'Well, I don't know that I did anything, but it's certainly viable.' I wrap my arms around his neck. 'And thank you for all your help with everything. I'd have been lost without you.'

He grins. 'Anytime.'

I wrap my arms around him more tightly and say, 'Good, because I'm probably going to need a lot more business advice in the days and weeks to come.'

He nuzzles into my neck. 'I always fancied being a PA.'

At that, I snort and ease him away from me. 'I can't imagine anyone who looks less like a PA.'

His eyes brim with amusement. 'I could carry off the sexy secretary vibe quite well, thank you very much.' He puts his hands on his hips, making me splutter with laughter as the bell over the door announces someone's arrival.

'See you later?' I say as Jean-Luc retreats.

'You can count on it.' He backs out of the boulangerie, not taking his eyes off of me.

As he heads back to the *fromagerie*, I hug to myself the fact that perhaps all my dreams are about to come true, including those involving Jean-Luc.

Chapter Twenty-nine

This is the earliest I've been up on a Saturday in, well, forever, possibly. I got up at five o'clock, suited up, and am in the bakery preparation room, watching Suzanne at work. She has been making today's batches for the boulangerie as Matthieu isn't due back until tomorrow. She'd stayed at her own house with Patrick until late evening yesterday then arrived back whilst I was out with Jean-Luc – we'd gone to a bar near the Garonne and then for something to eat, but not back to his place. If we had done, I'd have jumped him straightaway I'm sure, but I'm glad we didn't – yesterday was about much more than that; it was pivotal for me in so many ways and underlined the beginnings of my new start in France.

Plus, Matthieu had called when we were in the restaurant, just as I was about to bite into my scallops, to tell me he'd managed to talk to Bernard, who'd confirmed there should be no issue, which means we're full speed ahead. I couldn't be more delighted. So, buoyed up by this news, here I am, starting as I mean to go on, learning the trade with Suzanne, watching as she measures, kneads, rolls, dusts and sprinkles. It's fascinating and she's so precise, and fast. I'm tired just watching her, although that may have something to do with me not having had much sleep the past few days. I've been too excited. I lay awake last night after my evening with Jean-Luc finished, unable to sleep, thinking about the future and looking into *boulanger* courses. Since I want to become more creative, and be hands-on, that's important to me.

Suzanne has given me a section of the bakery where I can work on my own creations. She has been most emphatic, however, that we can't sell anything I create because I haven't qualified as a *boulanger*. I chuckle to myself. She has underestimated me. I already researched all this. I know I can't, but I'm delighted that I can have a bash myself. It's very rewarding. If nothing else, I'm looking forward to eating my own efforts.

We chat comfortably as we work, I do note, however, that Suzanne barely looks up from her creations, although her ears are clearly primed to take in what's being said. The couple of hours in the bakery pass quickly as we discuss everything from how she and Patrick are coping with all the upheaval of her grandparents being in hospital; what she thinks is the best *boulanger* course; anecdotes of Jean-Luc as they were growing up, to tales from when I lived here first time around, where I should visit outside of Toulouse on my days off, and where I could possibly look for an apartment now I'm staying here long term.

Suzanne has said she'll work in the boulangerie for a couple of hours this morning so I can browse the markets. I'm particularly keen to visit the *Marché des Bouquinistes* – the book market – in one of the oldest streets in Toulouse, Rue du Taur. I haven't been since I returned to Toulouse and I have such fond memories of it, leafing through books laid out by the booksellers of Toulouse's six bookshops. I love the tradition and how it's so quintessentially French. If we had markets like that back home, everything would be soaking wet. When I told Jean-Luc of my plan, he was miffed that he couldn't come too; he doesn't get to go very often as the *fromagerie* is always open during the hours the market is on, but he said he'd try to accompany me on a future occasion when he can ask his assistant to work on Saturday morning.

I didn't like to tell him that when I look for books, I like to browse on my own. That said, I'm sure it would be lovely to have him alongside me, recommending books to me.

Once the boulangerie opens, the morning passes quickly, and I find I'm even breezier than usual, my smile that little bit wider as I hug to myself the secret knowledge that I'll soon officially be involved in this business and that it's part of my long-term future. It does remind me, however, that I'll need to speak to Eric and see how the land lies. I still have holidays due, so it shouldn't be an issue, but I need to ensure everything is in place legally, particularly as I want a clean break, and then my new start here, which will again involve solicitors. I wonder if Jean-Luc knows anyone I could use, especially since using Matthieu's would be a conflict of interest.

When I leave Suzanne to her own devices, she's busy talking to a father who comes in with his brood every Saturday. Each child has a *pain au chocolat*, and their faces are various degrees of messy, from a spot of chocolate to chocolate-smeared.

I take my time, meandering along Rue de la Balance, appreciating how quiet it is, until I reach the noticeably busier Place Arnaud Bernard, which leads down to a series of shops, bars and cafés, then I head round past the imposing structure of the cathedral of Saint Sérnin, with its octagonal tower and impressive spire, until finally, I reach Rue du Taur.

Some things have definitely changed. There's a bagel shop and a pizzeria that I don't recall from my last trip, and it definitely has a busier vibe, but like I remember, there is a medley of canopied stalls, where book lovers are jostling to see the day's offerings. Beige, green and white canopies vie for prominence in this beautiful street, with some of the pink city's most incredible terracotta façades here or within a stone's throw.

The bookseller at the first stall I stop at acknowledges me with an incline of his head after accepting payment from a client. I leaf through the contemporary volumes, looking for those with spines that are a little less creased, a little less well worn, whilst trying to select something that appeals and that I'll be able to understand.

Moving on, I note a crowd around one particular stall and gauge it's either a large group of friends or family or this bookseller has the most interesting finds. It turns out to be the latter, as the quality of the books, the condition, as well as the pricing, when I ask, are far superior to that of the previous stall.

By the time I return to the boulangerie, I'm in possession of four books for myself; one by a French novelist I know Suzanne likes; and a book about the history of Dutch cheeses – my little joke – for Jean-Luc.

Over lunch, Suzanne and I discuss the books I've bought and when she asks me if I noticed if much had changed in the area, I tell her that whilst a lot has indeed changed, and not all for the better, if I'm honest – there are more chains, principally food and clothing franchises, rather than independent boutiques and cafés – much of what enchanted me about *la ville rose* when I lived here years ago remains the same.

After lunch, Suzanne sets off for home, saying she'll see me on Monday and that her parents will be back this evening. I didn't make concrete plans with Jean-Luc yesterday, but I'm hoping he's around tomorrow – I guess it's time to see. I love Sundays in France. They're so much quieter than back home.

Following my relaxed morning, my mind begins to buzz again with all the chatter around moving to France and setting up as a business partner. How many times will I have to return to the UK until I get a work permit? Can I work before I get the official work permit or will I be a sleeping partner for a while? The makings of a headache begin to pound at my temples and the brilliant sunshine isn't helping.

The *fromagerie* closes, for some reason, an hour later than the boulangerie on a Saturday, so whilst I've been talking to Suzanne, Jean-Luc has been hard at work. When I enter the *fromagerie*, the smile he gives me makes me feel like I'm floating. I was already halfway there with the news about the boulangerie, but to have the possibility of something special with this wonderful, gorgeous, kind, caring man really does kick things up a notch.

'Hi.' He comes round the counter and kisses me on each cheek. He smells divine, like a lemon tree and a beehive made a baby. The scent of citrus with that touch of honey tantalises my senses and the heady mix combines to make me a tad light-headed. It makes me want to lick him, but I realise that would be a step too far. Maybe one day…

'Hi,' I say back, aiming for husky, but probably sounding like I have a sore throat. 'How was your day?'

He nods. 'Good. And hopefully about to improve even further.'

I tilt my head to the side and scrunch my eyebrows, batting the obvious compliment away. 'Really? Whatever could cause that?'

'I don't know, but maybe it could be what you're holding in your hand.' He reaches out for it, but I put it beyond his outstretched arm.

'Ah, ah, how do you know it's for you?' I say, teasing him.

'Hmm, since it's a history of Dutch cheese, I'm guessing it's not your bedtime reading.'

'Hey!' I say, batting him with it. 'How did you know that's what it was?'

He grins. 'Because I'm exceptionally good at reading writing upside down.'

I roll my eyes. 'Bang goes my surprise. Yes, you're right. It was a little joke present. Here you go.'

'Thank you. I'll add it to my collection of cheese books.'

'Collection of cheese books?' I say incredulously.

When he nods vehemently, I realise he isn't kidding.

'Well, I am a master cheesemonger.'

I'm sure he's a master at other things too, and I'm hoping I'll get to experience those soon, as a girl can only have so much patience … and self-restraint. As I bask in the warm glow of his gaze, I know it's going to be fun finding out.

Chapter Thirty

'So, are you free this afternoon?' I ask as Jean-Luc leafs through his book.

'Yep. And I had an idea. I know you've already had a walk through town today, but I had a different type of walk in mind, if you're up for it, since it's such a nice afternoon.'

I pause then say, 'OK, hit me with it.'

He smiles and my insides melt again. I know I have a lot going on, but seriously, when am I going to get this man into bed? I'm not a saint, nor in the religious orders, and I have needs.

'Well, it's in the old town, and it's kind of a surprise.'

Now I'm intrigued. 'Fair enough. I like a good puzzle. I'm in. Are you done here?' I ask as he washes his hands at the sink, his eyes barely leaving mine.

'Yep, ready to go.'

'Have you eaten?' For a second, I feel guilty that I was so busy chatting with Suzanne over lunch, it didn't even occur to me to bring Jean-Luc some, despite him finishing an hour after us – particularly with him having been a total gem in that department with me; he never lets me go hungry. That, I admire in a man. I like my food too much.

'No, but I had a big breakfast and I nibbled on some cheese.' He grins. 'Plus, I figured we could grab an early dinner whilst we're out, if you like?'

I very much like. 'Yes, that sounds good. Ready?'

As we walk through the streets of Chalets, Jean-Luc holds my hand and it sends a little thrill through me. How innocent, holding hands, but it occurs to me it's not something I did with Freddy; he was never that subtle. I shudder at the thought of him now. How things have changed in only a few short weeks. Thinking of him, though, reminds me I have to contact him again to see how things are progressing with the solicitors and the flat sale. I know we've had the offer, but I now, more than ever, need to know about the entry date, so I can work out when I'll receive the funds. For now, I put Freddy to the back of my mind, as I don't want thoughts of him to sully my day out with Jean-Luc. Instantly, my brain refuses to comply and compares both men; none of it is favourable towards Freddy, although that shouldn't come as any surprise. He was always too self-serving and narcissistic. Everything Jean-Luc isn't. In fact, he shares many traits with Théo; maybe that's why I was drawn to Théo. God, stop thinking about other men!

We emerge into the old town and as we pad down the streets, I take in the gorgeous pastel-coloured buildings with their white wooden shutters and wrought-iron balconies.

'OK, you can start looking now. We're here. From here on out is what I wanted to show you,' says Jean-Luc with a smile.

I look around me, not sure what I'm looking for, but when I glance back at him, he urges me on, and it's clear I'm not getting any advance on his cryptic clues yet.

'You're getting warmer,' he says as I approach the

entrance to a new street.

I scan around, stumped as to what I'm supposed to be seeing.

Stifling laughter, Jean-Luc says, 'Look up.'

When I gaze up at the sky, he bursts out laughing.

'Jean-Luc, I like surprises, but so help me, if you don't tell me what it is I'm meant to be looking for, I won't be responsible for my actions.'

He glides towards me in one fluid movement, then tilts my chin up with one hand. 'See?'

I'm staring at the street signs and another pastel-coloured façade with pale blue wooden shutters. Rue Peyrolieres.

'What am I missing?' I ask, frowning. 'The two street signs?'

He beams at me. 'Bingo!'

'In French and Catalan.' With Toulouse being so close to Spain, it's not terribly surprising that they're in Catalan as well as French, although I don't remember seeing these when I last lived here.

'A-ha! Not Catalan.' Jean-Luc folds his arms and looks smug.

My frown deepens. 'Well, it's not Spanish. At least, I don't think so. Is it?'

He shakes his head. 'It's Occitan.'

Realisation dawns. 'I didn't realise Occitan was still spoken, except by some of the older generation, like Alexine and René.'

'Actually, that's not pure Occitan. It's Gascon dialect, but it is related.'

I laugh. 'That's not at all confusing.'

Jean-Luc takes my hand as we stroll through the city's

streets, each of us pointing out more of the dual language signs.

'They weren't here until 2001, but you were here after that, right?'

'Yes, but I guess my priorities were different then as I don't remember them at all.' I almost feel as if I should apologise for not noticing. How self-absorbed I must have been back then. Now I find it endearing and sweet that there has been such an effort to bring the Occitan language to the forefront again.

We wander around for a while, Jean-Luc indicating some lesser-known landmarks to me, before we settle down at a pavement café with a fabulous view over the Garonne river.

My hand flies to my mouth. 'Oh my goodness, you haven't eaten. I was so caught up in, well, enjoying myself and wandering these lovely streets.'

Jean-Luc smiles that lazy, oh-so-sexy smile he has. 'Don't worry, but I *am* ready to eat now.'

He soon orders a plate of Iberian ham with tomato bread for himself, and I dither for a bit then decide, surprisingly, I'm still hungry and could easily eat some Iberian ham too. It may not be a French delicacy, but back home in Scotland, it's not as if I'm eating haggis every night, is it? So, in a nod to Spain, I allow myself this indulgence and we wash it down with a glass of crisp white burgundy.

When dark clouds spring up out of nowhere and a breeze starts to gust more than flutter, we decide to call it a day.

'Where to now?' I ask.

Jean-Luc's eyes are full of hope as he says, 'My place?'

Get in! I think, but I restrain myself and say, 'Why not?'

It doesn't take us long to reach his townhouse, which is as welcoming as it was last time. I can't help contrasting the immense space Jean-Luc has all to himself on this side of the city, versus the cramped, chaotic conditions at the Molins' back in Chalets, particularly when all the kids were still there and they had a part-time lodger – me. Yet, it was lived-in and a cosy home; it still is. Whereas their home is more traditional, Jean-Luc's hints at the modern, whilst still retaining elements of its history.

He puts some music on in the background – flamenco, certainly sounds like Spanish guitar – perhaps he's trying to extend the Spanish vibe from our late lunch/early dinner.

When he comes to sit beside me on the sofa, that's when I hear the rain. I glance up, as does he, to see the torrent thundering off the glass windowpanes and onto the paving stones on the street below.

Jean-Luc stands. 'Let me put the heating on.'

'No,' I say.

Startled, he stops and turns towards me.

'You don't need to.' Boldness and brazenness mix together as I take the final two steps towards him. 'I know a better way to keep us warm.'

At that, his eyes widen and as I raise my head for his kiss, his lips lower to mine. As soon as the softness and then the hunger of his lips touch mine, I'm lost, totally immersed in this man and the sensations he evokes in me, and I can only hope I make him feel the same way.

As he lowers me to the sofa, I moan, and he sighs. 'I love when you make that noise.'

I whisper against his neck. 'Then you'll have to keep

making me feel like this.'

He groans with desire and slips the strap of my dress down my shoulder, raining kisses along my jaw, into the crook of my neck and shoulder. Who knew those were erogenous zones? But whatever he's doing, he's doing it oh so well, and I hope he never stops. As I begin to undo the buttons on his shirt, his breath hitches and he raises his body off of mine a fraction to allow me easier access, and I make quick work of unbuttoning the rest. To be honest, I'm being very restrained; it's tempting to rip the shirt apart, but he may want to wear it again, so I resist.

It's like a pleasurable kind of torture, and as Jean-Luc's mouth trails its way down the dip between my breasts, and he drags my dress with him, I fumble with his belt, unbuckle it and pull it off in one fell swoop, eager as I am for our bodies to be closer, and quite frankly, for him to be wearing fewer clothes.

Soon, he's lying on top of me, and we're naked apart from our underwear. There's no questioning how much we want each other. I can almost see my own desire mirrored back at me in his lust-filled eyes.

With a daringness I didn't know I possessed, I pull his boxer shorts down, and then it's his turn, as he slides first my bra and then my briefs off of me. I'm so turned on, I might combust if we don't bring this to its natural conclusion soon, so when he melds his body against mine, but also takes me by the hand, all the while kissing me, I follow his lead, until we're in his bedroom and he's lowering me onto his bed, and it's all I can do not to pull him down onto me – the wait is over. Whilst he searches for a condom in the bedside drawer, it's my turn to kiss his neck, his jaw, his chest, every part of him I can, and he matches my earlier moans, which is gratifying to hear.

He turns towards me and we tumble into each other's arms for the main course of the banquet I've been waiting to feast at since I set eyes upon him in the Molins' living room.

When we surface a couple of hours later, all I can think is '*dix points* to the boy next door.' We spend the rest of the evening back in bed, occasionally rising to snack and drink wine – it's not a bad way to spend a Saturday night. As we make love – and I think of it as that – for the third time, I realise I don't only like Jean-Luc a lot, I don't just fancy the pants off him; I've fallen for him, big time.

Chapter Thirty-one

Stars are twinkling in the inky blackness as it approaches midnight, but the only sound is of the occasional vehicle passing below Jean-Luc's townhouse.

'Don't go,' says Jean-Luc as I shimmy back into my underwear and dress.

'I have to,' I say, leaning forward and kissing him gently on those heavenly soft lips.

'Why?' He throws out his hands. 'It's Sunday tomorrow. The boulangerie isn't open. As of Monday, it will probably get more frenetic, what with solicitors, looking at courses, managing the boulangerie, sorting out your flat, your work. Take some time now, whilst you can.'

He has a point. There's no rush for me to be back at the Molins'. It would probably give Estelle, and Matthieu, if he returns, time on their own. Suzanne's back home with Patrick. And it took all of my willpower to drag myself out of bed, away from Jean-Luc, a few minutes ago.

'You could text the Molins,' he says, his voice and his eyes pleading. When I don't immediately answer, he continues. 'OK, can I put my cards on the table?'

My heart thuds in my chest as I nod.

'I want you to stay. I really, really don't want you to go. I don't want tonight to end. It has been perfect.'

My heart starts doing a tango in my chest. If I was on social media, my status would say 'Lia Abernethy is feeling excited'. If I were in a romcom right now, Jean-Luc couldn't have phrased things better or used more meaningful words. And that settles it for me; I'm going nowhere.

I crawl over the bed towards him and kiss him full on the lips. 'You can be very persuasive, you know.'

His lips lift at the corners. 'Don't forget to send that text,' he murmurs as he nuzzles into my neck and pulls me down beside him into the tangle of bedsheets I left only moments ago.

I shriek as with one fluid movement he pulls my dress over my head again, then I lose myself in the happy oblivion that is being with someone you're crazy about.

The pealing of church bells wakes me next morning. Even before I open my eyes, I remember where I am and who I'm with, the sensation of Jean-Luc's warm leg over mine an instant and welcome reminder. Straightaway, parts of me that were asleep are wide awake. I feel like someone in a desert, who spied an oasis, drank from it, and now can't stop. Nor can I stop the smile that spreads across my face.

'What are you smiling at?' Jean-Luc says.

I open my eyes. 'Drat! You weren't meant to see me smiling.'

His brow furrows up. 'You don't want me to see you smiling?'

I burst out laughing, struck by the stupidity of my comment. Naturally, he had no idea what I was smiling at; he wasn't inside my head. A naughty little voice tells me,

'No, just inside your body.'

'Of course I do. Morning,' I say, running my tongue surreptitiously over my teeth, hoping my breath isn't terrible. How can he look so incredible? His hair is a little mussed and he has a fetching five-o'clock shadow, and he looks like he has had lots of sex – well, that is the case, but he doesn't need to advertise it so much.

I bet I look a state. I run my tongue over my lips, not in a come-to-bed teasing way, in a 'do I have the bee-stung lips of someone who has been kissing solid for a day' way? I do.

Whatever. It doesn't faze him, and I can't look a complete hag as he bends to kiss me, lips closed. Clearly, he has the same concern about morning breath, although whether mine or his, it's hard to tell.

'Let's freshen up and then we can grab some breakfast,' he says.

I almost feel insulted he hasn't tried to ravage me, but to be honest, I'm probably being greedy. He is in his thirties; no doubt he needs to recover from last night's exertions.

He kisses my neck, then my shoulder again, then as I'm about to make him tumble back into bed entirely, for round four, he leaps up and heads to the bathroom. 'Back in a second.'

I feel his loss as soon as he closes the bathroom door. I mean, he probably only needs to use the toilet – actually, so do I now – but he has also made me super horny.

I try to calm my racing heart and my raging hormones. God, you'd think I was a teenage boy the way my body is responding, not a thirty-six-year-old woman.

Whilst I wait for Jean-Luc to return, I check my

messages. One from Jules, one from Suzanne and one from Freddy. Ugh. How to spoil my mood, although I suppose it may be with news of a potential moving-in date for the new owners.

I reply to Jules, both berating her for not telling me before about Josh, and applauding her for finally getting together with him. After replying to Suzanne, I turn my attention to Freddy's message.

WTAF? No, no, no. This can't be happening.

Lia. I've told the solicitor we're not accepting the offer. The couple got a bit arsey and wanted quite a lot of the furniture included in the sale price, and in particular my sofa. Since it's mainly my furniture, and I like it, I've said no, so it's back to the drawing board for now. I'll keep you posted. F.

I can't help it. I begin to cry. Hasn't Freddy taken enough away from me? I'm so tired of it all. Jean-Luc comes out of the bathroom at that moment, strides across the room and takes me in his arms, concern written all over his face, clearly no idea what the hell is wrong with me. I'm so devastated – and angry. Jean-Luc rubs my back as hot tears roll down my cheeks then plop onto my chest.

Jean-Luc holds my hands and his gorgeous chocolate brown eyes stare into mine. 'What is it, Lia? What's wrong?'

'Freddy,' I sputter. 'He's turned down the offer on the flat.' I stare at Jean-Luc. 'What am I going to do? I'll no longer have the money to invest in the boulangerie. How am I going to tell the Molins?'

Jean-Luc's jaw drops, and I can tell how gutted he is by my announcement. I can almost see the speech bubble in his head. "How does this affect us? Will you have to leave France?" but good guy that he is, he doesn't voice any of that; instead he says, 'What can I do to help?'

'Jean-Luc, you're doing enough by being here. Thank you.' Then as he embraces me, I burst into tears again, overcome by emotion and by yet another obstacle in my path. Damn you, Freddy!

Once I've cried myself hoarse and Jean-Luc has comforted me, at his insistence, I head for a shower whilst he makes me some tea. As the water sluices over me, I cry some more, unable to believe the position Freddy has put me in. And over a sofa! He made me sell my sofa, for God's sake, yet here he is refusing an offer on the flat because the buyer wants his. Double standards, much?

I flit between devastation and rage, and end up staying in the shower far longer than necessary so that when I exit I'm able to at least fake a little serenity.

As I towel dry my hair, I wonder if it's too early to call back home to have a showdown with Freddy. Then I almost slap myself at my stupidity. Why should I care about the time difference? Freddy has trodden all over my dreams with a single decision he made without consulting me. Yes, the sofa's his, but the flat is ours, legally, thus the decision to sell it or not, or accept an offer or not, should be a joint one, whether we're still a couple or not. It's so typical of him. Selfish git. I take some calming breaths as I pull a brush through my hair.

'Here you go,' says Jean-Luc, when I reach his kitchen. He pushes a cup of tea towards me. English Breakfast, I note. I can't help wondering if he bought that for me, or if he usually drinks it. He's the thoughtful sort, unlike my expletive of an ex.

'Thanks.' I take a sip then worry at a fingernail as various scenarios cycle round in my head on a loop. Is there a way for me not to tell the Molins? Is there a way for me not to have to give up my dream of a life in France and a career in the boulangerie? Can I raise the money another way? I wonder how much my redundancy will be. I shake my head. It won't be anywhere near enough.

'How are you doing?' Jean-Luc says.

I shake my head and blow out a breath. 'Honestly? I don't know. I don't even know where to begin. Just as I was beginning to get excited about everything, it's like my whole world has come crashing down.'

Jean-Luc nods gravely and reaches across the table to take my hand. 'Lia, whatever I can do to help, I'm here. All you have to do is ask.'

I give him a wry smile. 'Thanks. That means a lot to me. I just don't know where I'm going to go from here.' I pat his hand. 'But one thing's for sure, I'm going to have it out with Freddy.' When Jean-Luc's eyebrows raise, I say, 'And that's not something you need to see, because there will be blood spilled. His.'

Jean-Luc's eyes bulge out cartoon-style and I laugh.

'I need to go to the boulangerie and tell the Molins, but first I'm going to call Freddy.'

'I'll come to the Molins' with you for support, if you like.'

Why couldn't Freddy have been like Jean-Luc? Dependable, thoughtful, caring. Chalk and cheese doesn't even begin to describe the difference.

'You don't need to do that,' I say, hoping he insists, but not wanting to appear that needy. I've only known him a couple of weeks, snogged him a few times and had sex with him on one occasion, and now he's being hauled into all my drama.

'I know I don't,' he says gently, 'but I want to.'

I squeeze his hand until he pretend yelps in pain, making me laugh. So instead I kiss him softly on the lips. 'Thank you.'

As we drink our tea, hashing over potential routes out of my dilemma, I curse Freddy to the darkest corners of the universe.

'Freddy, it's me,' I say from the courtyard of Jean-Luc's townhouse.

'Lia, what the hell are you doing calling me at this time on a Sunday morning?'

All my patience deserts me. 'Freddy, are you fucking kidding me? I have more to worry about than your beauty sleep. Did it ever occur to you that by turning down the offer on the flat, you are royally shafting me?'

'Shafting you? What are you talking about? And how does that make it OK to call me at this godforsaken hour?'

'Freddy, I had plans for that money, plans that I can no longer commit to because of your selfish action. You didn't even discuss it with me. It's our flat. I own half of it, so I have as much right to decide who buys it and when as you do.'

'They wanted my Conrad sofa, Lia. You know how I feel about that sofa.'

'I do know how you feel about that fucking sofa, Freddy. Certainly more than you ever felt for me.'

'Oh, Lia, let's not get into that right now.' Freddy yawns and a rage boils up from deep inside me as I think of how well he has clearly slept, not having considered for a second how his self-absorbed decision will affect me or my life. The bottom line is he doesn't care, and he probably never did.

'Freddy, I couldn't give a shit about you and how much you did or didn't care about me. Right now, all I want you to do is get on that phone and tell the estate agent you've reconsidered, or better still, tell them you've spoken with the *other* owner of the flat, and you're now both happy to accept the offer, and ask them to go back to the buyer. I don't care if you have to beg them or the estate agent does, but get that offer back on the table.'

He sighs. 'Lia, that's not going to happen.'

Not that I had any vestiges of patience left, but my reserves, those held deep down in my soul somewhere for a rainy day, well, they're now depleted too.

'Freddy, I'm not asking you, I'm telling you. I am not having you scupper my chances of making a go of my new life.'

'New life? What are you talking about?' I can almost see his scrunched-up eyebrows and his pout as he tries to rationalise what I've said. Damn! I didn't mean for him to know anything more about my life, but he has put me in an untenable position.

'Not that it's any of your business, but I'm buying a property in France.'

'France!' he splutters. I wish I could see him; he sounds like he has choked on tea, but since I know I've woken him up, that doesn't seem likely.

'What do you know about living in France?'

'Eh, well, I did live here before.' Again, his self-absorption means it's difficult for Freddy to recall details about facets of people's lives in which he doesn't feature, even if it's someone he's in a relationship with.

'You did?'

'Freddy! It's not important. What *is* important is that I need those funds releasing so I can buy the property I'd settled on here, which I agreed to buy in the past few days after you told me about the firm offer we'd had.'

'But they want my sofa,' he whines.

'Freddy, if you mention that sofa one more time, I swear I won't be responsible for my actions.' I'm breathing heavily now, but I can't help it. Can't he see how unreasonable he's being?

'Lia, I'll be in touch when we have another offer. Now I'm going back to sleep.'

It takes me a full ten seconds to realise he has hung up. Oh my God, I can't believe it. Self-centred, arrogant, narcissistic… I dissolve in a pool of tears.

There really is no hope. I would never have put forth my case to the Molins if we hadn't received a firm offer on the flat. Sure, the flat will sell in the future, but it may not sell in time for the Molins, and they have enough stress to deal with as it is, without wondering if my flat will sell and I can release capital to them.

No. I need to face facts. I have no choice but to tell the Molins our partnership is over before it's begun.

Chapter Thirty-two

The sun arcs high above us by the time we're ready to go and face the Molins and deliver the fateful news. Apart from Jean-Luc, it's the only sunshine in my life right now. How can I add to this family's problems? I'm going to pile on the stress further when I tell them this, plus make them look foolish to their solicitor, and I don't relish it one bit.

Although I'm gutted for myself and the fact my dream has been shattered, I'm heartsick at the thought of bringing this bombshell to their door. Just when they thought their money woes were over, I've not only raised their hopes, but shot them to hell.

As we approach the boulangerie, I visibly slow my steps, wanting to delay the inevitable as long as possible. But Jean-Luc guides me gently by the hand towards the side entrance.

I didn't call ahead as I couldn't trust my voice not to quiver and give me away. The smell of something tomato-based greets me as I open the door. Estelle must be cooking; Matthieu spends so much time in the bakery baking that Estelle does the lion's share of the cooking, even though he's a pretty good cook too.

'Lia!' Estelle comes towards me and envelops me in a hug. 'And Jean-Luc.' She gives me a sly wink out of his line of sight as she kisses him on both cheeks.

'How are René and Alexine?' I ask. By now it has become the common opener.

She raises her eyes to the ceiling. 'He had another minor relapse last night, but he's stable, for the moment.'

My heart drops through the floor. How can I tell her now and add to her worries?

'And what about Matthieu's mother?'

'No change yet.'

Anxiety twists in my gut as Estelle says, 'Lia, are you all right? You've gone quite pale.' She steadies me with a hand as I sink to the chair she holds out with her other hand.

Tears threaten behind my eyes and I glance at Jean-Luc, who gives me a sad smile then lifts his chin, urging me on.

'Estelle, is Matthieu here?'

She shakes her head. 'No, he hasn't returned from his parents' yet. Suzanne will be here soon, though. Why do you ask?'

My eyes meet hers then Jean-Luc's again. I can't wait. There's no possible way she'll allow me to wait; I'll only worry her more. Ha! As if that's possible.

I exhale then say, 'Estelle, I'm so sorry, but I'm no longer in a position to buy into the boulangerie. At least not right now.'

It takes a second for her to register what I'm saying, then a multitude of expressions flits across her face – incomprehension, dismay, disbelief, finally settling on what I can only imagine is dread, or perhaps fear, for the future – before she crumples, this time Jean-Luc steadying her as she eases herself into the chair opposite me.

'But what are you saying, Lia? Have you changed your mind?'

'No.' I shake my head emphatically. 'Not one bit.' I'm close to tears as I recount the whole sorry tale and Freddy's pig-headedness.

Estelle's shoulders begin to heave and I stand up and go round the table to her. I have never felt so awful in my life. I raised this family's expectations, this family which practically adopted me as one of their own. I have a physical pain in my sternum as if someone has punched me – hard. Well, Freddy *has* gut-punched me.

'Estelle, I'm so sorry. I'm wracking my brains trying to think of another way to get the funds in place, but so far, I haven't come up with anything that would raise anything near the amount needed.'

Jean-Luc places two cups of tea in front of us – clearly the English tradition of tea solving all problems works in France too – just as Suzanne breezes into the kitchen.

'*Salut, les filles. Ca—*' she calls, then stops mid-sentence when she takes in the scene.

'*Maman? Qu'est-ce qu'il y a?*' She rushes to her mother's side as I explain what has transpired and Jean-Luc fetches another cup of tea.

After listening to everything, and inserting a few choice comments, including 'entitled prick' – I couldn't agree more – Suzanne looks equally as dejected as her mum, whose hand she has gripped and whose shoulder she has been rubbing the whole way through my story. She reassures Estelle. '*Maman*, it will be OK. We'll think of something. We have to.'

Then she stands and walks back and forth, muttering to herself. She opens the external door to the courtyard, steps out and closes it behind her. I watch, casting the occasional glance at Jean-Luc as she paces the courtyard, still muttering under her breath. Maybe she's working out a hundred ways to kill Freddy. I can probably add a few suggestions of my own. We could join forces. Or, more likely, she's trying to come up with solutions. She clearly thinks better on her own, which is why she has sought solitude.

Finally, she re-enters the kitchen, almost slamming the door. 'No! I refuse to believe we're beaten. There must be something we can do.' She eyes me almost mutinously. 'We're not giving up.'

My spirits raise then plummet. Whilst I admire her resilience, I simply don't see how we can raise that sort of money. There's no way whatever my redundancy package is, that it'll be enough. I still need to find out how much that is likely to be, though. And I can't find that out until at least tomorrow when the office opens again after the weekend.

'Do you think we should call *Papa*?' Estelle asks Suzanne. In an instant, their roles have reversed, the matriarch seeking much-needed advice from the daughter.

'No, it's time enough when he gets back tonight; there's nothing he can do on a Sunday anyway. He'll have to call Bernard in the morning. In the meantime, I suggest we put our heads together and try to figure a way out of this mess.'

'Agreed,' says Estelle firmly. 'But first, lunch. Who wants to help me dish up? We'll work better once we have some food inside us.'

I'm not sure about that. The thought of eating right now makes me want to throw up, but Estelle is resolved, and given that I'm to blame for their despair – well, Freddy is, but I'm the one who offered to go into partnership with them – I decide to go along with her suggestion and not make waves. Let's hope inspiration strikes.

Two hours later, after lunch and much wrangling and tossing around of ideas, and Estelle doing calculations and me with my internet banking app open on my laptop, and checking law on garden leave and on redundancy packages, and how much I'm likely to get, I stand up and say, 'I need some air. Perhaps some time away from the figures will help. Does anyone want to come for a walk?' Really, I want to be alone, but I brought Jean-Luc with me, so I can't exactly ditch him now, can I? However, like Suzanne, I do my best thinking when alone.

Suzanne looks at Estelle, who shakes her head.

'I'm going to keep poring over these figures with Suzanne until they give me better results,' says Estelle. 'There must be something we can do.'

'OK. Well, I won't be too long, maybe an hour or so.' I bend to kiss them both on the cheeks, then Jean-Luc and I head out.

Once we've closed the door and are back out in the street, I sigh and turn to him. 'It's hopeless, and now I have them almost demented going over figures they'd already gone over before they decided they needed to sell the boulangerie in the first place.'

Tears brim in my eyes and I blink them away. Now is not the time for weakness. I need to get through the pity stage and onward to the sort-this-problem-out phase.

Jean-Luc takes my arm. 'Let's walk. Sometimes ideas appear when we least expect them to.'

I raise my eyebrows and hope he's right.

As we saunter along the dusty streets of Chalets, the sky darkens and I pray I haven't been hasty in suggesting a walk to clear our heads. The last thing I need right now is to get caught in a thunderstorm, not with the internal one I have going on.

We walk in silence for a time, then Jean-Luc says, 'What will you do if you can't buy the boulangerie?'

I turn to him and stop for a second, then throw up my hands. 'I honestly don't know. It seemed like the answer to everyone's problems, mine included. I loved my job as a graphic designer, but the pressure the past couple of years has been sucking the joy out of it. This opportunity with the boulangerie felt so right. I had the possibility to pursue something completely different, but that's looking less likely by the second.'

'Will you still think of staying in France if you can't buy into the boulangerie?' His voice is soft and I gaze up at him to see an earnestness, a longing in his eyes. Not a sexual longing – we've already addressed that part – but something more. Doesn't he want me to leave? Hell, I don't want to leave, but in all of this … fiasco, I haven't even had time to think what it might mean for my and Jean-Luc's fledgling relationship.

I hesitate then say, 'I don't know. I haven't got that far in my train of thought.'

We reach the Canal du Midi and follow the path. Jean-Luc's trying to lift my spirits to make me laugh when a voice cuts through my laughter.

'Hi, Lia.'

I look up to see Théo in front of me, and Gloire is beside him. Oh my God. Am I hallucinating? Could things get any worse?

'Jean-Luc.' Théo says his name but barely glances at him, his eyes fully on mine. However, I can't help it; my traitorous eyes slide over to Gloire. Is she Théo's newest girlfriend or acquaintance or whatever? Gloire, who gave me such a hard time over Jean-Luc.

No, I don't get that vibe from them, and also she's glaring at me the way someone might if they'd won second place in a competition, where first place was a week in Hawaii and second place was a set of power tools. She reminds me a bit of the Tasmanian Devil, from the cartoons, all snarls and spikiness.

'Théo,' I say, not offering anything else.

'Good to see you, Gloire,' Jean-Luc, always polite, says, but Gloire doesn't look particularly mollified. 'But we really must be going. We have a lot to do,' he continues, and I could kiss him. The last thing I wanted was to make small talk with those two.

We pass them on the canal-side and for one worrying moment, I fear Gloire is about to pitch me into the canal.

Jean-Luc's grip on my fingers tightens as we walk away from them, without glancing back, although I would bet the whole of my upcoming settlement that they are staring at us, as I can feel the daggers in my back.

'Well, that was uncomfortable,' I say once we're out of earshot.

Jean-Luc sighs and gives me a tight smile. 'Yes, on so many levels.'

'Do you mind me asking you something?'

He purses his lips. 'No, not at all.'

'What happened between you and Théo? The animosity between you is as positively charged as two protons.'

He chuckles. 'That's pretty accurate. It's no secret we don't get on, and we haven't done for a long time. We stopped being friends after what happened with Suzanne.' He stops and looks at me intently. 'You know about Suzanne?'

I nod. 'Yeah, she told me, but only recently and only after I'd been out with him a couple of times. Of course, she didn't know I'd been out with him – until then.'

Jean-Luc gives a sad smile. 'Life can be complicated.'

'Indeed.' It's my turn to smile as I think of how complicated things have been since I got here.

'But there were other incidents too, where he was unnecessarily cruel to those less fortunate or well off than himself, where he didn't allow someone to go to an event with our group because they didn't have parents with the right connections or jobs. People whose parents didn't have their own businesses. He looked down upon them.'

'He certainly rates appearances very highly,' I agree.

'Then there were numerous other, more minor incidences, where his behaviour was … how can I put this? Less than ideal?'

'Yes, I'm beginning to build up a bit of a picture of the real Théo, from my own experiences, what Suzanne said and now you. It's not a flattering portrait.'

'He wasn't always like that, and I don't know what changed him, but I couldn't forgive what he did to Suzanne. Suzanne and I have been friends since … well, since I can remember.'

'To me your relationship comes across like that of brother and sister.'

He nods. 'That's exactly it. We all grew up like family together, and Estelle and Matthieu have always been like an extension of my own.'

'So, do you think Gloire is Théo's newest love interest?' I ask, my nosiness getting the better of me.

Jean-Luc laughs. 'I hope not.' When my eyebrows shoot into my hairline, he slips his hand in mine once more and goes on. 'Théo is Gloire's cousin. No, much though I hate to say it, Gloire still holds a torch for me, despite me telling her we will never be together again. Never,' he says emphatically.

'I see. Well, that explains the doubly uncomfortable situation back there. To let Théo down gently, I told him I had no time for a "friendship", given everything going on with the Molins, and I imagine he probably saw us holding hands, and perhaps Gloire did too. We better hope they don't murder us in our sleep!'

Jean-Luc laughs. 'Yes, they can both be a little intense.'

I pause but Jean-Luc sees me hesitate and prods me. 'What? What is it?'

I shake my head. 'Nothing important. Funny story, actually. I met Gloire outside the church last Sunday and she warned me to stay away from you. She was really quite threatening.'

Jean-Luc's mouth falls open. 'You're kidding me! Oh my God, Lia. I'm so sorry.' He entwines his fingers more with mine and strokes the back of my hand.

'What do you have to be sorry for? It wasn't you who threatened me.'

'No, but if I hadn't had a delusional ex-girlfriend, you wouldn't have been threatened.' He pauses and shakes his head. 'I can't believe she did that. She has definitely reached a new low.'

I can't argue with him there; she's truly deluded. Poor

Jean-Luc that he has to put up with her. It does beg the question, though: why was he going out with her in the first place? But I'm not brave enough to ask him that. I guess we all make mistakes.

Chapter Thirty-three

Next morning, I'm in the boulangerie, on tenterhooks, waiting to hear the update from the solicitor. When Jean-Luc and I went our separate ways on our return from the canal yesterday, Matthieu arrived not long after and he, Estelle, Suzanne and I talked long into the night. The crux of the matter is we need to see what the solicitor says. Currently, I can't see any way I can invest significantly enough in the boulangerie for my contribution to have the desired impact and allow the Molins to release funds from the boulangerie to help them. However, I also emailed my office to see if they have news on my remuneration package yet – and when I'm likely to get it. Hopefully, they'll get back to me later today.

Suzanne gave me some time this morning in the bakery to knead some dough and make a batch of croissants, for our own consumption, as she could tell I was as tense as an overly stretched elastic band.

As I serve the customers, still with a smile but a little on autopilot, I wonder how René and Matthieu's mother are doing. This is, ultimately, all to help them. It will become a large part of Estelle and Matthieu's daily routine to be in Saint-Sauvy and Verfeil, helping with their parents. I can only pray nothing more happens to Alexine or Matthieu's father.

I texted Jean-Luc this morning to fill him in on what I discussed with the Molins last night. He'd suggested I come over, but I needed to be focused this morning, as well as to have a good night's sleep. Now, however, I'm regretting not having spent time with him. Who knows how much more time I have in France? I can't help feeling a bit low this morning.

At eleven o'clock, when Matthieu returns to the boulangerie, a wave of foreboding washes over me. His smile and greeting are strained, and the muscles in his face are taut. Suzanne and Estelle have already left for the hospitals. Poor Suzanne. She has barely seen Patrick these past two weeks and I can't imagine it getting any easier.

Matthieu clears his throat, signalling he's standing behind me in the living room. I pop my head through the beaded curtain and he says, 'Why don't you come in for a second whilst it's quiet?'

We both know the doorbell will jangle if anyone comes, so I sit opposite him, my heart racing.

'Lia.' Matthieu nods at me. 'I've spoken to the solicitor and he thinks he may have an interested party – one who'll be happy to keep the boulangerie as a going concern.'

My mouth falls open automatically before I can school my response. The boulangerie, Jean-Luc, the Canal du Midi, the neighbourhood of Chalets, Place du Capitole, they all fight for position in my mind in that one second.

'Matthieu, that's great,' I say finally. 'At least you'll still have the funds you need.'

He gives a sad smile. 'I'm so sorry. I was so excited by your plan and in the possibility of keeping Suzanne on as staff and in the potential partnership, but I have to consider what the family needs, and unfortunately that's capital, and quickly.'

His shoulders are hunched and the air of defeat encircles him so completely it makes my heart ache. This big, gentle giant of a man only wants to look after his family, his whole family, and here he is, concerned he's quashing the pipe dream I only came up with a little over a week ago.

I lean forward and place my hand over his. 'Matthieu, you're doing the right thing.'

His eyes meet mine. 'I hope so, Lia. I really do, and I'm so sorry.'

'Matthieu,' I say, my eyes holding his, a forceful note in my voice. 'You have nothing to be sorry for. Nothing. My ex-boyfriend, on the other hand…'

We both laugh but there's no mirth in it.

'I had better call Estelle. She was waiting to hear from me.'

The doorbell jangles at the same moment and I smile and say, 'That's my cue,' although I can't help wondering for how much longer, given the news Matthieu has just broken.

As I serve the next run of customers, I flip between elation that the Molins' money problems are solved and despair that I won't be part of the boulangerie after all and that my future in France is more or less decided. How can I stay now I have no prospects here? Much as I want to be with Jean-Luc, my in-built self-preservation system won't let me stay in the country solely because of a man. The boulangerie gave me a bigger reason to stay, and now I don't have that. Plus, since the flat sale fell through, he hasn't asked me to stay or given any indication that's what he'd like to happen. Would I stay if he asked? Tough one.

But the instant a negative, depressed thought enters my mind, a happy, delighted one replaces it. I'm elated that the boulangerie will be kept a boulangerie, since that was one of the crucial points for the Molins. As it has been in the family for such a long time, they'd decided they wouldn't sell to anyone who didn't share the vision of keeping the business as a boulangerie, serving the neighbourhood of Chalets. At least their plans are coming to fruition, and that's all that matters. My wants weren't anywhere near as important as their needs, so I can only be happy that at least their needs have been met.

I haven't been able to face telling Jean-Luc, so when he comes in a little before lunchtime to invite me to the *fromagerie* for lunch, I almost feel like I'm going to the Last Supper. Or one of the last lunches. The sensation of dread in my stomach intensifies.

'Hey, what's up?' he says.

I sigh then look into his eyes. 'Matthieu's had another offer.'

'What?' Jean-Luc's mouth falls open and my eyes focus on the tiny chip on his tooth, which I find adorable. He's almost but not quite perfect, which makes him perfect to me and for me.

'He spoke to Bernard this morning. He's had an offer from someone who's happy to keep the boulangerie as a going concern. I can't expect them to turn that down. Keeping the boulangerie going and serving the community was one of his key requirements.'

'Always thinking of everyone else. That's Matthieu,' Jean-Luc says.

I nod, agreeing. 'I guess the finality of it all sent off

some message to my synapses and they stopped firing.'

He squeezes my fingers, as if understanding how devastating this is for me.

'I'd really begun to think I could stay here.' Tears plip down my face as the reality hits me with the force of a high-speed train hitting a crash barrier head on.

'I'm so sorry, Lia.'

When I look up, my own sadness is reflected in the dark pools of Jean-Luc's eyes.

I squeeze his fingers back. 'So am I.'

We each keep looking at the other, and if I could hazard a guess, I'd bet my redundancy package on us both not only thinking of the lost opportunity of the boulangerie venture. Where do we go from here?

In the evening, Matthieu tells Suzanne, who has returned from seeing Alexine. I'm sitting out in the courtyard to give them some privacy and to try to figure out what to do with my life. I'm coming to the conclusion that I'll stay for as long as the Molins need me to help out, then I'll have to go home, at least to make some choices about my future. If I'd been buying into the boulangerie, it'd have been different, but as things stand, I don't see any other option.

Suzanne's raised voice glides out through the open window. 'You can't do this, *Papa*. We'll think of something else. Just give us a little more time. Maybe Lia will get a different buyer.'

My heart almost tears in two. Yes, my dream of an idyllic life in France has come to an end, but for Suzanne the fear of losing her job, her income, her whole way of life is on the line. What if the new owner doesn't need staff?

Plus, how would Suzanne react to a new boss, after living here all her life?

Matthieu murmurs something that I don't quite catch, then the door to the courtyard slams open and I jump back in my chair as Suzanne storms out, tears cascading down her face. She paces up and down for a moment, muttering '*Merde,*' '*Putain*' and various other obscenities in French that I can't totally make out. I'm not even sure she realises I'm here. Then she stops, looks at me, her eyes full of sorrow and despair. She scrapes out a chair and plonks herself down on it.

'Sorry.' She swipes away her tears.

I rest a hand on her arm. 'Don't be. It's me who should be sorry.'

She shakes her head vehemently. 'No. It was a good idea, Lia. And it could have worked. Except…'

'…for Freddy.' Anger bubbles up within me again. Not that he would care, but he hasn't just ruined my future, but the lives of all the Molins too. Yes, they'll be financially free once they receive the funds, but they'll have to entirely give up the business they worked so hard to build, which they intended no doubt to pass to Suzanne when they retired, probably with some payments to her siblings. Plus, they'll lose their home, where they brought up their children, and they'll possibly lose their community, as who knows if they'll be able to find another property in Chalets, or one that's suitable?

As Suzanne continues to vent, I once again curse the day I met Freddy McKenzie.

Chapter Thirty-four

The email finally arrives from Eric, informing me of the amount of my redundancy. It's a decent package and will see me all right for a good while, but it's not enough to allow me to invest in the boulangerie. That was my last shred of hope. Last-chance saloon, if you will.

I wear my bright and cheery mask for the customers, but inside it's as if my heart has been hollowed out with a spoon.

Suzanne and I talked way after midnight, about what she would do for work, where her parents would live – they'll need to buy something much smaller, but potentially equidistant from their parents. Unfortunately, neither of their parents' homes have enough space for them to move in long term, although quite frankly who would want that? We all value our own space.

Today, Suzanne's in the living room, tapping away at her laptop, updating her CV and checking out situations vacant. We don't know how quickly the sale will go through. Matthieu has another meeting with his solicitor late this afternoon, when he returns from the hospital. Not even Jean-Luc's impromptu appearance in the boulangerie this morning with a cheese selection for Suzanne and me for lunch, or his multiple texts last night after we went our separate ways, has alleviated this feeling of dread inside me. Knowing soon I'll have to return to Scotland and leave behind Jean-Luc is also adding to my stress and devastation. It seems so unfair. I know I'd sworn off men once Freddy and I split – who doesn't in the moment? – but finding someone as amazing, kind, funny, sweet and bloody well gorgeous as Jean-Luc so soon after having my boyfriend cheat on me and making me lose all faith in men, only to then have the possibility of happiness whipped away from me is too much to bear.

A message pops up. Jules. *Morning! How is my favourite boulangerie owner-to-be?*

God, so much has happened since Friday when I told her I was buying into the boulangerie. I don't even know where to begin with the update. She'll be furious with Freddy, that's for sure. She'll probably offer to go round and rip his head off. And I'd be sorely tempted to accept.

With shaking hands, I type back. *Not going ahead. Can't go into it right now. Will call later. Hope all well with you x*

Immediately, I see her typing. *WTAF? Are you OK?*

She won't give up until I tell her something, so I reply, *No, but I will be. Freddy didn't accept the offer on the flat x*

Her response arrives: three angry face emojis. I couldn't have put it better myself.

Over lunch with Suzanne – the cheese Jean-Luc brought was incredible – she shows me some of the apartments she has found for her parents. Estelle couldn't bring herself to look, not yet, at least. So she'd tasked Suzanne, who is also better on a computer, with doing some research.

'Look at this,' says Suzanne. 'The properties cost double for half the space we have here.' She sighs. 'One of the biggest problems we have is because we can't separate the boulangerie and our home. They need to be sold together since they're joined. If they weren't joined, we'd be able to get so much more for each of them.'

I nod, as I have no expertise in this area, and certainly not in France, but her rationale makes sense.

'What about the job hunting?' I say, half afraid to ask, but knowing I need to.

'Don't even get me started. There's hardly anything and what *is* available is for entry-level bakers, not for someone with my level of expertise, so as you can imagine the salary is peanuts.'

That's what I'd feared.

'I simply can't believe this won't be my future. All my life I've thought that when *Maman* and *Papa* retired, I'd take over, and then if I have kids one day, they would take over after me.'

I shoot her a rueful look and once again guilt overwhelms me. I know it's not my fault, but I got their hopes up, only to dash them again.

It's hard to describe the next few days. They passed so quickly and in a whirl of activity. When Matthieu returned on Monday night, after seeing Bernard, it was pretty much a done deal, only a few 'i's to dot and 't's to cross. Then the new routine kicked in: hospital visiting for the four Molins, with Suzanne also house hunting for her parents, job hunting for herself, as well as alternating shifts with her father in the bakery preparing the bread and pastries. I split my time between the boulangerie during the day – effectively running it as I had been for the previous days – and Jean-Luc's townhouse and the Molins' at night.

I'd had a few messages from home: emails from work regarding my final termination and payment dates; Jules checking in, even one from my neighbour, Josh, but in the recesses of my brain, I knew I'd need to start making plans for going home. I just wasn't ready. I'm still not.

'Matthieu, there you are!' I say as he breezes into the boulangerie on Friday. Then I realise he hasn't breezed in, but stormed in. His face is as black as a gathering of storm clouds.

'Lia,' he says, his tone clipped. He looks a man on a mission and I, for one, don't want to get in his path. I've never seen him like this. I could quite easily believe he could rip an oak tree out of its roots with one hand, given the anger emanating from him.

'Are you OK?' I ask. Stupid question, I know, but I have to say something.

He turns to me. 'No, I am most definitely not all right.'

Well, that's pretty definitive.

'Can I help?' I ask, fully expecting not to be able to, but feeling I should offer assistance.

Matthieu's eyes soften and he deflates in front of me. 'I'm sorry, Lia. I'm just heartsick of all this … *merde*.'

I pat his shoulder. 'Tell me, but you may have to be more specific.'

He gives a wry smile. 'True. So, the latest is, the "buyer" doesn't want to keep La Boulangerie au Coin de la Rue as a boulangerie.'

'But—'

He holds up a finger and I let him go on. 'Yes, I know. Bernard told me they agreed to maintain the use, but they've apparently already applied for planning permission for change of use.'

'But that's outrageous,' I cry.

'I know. Hence, I'm not very happy.' Understatement. His eyes crinkle at the corners with dry amusement.

'What are you going to do?'

His face sags. 'I don't know. All I do know is I need to come up with a plan before Estelle and Suzanne get back, as I feel I've already let them down too much.'

'Oh, Matthieu, you haven't let them down at all. Please don't think that.' I rub his arm reassuringly. 'I know *they* don't think that.'

'Thanks, Lia.' He shakes his head. 'There has been a boulangerie here for fifty-two years. I don't want to deprive the community of that, but likewise I need to think of the family.'

'I know. Did your solicitor tell you why the buyer originally said they would maintain the use then changed their mind?'

He purses his lips. 'No, but I would bet it was intended all along, which now makes me not want to sell to whoever it is.'

I screw up my face. 'So you still don't know who the buyer is?'

'Nope. And I don't like that one bit.'

I exhale slowly and say, 'I wouldn't either. Sounds very mysterious and more than a little shady.'

Matthieu's lips set in a firm line. 'My thoughts exactly. Right, I need to think about what to do next. This calls for a cognac.'

My eyes widen. It's a bit early in the day.

'Will you join me?'

I glance back at the boulangerie, mindful of the fact customers may come in and I may have to serve them with alcohol-infused breath. As if sensing my hesitation, Matthieu nudges my elbow and says, 'Lia, live a little. It looks like it won't be ours for much longer anyway.'

Fair point. 'Sure.'

'Excellent. Two large cognacs coming up.'

By the time Estelle returns later, Suzanne having gone to see Patrick for a bit, it's almost time for the boulangerie to close. As if its patrons had sensed we needed some discussion time, it was mainly devoid of customers in the latter part of the afternoon.

Jean-Luc also reported less footfall when he came in to see how things were going a couple of hours ago, and joined us for a cognac too. We had quite the little party. Or rather, Matthieu did. Jean-Luc and I stuck to a cognac apiece, with me keeping one ear out for activity from the boulangerie and Jean-Luc putting an 'I'm in the boulangerie. Find me there' sign on the *fromagerie*.

We'd listened to Matthieu's woes and Jean-Luc had been appalled at the buyer's behaviour, wondering who would be so duplicitous and agreeing it left a bad taste.

'Couldn't you play for time?' Jean-Luc had asked, which had Matthieu eyeing him thoughtfully.

'You might have hit on something there. Good man!' Matthieu had slapped him on the arm in thanks.

When I enter the kitchen after closing the boulangerie,

Estelle has her head in her hands and Matthieu is standing behind her, rubbing her shoulders. He raises his eyes to mine and says, 'Hi, Lia. I've told Estelle about the change of use.'

Estelle lifts her red-rimmed eyes from the table and sighs. 'Everything OK with the boulangerie today, Lia?'

I nod, worried she hasn't responded to what Matthieu said. He glances at me, a look of alarm on his face.

'So, Matthieu, do you think Jean-Luc's idea of trying to stall for time could work? You could have Bernard tell the buyer you need time to think it over, or you could play up the community angle, talk of the history of the boulangerie here in Chalets, that sort of thing.'

Matthieu chews his lip as he mulls this over. 'It's certainly worth a try. Hell, anything's worth a try at this point.'

'Have you told Suzanne yet?'

He blows out a breath. 'No, that can wait for tomorrow. I'll be here tonight as Sarah is at my father's.'

I can't help thinking how complicated the logistics are for everyone. It's hard enough with them all running the business and visiting two parents in hospital, whilst trying to care for two other parents in different regions from each other, but Sarah has three school-age children. The upheaval must be unsettling for them too. What they all need is a good dose of stability and certainty, and this offer doesn't provide that. It also comes with an unhealthy helping of unease.

Later, as we head off to bed for the night, I pray tomorrow brings good news.

Chapter Thirty-five

Early on Saturday morning, Matthieu trundles off to meet his solicitor to see if he can delay the date by which he has to accept the offer. Whether this is to allow time for us to raise funds, him to find another buyer who won't change the use, or a bit of both remains to be seen.

Since I don't know how much longer I'll be able to stay in Toulouse once things move forward, I want to make the most of my time here, so Jean-Luc and I have agreed to go to the *Jardin des Plantes* – Toulouse's botanic gardens – once our shops close.

Suzanne returns mid-morning and helps me for the last few hours in the boulangerie whilst Estelle catches up on some paperwork. Suzanne spent the night at home with Patrick, but Matthieu asked her to be home earlier than initially thought so he could speak to her, presumably about the offer now stating change of use was likely.

When she comes in, I don't think she knows about the offer dilemma and I'm a little wrong-footed, having this knowledge she's not privy to, so I dodge the topic as much as I can, until I breathe a sigh of relief when Matthieu arrives.

Soon after, her shout and a stream of swear words reaches my ears from the living room. I'm glad the boulangerie is empty of customers.

When Suzanne ducks her head into the boulangerie through the curtain and says, 'Come here a moment,' she has a look on her face like she's about to knock hell out of me, or out of someone, at least. She's very scary when she's like that.

'I believe you know some of this.' She scowls at me. Oops. What did I do?

I nod.

She scowls again. 'You should have told me.' She turns to her father, '*Papa*, I know Lia is almost like family, but I *am* family and this boulangerie is *my* livelihood. Please, in future, don't leave anything out or make me wait to hear any piece of news about it.'

Matthieu hangs his head then raises sad eyes towards Estelle before finally looking at his daughter. 'Sorry, Suzanne.' He turns to me. 'Lia, I think you should sit down. There are a few things you need to know.'

Now I'm intrigued and a little puzzled. I do as I'm bid and wait for Matthieu to elaborate.

'I spoke to my solicitor.' His glance moves between me, Suzanne and Estelle. 'I told him I want to hold out for another offer, as I'm not happy about the change of use, and I thought I was quite clear about that in our initial conversations. The legacy my family has here means a lot to me, plus I don't want Jean-Luc or any of our other neighbours to have just anyone next to them – imagine, they could have a tattoo parlour or a pawnshop. I would never be able to forgive myself. Besides, I want the people of Chalets to always have a reputable boulangerie they can come to.'

I dip my head in acknowledgement before Matthieu continues.

He takes a deep breath as if readying himself to deliver some unwelcome news. To be fair, what could be more unwelcome than what has already happened?

'Bernard has told me the change of use they've applied for is to turn it into a hairdressing salon.'

'What?' My eyes scrunch up in incredulity. The boulangerie and apartments don't lend themselves particularly well to that type of use. 'Surely there are other more suitable places.'

Matthieu rolls his eyes heavenwards. 'You'd think so, wouldn't you? But Bernard was very specific. In fact, so specific, he also told me they've asked for it to have future potential to house a nail bar and beauty salon too.'

I can see the attraction for the buyer. There isn't one in the immediate vicinity. The nearest I spied was much closer to Place du Capitole, but it still makes little sense.

'And who is the buyer?'

Matthieu glances at Estelle as he clasps his hands together, circling his thumbs. 'Well, that's the interesting thing.'

'Oh?'

'Yes, the mysterious buyer, or should I say buyers, is maybe not quite as mysterious as they think.'

My brows knit and Matthieu goes on. 'Bernard was able to tell me the hairdressing salon will be managed by a certain Mireille Dubois.'

I shake my head. 'Should I know who that is?'

'Dubois?' says Suzanne. 'Mireille Dubois as in Gloire's best friend?'

When Matthieu nods, my eyebrows must disappear into my hairline. 'Gloire, as in, Jean-Luc's ex?'

'The very same,' Estelle says, her lips set in a thin line.

'But why all the secrecy then and why all the lies?' I ask, my brow creased in confusion.

'That's what I'd like to know.' Matthieu stands up and pours himself a glass of wine then gestures to everyone else. The other two accept whilst I wag a finger no. It's not midday yet and the boulangerie is still open.

'And that's not the best part. Ha!' He downs half of the glass's contents in one go. 'Bernard had to leave the room unexpectedly for a moment as someone kept banging at his door and his receptionist doesn't work Saturday morning. I happened to notice–' he eyes us a little sheepishly '–some paperwork on his desk that mentioned Mireille, Gloire and…'

I urge him on with a nod.

'Théo Martin.'

'Théo?' I say, unable to utter more than that single word.

Matthieu nods. 'Yes. I know the way I behaved isn't who I am, but I need to protect my family.' He turns to each of them and stands straighter and taller. 'And my neighbours.'

Again, I wait when he pauses then downs the other half of the wine. We may need to have a word with him about his alcohol intake soon.

'So I did what I've seen them do in the spy movies … I photographed the paperwork before Bernard came back.'

Estelle covers her mouth with a hand. Looks like she didn't know that, although a quick glance at Suzanne confirms *she* did, and wholeheartedly approves of her father's genius. Honestly, I'm impressed too. He thought on his feet.

'What did you find out?'

Matthieu turns three sheets of paper towards me. 'I printed them off from my email when I got back,' he says, clearly proud he has learned a new skill, but whether that's the espionage or the printing isn't initially apparent.

I glance over the legal documents. My French isn't refined enough to grasp all the legalese, but essentially, Théo is putting up the majority of the money with the aim of being a sleeping partner in a hairdressing business that Mireille and Gloire intend to set up – here in Chalets. Here, at what would be the boulangerie's old premises. The question is why. I mean, I don't think my recent exploits with Théo have anything to do with it, I'm not that self-absorbed, but the timing is a bit suspect.

Could it be because of what happened with Suzanne? Is he rejoicing in being able to drive in the knife just that little bit more? Surely not. Surely he's not that malicious. Yet, from what others have told me – people I trust – the Théo I knew was a façade, a construct, and he bears quite the grudge, as well as hating to lose.

But their families go back decades, the grandparents, all living in the same village of Saint-Sauvy. God, I hope news of this doesn't get back to Alexine and René. That's all the family needs – more stress, more pressure.

I don't quite know what to do with this information, but I do know I want Jean-Luc's take on it, so I ask, 'Matthieu, I'm honestly blindsided by this. I'm guessing you are too. I've arranged to meet Jean-Luc when the *fromagerie* closes and go to the *Jardin des Plantes*. Would you be OK with me speaking to him about this? I'm hoping he can shed some light on it or give us some advice, and quite frankly, the more we can understand what's going on, from whichever source, the better.'

Matthieu nods. 'Of course. For now, all I can tell you is I have asked for two months to consider the revised proposal.'

I hear my own sharp intake of breath. 'And you think Théo will go for that?' I'm hazarding a guess Théo is the driving force behind this operation, although I can't quite tell if it's purely that he has good business sense, saw an opportunity and didn't want it to pass him by, or if he's being manipulative and wants to get his own back for some perceived slight or a long-standing feud.

'I don't know, but I have the feeling whatever I ask for, I won't get. I reckon we need a month as a minimum. I'll know more on Monday once Bernard has had a chance to speak to "the buyer".'

No mystery which of the three he'll be talking to. Nobody rocks confidence like Théo.

When the boulangerie door jangles, I rush off to serve the customer, leaving the others to ruminate over the latest twist in the tale.

Chapter Thirty-six

'You're kidding me!' Jean-Luc looks horrified as he stops and takes me by the arms. 'Gloire? And Théo?'

'Yep.'

We stand there in the *Jardin des Plantes*, among all the families and young couples, our faces mirroring the dismay and disbelief on the other's.

For a moment, Jean-Luc can't even speak. He shakes his head as if to clear it, or as if to wake himself from a bad dream, but it's real; this is happening. Gloire, Mireille and Théo could be how and why Estelle and Matthieu lose their business and their home, and Suzanne her livelihood. I don't even add me to the list, although I am narked about me too.

We're standing in front of the largest of the fountains, Wallace, I think it's called, as toddlers waddle in front of their parents, connected by a set of reins; dogs are on model behaviour, clipped on leads; and a group of children play a game of tag.

The earlier coolness has lifted and the sun is shining in all its springtime glory. On checking my phone, I noted it was an unseasonably warm 21 C. Perfectly pleasant for a stroll in the park, or the botanic gardens; just a pity about the topic of conversation, which still has Jean-Luc floored.

'But why all the subterfuge?'

I raise my hands out in front of me. 'Who knows?'

His face turns as white as an alabaster statute. 'You don't think this has anything to do with you and me, do you?'

I purse my lips. 'The thought had crossed my mind, but somehow I don't think so. I was wondering if it was more to do with his and Suzanne's history.'

Jean-Luc exhales heavily. 'With Théo anything's possible. She really hates him, and Théo likes to be adored not hated.'

I know that much to be true. 'But how could they have moved so quickly? Théo doesn't seem like the type of person solicitors put feelers out to.'

Jean-Luc shrugs and says, 'He's a businessman. Why not?'

I have to concede that, but then say, 'OK, well, did the solicitor contact you?'

'No, but my family hasn't used Bernard for any business. He's also Théo's family's solicitor.'

Well, at least that piece of the puzzle makes sense now.

'What I don't get is why Théo wants the boulangerie,' I say.

Jean-Luc shrugs. 'It could be any number of reasons, but first and foremost Théo is a very astute businessman. There must be a demand for a salon there or he wouldn't be interested. You can bet he's expecting to make a killing.' He pauses. 'And I'm sure the fact he'll be sticking it to Suzanne is a bonus.'

'But why? He was the one who wronged her.'

'Like that matters to Théo. If someone gets in his way or doesn't meet his expectations, he swats them as if they're a fly. Mark my words, we don't want Théo getting his claws into the boulangerie.'

I nod at him sagely then we continue our walk through the *Jardin des Plantes*, admiring the incredible, eclectic mix of flowers and plants, I appreciate the surrounding beauty even more. It's in such contrast to our current situation, which isn't sweetness and flowers. I stop by a particularly spiky plant and study its unpronounceable Latin name, then say, 'I think we should call it either Gloire or Théo.'

Jean-Luc laughs, a great belly laugh, which makes me giggle.

'Definitely Gloire,' he says. 'She can blank someone at a hundred paces.'

I smile and as we pass some more beautiful plants, I stop by another, rather over-the-top creation. 'Then this one can be Théo.'

Jean-Luc and I look at each other and burst out laughing, bending double and having to hold on to each other. Being able to find levity and amusement in the middle of such a gloomy situation surely bodes well for us.

In the *Jardin Royal*, we pause at the statue of Antoine de St. Exupéry. I only stop because I remember reading a translated version of his *Le Petit Prince*, *The Little Prince*, when I was at primary school. I had no idea he was connected to Toulouse.

After doing a tour of the *Jardin Royal*, taking in the duck house and admiring the statues of various composers, I decide I've had enough culture for the day and what I'd like right now is a bloody big glass of white wine, since perspiration is beading on my brow and I feel sticky.

As we walk towards a bar Jean-Luc recommends, I notice a colourful sign on a nearby brick wall which reads '*artisanal*'. When I stop, Jean-Luc almost runs into the back of me.

'What is it?'

I nod to the poster, which shows an image of a basket of bread, cheese, wine, hams, olives and other artisan products. 'Does that say Gastronome artisan produce competition? And is that a prize fund? Sorry, my French is letting me down here.' I move out of his line of vision so he can read the sign.

'It says "Calling all artisan producers in the Haute-Garonne region. If you have a new product, put it to our taste test and win our grand prize of €50,000. Closing date for entries 30 April. Join our festival on 15 May at Place du Capitole where the winners will be revealed."

'Jean-Luc, have you heard of this festival before? Is it legit?'

He nods. 'Yes, it has been going on for quite a few years.'

'But you've never submitted to it?'

He purses his lips. 'No, I haven't had time, nor have I had anything to submit.'

A ghost of a smile dances across my lips. 'But what if we made time and what if we did have something to submit?'

His brow creases, so I rush on. 'What if we could have the Molins enter this competition, perhaps with a new bread or pastry, and see if they could win it? If they did, it could be the difference between them keeping the boulangerie or not.'

'And letting Théo win or not,' Jean-Luc goes on. 'I bet I know one person who'll be in.'

I scrunch up my face. 'Who?'

'Suzanne. There's no way she will let Théo take the boulangerie and her home from her without a fight.'

'Come on.' I snap a photo of the poster then drag Jean-Luc by the hand. 'Change of plan. Back to the boulangerie.'

We tumble through the door to a bustle of activity in the Molins' kitchen. Estelle is cooking, Suzanne is baking a cake, not for the boulangerie, I imagine, and Matthieu is sitting at the table, elbow deep in paperwork.

'I have news,' I announce.

Three pairs of eyes turn to stare at me, so I whip out my phone and ask Jean-Luc to read it, as it sounds better when said in a proper French accent.

Matthieu stares at me and shrugs, Estelle frowns and Suzanne grabs me by the hands, not bothering to wipe the flour from hers, and dances me round the kitchen.

'It's ambitious, but it's got to be worth a try,' she says.

'What's worth a try?' say Estelle and Matthieu in unison.

'*Papa*, *Maman*, don't you see? If we can bring out a new Molins artisanal product, we could enter this competition. The winner gets fifty thousand euros.'

But Matthieu is dismissive. 'Pah! There must be some catch.'

'Suzanne, it probably has hundreds if not thousands of entries,' Estelle says.

'*Maman*, *Papa*, you have always instilled a great work ethic in me and a firm belief we should never give up. Now it's my turn to say to you, "please don't give up". We can do this. I feel it. We want it. We need it. Why shouldn't it be us?'

Estelle and Matthieu share a look then turn to their super-energised daughter and say, 'OK. Let's do it.'

'That's the spirit.' Suzanne kisses both parents on the cheek before quickly washing her hands of the flour, then reaching for her laptop. 'Now, what we need is a plan. Is everybody sitting comfortably?'

Jean-Luc and I take a seat at the table as Matthieu hastily rearranges his piles of paperwork. Estelle removes from the hob whatever she was cooking. It smells delicious; definitely something else tomato-based – ratatouille?

When Suzanne is on a mission, there's no messing with her. Straight off, she starts firing questions at us.

'*Papa*, if we had to come up with a new product, what could it be? Get your thinking cap on. Jean-Luc, can you help *Maman* with the entry form? Lia, can you go to the website and print that off? Then I'll look at timelines and what's required from entrants regarding a stall and how we could make that happen in the time, whilst you look into the history of the festival – how many entrants, how many prizes, what percentage of each type of artisan product has been featured, that kind of thing.'

By the time an hour has passed, we've all been engaged in various activities, whilst Suzanne checks them off or writes them into what looks suspiciously like a PowerPoint presentation.

'Right, what have we come up with so far? Let's do some brainstorming,' she says.

'She'd have made a great schoolteacher,' I mutter to Jean-Luc, who snorts beside me. I catch Matthieu's eye. He's smiling. Yeah, he overheard.

'Well, the entry form, although a bit complicated, is ready, we believe.' Estelle looks to Jean-Luc, who nods his agreement.

'There's a five hundred euro participation fee. I imagine that must go towards the prize pot,' says Jean-Luc, glancing round at everyone.

'Although it looks like there are some big sponsors, too, which accounts for the generous cash prize,' adds Estelle.

'Good. Progress.' Suzanne claps her hands together. '*Papa*, thoughts? Ideas?'

'This girl has missed her calling,' I murmur under my breath to Jean-Luc, who smirks. His face soon returns to a more serious expression when Suzanne glares at us both. Duly chastened, we listen up.

Matthieu blows out a breath and glances at us as if showing his appreciation for the slight delay. I have the impression his answer isn't going to be as favourable as the last one.

'First of all, the entry fee is steep, but given what's at stake, I think it's worth it.'

'*Papa!*' Suzanne rolls her eyes. 'Ideas for the artisanal product.'

'Oh!' Matthieu laughs, realising his error. Then he rubs his chin. 'Well, I had been thinking recently of a couple of new bread combinations and I wonder if maybe one of those could work.'

Suzanne stares at her dad. '*Allons-y*. None of us is getting any younger. What's your idea?'

'Forget schoolteacher, she should be in the army,' Jean-Luc mutters behind his hand.

I snigger then cough to cover it up when Suzanne once again shoots me a look.

'OK, how about a *fougasse*?'

'*Fougasse*?' Estelle scrunches up her forehead. 'But that's mainly associated with Provence not Haute-Garonne or Gascony.'

'True, but why? Do they have a trademark on it or something?' asks Matthieu. 'No. So, how about a *fougasse* with figs and walnut?'

Suzanne mulls this over as Estelle says, 'That sounds like a great idea,' then both Suzanne and Jean-Luc say, 'No,' and 'Not quite,' respectively.

Matthieu gives Suzanne an almost injured look. 'What's up with that idea?'

'Giving nuts to a judging panel isn't the best. We don't know who has allergies, nor if they will test it on the general public,' explains Jean-Luc. 'But the fig is a really good idea.'

'Yes, *Papa*, I was thinking the same thing. What else could we marry fig with?'

I quickly Google recipes with figs and am about to say soft cheese when Jean-Luc beats me to it.

'A Berger cheese would work wonderfully with figs.'

'Of course it would.' Matthieu slaps Jean-Luc on the back.

'But then it wouldn't be solely our product,' says Estelle.

'Well, we didn't plant the wheat, nor mill the flour. It's the same thing. It's the end product, baked here in our boulangerie, that counts. Isn't that right, Lia?'

What? Why's he asking me? How would I know? I'm a foreigner. Fortunately, Jean-Luc rescues me. 'Yes, that's exactly how it's viewed. The end product. Let me double-check, but I'm pretty certain that falls within the rules.'

'OK, *Papa*, but in case it doesn't, what else do you have?' Suzanne asks.

After teasing a couple of new pastry variants out of Matthieu, we all still believe the *fougasse* is the way to go, and with the steep entry fee, we're inclined to enter only one product.

'Do producers usually enter one or more products?' I ask.

Suzanne scuttles off to find out and comes back not long after. 'A mix. Fifty per cent had more than two products, thirty per cent had two, twenty per cent had one.'

We spend the rest of the evening sorting out our plans for the artisan festival and the new product. Estelle promises to go get some figs from Alexine's orchard garden next day, whilst dealing with parents and hospital visits on a shift rotation, and whilst the boulangerie is closed.

Jean-Luc, Suzanne and I agree to collaborate on the admin and submitting the application form. We have a few more days before the closing date, but I think we'd rather get it off our plate and focus on the larger task.

We agree that Matthieu will do his hospital visit in the morning so when Estelle returns from Alexine's with the figs, he has plenty of time for practising. Jean-Luc has promised to provide a supply of the Berger cheese he mentioned, which he has plenty of in the cold storage at the *fromagerie*.

Jean-Luc and I leave to return to his for the night – I need the walk and the Molins need a little time as a family to discuss things without an interloper, however well-meaning that interloper may be, plus, frankly, I'm energised, and I also want to rip the clothes off this man, who has been an absolute star through this whole process.

Chapter Thirty-seven

The sound of the birds twittering in trees right outside Jean-Luc's townhouse jolts me into wakefulness. I smile lazily as I open my eyes and catch a glimpse of Jean-Luc's toned torso partially uncovered, his legs entwined with my mine. I could get used to this, and to the view.

I'm not sure if it was yesterday's brainstorming session or last night's lovemaking, but I had the best sleep I've had in weeks, months possibly. Perhaps the fact we have a potentially workable plan, a ghost of a possibility of reversing the Molins' luck, is what's causing my brain to fully engage.

Last night was wonderful. We were both so on fire, in more ways than one. We couldn't get enough of each other. Jean-Luc was tender, thoughtful, giving, loving. There's no way I can leave this man behind and return to Scotland. I'm in too deep. There's no getting away from it – I love him. I love everything about him. Oh God. This plan needs to work.

After a leisurely breakfast and another lovemaking session – OK, two – we head over to the Molins, making a brief detour via the *marché aux puces* at Saint Aubin. I've been to a lot of the flea markets in Toulouse, but some have changed, and bizarrely, I'd never been to this one, so last night, whilst we came up for air, Jean-Luc stroked my bare arm and told me he'd take me today.

We spend an hour perusing the fare at the market, with Jean-Luc even buying a couple of soft cheeses for Matthieu to try, in case he prefers them with the figs instead of his own product. I pick up a few bits and pieces to try, and some canteloupes, and even though it hasn't been long since breakfast, it doesn't stop us sampling some of the incredible street food on offer: Syrian *fattoush*, Algerian *mahjouba* and Greek *spanakopita*. The Greek spinach pie was my favourite, but the Syrian salad was definitely moreish, and we also bought a *mahjouba* for the Molins, almost as an inside joke – buying a flatbread for a *boulanger*. All of the street food was mouthwatering and had me groaning with pleasure. I'm going to have to stop doing that; it happened a lot last night too. Jules would be so proud of me.

We arrive at the boulangerie, laden down with supplies, to find the Molins household abuzz with activity. Sarah and Estelle are busy with tasks Suzanne has set them. Suzanne is clearly still directing things. Maybe she should be a filmmaker. She could definitely run the boulangerie and organise staff, too.

Matthieu is in the bakery with Suzanne, kneading the dough whilst she helps him by adding various ingredients to the prepared mixes, then scoring the dough and finally proving it. She pops another batch in the oven as I greet her through the bakery window.

A moment later, she opens the door and comes out. 'Hi, Lia, Jean-Luc.' Her face is flushed, but whether from the heat or the excitement it's hard to tell.

'You guys have already achieved so much,' I say. It's

almost like an industrial workspace but on a much smaller scale.

'Yep.' She glances back through the window to the bakery and says proudly, 'And I know it's going to taste amazing.' She looks at Jean-Luc. 'We tried it with the Berger we had in our own fridge – the one you gave us last week. Fingers crossed it tastes as good as it looks.'

'I'll get you some more from the *fromagerie* in a moment, then bring more from the Gimont facility if you need it. I see you have plenty of figs.' He gestures to the worksurface inside the bakery where bowls of peeled figs sit waiting patiently to be included in the bread-making process.

'Yes, *Maman* went first thing this morning.' She swoons. 'They are delicious. If I didn't need them for the bread, I'd eat them all.'

Jean-Luc and I laugh then I say, 'You'd have to fight me for them first.'

We'd read up more on the festival last night. After we submit the product to the competition, we'll then have a stall during the weekend of the festival in Place du Capitole where shoppers and passers-by can come and sample our wares. At the end of the weekend there'll be a ceremony where the judges taste test then declare the winners. Whatever happens, we'll be raising the profile of La Boulangerie au Coin de la Rue.

So, the organisers provide the stall, but we can decorate it how we like. The festival runs from ten until five on Saturday and Sunday and we've come up with a schedule for how we can manage the boulangerie's Saturday opening hours, the hospital visits and the stall.

'It's all looking very productive,' I say to Suzanne.

'Here's something I drew up earlier.' I show her my plans and she reads, nods, bites her lip as if in concentration and then says, 'Yes, that should work.' She nudges me with her shoulder. 'Thanks, sis.'

Sis. Tears form behind my eyes and I clear my throat in an attempt to will them away.

'Well, I guess it's time for us to get cracking on ideas for the décor for the stall. Feel free to bring us samples to taste when they're ready.' I throw a grin over my shoulder as I walk away.

I corral Estelle and Sarah into helping with the ideas side of things, as despite being a graphic designer, coming up with something suitable for a 'country' market stall isn't my forte. Once we have a basic design, everyone gets to cutting, sewing or drawing.

We have a quick break half an hour later when Suzanne and Matthieu walk towards us, holding out the first *fougasse* the way a wine waiter holds the bottle in a posh restaurant. All Suzanne is missing is the white cloth over her arm and the matching white gloves.

'You try first, Lia. After all, the festival was your brainchild,' says Matthieu, offering me a slice of *fougasse*. I take the oval-shaped piece of bread in my fingers and admire it – it's almost too pretty to eat, and with its diagonal indents and the one down the middle, for some reason it reminds me of a Christmas tree. Random, I know, but I confess to not knowing what *fougasse* looked like until now. I savour the mouthwatering aroma for a second before biting into it. Oh my God! It is heaven in bread form. I'm not even hungry after first breakfast, then the various delicacies I sampled at the *marché aux puces*, but this is wow. I don't even have words to do it justice.

Suzanne, Estelle and Matthieu are all peering at me expectantly.

Finally, Matthieu asks, 'It's good?'

I nod, unable to speak for a second. Please let this be good enough to win.

'It's fabulous,' I say. 'So soft, yet crunchy, and the cheese is so gooey, the figs so oozy.'

Jean-Luc laughs. 'Here's to wonderful descriptions.'

'But perhaps a French person should try it. Let's not forget, I love French food, and much of it is so much better than Scottish food.'

'Most of it,' mumbles Matthieu, under his breath.

'Our Aberdeen Angus is pretty good,' I say.

Everyone laughs then silence reigns as they each take a piece of the *fougasse* Matthieu holds out.'

'Mmm,' Suzanne sighs. 'It's good.'

Estelle's eyes shoot into her hairline when she tastes hers.

Matthieu tries his and agrees. 'It's good … but it could be better. Suzanne, let's have a quick cup of coffee then it's back to the drawing board for us. Time to make a few tweaks.'

'Oh, I almost forgot,' says Jean-Luc. 'We brought you a few other soft cheeses from the market, in case you wanted to try something else, to give you a more rounded view.'

Matthieu's eyes light up. 'Thank you, Jean-Luc. That was very thoughtful.' He takes the bag of cheese then clarifies, 'Not that the issue is with the cheese.'

Jean-Luc smiles. 'God forbid!'

'More the balance of flavours.'

The two of them laugh then Matthieu says, 'Suzanne, we have plenty to work with here.'

After a few more hours' activity, we all sit down at the table. Estelle sets down a large ceramic pot whose delicious aromas waft towards me. '*Cassoulet*.' She pops in a huge silver serving spoon, about-turns and takes out a tray from the oven before setting it on the table too. 'And to accompany it, or if you're more in the mood for a vegetarian dish, Provençal tomato and aubergine gratin.'

She winks at me and I laugh. 'I'm sure they're both delicious.'

I tuck into the hearty *cassoulet* Estelle has prepared for us. It's incredible, and despite having eaten like it's going out of fashion today, I wolf the stew down. I do, however, conserve some space for the gratin.

Matthieu pours the wine – red, to complement the food – and we all raise our glasses at his behest.

'*A* La Boulangerie au Coin de la Rue,' he says.

We copy him as one and make the same toast. Yes, indeed. To the boulangerie on the corner. May it be victorious at the festival.

Once the plates are empty and we've cleared away, Jean-Luc and I decide to return to his for a while. Suzanne is heading to the hospital to see her grandmother, then staying at her grandfather's; Estelle to her mother's; Sarah is going to the other hospital to see René; Matthieu is staying here to make the *chocolatines* in the morning, early, before catching Bernard to see what the response is about delaying acceptance on the offer. We've all moved quickly on the festival front. I can only pray it hasn't been too hasty, but we were running out of time. If Théo, who doesn't know Matthieu knows who the buyer is, doesn't consent to a deadline extension of at least a month, our plans will be scuppered before they're out of the starting blocks. Time to keep everything crossed.

On Monday morning, I video call Jules before work and fill her in. We'd texted a few times last week, but not often. Perhaps she was leaving me to lick my wounds. Now, since I have some good news to deliver, I want to do it in person.

'Morning, gorgeous. Check you with your apron. You look like a chef,' she teases.

'Ha! Not quite. But yes, you're right. I rock this look.'

Jules looks effortlessly chic in her laid-back version of a business suit, with jaunty floral scarf. In fact, she looks more French than I do. All that's missing is the pout, although she could rise to the challenge if tested.

'So, to what do I owe this pleasure? Have you booked your flight home yet? How is everyone?'

'Actually, about that. No, I haven't booked a flight, because…'

Once I've regaled her with the weekend's exploits, she whoops with glee. 'No way, Lia. You are such a badass. Go you. Seriously, make these amoebas suffer. This Théo and Gloire. They sound like they need taken down a peg or two and also some life lessons in how to treat people.'

'Well, you won't get any argument from me there.'

'Hey, and Lia, when exactly is the festival?'

I rattle off the dates and she says, 'I'll look at flights.'

'Sorry, what?'

Jules quirks an eyebrow. 'Lia Abernethy, you didn't honestly think I'd miss your potentially life-changing festival, did you?'

I gape at her. I know she's my best friend and I've

known her for years, but she has just shown me she still has the ability to blow my expectations out of the water.

'But what about work?'

She waves a hand in the air dismissively. 'Details. I'll sort it. Look up a nice Airbnb for me. Right, I need to get to work. Meeting at eight thirty. Speak soon. Mwah!'

When I ring off, I stand for a few minutes in a daze. Jules is coming. Jules is coming to Toulouse. Somehow that buoys my spirits even more and I start my day with a spring in my step.

The boulangerie is busy from the off. It's almost as if customers sense there's something in the air, or maybe they simply need that sugar hit first thing on a Monday morning before work.

Once Matthieu had cleaned up after making all the *chocolatines*, he nipped out to visit Bernard, trusting he'd be able to get a straight answer if he saw him face to face rather than having to go through his receptionist. And he doesn't want to wait any longer. I don't think anyone's nerves can take it.

In the back of my mind, I still have to consider the what ifs. What if we don't win? What if I do have to return to Scotland? What will become of me and Jean-Luc? I don't really believe long-distance relationships work, and I know in my line of work, once you're involved in a large project, you've barely time to nip to the loo, never mind fly over to Toulouse at the weekend to pursue affairs of the heart.

So whilst Matthieu is off to see Bernard, I fret about that until Madame Leclerc breezes in with a '*Bonjour*' and a request for her usual.

'Is Matthieu around or has he gone to the hospital again?' she asks.

'No, he's gone to see…' I stop myself just in time. I almost said he had gone to see Bernard, but that's not my business to divulge.

Madame Leclerc raises an eyebrow. 'Who?'

My mouth downturns and I say, 'Oh, some business thing. I can't recall what he said exactly. Do you need him for something?'

'No, it's OK. I got what I came for. *A demain*.'

As the door closes behind her, I wonder what all that was about.

Chapter Thirty-eight

Matthieu bustles in an hour later, beaming, then dances me round the boulangerie. Thankfully, there are no witnesses.

'Can I take it we've had good news about the extension?'

He stops and smiles. 'Yes. Ah, I should have been a poker player,' he says, evidently delighted with himself.

'How come?' I lean against the counter, also to avoid him dancing me round the room again as I note passers-by in the street taking an interest.

'Because, dear Lia, we have exactly one month, which gives us until two days after the festival to find another buyer.'

'Yes.' I pump my fist in the air, then at the alarmed glance from a woman walking in the street, who's looking in the window, I lower my hand and say, 'That's wonderful.'

'Isn't it just? I knew suggesting two months would work. Bernard said he told Théo – although he still thinks the buyer's identity is unknown to me – to meet me halfway, and Théo went along with it.'

'Thank goodness for that. Now all we have to do is have the best product at the show.'

My attempt at exuberance falls flat as Matthieu's face

falls and he says, 'But what if it isn't?'

'Matthieu,' I say sternly, 'it will be. With everyone behind it the way we are, it has to succeed.' Strong words. I just hope I'm not setting us up for failure. But if we don't believe, who will?

And those are exactly Jean-Luc's thoughts when I tell him of my conversation with Matthieu.

The next ten days or so pass more quickly than we could possibly have imagined. Life is a whirlwind of preparations, testing, tastings, hospital visits, minor issues at the boulangerie – a delivery that falls through, a first-time customer who slips on the floor and talks of suing the boulangerie, and a whole load of logistical nightmares for the family to navigate as they slowly gain more updates on René and on Matthieu's mother's health.

It also represents a deepening of my affection for Jean-Luc, as well as a new stage in our relationship. I spend most nights at his but come back in time to open up the boulangerie.

Matthieu has decided today is the day we're going to announce to the world, or at the very least the clientele of the boulangerie and the area of Chalets, that we are entering the Gastronome artisan food festival. To showcase this, Suzanne has created an A1-sized poster, which she taped to the wall in the boulangerie at closing time last night.

It's quite exciting thinking of what the customers will say. It's even more exciting realising it's now only a little over two weeks until the festival. I'm so excited about it, and Jules is coming for a few days. I can't wait to see her.

It's only now, knowing she'll be arriving soon, that I realise exactly how much I've missed her, plus I'm so looking forward to her meeting Jean-Luc.

The boulangerie is uncharacteristically quiet this morning. Maybe the fine weather has drawn people to the parks and squares instead of to their usual haunts on this, the final day before the weekend. The glare of the sun dazzles me as I work behind the counter, and I wish we had blinds for the boulangerie's windows, although that would rather spoil the effect.

The mum who regularly comes in with her twins orders three *pains au chocolat* and a baguette. Whilst I'm popping them in paper bags and slipping napkins in each one, she notices the poster.

'Oh, you're doing the festival this year. How exciting. We go every year. Have you ever been?'

'No, it wasn't on during the months I lived here before.'

'In that case, you're in for a treat.' She takes a twin by each hand. 'Look forward to seeing you there then, and tasting the new product.'

I'm reflecting on her words when I look up to see Madame Leclerc standing in front of me. She has a Maltese with her.

'Oh, Madame, I'm sorry. We don't allow dogs in the boulangerie.'

'No problem. I will tie him up outside. Can you get me my usual whilst I do so?'

I oblige, but can't help feeling bad. She's not exactly the right side of eighty and here am I, not even the owner, telling her to keep her dog outside.

When she returns, I hand her the package and say, 'I

didn't realise you had a dog.'

She rolls her eyes. 'I don't. My neighbour had to go into hospital and I promised to look after Hugo.'

As I pass her change to her, she glances at the poster. 'What is this? The boulangerie is competing at the food festival?'

'Eh, yes.' I clear my throat. 'I saw an advert for it and thought it was a good idea for the Molins to enter.'

'And Matthieu has a new product for this?' She raises an eyebrow.

'Of course. It's only for new products.'

She looks at me as if to see if I'm suggesting she's stupid.

'Interesting. Naturally, I will be there. I go every year.'

'Yes, it seems very popular. The lady who was here a few moments ago said the same.'

'Really?' She weighs this up then says, 'I must be going.'

'Have fun with Hugo.'

She looks at me as if that's unlikely then throws me a '*Bon weekend*' before heading off in the direction of Place du Capitole.

I hope it is a good weekend. As I bring another tray of *chocolatines* through from the bakery, I stop in my tracks. Is that Théo? No, it can't be, and at this time of day. What would he be doing here?

I place the tray of *chocolatines* in their spot below the counter then half jog to the door, but there's no sign of anyone. I must have imagined it, although I'm a bit young hopefully for my mind to be playing tricks on me.

I'm about to reopen the boulangerie for the afternoon when a car door slams in the courtyard. I rush back through the living room, and I'm about to enter the courtyard when Matthieu flings the door open, almost taking me with it.

'Matthieu! What's wrong?'

His teeth are gritted so tight I worry he'll give himself lockjaw.

'That snake Théo has told Bernard he needs the decision date moved forward by a week. A week! We don't have a week to play with. We have two days.'

I think back to my imagining I'd seen Théo earlier.

'Surely he can't do that. You had a deal.'

'Yeah! And do you think he has any sense of honour? To think, I always gave him the benefit of the doubt in the past. Well, mostly.' He stops and looks thoughtful for a minute and I wonder if he's referring to what happened with Suzanne.

'Matthieu,' I say, interrupting his thoughts. 'I thought I saw Théo earlier.'

'You did?' He frowns. 'Here?'

I shake my head. 'Not quite. He wasn't in the shop. I'd served Madame Leclerc and was bringing a new tray of *chocos* through when I thought I saw him through the window.'

Matthieu purses his lips then walks through to the boulangerie, me at his heels. His eyes fly to the poster on the wall, then he asks me for the keys – it's time to open up anyway – unlocks the door and stands outside. What's he doing? He looks in the window, from various vantage points, craning his neck, but with what aim, I have no idea.

'Matthieu?' I say when he returns, colour high in his cheeks.

'Lia.' He sighs. 'I think somehow Théo saw or heard

about us participating in the festival. And maybe he has put two and two together and realised we're trying to raise the money.' He blows out a breath.

'So, what are you going to do? What did Bernard say? Can he change the details of the offer at this late stage?'

He huffs. 'Apparently so. Nothing was signed. It was a gentleman's agreement pending my decision in two more weeks. Oh my God, I could kick myself for being so stupid.'

'Matthieu, you weren't to know. Théo is clearly very devious.'

'I hate being outwitted by him.'

The doorbell jangles and we look up, expecting to see a customer, but it's Suzanne, all beaming smiles, until she sees our faces.

'What's going on?'

Her father looks at her and says simply, 'Théo.'

'Why don't I make some tea whilst you two have a chat?' I say. 'When it's made, I'll take over in the boulangerie.'

As I half-listen to their raised voices from the kitchen, I can't even smile at the fact I just know when Matthieu is gesticulating with his hands.

I almost have to cover my ears at the string of swear words that Suzanne lets rip. It's an impressive list.

'Tea,' I say, when I return to the boulangerie.

'We'll have it in the living room, so the three of us can talk,' says Matthieu. 'Suzanne has raised an interesting point.'

'Oh?' I ask, following them back into the living room.

Once we're seated, Matthieu looks thoughtful. 'What if I call his bluff? What if I say I have someone else interested, or say no to the tighter timeline? After all, it's not good business to chop and change like this.'

I mull this over for a second. 'That's a valid point. But, you have to think about one thing.'

Suzanne raises her chin. 'What?'

'Can you afford to let the deal fold? What happens if he calls *your* bluff? You don't have any other potential buyers and you said yourself, you're running out of time.'

'But if we win the competition…?' Suzanne says.

'I know, Suzanne,' I interrupt. 'But what if you don't? I mean, I have great faith in the product and in us, but what if we don't win? We don't even know who else is likely to be in the running.'

Suzanne glances at Matthieu, who looks at her solemnly, then she raises her chin again. 'I don't care. I don't think we should let ourselves be bullied by him. He did it to me. I won't let him do it to us. *Papa?*'

'We need to talk to *Maman*, but I'm with you, Suzanne. I don't appreciate being bullied.'

'Then it's settled,' says Suzanne. 'I'll talk to *Maman* later. No change to the deal or it's off.'

I give a wan smile. I admire their courage, but I hope they know what they're doing.

Chapter Thirty-nine

'Jules!' I run towards her at the baggage carousel and fling my arms around her. Jean-Luc hangs back, not wanting to intrude.

We hug like we're sixteen not thirty-six, or in her case thirty-five, but I don't care. Having my best friend here for this rather important occasion means everything to me and underlines once again why she *is* my best friend.

Behind her hand, as we approach Jean-Luc, she whispers, 'Oh my God, he's phenomenal, like a work of art.'

A broad smile spreads across Jean-Luc's face. 'Hi, Jules. I'm Jean-Luc, and Lia has warned me all about you.'

Jules bursts out laughing and accepts his kisses on both cheeks, then fans herself. 'Wow! I could get used to this. Who else can I get to kiss me at baggage claim?' She scans around as if actively seeking unsuspecting victims.

'Anyway, Lia, chilli pepper hot, like I said,' she whispers again as she loops an arm through mine.

Now it's Jean-Luc who laughs. 'I also have exceptionally good hearing.'

Jules turns around. 'You were meant to hear.'

'I did tell you she's an outrageous flirt,' I say to Jean-Luc, looping my other arm through his.

'Too right,' says Jules. 'We should all live a little. Life's too short.'

'But you live a lot, Jules,' I say, watching Jean-Luc take in our banter.

'You'd better believe it. And I wouldn't have it any other way. Right, lead the way. Take me to the French people!'

Oh God. What have I done? What did the poor people of Toulouse ever do to deserve this?

Jules settles in well. Estelle insisted she stay at the boulangerie, and although she doesn't speak any French beyond about five words, she has been enchanting my 'adoptive' family with tales of life with and without me, and Jean-Luc and I, and Suzanne to a certain extent, have been translating. We're all gathered together having dinner the night before the festival starts. Estelle, with help from Sarah and Suzanne, has excelled herself, and even I've had some input.

At my insistence that we don't care about the food being right for the weather, as long as it's tasty, Estelle suggested *l'alicuit de canard* – another dish I'd never heard of, but which I've greatly enjoyed being instrumental in preparing for this evening's meal.

Although the duck dish is made from the wings and neck – I initially thought 'bleurgh' – it's super tasty since the meat has been simmered for so long. There's now hardly any left as we've all helped ourselves to generous portions.

Over only a couple of glasses of wine – we want to be fresh for tomorrow – and the fabulous food, we all talk, laugh and share stories and anecdotes of life in Gascony, and in Scotland. There are promises of more visits here by Jules, longer ones, and a half-baked promise from Estelle to visit Scotland; it will never happen. She is too much of a homebody. She might like the idea but not the reality, and what would she eat?

'So you told Bernard you wouldn't move on the date?' Jules says to Matthieu, and I then translate.

He nods and Jules beams at him. 'Matthieu. Respect. You are a total badass!'

I translate that as best I can, with some help from both Suzanne and Jean-Luc.

Soon it's time for us to go our separate ways, and I take a few moments outside in private with Jean-Luc.

'I'll see you in the morning,' he says, kissing my cheek when we pull apart after some rather passionate kisses.

'You will.' I kiss him once more on the lips, trying to imbue in that one kiss how much he means to me.

This morning has been absolutely crazy. I don't know what I expected from the food festival, maybe that it would look similar to the *marché aux puces*, but it's nothing like that. As well as all the food stalls, there are fire eaters and jugglers and men on stilts wearing striped blue and yellow trousers.

'They like to go all out for the opening of the festival,' Jean-Luc shouts in my ear over the noise.

They don't half. Everywhere I look there is something going on. Crowds have gathered since early. We arrived at eight thirty to set up, but from long before the festival opened there has been a steady stream of people walking past. Now that the organiser has declared the festival open, people are swarming everywhere. It's a sight to behold. There are around forty tents, each with two or three tables, depending on the number of products, from what I can gather, that each artisan is exhibiting. I try to do the maths with regards to how much the organisers have taken in entry fees, but I don't manage to finish that thought before someone says, 'Can I try some, please?'

It's a little boy, about ten years old, and he's pointing at the *fougasse*. '*Absolument*,' I say, smiling at him and passing him a slice on a paper plate.

'Mmm,' he says as he takes a bite. '*Maman, c'est bon.*'

His mother appears at his side and asks if she can have a slice.

'*Mais oui.*' I place a piece on a plate for her too and pass it across.

She bites into it and exclaims. '*Oh, c'est magnifique.*' Then she rat-a-tats a lot of very fast French at me and I panic, but Jean-Luc answers her and I breathe a sigh of relief.

'She wanted to know what was in it exactly.'

'Oh?' I say. 'You didn't give away any trade secrets, I hope.'

He laughs. 'No, in fact, I told her about the soft cheese and told her there were figs in it too, but I didn't tell her it was *my* soft cheese.'

'Ha! You're still so proud of Matthieu choosing your cheese over all the cheeses we brought him, aren't you?'

'But of course.'

Since this is the first time there has been a gap in visitors, I say, 'Can you mind the stall for five minutes? I'd quite like to have a look around. This is such a big set-up and it's so busy, I can't even see half the stalls.'

'No problem. Take your time. I'll hit the panic button if it gets too crazy.'

I smile as I walk away. God, I love this man. God, this plan has to work, *because* I love this man.

I want to shout it to the crowds in Place du Capitole; that's how much joy I feel when I'm with Jean-Luc, but I don't want to frighten any passers-by, or more importantly, any potential customers, nor do I want people to think I'm nuts.

I take in the vast array of stalls, with striped canopies, those made of sailcloth, even voile. Each gives a different effect. We opted for something very simple: cream tablecloth, straw baskets with bread sticking out, as well as jars of Alexine's fig jam to showcase how homegrown everything is. And Suzanne, who it turns out is a skilled artist, sketched a few boulangerie scenes from La Boulangerie au Coin de la Rue – its location in the Chalets area; the layout of the shop; the layout of the internal bakery. And I have to say it looks fantastic.

The stall next to ours is another artisan cheesemonger, whom Jean-Luc knows. Beyond that there's one with jams of every type imaginable. I stop by to have a taste. Mmm. Good, but not as good as our fig jam.

There's one with patisserie, and I don't mind if I do try some of those. They are so petite and delicious, flaky and sweet. Yum! I pass by the vegan food stall, then feel rude for not having tasted anything so I go back and try some chocolate. I smile politely. Yep, not a substitute for the real thing, I'm afraid, although the hint of chilli was pleasant.

I come across a gin stall next. The vendor waves me over, but I dismiss him with a polite wave. Gin and I are not friends. I have had many horrific hangovers that attest to that. I am swayed by the organic wine producer, who offers me a crisp white in a long-stemmed glass. I've just raised it to my lips when I sputter. Arriving at the stand is Théo.

'Lia. How do you like the wine? It's my family's newest creation.'

Recovering myself, I say, 'Hi, Théo. Yes, it's delicious. Congrats.' I hastily down the wine, make my excuses and perform a quick circuit of the rest of the square as I try to figure out both who our greatest competition is and how to tell the Molins that Théo has entered the competition with one of his family's wines.

'Lia,' says Jean-Luc when I return to our stall. 'We'll need to get more samples. We've almost run out. Everyone's loving the *fougasse*.'

Jean-Luc's expression of delight soon curdles when I tell him about Théo. I have never seen Jean-Luc angry, but right now, the storm behind his eyes shows me he'd like to rip Théo's head off and feed it to a Doberman.

Finally, Jean-Luc sighs. 'We have to tell Suzanne, and Matthieu. They need to know. Théo's probably laughing right now. In my mind there's no doubt at all that he entered, hoping his wine, and his family name, would win and that would prevent Matthieu from having the necessary funds to keep the boulangerie going.'

'I'm inclined to agree.' I lean against one of the chairs supplied.

'Best-case scenario, he'll make the offer again, but a lesser offer. Worst-case scenario, he won't make the offer at all. It depends how much he wants it.'

I huff out a breath. 'Well, I guess there's nothing for it. I'd better make that call.'

When Matthieu and Suzanne arrive, with Jules in tow, they cast furtive looks towards where Théo's stand is situated. Throngs of customers block the view, so fortunately he can't see us, but neither can we see him.

'So, this is the new product, Matthieu?'

I turn to see Madame Leclerc, in her usual dog-tooth coat. She's carrying various bags, which appear to be bursting at the seams. She's obviously had a busy day shopping.

'Would you like a piece of *fougasse*?' I say.

'Of course. Why else would I be here?' she says, staring evenly at me.

I redden slightly and clear my throat. 'Here you go.' I hand her a piece on a paper plate, and a napkin.

She takes a delicate bite then her eyes boggle a little, and she turns to Matthieu. '*C'est superb*.'

Matthieu lets out the breath he'd clearly been holding as he'd almost turned purple. '*Merci*, Madame Leclerc. I'm glad you like it.'

'Will you be making more of this after the festival?' she asks.

Matthieu glances first at Suzanne then me, and Suzanne rushes in with, 'Yes, we plan to offer this as a new product going forward.'

She sounds so businesslike.

Madame Leclerc dips her head. 'Good. It will sell well. I hope the rest of the festival is a great success for you.'

Once Madame Leclerc leaves, I'm just agreeing to return to the boulangerie to relieve Estelle so she can visit her father, when a silky voice says, 'Please may I have a slice?'

All of us turn to see Théo's smug face staring at me,

then indicating the *fougasse*. 'Of course, Théo,' I say, trying to fight down the urge not to shove it down his throat. How could I ever have allowed myself to be taken in by him? Now he's showing his true colours and I really don't like what I see. He's clearly here to gloat, even though he still doesn't know we know where the mystery offer originated from.

I hand him a plate and he bites into the *fougasse*. 'It's good.' He looks at me, then Matthieu. 'Figs and soft cheese. This wouldn't be your Berger, would it, Jean-Luc?'

Jean-Luc doesn't reply, simply glares at him.

'And something else I can't quite identify. All in all it's good.' His mouth downturns. 'But unfortunately I don't think it's going to quite cut it this year.' He glances around. 'So much competition. But hey, I like a little competition; that's why I entered our latest, not yet released wine the day before entries closed. I always fancied doing the festival, but you know how it is. I'm always so busy.'

Suzanne looks ready to pounce, so I give her a warning signal to retract her claws and breathe a sigh of relief when she unclenches her fists.

'Oh, I'm sorry,' says Jules in English as she pretend-trips and spills her Coke all over Théo's trousers.

'You…' His tone changes as he looks up and spies Jules. I try not to roll my eyes. He really does never change. It was clear as day he was about to go off on one there, and then he spotted how gorgeous Jules is, with her long, blonde curly hair and her big blue eyes and his attitude and demeanour changed entirely. How predictable. But Jules doesn't suffer fools gladly.

'I'm sorry there wasn't more in the can.' She flashes him a look suggesting he shouldn't mess with her.

Even I know Théo's English is up to understanding that.

Théo looks at her in disgust, then me, then turns and walks off, shaking his Coke-drenched trouser leg as he goes.

'You're my hero,' I say to Jules.

'What did you ever…?' she asks but then catches my warning glare. Jean-Luc *is* in earshot, after all.

'*Connard!*' mutters Suzanne, her jaw clenched.

'Suzanne, language,' says Matthieu. 'And remember there are potential customers around. Now, paste a smile on your face and let's offer these *fougasses* around.'

'I agree. And as we say back home, "The show ain't over til the fat lady sings."'

As Jean-Luc and I walk back towards the boulangerie, I say, 'Poor Matthieu, and Suzanne. Théo was intentionally niggling them. Did you hear his veiled barb about entering the competition last minute?'

Jean-Luc nods. 'Yeah, unfortunately, that's classic Théo. We'll just have to keep our fingers crossed the judges like the *fougasse* better than his wine.'

'I had some,' I say. 'Before I realised it was his stall. It's really good.'

'So you think the Molins have reason to be worried?'

I sigh. 'I don't think they ever weren't worried, and they'd have been foolish not to be, too. Nothing is certain about this. We've given it our all, but now all we can do is wait and see how the judges vote.'

Jean-Luc puts an arm around me and pulls me to him. 'Lia, whatever the outcome, please know no one could have done more for them than you did. You're a true friend. A true daughter to them.'

My throat constricts and tears prick behind my eyelids. I squeeze Jean-Luc's hand a little tighter as we approach the boulangerie.

Chapter Forty

On Sunday, the weather is not so kind to us. Rain began to drum on the windows of Jean-Luc's townhouse in the middle of the night and hasn't let up. By the time we head to Place du Capitole, everything is soaked and I fear the organisers might call off the second day of the event, as everything is so waterlogged.

Fortunately, we don't cross paths with Théo again, although I'm sure I pick out the mystery judges at one point. The clipboard may have been a giveaway. Are they verifying that what we submitted to them is what we're offering the passers-by or are they checking footfall around each stall, perhaps grading the public's responses? That part of the process remains cloaked in secrecy.

Foot traffic is far less than yesterday and many of the stallholders struggle to keep up a bright façade as patrons splash around, clashing umbrellas with each other, and tempers fray. The day passes slowly and we don't have to return to the boulangerie for another batch, which means we'll be eating *fougasse* for a fortnight.

Bernard stopped by the stall today. I know Matthieu appreciated his presence. Every time a regular customer from the boulangerie came to the stall, Matthieu spent as much time as he possibly could chatting with them, not focusing simply on them tasting the *fougasse*, but seeing how they were doing, what was going on in their lives, and I believe that's one of the reasons the boulangerie is so popular. The Molins have heart at the centre of everything: their family, their community, their food.

The terrible weather and greatly reduced passing trade has allowed us to make friends with the stallholders on either side, Jules, in particular having caught the attention of the stallholder on our right. He's pretty easy on the eye, so Jules finds a way to get over the language barrier and makes his day pass a little quicker with her scintillating chat. Thank goodness for translation apps.

At five o'clock, the president of the festival arrives, with his officials, to declare the winners. Now that the stalls are closed and the festival has finished, the rain decides to let up.

The eighty or so stallholders gather around the central podium in a circle, waiting to hear their fate. Suddenly, I spot Théo off to the right, watching me. A shiver runs down my back. He's freaking me out. How could I have found him attractive? I think part of me always did think he was a little superficial.

The organiser launches into a huge speech about the festival and I note our little group unconsciously hold hands. I grasp Jean-Luc and Suzanne's; Suzanne has Jules'; Jules has Matthieu's; Matthieu, Estelle's and Estelle, Sarah's.

'In third place, Raspbois, for their raspberry-flavoured gin. Well done.' The organiser shakes hands as the third-placed entrant accepts their prize.

'In second place, with the most magnificent *fougasse* is La Boulangerie au Coin de la Rue. Well done.'

Estelle nudges Matthieu, who has frozen. I can't speak. I feel like I'm about to throw up. I can't even turn to catch anyone's eye as my heart is breaking. It has all been for nothing. All that effort. All that time. All that hope. For nothing. And once again I feel responsible. I turn away, unable to look as Matthieu pastes on a smile and shakes the organiser's hand.

'And finally, our winner of the twenty-fifth Gastronome artisan food festival is Delicaces with their peach and apricot upside down *mille feuille.* Congratulations.'

The small saving grace is that at least Théo didn't win. However, that pales into insignificance when compared against the fact the Molins will either have to sell to him anyway, or worst case, they have no offer at all, and have to go back to looking for a buyer again.

We all clap the winner, a young girl who looks like she has her whole life ahead of her and who is probably already spending the fifty thousand euros. I wish her all the best even though I wanted the Molins to win that prize fund. I hope she spends it wisely.

As we all head back towards the boulangerie, dejection hangs over us like a rain cloud. The irony of the sun beating down on our backs as we trudge back isn't lost on me.

Once we enter the Molins' kitchen, Matthieu says, 'We'll talk about it tomorrow. I'm going to bed.'

Estelle gives Matthieu a look and a nod before turning to the rest of us. 'Who wants a drink?'

'I thought you'd never ask, *Maman*,' says Suzanne.

We all raise a small smile at this and gratefully accept the glass of wine she offers each of us. Even Sarah has one, although Florian is on his way to pick her up with the kids, so she says that will be her only one.

On Monday morning, we're all a bit subdued and it's not only due to the stonking hangovers we have or the fact Jules has gone, having taken a taxi to the airport around 4 a.m., to catch a super-early flight. I'd originally offered to go with her to see her off, but now I'm so glad she dismissed that suggestion.

We sank quite a few bottles of wine last night. Just as well Matthieu went to bed when they did, otherwise there would have been no products to offer customers. I overslept, as did Suzanne.

When I finally haul myself to the bathroom to shower, I wince at the image staring back at me. I feel horrendous and I look it too.

Post-shower, I'm marginally more human, but I can't face any food, and when Estelle tries to shove a croissant in my mouth as I pass through to the boulangerie, I almost gag.

In the boulangerie, the poster of the festival seems to mock us, and I'm about to take it down during a lull in the rush when a voice says, 'Perhaps you should leave it up.'

I turn to see Madame Leclerc. It was nice of her to come and support us at the festival on Saturday; even if we didn't win, it shows we have a loyal clientele. The twins' mum was there too, and quite a few of our other regulars, although whether they were simply passing through, checking out all the stalls, or were keen to see our latest product will remain a mystery. There I go again, 'our'. Not only is it not 'my' boulangerie, soon it won't even be the

Molins'. My throat catches at the thought and I cough.

'Are you all right, Lia?' asks Madame Leclerc in a gentle voice.

'Yes, thank you. I must have inhaled some icing sugar or something.'

'Ah, I see.' She gazes at me with those gimlet eyes and I have the sensation she doesn't miss much. Shrewd. That's how I'd describe her. Like with Jules, I wouldn't like to get on her wrong side.

The doorbell jangles again and I look up to see Bernard, Matthieu's solicitor, whom I met for only the first time on Saturday at the festival. It was also nice of him to come show some support. Belatedly, I wonder how Théo felt about that. Or maybe he also went to Théo's stall and stood talking for half an hour.

'Hi, Lia. Is Matthieu in?'

'Hi, Bernard. I think he's in bed. He was up early making the *chocos*. Do you want me to wake him?'

I fully expect him to say no, but when he says, 'Yes, please,' I turn to Madame Leclerc and say, 'Excuse me a second.'

'No problem.'

I whizz through to the kitchen and Estelle looks up. 'Bernard's in the boulangerie, looking for Matthieu.'

Estelle gapes. 'Matthieu? But he's in bed. What does Bernard want? Is that Théo wanting to rub our noses in it, by advising us he's now making us a greatly reduced offer? I'll—'

'Estelle, calm down. We don't know why he's here, but can you go get Matthieu?'

Estelle takes deep breaths, then says, 'Of course.'

I return to the boulangerie where Madame Leclerc is

regaling Bernard with some tale.

'Sorry to interrupt. The usual, Madame Leclerc?'

'Lia, call me Selene.'

I stare at 'Selene' as if I've been Tasered. She has never told me to call her Selene before. Why now?

'And today, I'd like one of those flaky almond pastries.'

'Oh? Another visitor?'

She shakes her head. 'No, I just fancy a change.'

I try to hide my surprise. She almost never changes her order.

Selene and Bernard keep chatting and laughing together, until Matthieu steps through into the boulangerie, his hair still sticking up in tufts. I hide a smile. I've seen him numerous times trying to tame his unruly hair when he gets up; unless he is fresh from the shower, it doesn't do anything he wants it to.

'Bernard. What a surprise? Have I forgotten an appointment? You should just have called.'

Bernard looks at Madame Leclerc – Selene. This is going to take some getting used to. Selene nods then says, 'Sorry, Matthieu. That's my fault. I insisted he meet me here as I wanted to talk to you.'

The frown lines in Matthieu's sleepy, lined face deepen. 'Sorry?'

'Matthieu, may we come in? I'd like to speak with you and Estelle.'

Confusion written all over his face, Matthieu, as if he's living in a parallel universe, ushers first Selene then Bernard into the living room where Estelle looks up from her knitting.

'Madame Leclerc,' she says, her mouth agape again.

'Selene, please. Estelle, Matthieu, I have something I'd

like to discuss with both of you.'

I turn to head back into the boulangerie, but Selene stops me. 'Lia, please stay. This concerns you too.'

Me? Now I'm really confused.

When she's assured of our complete attention, Selene says, 'First of all congratulations on second place in the festival. Very much deserved.'

'*Merci*,' we all say.

'And now to the reason I am here.'

We wait as Selene pauses. 'Matthieu, Estelle, I have always admired your work ethic and the community spirit you have instilled in this neighbourhood. I heard that you had plans to sell because of what is going on with your parents – I'm truly sorry they are so ill. Please pass them my best wishes.'

Matthieu looks at Estelle, who looks mystified, then they both glance back at Selene.

'I understand young Lia had been hoping to invest.' She smiles when she sees my incredulous look. 'But that something happened to derail that. Lia, I do not know everything, but sometimes you do not have to.'

With that cryptic comment, she continues, 'Then I heard the dissatisfying news that another party was interested and that they would retain the building as a boulangerie, and although I was saddened that you would be leaving us, I was mollified that at least the community would still have its boulangerie.'

I cannot believe or understand how she knows all this. Does she have friends in the French version of MI5 or is it 6? I can never remember which is which.

She glances round at the three of us, and then at Bernard. 'But then I heard the unwelcome news that someone had applied for a change of use, and I was not so happy with that.'

She pauses again and this time Matthieu says, 'Madame, whilst I value your support, and indeed your custom over the years, I'm at a loss as to why we are here now.'

Selene smiles. 'Because, my dear Matthieu, I'd like to make you an offer. I'd like to buy the boulangerie as a going concern, keeping Suzanne and Lia – if she's staying – on as manager and staff, and if either one wants to invest, whether in the near or distant future, I'm happy to write that into the contract too.'

We all stare open-mouthed at Selene, then Matthieu glances at Bernard, who nods then says, 'Madame Leclerc suggested this to me a few weeks ago, but she wanted it kept secret until the right moment. She knew there was a deadline from the other party and who it was…'

'Théo,' Matthieu, Estelle and I say in unison, which has Bernard's mouth falling open.

'Yes, but how did you…? I didn't tell you…'

Matthieu finally smiles. 'No, you didn't tell me, Bernard, but like Selene, I keep my ear to the ground and listen to what's said.'

I stifle a grin, knowing all about Matthieu's amateur espionage moment, but Bernard doesn't need to know that.

'Right.' Confusion clouds Bernard's features. 'Anyway, Madame Leclerc wanted to hold off on making the offer, because once she saw the poster for the festival, she knew you were trying to raise the money, and she decided that if you were able to raise it, you wouldn't need her offer.'

'That's right,' Selene breaks in. 'At the end of the day, all I want is somewhere to get excellent quality bread and pastries.'

I glance at Matthieu and Estelle, and their matching looks of incredulity and disbelief have me biting my lip so as not to smile.

'So, Matthieu, Estelle and Lia, what do you think? Do we have a deal?'

'Yes, I believe we do indeed have a deal,' comes a voice from behind us.

'We turn to see Suzanne outlined in the doorway, her hair still damp from the shower. Although she looks exhausted and hungover, as I was, her determined expression is every bit that of a shrewd businesswoman. Just like Selene obviously is.

'*Maman, Papa*?'

They nod mutely at her.

'Bernard, if everything is in order, in principle we have a deal. Selene, please can you give us twenty-four hours to look over the paperwork and return it to Bernard, but, essentially, we look forward to working for you.'

Selene leans forward to shake her hand. 'With me, Suzanne. Not for me. With me.'

Suzanne's eyes light up and Madame Leclerc turns to me and says, 'And well done on your idea of having them enter the festival. That was the pièce de resistance for me. That's when I knew I was making the right decision. You never gave up.' She pivots. 'None of you gave up. You gave it your every last shred of energy, and that's how I knew you were a business I could invest in.'

'Pardon me, Selene,' Matthieu says. 'But have you ever owned a business before?'

Selene laughs and she and Bernard share a complicit smile.

'My dear Matthieu, I own twenty-four companies already. Yours will the twenty-fifth.'

We all stand and stare as she bids us goodbye and tells us she'll be in touch once Bernard receives the paperwork.

'Lia, where's my pastry?' she calls as she enters the boulangerie again.

I rush after her and pass it to her before she and Bernard exit the boulangerie and she waves a goodbye to me.

When I re-enter the living room, Matthieu has his arms around Estelle and Suzanne has her arms around both of them and they are jumping up and down in a bouncing group hug. I move to leave, but Estelle spots me and invites me in, so I join the group hug and bounce along with them as tears of laughter and happiness cascade down my face. The dream isn't dead, after all. In fact, the dream is only just beginning.

Chapter Forty-one

'Jean-Luc, come on, keep up,' I say as I cycle along the Canal du Midi, Suzanne right behind me.

Suzanne laughs as she pedals along. 'He's such a slow coach.'

'Yep, but Patrick's even worse. Look at them. They're like two old women, chatting away, taking their time, no sense of urgency.'

We've taken to cycling this route the past few weeks. With the boulangerie closed this afternoon, we're making the most of the opportunity to bask in the sun's glorious rays as tomorrow we're helping René settle back into his house in Saint-Sauvy and having a welcome home party for him. His recovery may be long, but at least he's finally out of hospital and that should take some of the strain off both Alexine and the Molins. *Mamie* is still in hospital, but she's getting the best care possible and all the Molins, Jean-Luc and I can do is continue to support each other until she's better and in a position to come home.

Madame Leclerc delivered on her promise and on Monday she will officially become a sleeping partner in the boulangerie, having invested enough funds to keep it running comfortably whilst also allowing the Molins the opportunity to still live in the accommodation attached and

Suzanne and I to still work there, although I'll be going off to do my official training soon, whilst working part-time in the boulangerie.

It was a great shock for us all to learn that contrary to the relatively modest existence we all assumed Madame Leclerc to lead, not only is she a millionaire, but a multi-millionaire with a thriving business portfolio. She also owns one of Toulouse's finest homes, one of my favourites in this part of the city, which I'd shown Jean-Luc on one of our walks, and which he'd also admired. Until now, I had no idea it belonged to Madame Leclerc.

Estelle and Matthieu are already in wind-down mode, which is lovely to see as they need it. Maybe this was all a blessing in disguise. They've already spent more time at their parents' country homes than at the boulangerie the past few weeks. I, for my part, along with Suzanne, have stayed here, some of the time. The rest of the time I've stayed over at Jean-Luc's.

Jules called to say she thought she saw Théo at the airport. Perhaps he boarded a flight to take him away from the humiliation of being gazumped by an eighty-year-old. It's a fool who underestimates Selene Leclerc.

Freddy finally accepted an offer on the flat. Fortunately, it was for the same price as the previous offer – and they didn't want his sofa. I always hated that sofa. So I already have the funds to pay into the business and become another co-owner. The legal paperwork is currently being drawn up.

'Lia, wait up!' says Jean-Luc as he puts on a spurt and breezes past me. As he does so, I notice something white fluttering behind him. It seems to go all the way back to Patrick.

'What is that?' I ask.

Suzanne frowns. 'I don't know. It's got writing on it, though. "I … you." Nope, I can't make it out.'

Patrick reaches us and stops. Then he grins at me. 'Maybe get off and walk for the next ten metres or so.'

I shrug then do as I'm told. Then the white paper he and Jean-Luc are holding flips over and I read: "I love you, Lia Abernethy. Will you move in with me?"

My heart soars and I almost cry with joy. Then I drop the bike I'm on, skip over it and in two strides I'm in Jean-Luc's arms.

'I love you, Lia Abernethy.'

'I love you too, Jean-Luc Rochefort, and the answer's yes.'

He cups my face, looks into my eyes as I stare into his then he leans forward and kisses me. I'm only aware of how lost in our kiss we are when Suzanne shouts, 'Get a room.'

I shout back, 'No, I'm not getting a room, I'm getting a whole townhouse and I can't think of anyone I'd rather share it with.'

I nuzzle into Jean-Luc's neck as he says, 'Was the banner too much?'

'Not at all. I loved it.' Then I kiss him and I kiss him, and I kiss him some more.

Vive la France!

Author's Note

I hope you enjoyed your stay with Lia and the Molins family and your visit to Toulouse. I absolutely loved writing this book. When I was 19, as part of my university degree in French and Hispanic Studies, I had to do a three-month residency in France. The university arranged for me to stay with a French family to become fully absorbed in all things French and to experience the French way of life. I have so many memories from those days, but most of them revolve around this family.

The internal layout of the boulangerie and the Molins' house, the countryside residence in Gascony, Place du Capitole in Toulouse, where I attended the Alliance Française for three months and where the market was held – all of these things stem directly from my memories.

The deep affection Lia feels for the Molins family mirrors the respect I felt for the Molins family, the laughs we shared and the joy they brought me.

Thirty years after living in Toulouse, I contacted the Molinières family and told them I intended to write a book inspired by their boulangerie and my experience of living with them.

To the Molinières, I say, once again, thank you and I hope we meet again in the future.

Did you get your free short stories yet?

TWO UNPUBLISHED EXCLUSIVE SHORT STORIES.

Interacting with my readers is one of the most fun parts of being a writer. I'll be sending out a monthly newsletter with new release information, competitions, special offers and basically a bit about what I've been up to, writing and otherwise.

You can get the previously unseen short stories, *Mixed Messages* and *Time Is of the Essence*, FREE if you sign up to my mailing list.
www.susanbuchananauthor.com

Did you enjoy *The Boulangerie on the Corner*?

I'd really appreciate if you could leave a review on Amazon. It doesn't need to be much, just a couple of lines. I love reading customer reviews. Seeing what readers think of my books spurs me on to write more. Sometimes I've even written more about characters or created a series because of reader comments. Plus, reviews are SO important to authors. They help raise the profile of the author and make it more likely that the book will be visible on Amazon to more readers. Every author wants their book to be read by more people, and I am no exception!

You can find all of my other books at
www.susanbuchananauthor.com

Happy reading! Susan x

Printed in Dunstable, United Kingdom

84418876R00197